DESTINY

LOUISE
Bagshawe

DESTINY

headline
review

Copyright © 2011 Louise Bagshawe

The right of Louise Bagshawe to be identified as the Author of
the Work has been asserted by her in accordance with the
Copyright, Designs and Patents Act 1988.

First published in 2011
by HEADLINE REVIEW
An imprint of HEADLINE PUBLISHING GROUP

1

Apart from any use permitted under UK copyright law, this publication
may only be reproduced, stored, or transmitted, in any form, or by
any means, with prior permission in writing of the publishers or,
in the case of reprographic production, in accordance with the terms
of licences issued by the Copyright Licensing Agency.

All characters in this publication are fictitious and any
resemblance to real persons, living or dead, is purely coincidental.

Cataloguing in Publication Data is available from the British Library

ISBN 978 0 7553 3616 6 (Hardback)
ISBN 978 0 7553 3617 3 (Trade paperback)

Typeset in Meridien by Avon DataSet Ltd,
Bidford-on-Avon, Warwickshire

Printed and bound in Great Britain by
Clays Ltd, St Ives plc

Headline's policy is to use papers that are natural, renewable and
recyclable products and made from wood grown in sustainable forests.
The logging and manufacturing processes are expected to conform
to the environmental regulations of the country of origin.

HEADLINE PUBLISHING GROUP
An Hachette UK Company
338 Euston Road
London NW1 3BH

www.headline.co.uk
www.hachette.co.uk

This book is dedicated to Alex Timpson, who is nothing like the character named after her! Mrs Timpson won the prize of a character named for her in a charity auction, and chose a villain. She has dedicated much of her life to charitable works including the fostering of children. I hope she enjoys *Destiny* as much as I enjoyed writing it.

Acknowledgements

Special thanks to my wonderful editor Marion Donaldson, whose light touch released a far better, tighter story for this book; to my agent Michael Sissons, who has guided my career from the very beginning, and on whom I rely completely; to the entire team at Headline, Kate Byrne, Frankie Gray, Laura Esslemont, Emily Furniss, Vicky Cowell, Siobhan Hooper and the whole Sales department; and to Fiona Petheram at PFD for always taking care of me.

Prologue

'And there he is.' Kate Fox breathed out.

Across the room, surrounded by sycophants and hangers-on, stood Marcus Broder. Wearing an impeccably tailored suit, and a confident smile. One of the richest men in the city.

'That's him,' she said lightly. 'My future husband.'

'Are you sure?' Emily asked. 'I don't like him.'

Kate smiled. 'But of course,' she said, lifting her champagne flute to her lips. It was antique Baccarat crystal, filled with vintage Pol Roger. 'Honey, men like him aren't meant to be *liked*.'

She would take only a few sips. She was always in control.

The party ebbed and flowed around them. They were standing in the great ballroom of the Victrix, the most opulent hotel in Manhattan. The enormous gilded space was made almost intimate by the crush, the press of bodies. Half of Wall Street's finest were here tonight. Just glancing around, Kate spotted four supermodels, a senator, two members of the New York Yankees, and a late-night TV host.

The social registry and the powerbroking elite were equally well represented.

Marcus Broder knew how to party.

It was his birthday. Not a milestone; just a regular birthday.

But nothing in the life of the great media mogul went unremarked. Invitations thudded on to the doormats of New York's priciest Fifth Avenue penthouses and Greenwich Village mansions, unsubtle things in thick, creamy envelopes, stiff cardboard edged in gold.

The A list all got one.

They were both an acknowledgement of the recipients' sure social standing, and a command to pay homage. Not many who turned Marcus down would be invited a second time.

'So is he going to be your boss, too?' Kate turned to her friend, her green eyes alight with interest.

Emily shook her head. Kate had known her since school, and supported her as she climbed the ladder. They'd always been close, despite their obvious differences. Kate was the butterfly, Emily the moth. Whereas Kate was slim, blond and startlingly pretty – and careful to maintain it all – Emily was short, dumpy and possessed of an untamed mane of curly brown hair. They had both lived their passions.

Emily's was magazines.

Kate's was money.

Kate wanted no part of Emily's hard-working life. But she still admired her for it. Emily got up early, not to jog or hit a Pilates class, but to cycle up to midtown and the dingy offices of her little publication, *Lucky*. It was a magazine version of the *Village Voice*, and produced clever writing on everything from alternative rock acts to global warming. Readership was small but loyal, and Emily was making a living out of it. *Lucky* was her baby, so she had no time for romance, apparently.

That was OK. Kate had dated enough for two.

Kate was also in magazines. At *Cutie*, the huge-selling women's title Marcus Broder had taken over a few months back. She was a contributing editor, on a nice safe salary. She wrote lots of stylish features on fashion, and a devoted coterie of readers followed her every word. But it was not entrepreneurial, not risky. Kate Fox was not a career girl. She had her eyes on something easier and far more lucrative.

Like a big diamond ring and the man who went with it.

'No.' Emily shook her head. 'I decided not to sell.'

Kate's eyes widened. 'But Em, Broder was offering you a ton of cash. He'd have made your fortune!'

'And taken *Lucky*.'

Kate shrugged. 'You could start another magazine.'

'It wouldn't be the same,' Emily said doggedly. 'We're unique. Everything's so conformist these days.'

'Then edit it for him.'

'It would just turn into another Broder title. Bland and big-selling. He puts his own stamp on everything he owns, or haven't you noticed?'

Kate nodded, slowly. Indeed she had noticed. Maybe Emily intended to put her off. The trouble was that she found this arousing. Marcus Broder didn't care what the world was like. He just shaped it the way he wanted it to be.

His third divorce had been Manhattan's big news of the summer. Yet another Mrs Broder tried and found wanting. Marcus had sued in Connecticut for unreasonable behaviour, and his Costa Rican ex-supermodel wife had not contested it. She would never have to lift a finger for the rest of her life, and besides, you didn't make an enemy of Marcus, not if you were smart.

Broder was back on the market. As Kate glanced around the party, she saw the excitement crackling through the young women. Models and socialites had come in their skimpiest dresses and largest jewels. There was enough hairspray and scent in the room to crack the ozone layer. No surprise; ever since the Broder divorce broke on the *Post*'s Page Six, you could hear the sound of garter belts snapping and push-up bras clicking all over town. He was the biggest lion in the jungle. The next Mrs Broder would live a life of unimaginable luxury.

Every gold-digger on the East Coast was on the prowl.

Kate could see Marcus now, across the room. He was standing talking to Liana Forrest, an Emmy-award-winning actress from a police procedural possessed of eye-popping fake boobs and glossy black hair. His body language was predatory. She could tell he was planning to bed her. A second later, he turned to talk to the tall, slim figure of Alexandra Timpson, the legendary fifty-something socialite who ruled the Manhattan scene with a rod of iron. Mrs Timpson hosted parties; she rarely attended them. Her presence here was a sign of Marcus Broder's massive reach. He was speaking to her warmly, deferentially. Keeping the actress in her place, waiting.

Kate took another sip of her champagne. Liana didn't matter. None of them did. She was about to brush her aside. *She* was going to marry Marcus Broder. She, Kate Fox, was going to live that life, the one they all lusted after. And she was going to do it brilliantly. Kate would be the wife who stuck.

They called them trophy wives, but it was the other way around, wasn't it? The men were the trophies. The women were out there, hunting the big game. And Marcus Broder was the head she wanted mounted on her wall. The biggest prize in New York. The gold ring . . .

Emily followed Kate's eyes, and sighed. She was used to seeing her friend get what she wanted. Even if it was wrong for her, even if it ate up a little bit of her soul, every day.

'You're certain you want to go out with him?' she protested. 'He's got such a bad reputation . . .'

Her friend turned those emerald eyes towards her and smiled, and Emily felt her reservations evaporating, the way they always did.

'But so do I,' Kate laughed.

She glanced back at Marcus. In a second, she would go over there, bold, fearless, a natural beauty, confidence and *joie de vivre* making her irresistible.

'I'm not just going to date him, Em. I'm going to marry him.' Kate smiled. 'He's my destiny.'

Chapter One

'I'm so sorry,' the nurse said again. 'There was really nothing we could do. She was DOA.'

Kate looked at her mom. She could barely recognise her, covered in tubes, her head and face spattered with blood.

'I'm sorry, miss.' This time it was a doctor, an Indian guy. 'If you can make a formal ID now, we can spare you going to the morgue later.'

Kate swallowed. 'That's her – that's Mom.'

Her voice was barely a whisper. She stood there in her school uniform, her eyes red with crying. A car accident, that was what they said. Joyriders, drunk after the Yankees game, tearing down Grand Concourse Avenue in the Bronx. Wiping her mother out as she crossed the street. They said it had been instant. But that was something Kate would never know for sure. Because her mom had died alone.

She felt a sudden, violent surge of rage mixing in with the grief. Fury at the selfish punks driving that broken-down car. Would they get justice? Rot in jail for the rest of their miserable lives? She would see to it, she would testify in court . . .

Oh, shit; what the hell did it matter. She looked back at her mother's corpse. Mom would still be dead.

Kate turned away. A deeper anger was bubbling up inside

her now. Forget those punks. Her rage was at a man she hadn't seen for years.

Her father.

Asshole. Deadbeat. Traitor.

Dad – if she should even think of him that way – had bailed on them when Kate was four. She had memories, fuzzy ones. A big, strong chest. Arms picking her up. Being carried to her little bed, the one with the special pink eiderdown with little white geese on it.

And then crying, because he went. And didn't come back.

For the first couple of years he sent birthday presents, something at Christmas. A few hastily scrawled letters to Mom. That he was working things out, finding himself. He'd be back when he had figured it out. Kate had a vague recollection of waiting, hoping. Maybe he'd be back for the Fourth of July. Or Thanksgiving – he'd just walk through the door and sweep her up into a bear hug.

But he didn't walk through the door. And the presents turned into cards, and then they stopped.

There was no more contact.

And there was no money.

Mom did her best. She kept Kate tight and close. She worked real hard at providing a normal home. The apartment was small, but it was clean and cosy and Mom made the rent right on time, every month. Dad was a building contractor with a good job, and there were some savings, and health insurance. Kate even went to a little parochial elementary school, where they charged a fee and there was a good mix of kids.

When she was six, though, the savings were done. Dad had evidently worked for his boss for a while after he left, so the insurance kept up, but then a letter landed on their doormat telling Mom that he had quit and there was no more healthcare. Her mom sat her down at the kitchen table, her voice falsely bright over their dinner of pasta and sausage with tomato sauce, and told her that Mommy had to go to work now, and that when Kate got back from school she needed to be the big girl of the house and let herself in. The key would be with their neighbour. Kate had to do her homework for a little while without Mom being there. That way, they could still make the rent and have their home . . .

As Kate stared at the motionless figure on the bed, her own words drifted back to her, down the years. 'I'll be fine, Momma.' Both of them trying so hard to be upbeat. 'It'll be great. I'll get all my work done, I promise . . .'

And then, everything blurred: the years of anxiety, always accompanied by the ache in her stomach, the nerves. Would Momma's new job keep them safe? It was a bad time in the Bronx, lots of layoffs. Every few months her mother came back in tears, with a severance payment. She tried everything: she bagged groceries, worked in a pharmacy, waitressed for a while. But she was a stay-at-home mother, abandoned; she had no skills to speak of. It was low-grade stuff, bad pay. She took two jobs, one at daytime, one at night. Kate seldom saw her. Sundays together became very precious, and she tried not to show how her mother's exhaustion worried her.

Kate did her bit. She worked on her grades, because when she came home with an A, Mom's smile reached all the way to her eyes, for once. She kept the house clean, vaccuming, even dusting. And she kept herself pretty.

'I want better for you.' Mom rarely talked about it, but when she did, her bony hand gripped Kate's shoulder, and her tired eyes grew hard as flint. 'You do well at school. You promise me.'

'Mom, I promise. I *am* doing well . . .'

'And stay beautiful, Kate. That's the real deal, right there. What they won't talk about. But it's true.'

'Sister Francis says that true beauty is on the inside,' Kate ventured. She was eleven then, brown haired and cute, with a dusting of freckles over her nose and creamy white skin.

'Sister Francis is married to Jesus. And he ain't particular about looks.'

Kate snorted with laughter. She loved it when her mother joked; it was so rare, these days. Mom was too drained to laugh.

'But other men are, Kate, remember that. You need to find somebody who will take you away from all this. Pay your mortgage. I don't want you renting, you hear me? You don't go out with anybody from round here.'

Kate swallowed. She kind of liked Freddie Ciccio, her best friend's older brother. But she knew better than to bring that up.

'You date men with *money*. You're going to be a real pretty girl. He should live in Park Slope. Or even Manhattan. And don't give him too much; make him marry you. The kind of man, if he leaves, you get a lawyer.' Mom's fist curled into a ball. 'And you take him for all he's worth.'

'So.' Kate tossed her little brown bob. 'If you want me to marry for money, Momma, why do I have to study so hard in school? I mean, what's the point? Cinderella didn't go to college, you know.'

She smiled, pleased with that little sally. But her mother's grey eyes clouded.

'Because sometimes things don't work out, honey. And if you can't marry the right guy, you need to have a backup. You know, work at better jobs than your momma.'

'You do great, Mom.' The fun was gone from the conversation now, Kate wanted to cry.

'No, I don't, honey.'

A tear trickled down Kate's cheek, and she swallowed, hard. Her mother relented, reaching out her bony hand and tucking a lock of chestnut hair behind her daughter's ear.

'OK, darling, don't cry. I do well enough, I guess. We have our place. We make the rent.'

'That's right.'

'And I keep you in private school. Understand me, sweetie.' Her mother's eyes were fierce. 'That's what keeps me going when I'm tired enough to just drop. That we don't have anything, but you're educated. If you can't marry well, after all that, you can work. White collar. Better than me. Better than Dad, even.'

'I don't have a dad,' Kate said, and her voice was ice.

'Don't be like that,' Mom replied, but her protest was half-hearted.

'I just have you, Mom. And you're all I need. I'm making good grades, aren't I?'

'The best.' Her mother cracked another smile and ruffled her hair.

'I'm going to go to college. Scholarship.' Kate tossed her eleven-year-old curls. 'Ivy League, maybe. Maybe Harvard.'

Her mother was delighted. 'You keep dreaming, honey. College is great. Any college.'

And there it was. Kate heard the words in the back of her brain, even as she stared at her mother's lifeless body. Their plan. Their pact. She, little Kate Fox, was going to be the one-two punch, the complete package. A brainbox on her way to college, clawing her way out of the neighbourhood, doing whatever it took. And yet she wouldn't be like the other geeks in school, with their thick glasses and their retainers and their pudgy, soft bodies. She would work at having the face of a model and the body of a cheerleader. There was no money for designer clothes or shoes, but drugstore cosmetics came cheap, and you could buy blond hair dye by L'Oréal, in a box, for less than ten dollars. Mom would manicure her nails and pluck her brows. And that was what Kate Fox would be to the world.

Obviously, too good for the Bronx.

Obviously, on her way to Manhattan.

She didn't need to be told twice. As Mom slaved away, Kate eagerly, frantically put the plan into action. Her grades improved still further, but so did her beauty. At twelve, she was already jogging around the block and blow-drying her hair. When she hit puberty, she really pulled out all the stops. Lipstick and perfume, and make-up that the other girls in school envied and didn't understand. When Maria and Elizabetta were lashing on four coats of mascara and fire-engine-red lips, Kate was experimenting with tinted moisturiser and bronzer used as blush. She had a healthy, athletic glow, big hair, and very white teeth, and she smelled of mouthwash and fresh shampoo.

The boys clustered around like flies.

Mom was so proud. Even as she got older, and more exhausted, and her back started to stoop a little, watching her daughter blossom filled her with a kind of inner glow. Kate was so desperate to please her, she took all her advice, wholesale. She treated the guys from school with the same contempt her mom did. Tempered with politeness, but they knew when to back off. And few of them fought it. Kate Fox was so clearly not for them. Obviously destined for bigger, better things.

They got by, Mom and her. At Kate's own insistence, she worked Saturdays at a small clothing store down the block, behind the counter, selling summer T-shirts to her schoolfriends and others. Cheap stuff from China, that turned into woolly hats and gloves in the freezing New York winters. The boys on the block used to come in and spend more than they could afford, just to impress her. But it was hard, dull work for peanuts, and doing it made Kate love her mother even more. Because this kind of grunt work was what her mother slaved at daily, just to keep them housed and fed.

It also made her hate her father.

He'd left. Abandoned them. And he was the kind of scrub who couldn't provide for his ex-wife and daughter. Momma was doing all this because she'd married a loser. Simple as that.

And now here she was, and her mother was dead. What would happen now? What would happen to the plan? What would happen to Kate?

She turned sharply on her heel, and walked away from her mother's body. She just could not bear to look at it any more.

'You. Miss.' The doctor came running after her. 'How old are you?'

She drew herself up proudly. 'Sixteen.'

'You're the only relative listed on the contact sheet. Do you have someplace to go, honey? A grandma, something?'

'It's Kate Fox,' she said, coolly. 'And I'm going home. To organise Momma's funeral.'

The doctor was unfazed by the rebuke. 'Well, Ms Fox, if you're a minor and you have no adult relative to look after you, I have to contact children's services, it's the law. You understand . . .'

'Oh, you're doing your job.' She turned then, and smiled at him with an open confidence that was completely charming. The doctor returned her smile, almost helplessly. 'That's fine, Doc. But I have a dad. I was living with Mom after the divorce, but now he's coming back to look after me.'

'Do you have some contact details for him? For release of the body?' the man attempted, feebly.

Kate brushed it aside. 'Well, they *were* divorced. I'm next of kin. I'll fix it up with Father Peter, he's our priest. At Mary Star of the Sea?'

'Uh . . . yes. I know the church. But . . .'

'And then I'll go live with my father.' Kate nodded firmly. 'That's what Mom would have wanted. She wouldn't want to see me fall apart. My dad works in Manhattan, you know,' she said, importantly. 'He's an engineer.'

'OK. OK.' Beaten into retreat, the doctor smiled weakly back. 'If you're sure . . .'

'Somebody will ring you tonight about Mom,' Kate said. 'Thank you, Doctor.'

And he was left staring after her back as she marched out of the ward.

Kate didn't dissolve. Not in the hospital grounds. Not on the bus, on the way back home. Not until after she had actually called the church, and gotten a discount from their local funeral parlour; Father Peter, distressed beyond belief, rang them and told them that if they didn't bury Mary Fox for next to nothing, he would see to it that all his elderly parishioners started to switch their burial arrangements to the more modern establishment a few streets away.

Only that night, once everything was in place and her mother's body had been properly removed for burial, did Kate fling herself face down on Mom's bed, wailing as though her heart had been ripped from her chest, as though she would never, ever recover.

That was the weird thing about a broken heart, Kate thought; it actually still worked. Even if you didn't want it to. It still kept right on pumping that blood around your body. When you longed to close your eyes and sink into darkness, you still woke the next day, seeing the harsh light of morning, hearing the cars honk, smelling the bagels cooking in the coffee joints. Every day, just the same. Her mom was still dead. And she was still here.

She tracked her dad down. It didn't take too long, if you called his old workplace, made a concerted effort. There was a real awkward telephone call. Great to hear from her, he said, with false heartiness. He was sorry about her mother. Kate's accusatory silence hung heavy in the air, and her father started talking to fill it, the hurtful words tumbling out of him, telling her about his life as though she were some distant cousin, some old acquaintance. He was living in Florida, had remarried. Got three little boys. Thing was, they only had a four-bedroom house and his wife Georgette was knocked up again . . . a surprise stepdaughter would be stressful to a pregnant woman . . .

Surprise?

Yeah, well. He hadn't told her. Clean slate, all that stuff. Better for everybody . . .

Kate didn't bother to argue. What was the point? A tiny flicker of hope against hope, that she'd carried for a long time, died in her, but it was nothing compared to the ongoing pain of Mom's loss. Quickly she turned things around. He would send her twenty thousand dollars, she said.

He laughed. He didn't have it.

That laugh was a mistake. Driven to fury, Kate made him a promise. That if he did not send it, she would turn up in Florida. On his doorstep. To say hi to her stepmom and half-brothers. Oh yeah, and she'd bring the cops with her, for non-payment of child support. He owed her.

'Wait,' her father whined. 'I need time, baby. Gimme some time . . .'

'Don't call me baby. It's Kate. And you can have time.'

'OK.' He exhaled, let off the hook. 'OK . . .'

'Until Friday. That's four working days. Meaning you wire the money tomorrow, three days for it to get to my account. I don't want to be behind on the rent. Mom never was. And I can't work, I've got to go to school. Go to college.'

'I can't get it that quick,' he protested. Kate noted how he didn't ask her about college, about her dreams. He didn't give a damn.

'OK, Daddy. Guess I'll see you on Tuesday.'

'Fine. You'll get the money.'

'If I don't, you're going to find yourself all over the front page of the local paper, and in court. Oh, and looking after me till I turn eighteen. It's a deal, Father. Jump on it.'

She hung up.

The money turned up in her account on Friday, buffering the paltry bit of cash Mom had had left over at the end of the month. It was enough; two years' rent, to see her through to eighteen, and whatever came next.

For the first time in her life, Kate Fox felt a little bit of power.

It was there, in between all the sadness, like a dandelion poking up through a paving stone. She'd taken on her little weasel of a father and she'd crushed him. And one phone call had gotten her what she needed. She thought how proud her mother would be.

They still had the plan. No way was Kate going to waste what Mom had done for her, what she'd fought for all these years. It was a sacred compact; she was sticking to it.

She took a little out of her account and walked it over to her landlord, paid him in cash, got a written receipt. Then she went home. On Monday she was back at school, working hard. Harder than she ever had before.

Chapter Two

'I don't know what to do with you,' Sister Augustine said.

She stared across her desk at the young woman sitting in front of her. Looking her over with deep suspicion. Everything was right, on paper. The girl was effectively an orphan – her father had abandoned her – although there was apparently a little money. Her attendance record was one hundred per cent. The teachers reported that she tried her best in class; she was not one of the most academic students, perhaps, but she was bright, and she worked with dedication. Really, waiving the fees was a no-brainer.

Still, Sister Augustine had run this school for fifteen years, and she knew a faker when she saw one. Beautiful Kate Fox sat there demurely, but her heart wasn't in this. The school had a small endowment; it ran a debt most years. Bursaries were strictly limited. And Kate Fox . . . Her body sat there in class, but her head was somewhere else.

It was her beauty. It was devastating, really. Sister Augustine was surrounded, in her vocation, by the health and lightness of youth. Kate Fox was different, though. In her hands, beauty was a weapon. She never actively flouted the dress code; unlike some of the girls, she didn't roll up her waistband to shorten her skirt, or thrust down her socks to bare her calves, or leave the top button of her cheap blue school blouse undone. There were no pierced ears or lipstick or eye-shadow.

But Kate Fox was working it.

The hair. Dyed, cheaply but well, to a glossy, butter-scotch blond. She always came to school with it shimmering down her back. Blow-dried three times a week for a discount at the cheap place near the deli. Perfectly conditioned, the ends cut razor sharp, so it moved around her face like a shampoo commercial. The principal had watched boys younger and older sigh after Kate Fox's golden hair. Her face was free of make-up, but her skin was exceptionally smooth – yet how could she fault the girl for eating well and sleeping properly? Her nails were manicured with an elegant, traditional French polish. Since lipstick was banned, she applied a clear gloss – perhaps it was just a dab of Vaseline – that gave her full, soft mouth shine and plump-ness. Even Sister Augustine could tell it was begging to be kissed. She chose shoes with the tiniest of heels, that threw her ass out in the little pleated skirt when she walked. A healthy appetite, lots of protein and fruit, and the girl flung herself into sports; as a result, while her contemporaries were getting spots from Dunkin Donuts or trail mix, or sallow teeth from smoking, Kate Fox positively glowed with vitality.

Sister Augustine glanced involuntarily at the full breasts jutting forward under the shirt. She realised that Kate was hardly responsible for these. But add in the hair, the lips, the shoes, the uniform worn tight against the body; the kid was dynamite. Teachers had complained to her that Fox in class was worth one grade less for half the boys that attended. She was bad for concentration.

Sister had quietly ordered that Kate Fox always be assigned a desk at the back.

There were no boyfriends. Kate had a group of girls you might call friends, but they weren't truly tight. She was too pretty to snub, and always got a place at the refectory table at lunch, but apart from little chats in the hallway and recess, and pleasant conversation at meals, the girl had no close connections. Nobody seemed to know what she did with her break times. Weekends were a mystery. She wasn't going to the bowling alleys with the rest of her working-class friends. She didn't queue up for the cinema or attend pop concerts. In fact Sister Augustine detected a strong current of resentment towards the girl. She was holding herself aloof, apart. Like she was too good for the kids, too good for this school. Even for Sister Augustine.

Kate returned her gaze, politely but firmly. There was a steel there. Sister had seen it before, with certain of the other sisters back in the convent house. They usually went on to bigger things. One had risen to be prioress. Sister Augustine tried not to resent that look.

'I don't understand, Sister.'

'You have a good record.' She hated how clipped and cross she sounded. Was it the sin of vanity? The young woman's lushness . . . was she seeing it as a challenge? She was meant to be above such things. 'But I feel that your mind is unfocused.'

'But my record.' The green eyes widened innocently. 'You know I always attend, Sister, I make good grades . . .'

'You're a B student in everything except business studies.' Sister Augustine sighed. 'I have applicants for this bursary who make A's, Kate.'

'Yes, Sister, but I try my hardest. I might not be as clever,

21

but I'm harder-working. And I don't have help with my homework,' Kate added.

For the first time in the conversation, Sister Augustine cracked a slight smile. Grudging admiration. What a beautifully subtle way to remind the nun that she was, in fact, an orphan. Kate Fox might not be the most studious girl in the building, but she had incredible low cunning.

'I find your appearance disturbing,' she said. 'Kate, you must remember that you are here to study.'

'But Sister, my attendance and—'

'And so are the young men that come here.'

Kate glanced down at her uniform. For the first time Sister Augustine noticed that it was freshly ironed. She imagined the kid, in her apartment, pressing her shirt before school. Kate Fox was on a mission in life, and not the kind that ended tending to the sick in Africa. On the other hand, as a woman who rose at half-four to sing Matins, she had to appreciate the discipline. But in the service of what, my dear, in the service of what . . .

'I hope I haven't broken any rules, Sister,' Kate said.

'Of course not. That would give me an excuse to deny you this bursary.' The nun sighed, and surrendered to the inevitable. How could she refuse a place to a teenage orphan with a good record? Impossible.

'Excuse me?' Kate replied.

'Don't play games, young lady. I don't understand exactly what you are doing, Kate. I think you could apply yourself more. You seem to concentrate on looking beautiful as much as on your SATs. And I'm sure you are well aware of your reputation for being a distraction. To our male students.'

'I haven't even got a boyfriend,' Kate protested.

'And apparently you do not intend to get one. No, don't

say anything, Kate. Credit other people with some perception, as well as yourself. There is no need to torture our young men. I have the sense you are using them for . . . for *practice*,' the nun said, with a sudden flash of insight.

The young girl dropped her eyes, and a blush crept up the creamy skin of her neck, suffusing her cheeks. Sister Augustine felt a small burst of triumph, as though she had won a game of chess with a master.

'You will wear your hair tied back in a ponytail. Drop the lip gloss.'

Kate nodded. 'Do I get the bursary, Sister?'

'Of course you do, Kate.'

Kate sighed, a deep, long breath, relief suddenly evident in her whole body, and the nun was slightly ashamed. The girl was an orphan, truly, looking after herself, and she needed to stay in this school.

'Keep out of trouble, and you will have a first-class recommendation to any college you want to attend. You can do better in your studies, too.'

'I really don't want to be a professor, though, Sister.'

'I'm sure you don't. But you meet a better class of man at the good universities. Remember that, Kate.'

A sheepish grin. 'Yes, Sister Augustine. And thank you.'

The young woman reached into the pocket of her pleated skirt and took out a small pink hairband. She carefully twisted her glossy mane, once, twice, three times, tying it high on her head into a sleek ponytail that swung as she moved, making her look sporty and sexy. Then she stood up, and left the office.

Sister Augustine didn't bother calling out to remind her to wipe the gloss off her lips. She knew when she was beaten.

* * *

Kate was a model student after that. Playing by the rules, mostly at least, showing up early, toning down the flirting. But as Sister Augustine kept an eye on her, she wondered what it was that still disturbed her.

'Kate Fox. There's something wrong there,' she said aloud in the staff room one morning.

'Kate?' asked Sister Francis immediately. 'The girl has no friends.' She stirred her coffee, indulging in an unusual luxury.

The older woman raised a brow. 'Surely that's not true. She remains popular. Always sitting at a packed table at lunch, always in the crowd . . .'

'Yes, and never actually *with* anybody. Fox has nobody special. She was always focused on her mother, and the boys. It's not healthy. Less so now.' Sister Francis took a sip from her mug, mulling the problem. 'But what can we do? We can't make her sociable.'

'Time for a prayer to St Jude,' Sister Augustine joked. He was the patron saint of lost causes. But the younger teacher's words stayed with her all afternoon.

What did Kate need? This was hard for the old nun, who long ago had chosen such a different path to this young butterfly of a woman, this sparkling beauty who was so full of life, so vibrant. Yet she was sure that Kate had suffered more, of the two of them. And under all her asceticism and discipline, Sister Augustine struggled to empathise.

She was not of the world, as Kate was. And that brittle determination Kate wore all about her, like a suit of armour, was alien to the nun. Not for the first time, Sister Augustine wished she had known Kate's mother. She might get a better read on her pupil. Kate was so hard . . . She refused all help. What did she need, this girl who was so forcefully self-sufficient?

And suddenly it came to her, in a brilliant flash. Kate refused to *accept* help. But maybe she would not refuse to *give* it. Kate Fox needed softening, needed exposure to somebody who was not like her, who was vulnerable, who could use some of that extreme sass and devil-may-care attitude. Sister ran through the girls in Kate's class. Ordinary, most of them, distinguished now only by the extreme beauty of youth, which they would grow out of, and then grow into very average lives, she feared. There was the usual motley crew of common or garden sins. Arrogance and vanity, that teenage cruelty of cliques and exclusion, one-upmanship that would shame a French Renaissance court. And of the kids on the outside . . . she couldn't see Kate forming a true connection with any of the stupid ones. The girl was too bright for that. Which left one candidate. And immediately Sister Augustine had the girl in her mind, she smiled. It wasn't the obvious pairing, but she somehow sensed they would be very good together.

Chalk another one up to St Jude.

She scribbled a note to Kate's form teacher.

'Yes, Sister?'

Kate hovered in the doorway. She must be nervous; even the lip gloss had vanished. Sister Augustine felt a crunch of pity in her heart.

'Don't worry. You aren't in trouble, yet. Take a seat.'

Kate slipped into the chair in front of the desk, breathing out.

'I want you to do something for me. It's a little delicate.'

Now the young face was interested. Kate tilted her head slightly. Good Lord, but she was a pretty one.

'Emily Jones is applying to colleges. I'd like you to discuss her options with her. As far as I can see, she has no close friends.'

'That's right,' Kate said, at once.

'You know Emily?'

Kate grinned. 'She edits the magazine. Of course I know about her.' And to the nun's amazement, Kate rattled off a string of facts about her classmate, her family, her interests.

'So you're friends?' Sister Augustine blinked. 'I haven't noticed you together.'

'Not particularly.' Kate shrugged.

'Then how do you know so much about her?'

'I'm interested in people,' her pupil replied simply.

Sister Augustine suppressed a smile. That was an excellent sign; interested in people was almost as good as interested in God.

'Well, between you and me, my fear is that Emily's parents may be forcing her down the wrong path. Why don't you intervene?'

Kate squirmed a little. 'Like I said, Sister, we're not friends. She might not want . . .'

'Please. No excuses. The school has accommodated you, Kate. Now it's your turn. That's all. Shut the door when you leave.'

Emily Jones was sitting in the school library when Kate Fox walked in. Almost unconsciously, she straightened her dumpy body. Kate just had that effect on everyone, even the girls, really. Walking everywhere like she carried a pile of books on her head, like this was the best finishing school in Switzerland or something, not a little parochial joint in the Bronx.

For a second Emily felt a pang of envy. Dislike even. The

girl was so confident, so cool. The little cruel games of cliques and favourites that the other kids played, Kate just didn't get involved in. When one of the popular chicks tried to snub her – she was orphaned, she was poor, she lived in a crappy rental apartment somewhere on Grand Concourse; hell, at lunch she only ever bought a cheap tray of stuff, no frills, almost like she was on food stamps – Kate just smiled pleasantly, and the insult sailed harmlessly over her head.

Emily's life was made miserable by those girls. They laughed at her weight, her braces, her greasy hair. Even her grades. She was a geek, she was a loser. And even though Emily had two married parents and her pop was a dentist in Westchester, she had a baby sister, a dog and a fish tank – prosperity, a full family, money for college, the works – she would happily have traded places with Kate Fox in that moment. Real happily.

She sighed.

Kate looked her way. 'What's the matter?'

Oh, man, Emily thought, wearily. Did I do that aloud?

She shrugged and tried to recover. 'It's all this stuff. It's overwhelming.'

Kate walked over and hovered by the table. 'Mind if I sit down?'

Emily was flattered. The blonde bombshell wanted to sit with her. Her jealousy evaporated. 'Hey. Sure you can.'

Kate glanced at the pile of glossy prospectuses surrounding the other girl. 'What's this stuff?'

'College. I have to pick.'

'Exciting,' Kate said, and she looked like she meant it. 'Can I help?'

'Help?' Emily blinked. 'Like, help me pick a college?'

'Sure. You've got money, right?' That smile again. Kate

waved away Emily's worry like it was nothing, this was simple. 'I know where all the good ones are, depending on what you want to major in. Like, which places are social, what's good for politics, arts, pre-med, that sort of stuff. What they don't write in these things, too.' Her manicured hand patted the Yale prospectus. 'Which have the best hiring prospects, the affirmative action programmes for women; where the kids are stuffy, where they're rich liberals, or social-register Republicans . . . the drug campuses, the sports franchises . . . pretty much everything.'

Emily looked at Kate's beautiful face, as though she was seeing her for the first time. It was like that detached mask had slipped. She was passionate, engaged. And looking at Emily as if she wanted to help.

'How do you know all that?' she asked, timidly.

'I've been studying up. Weekends, evenings. Deciding where I want to go. You know, when we get out of here.'

She talked about it like it was a prison cell.

'I thought you loved the school,' Emily ventured. It had been all round the place that Kate Fox picked up the bursary last year. Over some guys with better grades and parents on welfare. She was like this unstoppable force of nature.

'It's what I can get,' Kate said, and for the first time there was a touch of bitterness. 'All my mom could afford. And when she got killed . . . I needed somewhere I could reach cheap, on the bus, and I kind of knew this place. She thought it was good enough. Food's cheap. Plus, they were gonna have to let me stay. So it'll do, because it has to.'

'But you want to go on to bigger things?'

Kate rolled her eyes. 'Of course. What, you don't?'

Emily looked at the glossy prospectuses. They all seemed

intimidating to her. Ivy League kids, all skinny and driving rich-kid cars, and her, the dentist's daughter, scraping in on the back of good grades. It would be school all over again. No different.

'My dad wants me to do science, so I can be a dentist, like him.'

Kate looked at her. 'You don't sound enthusiastic. A lifetime bending over people's mouths, wearing rubber gloves and breathing their skanky breath?'

Emily giggled. She'd never have dared say that to her dad, but she pretty much thought it every day.

'Come on. Tell me your dream.'

'I don't do dreams. I do a nice house in Bronxville at best. Suburban Westchester at its finest. Ducks in the park, a ball game twice a month. That sort of life.'

Kate stared. 'When you were a kid, didn't your mom read you "Cinderella"?'

Emily's confidence was growing. Kate Fox wasn't so bad; she wasn't eating her alive.

'Don't be dumb.' She gestured at her own dumpling thighs and soft stomach. 'You're Cinderella, babe. I'm an Ugly Sister. Prince Charming isn't in the plan.'

'I can make you over,' Kate offered.

Emily shrugged. You couldn't make over her heavy body or ordinary face. But she had learned a while ago not to complain about it too much. Any man that was going to love her would want her for her mind. She didn't have great expectations.

'You can give it a shot. I'm not one of those babe types, like Priscilla.'

'Priscilla!' Kate's nose wrinkled. The polished brunette led the most popular clique in school. She was a rich girl from

Scarsdale; her daddy worked in a bank. She had tried, and failed, to crush Kate Fox. Other chicks lived in fear of her cutting remarks and the sniggers of her little crowd of sycophants. 'Thank God you're not. Believe me, she's going to wind up a fat housewife.'

'You think so?'

'Look at her ass.' It was true Priscilla was voluptuous. Her ass and tits hung right out there, and her shoulders were softly rounded. 'It works, at sixteen. By twenty-six she'll already be droopy. By thirty her thighs will look like cottage cheese and that ass will have its own zip code. Mark my words. And she'll have married some poor schlub from down her block, and the best she'll do in life is be, like, president of the PTA. And bully all the other moms.'

Emily chuckled. Yes, Priscilla did have a certain overripeness to her look. Maybe she *would* wind up fat and desperate. It was a cheery thought.

'But I'm never going to appeal to the jock crowd, face it.'

Kate looked at her shrewdly. 'You weren't made for the jock crowd, Emily.'

Emily's eyebrows lifted. So Kate Fox knew who she was? That surprised her. Kate was surprising her.

'And you weren't made for the dentist crowd, either. No disrespect to your pops. But you obviously hate Westchester and you don't much like it here. And they're trying to shove you into being something you're not.'

'So what am I?' Emily leaned forward. She hadn't had this much attention for years. She was really warming to Kate, beauty or no beauty. The girl was a people-watcher, she was quiet, but she was soaking up information like a sponge. And she had good judgement. Didn't like Priscilla, that had to be a great start, right?

'Don't be offended,' Kate warned. The gorgeous eyes twinkled.

'I'm not making any promises,' Emily said, but it felt good to wisecrack. Kate wasn't making her feel small.

'You're a bluestocking. A classic academic, the type these teachers are always saying they want, but they don't know what to do with when it turns up. Only thing is, you're also kind of a rebel. You're bohemian. Real liberal. You're the opposite of "dentist in Westchester", actually. You're more "artist loft in Tribeca" and having an intense romance with a physicist from MIT or something.'

Emily's eyes rounded, and she laughed aloud. 'Jesus.'

'Blaspheming? See, I got you pegged. Rebel.'

'You know what? I think you actually do.' Emily sat up straighter, and unfamiliar sensations ran through her body. Adrenaline, maybe. Excitement. Just talking to Kate Fox, she had the sense that anything was possible – amazing things, stuff she would not have believed could come her way. She might never be a model, but that didn't interest her. Kate was showing her a vision of what Emily Jones could be – not trying to make her into a Priscilla clone. Just a more thrilling version of herself. 'What made you think I was a liberal?'

'You don't mix with the standard cliques. You study, but I've seen you reading graphic novels and Kerouac and Douglas Copeland. You read the *New York Times*. You have just one ear pierced, you let the other one close up. And you edited the school magazine.'

'For one semester.' Emily frowned. 'Then the sisters took it away from me.'

'Of course they did. You put in articles about modern art and censorship. You ran a photo of a nude model. You wrote about rent control in the city. You had a long piece about gay marriage. This is not the mix they want in a Catholic parochial school.'

'Guess not.'

'But you made the damn thing interesting. And there's something to be said for that, Em.'

'Em, is it, now?'

'Why not? We're going to be friends, aren't we? Two freaks like us?' Kate said disarmingly.

'Yeah.' Emily nodded. 'We sure are. I can't believe I never talked to you before now.'

Kate shrugged. 'I won't dwell on the past if you won't.'

'So tell me where I should go to college.'

'Columbia or NYU,' said Kate, instantly.

'Because?'

'It's Manhattan. And you need to be in Manhattan. The art, the journalism you love, it's all there. All the big glossy magazines are there. Fashion Week is there. TV. OK, not Hollywood movies, but indie movies, they shoot plenty of those in the city. Plus you got your liberal arts professors, your museums, the Metropolitan Opera. You'll love it there, Em, you'll spread your wings. Maybe Columbia is a better school.'

'So I should apply there?'

'No. You should go to NYU. Because that's where I'll be going,' Kate said, smiling disarmingly. 'They have better financial provision, better scholarships, and I can't afford Columbia, even if they waive tuition. Too many extras and suchlike. Besides, even if Columbia is an Ivy League school, NYU is the place for the arts, you know. It's got the film school and the fashion design and lots of liberal creative types turn up there. I think it's your destiny. You could make movies or be a fashion designer. Something like that. And it's the kind of place you'll find a guy that fits you, too.'

'OK,' Emily said, and it was like an anvil lifted effortlessly off her back. 'OK.'

'Just like that?'

'You've convinced me. It sounds a lot of fun, the way you sell it.' Emily reached out and pushed the rest of the shiny brochures to one side. 'I didn't want to do any of them, you know? Go away from home to some place with a bunch of Barbie doll girls and jocks.'

'You want adventure, Manhattan's far enough.'

Emily smiled. It was so true. Barely twenty-five minutes on Metro North, but an entirely different world. She looked at Kate Fox, and suddenly a golden future spread itself in front of her. Art, music, bohemian guys with dark eyes and bad attitudes. Freedom. And a real friend, to go with it. A surge of gratitude washed over her. She stuck out her hand, and Kate shook it.

'I'm glad you came into the library,' she said.

Chapter Three

Their friendship deepened at college. Emily's parents tolerated NYU, although her dad was upset she hadn't chosen Columbia, and was only working at a liberal arts degree. But she called home three times a week and went back regularly for Sunday lunch, and they were indulgent, covering tuition and paying for a small apartment. Kate shared it. Rent-free.

'It's beautiful,' she said wistfully, when Emily showed it to her. Downtown, with two tiny bedrooms and a sitting room with a kitchenette. It had a huge mirror over the fireplace, edged with cracked gold paint, exposed brick walls and dusty wooden floorboards, giving it an air of faded glamour, like a Parisian attic in a good building. Kate loved the big windows and high ceilings that helped the small space not feel cramped. The bathroom was tiny, just a shower cubicle, but you couldn't have everything, and it was a short walk to campus, with all the artists and musicians and banking millionaires of Greenwich Village on their doorstep. 'You've even got a spare room.'

'Spare?' Emily blinked. 'That's your room. We're going to share.'

Kate flushed, unusually discomfited. 'Oh no, Em, I can't afford to pay rent on somewhere like this. Even sharing. I'm

35

going to look for a cheap studio in Red Hook and get the train in.'

'Red Hook?' That was in Brooklyn, and one of the roughest parts of the city. But it was about all Kate could afford with her new job at Bloomingdales, working shifts on the cosmetic counter to fit around her tuition. She was on a scholarship, but still had to work to make living expenses. 'Don't be an idiot. You stay with me. No charge, I mean, come on, we're friends.'

Kate breathed out. 'You're kidding. I mean, Em, I can't accept that.'

Now it was Emily's turn to blush. 'But you have to – or I don't get to stay here. Please, Kate. My parents . . . They want me living with somebody they trust.'

'I don't even know your parents.'

Emily brushed it aside. 'They saw you at graduation day, remember?'

'Well, just to shake hands.'

'That was enough. They're paying for this place. I mean, I don't have a job, they're covering tuition, the whole bit. They weren't happy I don't want to be a dentist. But they are letting me do this, providing I'm chaperoned. You're a girl from school . . . I've talked about you,' she added, understating it quite a bit. The friendship of glamorous, popular Kate Fox was a major thing in Emily Jones's life. 'Dad doesn't care if you don't pay rent, he just doesn't want me falling in with a bad crowd. Sharing digs with a model with a coke habit, you know? He understands you got a scholarship and you work. See, he thinks you're responsible.'

Kate laughed. 'Your poor dad.'

'You kind of are responsible, you know.'

She tossed her head. 'I'm focused,' she said. 'It's different.'

'Anyway, you'll stay here.'

Kate beamed with joy. No point playing hard to get; she loved Emily, and she'd be living in Manhattan, and with tuition covered by the scholarship . . . immediately she started to spend her tiny salary in her head, a few good dresses, some nice make-up, all on an employee discount . . .

'Then thank you, sweetie,' she said, giving Emily a big hug. 'I'm so grateful.

It was unspoken, the bargain between them. Emily shared the good things her parents could give her, and her brains and hard work. She helped Kate with her grades and papers. And Kate, glorious, smiling Kate, freed from the strictures of high school, just sprinkled a little of that pixie dust over Emily.

Not that Em could ever compete. But she didn't want to. Kate, in her sprayed-on jeans, with her glossy mane of blond hair, her tight little sweaters, teetering ankle boots; the boys panted around her like dogs, all the jocks and the rich kids. And she went through boyfriends like a laser beam. Lots of dates; many guys never made it to a third or fourth. Emily watched her like it was a science experiment. All of them had money, but somehow Kate was never satisfied. It was as though she were fishing for some major target, and the sons of lawyers and plastic surgeons, the comfortably off film-makers with their bachelor-pad studios in the Village or the Upper West Side, they just weren't cutting the mustard.

But Kate was having fun. It was like watching a movie, Emily thought. She was like the Queen of England, never carrying any money to speak of. The boys always paid. There were presents, too; jewellery and flowers, champagne at dinner, ski trips to Aspen. Kate received everything with a light laugh, a kiss on the cheek. Her heart was a fortress. Young men flung themselves at it like waves breaking on a cliff. But Emily detected nothing, no real love, no passion.

Kate never brought boys home to their apartment; that space was sacrosanct. Emily's dad would have approved. And from what Emily could see, she rarely slept with them. Sometimes, if a boy lasted several months, Kate would give in. If it had the makings of a serious relationship. But few did. She was jealous of her reputation, and as the years rolled by at college there were lots of boys but few bad stories. Kate Fox was not easy. The ploys men used were legendary: flowers, dresses, a weekend at a country estate in Dutchess county where she was picked up by helicopter. But she would come back with her heart intact and the young man frustrated.

Sometimes Emily wondered why the boys put up with it. But they seemed to have a sneaking admiration for Kate. She was holding out for something major. And as word got around, more and more of them wanted to try their luck at being the one . . .

As she dazzled at the centre of the whirlwind, Kate didn't neglect her best friend. She insisted on making Emily over, despite her protests, so that the worst of her laziness got masked; her short brown hair was cut into a chic bob, and Kate found her some fitted pantsuits and even, despite her protests, a couple of dresses, tight round the waist, making the most of her large breasts and covering her ass and thighs. When Kate hit the gym at the YWCA regularly every morning, Emily was shamed into taking a relaxed stroll around the city. She never got thin, but at least she never ballooned. And Kate didn't make her feel bad about her body. She taught her basic make-up, even bought her a little bag of cheap cosmetics.

'Takes the guesswork out of it,' she said. 'You moisturise. Oil of Olay, OK? Can't go wrong. Then foundation. Takes ten seconds. I like this shade on you, Maybelline, they're cheap but they're good. Neutral eyeshadow. Like a biscuit shade.'

'OK,' Emily said, feeling alarmed.

'Don't panic, I'm almost done. Here's a bronzer. You sweep it over the cheeks, like blusher. Instead of blusher. It's failsafe. I learned that from Bobbi Brown.'

'Who's he?'

'She.' Kate rolled her eyes. 'The make-up woman? Look, don't worry about it. Just use it, the brush is right there. Finally you can put some mascara on, Great Lash waterproof. The whole thing costs under twenty-five bucks and it'll last you all year.'

Emily looked dubiously at the array of lotions and compacts before her, neatly ranged inside a clear Sephora plastic make-up bag.

'Try it.' Kate was implacable. 'You liked those Levi jeans I put you in last week. Let me see you do it. It's easy. Em, even professors wear make-up.'

'But . . .'

'No buts. Put it on. Hell, you should see me without make-up, I'd frighten small children, sour the milk.'

Emily laughed. 'Sure. Right.' Kate natural was gorgeous; Kate made-up was stunning.

'Waiting,' her friend said, impatiently.

Self-consciously Emily squeezed out the moisturiser and smeared it across her face; then, since Kate showed no signs of backing off, she did her best with the rest of it.

'Perfect. I'll show you.' Kate took her by the shoulders and marched her off to the huge mirror over their tiny fireplace.

'Wow,' Emily breathed. The face that looked back at her seemed so different. At school she wasn't allowed make-up; at home, on the weekends, she'd never dared. Any attempt to look pretty was just licence for the cruel girls to make fun of you. But this, this was . . . hell, it was really cool. She was still Emily, but smoother, better, with a suggestion of cheekbones, and her large eyes popped in her face, and she was almost . . . how to put it? *Attractive*. Maybe. To a certain type of guy. Hope and pleasure welled up in her. It wasn't difficult; Kate gave her the stuff, she could put it on. Between this and the good-fitting jeans and the tight sweater – and her body was firming up from the walking – well, Emily knew she wasn't Marilyn Monroe, but then again, the guys she liked weren't Clark Gable, either. They wore black-framed glasses, they were skinny, they had their hair long. And their intelligence was the most attractive thing about them. Men like that didn't date cheerleaders. Best part was, they didn't want to.

In her own crowd, Emily could rate as a sex goddess. The thought made her smirk.

'Kate, honey,' she said, with real affection. 'You are *such* a good friend.'

Kate had a date with Oliver Martin; he was studying economics and his dad was in Wall Street. 'Remember that,' Emily told her, floating towards the door, 'when you're rich.'

Rich.

That was the answer to the riddle. If you believed Kate's own testimony. That was the story she confided to Emily when they stayed in to study, slouching companionably on their white couch covered with its cosy red throws, hugging the real fire lit in their tiny grate as the winter nights drew in and New York was an icebox. Kate didn't spill her guts, not even after a glass of champagne from the various bottles, gifts from hopeful suitors, that nestled in their fridge. Emily never heard that much about the heartache of losing her mother, about the pain of struggling with rent and food and bus fares, keeping herself fit and pretty on a shoestring. Kate wasn't willing to talk, and Emily didn't push it. She feared losing her friendship. The girl was intensely private, and Emily judged she might withdraw everything if she tried to break down that wall.

But about her plan for life, Kate would talk. Studying hard on campus, working twice as hard on beauty. Learning how to be around men who wanted her without saying yes to them, or making them into her enemies. That was what school really taught her, she said. Kate Fox didn't want enemies. When it works, it's easy, she said, blithely. She was here, wasn't she? At NYU, where she'd wanted to be? Dating rich guys? None of them were quite *right*, not yet, but she was getting the hang of it, and her expenses were paid, and she was out there, being seen . . . See, she did believe in Cinderella, but nobody came to get Cinderella when she was sweeping up the ashes. She had to get all dolled up. She had to go to the ball. That was where the Prince saw her. So by working hard at school, Kate explained, she'd gotten invited to the ball.

'But Cinderella's coach was really a pumpkin,' Emily pointed out.

'I know. Isn't it great?' Kate asked, laughing. 'You know – fake it till you make it.'

'But why?' Emily asked her, one day. Kate was clever enough, not a superbrain, but Emily thought she could graduate top third of the class. Major in English, minor in media studies. You could get a great career with that. 'Why are you looking to marry money? You could make your own. You could do anything you want to.'

'Don't be naïve.' There was bitterness in that voice. 'How many women do you see in the Fortune 500? It just doesn't work that way. You can pass all the laws you want, Em, believe me, women are still going to be second-class citizens.' Kate exhaled. 'Look, you're a hippie, you should get this. It's Zen. I'm taking the path of least resistance. Riding the horse in the direction that it's going. A woman can slave her guts out her whole life in high heels and a business suit, and likely she'll be left with blisters and a middle manager's salary. When jogging, great hair, neat nails and intelligent conversation can land her in the middle of easy street just by saying "I do".'

'You don't really mean that,' Emily said.

'Really? Look at the average career woman. Her husband slobs around the house while she does the heavy lifting. Maybe he runs off with another chick. Leaves her holding the baby. She's working a job, maybe two, struggling with daycare . . . Even if he's there, he works less because she's helping, only she takes care of the kids *and* she cleans the house. You know what that sounds like to me? A really crappy deal.'

Emily shook her head, shocked. 'Feminism struggled for years so we could make our own way. What's marrying a rich husband? That's not success. That's being a lady who lunches. It's nothing. I can't believe that's your goal, Kate.'

'Believe it,' Kate replied, and she was deadly serious. 'A career woman with kids carries an anvil on her back. Whereas a girl who marries right . . . the only weight she has to worry about is the knuckleduster on her left hand.' And she laughed, and held her own, ring-free fingers up to the firelight. 'Can't you just see it sparkle already?'

When they graduated, Emily took her degree *cum laude*. Kate just got a good pass. Nevertheless, she was flooded with job offers. She took a position working as a staff writer on *Cutie* magazine, covering beauty and fashion.

'*Cutie*!' Emily remonstrated. 'That magazine's a bunch of crap. Pastels are in for spring and here's a feature on multiple orgasms. All they care about is shoes and bags. And maybe sex.'

Kate grinned. 'Wait, did I miss something? *Is* there anything else?'

'Kate,' Emily protested. 'Come on.'

'Look, I happen to like shoes and bags. And *Cutie* is a major player in the market. Sells a million copies a month.'

'Some women have no taste.'

'Don't be so patronising. Not everybody's into indie films and the *New York Times Review of Books*.' Kate was slightly annoyed, to Emily's surprise. 'Even some of your hard-nosed businesswomen like to switch off on the train on the way home. This job gives me a reasonable salary, I get the clothes for free, and there are plenty of guys swarming around fashion – all those models.'

'You're sexier than any model,' Emily said loyally.

Kate looked down at her body. She was slim, but she still carried her curves; nice breasts and a firm, flaring ass that jutted out a little from her waist.

'I'm not afraid of the competition,' she admitted, grinning.

Emily could not talk her out of it. And it looked as though there was no need. They got a flat together, and Kate made her share of the rent. True to her word, she acquired a closet full of designer threads and top-of-the-range shoes, well beyond her means. Her writing, which she sometimes showed Emily, was punchy and bright. And her boss seemed to like her, because she wasn't too ambitious. It was a placeholder job, like her placeholder boyfriends. Emily worried that she was waiting for Mr Perfect, and she might wait her entire life away. But Kate Fox would not be moved. The butterfly continued to dance in the sun. In the end, Emily stopped trying to fight it.

She worried about what to do with herself. She'd rather chew her own foot off than work at a place like *Cutie*. Her dad didn't understand, but dentistry was dead in the water. Guess that was one thing about living with Kate: you learned how to plough your own path. Emily had learned confidence at college; Kate had dragged her out of her shell.

'I like what you're doing,' she announced one night, as they sprawled on the couch watching the Yankees game. Kate's boyfriend of the moment had blotted his copybook by not requesting a Friday-night date four days in advance, and Kate was punishing him by saying she had other plans. Which involved a dressing gown and a home pedicure. Besides, Emily strongly suspected he was on the way out. He was a trust-fund brat, and Kate was already a little bored of him. She wanted to be a lady of leisure, but interestingly, Emily thought, on some level it wasn't money alone. She wanted an achiever.

'You like *Cutie* all of a sudden?'

'No. Not *that* magazine. It's a pile of crap,' Emily said, firmly. 'Glossy, best-selling crap, maybe. But that's still what it is.'

'Thanks for the vote of confidence,' Kate answered, smirking. She loved yanking Emily's chain, and they both knew it.

'Just a magazine. Maybe you were right the first time. Years ago.'

'The school mag, you mean?' Kate knew exactly what Emily meant. Emily glowed at the recognition.

'Exactly. It *was* good. Even for a teenager. And you know, there are people out there who do actually like indie films and the *Times Review*. And activism. And reviews of ethical restaurants and fashion that's sourced from micro-collectives. In New York, there are tons of those people. And quite a few of them have money.'

Kate looked at her, and put down her nail file. 'Sure. I've been to the West Village. All those limousine liberals. You think you could raise the cash?'

'I'd like to try. You could help, you know.'

'What, you're going to run features comparing five popular brands of mascara?'

'Not exactly. But I can see that a little populism might not hurt. You could take a look at layout, design. Mix something in there that's not quite so worthy.'

Kate sat bolt upright. 'I could totally do that for you, Em. I'd love to try.'

She sounded truly excited. Emily suddenly got excited too. When Kate Fox turned her energy to something, big things started to happen.

'Think of a sexy feature for the dummy issue,' Emily urged.

'I have it already.' Kate spread her hands. 'Call it "Nice

Guys Finish First". It's your standard "inside the home of a celebrity" feature, with the cool pics of their oyster-white living rooms and Italian designer couches, only you feature heroes of the revolution – liberal legends who've made it big. Sell your readers on the idea that they can be ethical *and* rich.'

'Wow.' Emily was taken aback. 'That might actually work.'

'Of course it'd work. Start with that guy from Ben & Jerry's ice cream; I hear he's got a mansion in the Hamptons. Plus, they might even give you some money towards the start-up. I can get people who'll write a business plan for you – magazine people – and you do the editorial.'

'God. Kate.' Once again, Emily found herself moved. Kate was just so enthusiastic, so ready to help. 'Would you? That'd be perfect. You don't want to be partners?'

'What, and quit *Cutie*? Hell, no. I like my life. I like trying out mascaras. But I'll help you get started, Em. And you take it from there.'

Emily worked round the clock, day and night. She went to banks and liberal arts foundations, charities and rich left-wing donors. She banged on doors and negotiated with printers. She talked to newsagents and magazine stalls. She hired writers, smart, funny kids fresh out of college. Her list of features was a mix: anarchic politics, quirky arts stuff, indie films and, thanks to Kate Fox, a whole dose of naked glamour. Maybe it was liberal glamour, but Kate poured the sexy, glossy magic into the worthy stuff, and Emily's dummy issue showed a New York that could have a con-science but carry a Prada backpack; Doctors without Borders by day, nightclubs and champagne at night.

And it worked. They sold ad pages. Not a lot, but enough to keep the magazine afloat. People talked. The *Village Voice* wrote about it. The target market was small, but sophisticated; they were taste-makers, they had money. The magazine would never be *Cosmopolitan*, Emily realised that, as she sat exhausted in her little apartment, cradling her phone in her hands. But that was OK. It had a niche. It worked.

'What are you going to call it?' Kate asked. 'You need a good title.'

'*West Village*?' Emily suggested. '*Your Take*? *Apple Core*?'

'Ugh, no. Those are all horrible. Look, your magazine's still really worthy, lots of upmarket articles, wordy stuff. You need to counter that, not just with the photo features, but with the title too. I know exactly what to call it.'

'What?' Emily asked, already preparing to surrender to the inevitable.

'*Lucky*,' Kate said triumphantly.

And so *Lucky* it was.

Within six months, Emily had moved out, to a place of her own near *Lucky*, and Kate had the apartment all to herself. She could afford it, though, with her generous boyfriends and gradually increasing salary. As *Lucky* continued to grow, and solidify, Emily found to her amazement that she was making a little money. Nothing crazy, but soon she was drawing down eighty thousand a year. And she insisted Kate stay involved. If money ever got tight, Kate was hired for some feature or other. A little glamour never hurt the mix, even if it wasn't Emily's own taste.

It worked. That was what mattered.

Their friendship continued, too. Over the next year they laughed and shopped and wrote together. Kate Fox was addictive, Emily thought, even as she herself became a successful magazine publisher. She was light, bright, determined. Emily didn't approve of her life plan – fine. But Kate forged her own path.

And then Marcus Broder came into their lives.

Chapter Four

'Kate!'

Marianne Jephson, the frosty secretary to Fleur D'Amato, Editor-in-Chief, stopped in front of Kate's desk, looking down. Her ice-blond hair was wound in a tight chignon, her pale skin and anaemic hazel eyes adding to her air of cold reserve.

'Yes?' Kate responded, looking up insolently. She stretched a little in her chair, an instinctive, feminine movement, displaying her lithe body and generous curves, contrasting her young figure with Jephson's older, skinnier, social X-ray sexlessness.

'Fleur wants to see you. In her office.'

'To what do I owe the pleasure of a personal visit?' Kate asked. 'You couldn't ring my desk?'

'No. I couldn't.' Marianne's clipped tones said she did not approve. 'Your phones have been going all afternoon.'

'Cosmetics companies want reviews.' Kate shrugged. 'The column's popular.'

'Well, if you could see your way clear to allowing the editor a moment of your precious time,' snapped Marianne. 'As in *now*.'

Kate stood, managing to slither in her dress, a tight

Azzedine Alaia bandage number that hit modestly above the knee and boasted tiny cap sleeves, yet nevertheless left nothing to the imagination; her tiny waist, her gorgeous flared ass and her curvy breasts were all on display like candy. Long hair fell down her back, gathered softly with a velvet ribbon. It was all Marianne could do not to blush. They were a fashion magazine; she could hardly complain if a features writer wore a hot designer. Yet Kate Fox was so unashamed, so lush, so in-your-face. It just wasn't right. Marianne thanked God her boss was a woman.

'But of course,' Kate said smoothly.

'This way.'

'I know how to get to the editor's office,' Kate answered.

Marianne pretended she hadn't heard her. Sassy little bitch. Well, hell, she'd eventually lose her looks like the rest of New York, and the way she dated around – bound to be left without a partner when the music stopped. And then she'd probably marry some blue-collar guy from Queens and spend her life slumped on a couch, watching daytime TV and getting fat . . .

An upbeat thought. Only problem was, Marianne didn't believe it.

Kate Fox was young. She wore borrowed clothes but had no real money. She rented an apartment, held a junior title. There were a million girls just like her in this city, and a million more who had better things going for them – doctorates, trust funds, big promotions.

But Kate was going places. That much was easy to see. Marianne hated to admit it. She gritted her teeth against the insistent thought that somehow, some way, Kate Fox would make it.

'Here we are,' she announced unnecessarily. 'Go in. You shouldn't keep Ms D'Amato waiting.'

'Thank you,' Kate said sweetly. Like she could read the older woman's mind. She walked confidently into her boss's office, and shut the door.

Fleur D'Amato was a wasp-waisted woman of a certain age, and thanks to some of the best dermatologists in New York, nobody knew quite what that age was. Botox and mini-lifts, peels and fillers gave her a smooth, permanently startled look. She never frowned, because she couldn't. But that didn't fool the staff at *Cutie*.

Her temper was legendary.

They lived in terror of her.

You could count the staff who survived more than five years here on the fingers of one hand. Fleur fired people with abandon. Her rule was 'one strike and you're out'. Everybody knew that the trick at this mag was to rise to a position where Fleur would tolerate you, then quit before you were kicked out. That way you could switch titles, go work for another top-rated magazine. Because if Fleur D'Amato got seriously pissed off at you, she would put the word out, and you'd never work again.

She looked serenely at Kate as she entered the office, but her eyes narrowed. Her gaze flickered up and down the younger woman.

'So apparently you've been making waves,' she said.

Kate felt her stomach turn over slightly. She could only just manage to keep up her rent, and grooming was expensive in this town. She liked her job at *Cutie*. It would suck to lose it.

'Really?' she said lightly. It was the old lioness versus the

51

young, and she couldn't afford to show weakness. 'I can't think that that last "Save vs Splurge" feature on lip gloss caused the advertisers a lot of sleepless nights.'

'It's not your work,' Fleur said. She waved her hand, annoyed. 'That's adequate.'

This was high praise. Kate relaxed slightly.

'It's your outside activities.'

'You mean my social life?'

'Quite so,' her editor replied.

Kate stiffened slightly. 'I believe I'm over twenty-one, Fleur. And entitled to date whoever I want.'

One steely eyebrow arched just a fraction. Kate Fox was close to defiant. Nobody ever spoke to Fleur D'Amato like that.

'*Cutie* has a certain image to uphold,' she said.

'Oh, that's OK,' said Kate. 'I don't wear the Gap when I go out. It's fashion forward all the way. I'm known for it.'

'You're getting a reputation,' Fleur stated flatly.

Kate smiled. 'Thank you,' she said.

Thank you. *Thank you*? The girl was acting like she'd just been paid a compliment. The sheer insolence, the rebelliousness of it. Fleur was momentarily taken aback. There was something admirable about the girl's chutzpah.

'I didn't mean as a fashion plate, Kate. I meant as a . . . a . . .'

Uncharacteristically, she blushed. She could not bring herself to look the girl in the face and say 'a gold-digger'. But that was what she meant.

'A playgirl,' she finished lamely. 'And I think you ought to be careful. Senior magazine staff don't get promoted if they start to become the story.'

Kate nodded. That, at least, was good advice. And if she

was truthful, perhaps it was just slightly embarrassing to have Fleur D'Amato call her out on the partying. She repented nothing, but if she had a reputation with women, she would shortly get one with men.

Mustn't damage the brand, she said to herself.

'I take your point. Thank you for the heads-up,' she answered the older woman.

Mollified, Fleur turned to a paper on her desk.

'But in fact, it may be somewhat helpful. I gather you attended a party at the Metropolitan club last Saturday.'

Kate tensed. Fleur's spies were everywhere. Yes, she had been there, on the arm of Bradley Winstone III, a WASP import from Boston whose father had grown very rich off parking lots in ten major markets. But Bradley was only the son, and it burned her that she'd been seen out with him. Really, she ought to be over the trust-fund brats. The Met party had tempted her, though. It was one of the most prestigious private members' clubs in the city, and the crowd there were diplomats and landowners, banking CEOs and senators. Old money, old power. Bradley had been attending a birthday party for the banker William Cabot, thanks to his father's connections, and was probably the least important man in the room. Kate, years younger than most of the rail-thin women in their chiffon and pearls, had attracted her fair share of admiring looks from men older than her father. Bradley had hated how she basked in their approval, but she could hardly help herself. She was light hearted, enjoying her own prettiness, like a butterfly on a warm stone, spreading its wings slowly back and forth in the sun.

Bradley's number was up. Kate resolved to dump him, that night. And maybe swear off men for a little while. She needed to work, keep her head down. The magazine was fun. And there was something . . . how to put it . . . unsatisfying about her current life. Dating dull, medium-level rich kids, fending off their sexual advances, breaking up with them when they began to demand her presence in bed – before they could choose to do the leaving. Any number of her men this past year might have married her. Sometimes she couldn't figure herself out. Why hadn't she bitten the bullet, and coaxed one to the altar? Then she would have the life she'd always dreamed of. The one Momma had thought she deserved.

'Yes, a birthday party for a friend of my boyfriend's.'

'And who is he?'

That was a little personal, but Kate surrendered. She did not want her boss as an enemy.

'Nobody important. I was planning to end it, in fact.' If that wasn't true then, it sure was right now. 'I might take a break from dating. I want to concentrate on my work at *Cutie*,' she said.

Fleur stared at her. She did not appear convinced.

'That's terrific. And meanwhile, I have a use for you. You were noticed by Marcus Broder, it seems. He asked a few people who you were. That kind of thing makes its way back to me.'

Kate's heart sped up. She didn't embarrass herself by asking '*The* Marcus Broder?' In New York, there could only be one.

Marcus Broder. Late forties, maybe even early fifties. Slim and dapper. Known for his flamboyant affairs and arm-candy wives. The gossip columns called him 'the tycoon's tycoon'. And he had interests ranging from real estate to . . .

To publishing. That's right, Kate thought, swiftly retrieving the key facts from her mental Rolodex. Broder, Inc. owned a small, chic little publishing house, one with slender but steady profits, that published a lot of Nobel laureates and literary prize winners. He also had a string of regional newspapers and a few radio stations across the north-east.

'Is Marcus Broder interested in magazines?' Kate asked. 'Does he want to buy *Cutie*?'

A grudging respect filled Fleur D'Amato's face. She had watched the pretty little kid make the leap. There were brains under that blond hair, if only the girl would let them do the talking.

'You won't know about the corporate structure of this magazine,' she said.

Kate shrugged. 'That we're owned by Horrell Media? Which is a subdivision of WorldNews, Inc.?'

Fleur blinked. 'Ah, yes.' She felt her annoyance returning. What was Kate Fox's deal? Was the social butterfly thing some kind of act? She doubted there was one other writer on the magazine who could have identified how they were published. 'Then you understand the reporting structure?' she challenged.

'You are Editor-in-Chief so you report to the board of Horrell. In reality, though, that means Claudius Sabrini, doesn't it? He's CEO. But obviously just of a division. That also makes him a senior VP of WorldNews. Reporting to Sir John Hoxton, the Brit. He came to the company from the film industry, ran Artemis studios at one point. And I guess he reports to the board of the global firm.'

Fleur was amazed. 'Who sits on that board?'

Kate shook her head. 'I don't know. I could Google it, I guess. Obviously Harry Burnstein has the majority stake in WorldNews, so they all answer to him.'

Fleur wanted desperately to ask how the hell Kate knew all that. *Why* she knew all that. She was a contributing editor, she worked for peanuts; the whole office – hell, half New

York's social scene – knew she was only interested in finding a rich man. But ask her a business question and she suddenly came off like the *Wall Street Journal* digest.

But Fleur had not risen to the top of popular magazines by showing weakness. She would not give Kate Fox the satisfaction.

'Claudius is interested in disposing of *Cutie*.'

'But we've got great sales,' Kate said. 'We're profitable.'

'In a declining market, my dear. Magazines as a whole sell less and less every quarter. Young women are on the internet now, they play with mobile phones. Books have been hit worst, but all print media is the same. Newspapers, magazines. Horrell Media wants to shift into computer game publishing.'

Kate was silent.

'You're right, though.' Fleur preened a little, catching sight of her reflection in the window that looked out over West End Avenue. 'We *are* selling well. We buck the trend. I know how to run a glossy title. It's what sets this magazine apart. All about the mix, staying fresh. And there are investors who want some of that.'

'Like Marcus Broder.'

'Exactly like Marcus Broder. He likes the idea of owning a woman's magazine.'

'Access to models?' Kate suggested.

Fleur frowned. 'Mr Broder is a very powerful man, Kate. I would not suggest you use that sort of levity with him.'

'With him?'

'He's already been to see me. I've taken a meeting with Mr Sabrini and some of his executives. Now Mr Broder has expressed a wish to meet a few of our top talents. I thought you could arrange to conduct him on a tour of the office.

Show him around. He tends to be fairly hands-on, so he informs me. He wants to see how we put our book together.'

Kate blinked. 'I'm only a contributing editor . . .'

'He wanted a junior staffer. And since he was asking after you at the party . . .'

It was Fleur's turn to shrug. A blush crept over Kate's cheeks. The older woman was offering her up like bait, she thought, just like bait. A piece of eye candy, if you buy *Cutie*.

She smiled back evenly. No way would she protest, give Fleur a chance to fire her. Her boss clearly thought of her as a worthless flirt. This was an opportunity, a chance to sell the entire magazine, to operate like a corporate executive.

Marcus Broder would not know what had hit him.

'I'm excited for you,' Emily said, when Kate took her out to dinner that evening. 'Marcus Broder is a big deal. Just be careful, OK?'

'What do you mean, be careful?'

'He's supposed to be a total bastard. Utterly ruthless. If somebody crosses him, they're finished in business, at least in New York. And he's predatory with women.'

Kate sighed. 'I don't care. He'd make a great husband, if he wasn't already married.'

'You hardly know him,' Emily protested.

'I know he's a self-made man. Not a trust-fund brat. You have to admire that. I know he owns half of New York.' Kate fell silent for a minute. The gossip columns talked about Marcus Broder's legendary parties, his Upper West Side mansion, his private jets, the helipad on his corporate offices, the estate in Mustique.

It was everything she'd ever dreamed of. What a cruel fate

that she only had the chance to impress him in an office setting. Kate wanted marriage, and all the economic security that came with it.

She wanted the ring. Marcus Broder's would be made out of solid platinum.

'And that's all I need to know,' she said. And sighed.

Chapter Five

It was a Tuesday morning. She remembered that later, the glorious feeling of spring in the city, the harshness of New York's long winter finally over. Now they were basking in sunshine, the trees on the block were in full leaf, the glass towers of the skyscrapers were drawing the warmth of the sun into them. Manhattan was flooded with light.

Kate had dressed very carefully. No jeans today. Since Marcus Broder wasn't on the marriage market, maybe she could impress him as a boss. It was time to grow up, perhaps. She had been setting her sights too low, Kate decided. That was why she wasn't married. Parties in the best nightclubs with rich, foppish young guys . . . a life she didn't like as much as she had expected. Now it was time to step up.

Of course, she believed in her life goals. Momma had been so clear. Work was just a smart girl's backup. But as a senior executive, not just a lip-gloss writer, more doors would open for her on the dating scene, too. Men of substance, men who sat on division boards. Guys whose woman would need to be accomplished, beautiful and discreet.

She was annoyed with herself for making her sexiness too obvious. She was annoyed with herself for selling Kate Fox short.

That stopped right now.

Kate chose a skirt suit. Jil Sander, cut with great elegance, but a daring shade of very pale lemon yellow; a fitted jacket over a white T-shirt, and a skirt that was tight around her curves but then kicked down into feminine pleats, just half an inch shorter than you might have expected. She teamed it with buttery mid-height heels from Jimmy Choo, and no jewellery except tiny, discreet canary diamond studs in her ears. The look was all youth and professionalism, light and very feminine. Her blond hair was highlighted by the daisy shades of her outfit; she'd had it styled and blow-dried that morning. Nothing on her face but tinted moisturiser, bronzer as blusher, and some Bobbi Brown neutrals on her eyelids. No eyeliner, no mascara. She used a clear gloss on her lips, something to set her apart from all the over-made-up model types a man like Broder would be used to.

Her reflection had reassured her. Chic, in control, perfect for a high-fashion office. She was elegant, now, not flirtatious. The worst Fleur would be able to say was that the bold choice of buttercup shades played up her youth. A small Michael Kors shoulder bag in sleek gold leather hung from one shoulder.

She was waiting outside, on the pavement, when Marcus Broder arrived.

And he arrived in style.

The limousine, black and sleek, washed free of any grime from Manhattan's roads, purred silently to a stop in front of the *Cutie* offices. Kate saw that the windows were tinted. Average people did not get to stare at Marcus Broder, just because he stopped next to them in traffic. Not that there would be much doubt, if you were up on things; the vanity plates said MARCUS1. And the car itself was the kind of gas-guzzling boat that environmentalists cursed at, enraged. A big 'fuck you' to balance and subtlety. Marcus had it. He flaunted it. Kate tried not to drool. The car was big enough for a medium-sized Jacuzzi and a full wet bar. Given Broder's reputation, she wondered wildly if it held both.

Kate smiled briskly as a uniformed chauffeur stepped out of the driver's side and went to open the door for his boss, as though Marcus Broder was a major Hollywood star, Brad Pitt arriving on the red carpet. Only he could buy and sell Hollywood stars if he wanted to. And the film studios that made them. Her heart thumped. She desperately wanted to impress this man. But he ate whole companies for breakfast, and she wasn't prepared to be just another notch on his bedpost. So what possible interest could she have for him?

The chauffeur stepped back. Broder stepped out.

He was tall, relatively slim, with a tight, hard body. His face was classically smooth and even featured. Dark hair, cropped close to the head. Very expensive suit, she saw at once, absolutely bespoke, and it looked like Savile Row. Hand-made John Lobb shoes. Piaget watch. In titanium, she thought.

Everything about him screamed money. Power.

She felt nervous, excited in front of him. What would it be like to be the wife of a man like this? Dripping in diamonds and South Sea pearls. Haute couture all the way. You could put up with a lot of affairs for that, she thought, and then chided herself. But still.

'Mr Broder?' she said.

His eyes swept over her, dark, assessing. 'You would think so, wouldn't you?' he said drily.

Kate flushed. Usually she was the most composed person in the room. Men sweated and loosened their collars just from being in her presence. Not today, though. For once, she was definitely not in charge. Marcus was letting her know the score.

'Good morning, sir.' Just the right note of deference in the 'sir'. 'Welcome to *Cutie*. I'm Kate Fox.'

'I know who you are.'

'I'll be taking you around this morning, if that's OK. Ms D'Amato thought you might want one of the junior staff showing you the office. I'm a contributing editor, so I'm part of the day-to-day. Will you follow me?'

Broder grinned. 'Certainly.' His eyes trickled down to her ass, tight in its snug yellow frame. Kate blushed. She had a vision of him following her up the stairs, his eyes fixed on her curves.

What the hell, he wouldn't be the first, she thought.

Kate led him into the reception area. She didn't bother to introduce Janet, behind the desk. It was immediately clear that Marcus Broder had no time for nor interest in the little people. His willingness to deal with Kate was limited to the fact that he found her fuckable. She got that. Her job now was to show him something else.

'The main editorial work happens on the sixteenth floor.' She punched a button for the lift. It arrived, empty, and they got in. As the steel doors hissed shut, Kate felt a frisson of enjoyment at being alone with a man like this. The biggest fish she'd ever been confined with.

'So you're a contributing editor?'

'Yes, sir. I write pieces. Popular ones. More reader letters are generated by my stuff than any other writer on the magazine.'

'And what precisely is your stuff?'

'Well.' Kate smiled disarmingly at him. 'It's not high-quality journalism, Mr Broder, but it's what the readers want. Celebrity houses, comparing mascaras, trends for less, spotting the cute bag that Beyoncé picked up before anybody else does. I've got a reputation for being on-trend. Girls love it.'

He smiled at her, cynically. A challenge.

'It sells magazines, Mr Broder,' Kate said.

'Does it?' The doors slid open, and they stepped out on to the floor. Kate felt the eyes of her colleagues burning into her back. This would not improve her popularity around the office, or the jealousy of her workmates. Now she was here with Marcus Broder, for crying out loud.

'This is where the features writers we keep on staff turn in their copy. We like to have them located in the building, so we can get their opinion on photo shoots to accompany the stories, stylists' picks, that kind of thing. It's unusual for a magazine but it works well for *Cutie*.'

He was supremely uninterested. 'How much do you make a year?'

'Excuse me?'

'Did you not hear the question?' Broder asked mildly. 'How much do you make a year? Give me an exact figure, including bonuses, et cetera.'

Kate flushed from the neck up. She should tell him to go to hell. But her whole job here was to please Marcus Broder. Fleur would be judging her on that. And more importantly, Marcus would too.

She looked him in the face. 'I make forty-five thousand. Which is excellent for a writer.'

He laughed. 'Forty-five thousand dollars a year? And you say you know what it takes to sell magazines? Why are you so unambitious?'

She stiffened. 'Unambitious?'

'If you can sell magazines, why aren't you in management? Hell, why haven't you started your own? Come on, Kate Fox. You're better than this. Being a staff writer and boasting about your really very tiny salary.'

'It's not bad for a first job,' she protested.

'It isn't?' He smiled wolfishly at her. 'My first job was at Goldman Sachs trading derivatives. I made a quarter mil a year. And that was in 1978 money. You could buy stuff with that back then.'

Kate coloured. A thrill of desire rippled through her. He was so boastful, so cocky. She loved it.

Her brain tried to imagine having that much money, what that must be like.

'And I was too young to figure out it was chump change,' Broder added dismissively, enjoying her reaction. 'What's your excuse?'

'I like writing.'

'About handbags? Try again, sugar.'

Kate squirmed. What could she say? That this job was a stop gap, something she did to mark the time until she could meet a guy like him? That she was studying hard for her MRS degree?

'Style is a passion of mine,' she said. 'Maybe I'm finding my feet.'

'Well.' He smiled again, backed off her. 'You're certainly stylish. Tell me more about this place. Why you think *Cutie* sells, other than your own pen and ink about shoes and purses.'

Kate took a deep breath and launched into her spiel. She had all the facts, all the figures right at her fingertips, and she was somewhat relieved to see Marcus Broder nodding thoughtfully as she talked. His mind had switched away from her now; he was considering the deal. It was awful that she felt so disappointed by that. For goodness' sake, girl, she told herself. He's married. *Very* married. To one of the most prominent socialites in New York. Broder would be a perfect catch, only he wasn't on the market. And she definitely wanted to be more than a one-night stand, even a mistress. Fobbed off with some sparkly earrings from Tiffany's and a bad reputation.

'So there you have it,' she announced, when she was done.

'Interesting,' Broader said. He looked at her again, and Kate could almost hear the wheels shift in his mind. His detachment was total. He was the type of guy who put things in compartments. She sensed that he had done the deal in his head, and now he was looking for fun again.

'Are you going to buy us?' she asked.

'Do you want me to?'

She nodded. 'Yes, sir. This place needs shaking up. Some more cash. Some attention in the market. If you buy us, advertisers will be more interested again. It'd be great to have that lift.'

'I'm thinking about it, yes.' He looked at her. 'Do you come with the deal?'

Kate smiled back, unafraid. Standing up to him. 'Of course I do. Like I said, I'm a staff writer here.'

'Would you like to have dinner?'

She shrugged lightly. 'Me and some of the team?'

'None of the team.' His eyes narrowed. 'Just you, Miss Fox.'

'No, sir,' she said.

'No?'

'You're married. I'm not looking to be anybody's mistress. Not even someone like you.'

65

He stepped back, surprised at her directness. He smiled a little. 'That's very raw. Besides, I haven't even made you an offer yet.'

'An offer without a ring isn't worth it. I want to get married, at some point. You want to talk about deals? That's the deal. It's pretty likely that no man would want one of your cast-offs, isn't it, Mr Broder?' Kate smiled flirtatiously.

'And what if I told you that my marriage was coming to an end? That I'm about to get divorced?'

'I'd say, that's a shame, feel free to call me after the paperwork's come through.'

'You're a feisty one,' he commented.

Kate shrugged again. 'By the way, Mr Broder, if you're looking at magazines to invest in, you should take a glance at my friend Emily's little independent, *Lucky*.' She heard herself say it, and almost winced. What the hell was she doing? Emily would never sell. She loved that magazine.

But she so wanted to impress Marcus Broder now, after all his sarcastic talk about her salary, and chicken feed, and how badly she was doing. She almost couldn't help herself. Anyway, it wasn't like Emily had to sell, and what harm could it do if somebody offered her a wad of cash? she rationalised.

'It's liberal news and high fashion,' she ploughed on. Well, it was when Kate was involved. 'Sells well in her niche market, but she needs better distribution. Maybe you could make a deal with her. It's different – but you have local papers that eat up a large share of a small market, so you're used to it.'

'*Lucky*, huh?'

'How can you resist with a name like that?' she flirted.

'You've got my card,' Marcus Broder said. 'Email me her details.'

His gaze swept over Kate again, like he could eat her, finish her off in two bites.

'Marcus!'

Fleur D'Amato, flanked by her assistants, swept on to the floor from the hallway. She smiled briskly at Kate, dismissing her. 'I see you've had your tour from our little contributing ed? Good to see how the lower ranks of the staff work?'

'Yes. Fascinating stuff. Kate's very up on her job here.'

'Glad to hear it,' Fleur said sweetly. 'Kate, you can go now. Back to work.' She laughed, a nasty, tinkling little sound. 'Got to write up that "luxe for Less" column. What is it this week, hats?'

'Coats,' Kate said, putting some warmth into her own smile. Like Fleur's venom just sluiced off her back.

'Well, off you go. Mr Broder wants to talk business now.'

Kate smirked. Fleur was so obvious. And so was Marcus Broder, but she admired it when he did it. He was so relentless, so amoral. He just didn't care. He focused on what he wanted, when he wanted it.

Money. Power. Women.

Her.

She extended her manicured hand to Marcus. 'Nice to meet you, Mr Broder.'

'Marcus, please,' he said.

The handshake was firm. 'We'll see each other again, Kate Fox. Sooner than you think. And meanwhile, I'm going to give your friend Emily a call. Tonight.'

That conversation had been four months ago.

Marcus Broder moved fast. And he was as good as his word. By the weekend, Emily was calling, full of excitement, to say that he had contacted her, come by the office, was interested in making a bid. Like Kate had predicted, she was lukewarm on the idea of actually selling, but still thrilled that Marcus was going to offer. It said that *Lucky* had worth.

'It's flattering,' Emily said simply. 'And it *is* a lot of money. Thanks for the tip, Kate.'

'No problem,' Kate answered, trying not to feel guilty. No harm done, right?

A few weeks later, the news of the Broders' impending divorce hit the gossip columns. It was all done, all finished, by the time spring changed into summer.

Broder bought out *Cutie*. Kate waited in vain for her phone to ring, for the front desk to pass her a message. Something, anything. A summons to the new CEO's palatial office across town.

Her phone stayed resolutely silent. Her email box was empty. She was forced to busy herself writing, reporting. Annoyed, she flung herself into her job. She wrote more pieces, styled more shoots, broke some new trends in the pages of *Cutie*. And when she went out, she did it with Emily. No men. No trust-fund brats or hedge-fund traders. The quietness of Marcus Broder annoyed her. Nobody ignored Kate Fox.

And then, finally. After the divorce and the takeover, after Marcus's company had finished talking to *Lucky*, just when her life was settling down . . .

The invitation to the party arrived in her mailbox.

Chapter Six

Kate thrust her way fearlessly through the crowds of women jostling for position near Marcus Broder. They were all sipping their Pol Roger and looking at him heatedly over the rims of their glasses, pretending to talk to each other, sending smoke signals. Nobody wanted to appear too obvious; only some slightly drunk, already married socialites were actually button-holing the host.

Kate pushed on. This was New York, and she was from the Bronx. You didn't get anywhere in this city by being a shrinking violet.

'Marcus,' she said, as he extricated himself from the bony grip of a sixty-something Boston Brahmin from the Upper East Side, dripping in diamonds and old-school mink. 'It's Kate Fox.'

'I know it is.' He grinned, and his gaze settled on her ultra-tight Badgley Mischka dress in pale pink and silver. 'So it's "Marcus" now, is it? Last time we met you were all "Mr Broder" and "sir".'

'That was in the office.' Kate returned the smile. 'Where you are my boss. But now we're at a party, and I'm your guest.'

'An excellent point,' he acknowledged.

Out of the corner of one eye, she noticed the scowls and frowns of the other young women in the vicinity. Well, if she had more balls than them, it wasn't her fault.

'Thank you for the invitation. And happy birthday.'

'You're welcome.' He tilted his glass towards her, and Kate noticed that he was drinking fizzy mineral water. Marcus Broder provided the finest vintage champagne and *grand cru* wines for his guests, but he himself stuck to the soft stuff. Rumour had it that he hated to be out of control. An attribute they shared. 'I was expecting to hear from you.'

Kate laughed. 'And I from you.'

'So it would appear that I cracked first.' Another grin. 'A battle I am happy to have lost.'

'You said you'd see me sooner than I thought,' Kate replied. With the slightest hint of a rebuke.

'I was referring to the divorce,' he said. 'You told me you wouldn't be my mistress. At any price. So there wasn't a lot of point in seeing you until I got that done.' Broder sipped his water. 'Which I did, in record time.'

She blushed. He was so direct, so insistent. 'You didn't do that for me?'

'Of course not.' He smirked. 'I just wanted to be divorced. The fact that you'd then be available was a delightful bonus.'

Kate felt a shiver run down her spine. The arrogance of the guy!

'It's been several months. How do you know I'm available? I could be with anybody right now.'

'You're not. You're available.' He said this with flat, calm certainty.

'How do you know?' She was challenging him. She felt a ripple of desire run through her. Broder was a force of nature.

She couldn't work out if he was sexy, or just a son of a bitch. He left the young, pale moneyed brats in the dust, that was for sure.

'For one, you're here. You came up to me, sought me out. That means you're not dating. For a second, ever since we met, you've been thinking about me.' She blushed scarlet, opened her mouth. 'Don't bother to deny it, sugar. I know women. For a third, I have lots of contacts in this town. People have kept an eye on you. Clubs you were at, who you were with. Your girlfriends, mostly. No single men.'

'You've been spying on me?'

Kate wasn't sure how she felt about that. But Broder was fixing his charming smile on her.

'My friends talk to me. That's all. I notice you don't deny it.'

She shrugged. 'I don't. I haven't dated recently.'

'Since we met?'

'A happy coincidence,' Kate replied, tossing her blond hair. 'Are you going to ask me out?'

Broder blinked, then laughed aloud. 'I don't think any woman has talked to me in quite that way before.'

'First time for everything,' Kate said.

'Yes, there is. My driver will pick you up at eight p.m. tomorrow. Don't say you have plans; I don't enjoy games.'

She inclined her head.

'And now I should mingle.' Broder took her hand, kissed it. Somewhere, she was aware of a flashbulb popping. 'See you tomorrow, Kate Fox.'

Kate watched as he turned away from her, one hand already extended to greet the Mayor and his latest wife. For a second she drank in the body language – how the powerful politician half bowed, lowering his head in front of Broder, how the city's First Lady simpered. Yes, they were sucking up to him. The aura of raw power was incredible. Half the men in the room wanted to placate Marcus Broder, to win his favour. And all the women in the room wanted to be with him.

Except maybe Emily, Kate thought, smiling.

But Kate was the one he had chosen. When they both knew he had had his pick. She glanced again at his back, his narrow shoulders encased in the dark cloth of his bespoke suit. He was shaking hands, holding court. He had moved on from her now. Time to go.

She moved back through the crowd to Emily and kissed her lightly on the cheek. 'You're going to network with the publishing crowd, right?'

'There are some of the biggest distributors in the city here.' Emily nodded at a group of suits standing in one corner. 'I was going to talk to them, if you don't mind.'

'It's fine. I'm actually getting out of here.'

'You're leaving?' Emily blinked. 'But the party's just getting going. Why?'

'Marcus Broder asked me out for tomorrow night.' Kate shrugged.

'So, what? That's misson accomplished?'

Emily was joking, but Kate wasn't.

'For this evening, at least, yes it is,' she said. 'I'll see you tomorrow, OK?'

Emily shook her head, but Kate was determined. 'OK.'

Kate squeezed her friend's arm and was gone, in a slither of silk. When Broder looked around for her, some minutes later, he would notice that. That she'd left. The same way he noticed everything about her. Kate Fox didn't hang around like a spare lemon. He had asked her out, so there was no point in staying, involving herself in conversation with the social X-rays, or lesser rich guys.

In the taxi on the way back home, reclining against the ripped black leather seat, Kate smiled to herself. This would become an infrequent mode of transportation for her. She was a limousine girl, all the way.

She was quietly sure that Marcus Broder was going to see to that.

He didn't do subtle. That was what she noticed on day one. The car came for her on time, complete with uniformed chauffeur and a chilled bottle of vintage Krug on ice in the back seat. Kate didn't touch it. Who knew what he would think of women who drank?

She also didn't ask any questions when the limo swung away from Manhattan and out of town. Rather she busied herself with emails on her phone. When Broder asked for a report from his driver, the guy would have to say she was cool. Anyway, she figured it out within fifteen minutes.

They were heading to Teeterboro – the small airfield where they kept the private jets.

A shiver of pleasure ran down her spine.

She looked great. She'd made sure of that. A silver wrap dress by Burberry Prorsum, with a square neckline and little cap sleeves. It sat modestly just above the knee, but it clung to every curve of her gorgeous body. Her long blond hair was washed and blow-dried. Her make-up was smooth – she'd used the Laura Mercier primer today, the custom-blended Bobbi Brown foundation, YSL bronzer on her cheeks, contrasting with metallic rose eyeshadow and Chanel's pink-silver Rouge Argent lipstick. Her purse was a Kate Spade hung with hundreds of tiny beads of mother-of-pearl, and her

Wolford stockings tapered down to teetering Manolo pumps in pewter. A soft grey lambswool shawl hung around her shoulders and she had perfumed herself with nothing but a spritz of rosewater.

It was a knockout look. The driver's eyes had almost popped out of his head as she slid gracefully into the back seat of the car. Getting into that dress was like putting on a suit of armour. This was the big one, and Kate Fox was headed to battle.

Marcus Broder was waiting for her on the tarmac, next to a gleaming Gulfstream IV. She walked towards him, smiling confidently, her purse swinging. He lifted his hands a little, as though in surrender.

'You look ravishing,' he said appreciatively. 'That's a hell of a dress.'

'And this is a hell of a date.' Kate made no attempt to conceal how impressed she was. Broder didn't like games; he'd said that already. 'I like your ride.'

He laughed, but he was pleased. 'It's the company's jet.'

'Is this business?' she teased.

'I'm the CEO. I do what I like. It's a short flight; we're headed to my house in Nantucket.'

'Sounds perfect,' Kate agreed. 'You didn't need to push the boat out for me, Marcus.'

'It's what I do,' he said, then added, 'if I really like a girl.'

The first date was blissful. Like all Kate's dreams had come true. The private plane took them smoothly down to the shore, and another short limo ride delivered them to Marcus's enormous ocean-side mansion, complete with private beach. It was tough not to stare, tough not to drool; she couldn't contain the waves of excitement. Oh God! This was it, this was everything she'd waited for, everything Momma dreamed of, all those years ago in the Bronx! And she was close, this close to it!

Servants laid out a dinner on a vast terrace overlooking the ocean: local lobster, some champagne, ripe strawberries, chocolates by Debauve & Gallais, Jamaican Blue Mountain coffee. Kate enjoyed the glow of outstanding performance. She felt like she was in the zone. She focused exclusively on Marcus, asking about his hobbies, his schooling, the history of his life, and she managed to listen to the answers as though they were the most fascinating thing she had ever heard. She laughed at his jokes, kept it light and fresh. If Marcus asked about her, she made the answers short. And to wrap up a perfect evening, at the end of the night he didn't even try to get her into bed.

Kate disembarked from the plane into the limo that would carry her back home, filled with a wonderful feeling of achievement. Marcus had liked what he saw. He didn't make an immediate move. Meaning, he saw her as a prospect, as a proper girlfriend, not just an easy lay. That was the first hurdle cleared. And if she hadn't exactly been thrilled with his conversation, so what? She could grow into him. She could grow into his *life*, real easy. The pleasure for her was being appreciated by Marcus Broder.

The great connoisseur approved. And he'd already asked for a second date . . .

Kate planned the whole thing meticulously, yet sometimes it felt as though he was sweeping her along. She made herself available whenever he wanted, whenever he called, accompanying him to private gallery viewings, charity balls, political dinners. At the same time, she went on with her work. The mutterings in the office reached fever pitch about a week in – Fleur and everybody else shot her the most venomous looks – but after that they subsided. Kate smiled to herself. That's right, they had all started to worry, hadn't they? What if Marcus Broder actually *liked* her? What if he decided to marry her? Then she would be somebody none of them could afford to offend.

That idea occurred to the entire office at about the same time. The nasty looks were replaced by warm smiles. Kate was invited to more meetings, and allowed to choose her own assignments each issue. Co-workers started to make her coffee. Her articles got prominently positioned in the new issue of the magazine. Fleur commissioned two major features from her, real articles, not just price-comparison stuff.

Kate just smiled serenely and said nothing.

She also behaved perfectly with the press. They swarmed around her flat, they waited outside nightclubs, they rang her mobile until she had to change her number. But she didn't give the paparazzi a passing glance, didn't give the gossip columnists so much as a 'no comment'. Instead, she just *didn't* comment. She waited.

And it got results. Marcus made his move on sex a month later. After a satisfyingly respectable period.

When Marcus Broder got tired of waiting, he made it clear. They were some way into dating, he'd shown her off in public, introduced her at dinners and lunches. There were the corporate jets, the exclusive resort islands, the best tables at New York's finest private members' clubs. Kate refused any gifts he tried to give her, though, even when they came wrapped in a little cardboard box of duck-egg blue tied with Tiffany's signature white ribbon. Her instincts prickled with danger; she could accept his hospitality, they told her, but never a gift, nothing to keep, nothing with value. She tried not to think about the diamond earrings and South Sea pearl bracelets she was giving up. A real huntress would keep her eyes on the ultimate prize.

And Broder was that prize. Kate Fox was shooting for the big game.

But he'd treated her with respect. And she'd stood up for herself, by not allowing him to say he'd bought her. It was clear to Kate that Marcus wasn't a 'no sex before marriage' kind of guy. He was more the 'try before you buy' type. She had to accept that. Once he was past the two-week mark, she upped the flirting. And when he showed signs of impatience, she allowed herself to be seduced. She suggested dinner at his place.

'Which one?' he asked, grinning. 'Nantucket? The Hamptons?'

'You have somewhere in town?' Kate asked, innocently. As if she didn't know.

Marcus barked with laughter, playing along. 'Sure. More than one. My main joint is the penthouse on Central Park West. Does that suit you?'

'Suits fine,' Kate said lightly. 'Anywhere we can be private. Anyway, I've got to go. I've got copy to file. Call me later?'

She blew him a kiss and hung up.

It was working. She could see it, sense it in her bones. He was like a big fish on a line, and she was reeling him in very slow, very carefully. Keeping the tension just right. Not letting anything snap. It was a balance, a game of psychological chess, she decided. Men like Marcus didn't want a gold-digger, but they *did* want her to be impressed. They wanted to show off. And her job was to be an appreciative audience, a shiny mirror that reflected Marcus Broder, the man he was, the man he wanted to be. He valued that she never pretended to be blasé about his wealth, but at the same time she never chased it. Kate was busy with her friends, her little job, her own life. And Broder enjoyed that.

Now he wanted to sleep with her. And Kate was ready. For weeks now, she'd been psyching herself up. Plenty of boyfriends and dates littered her past, but sex – not much of that. She had been so careful, parcelling herself out only rarely.

But she wasn't a virgin. And even though she'd never chosen to face it, to look deeply into the raw facts of it, she had learned something about men, especially entitled, rich men, the kind whose arm she appeared on at parties. Sex wasn't enough for guys like that – but it was required. There was simply too much competition out there, too many hot chicks ready to give it up at the drop of a hat. When the right man turned up, he would want sex. And plenty of it.

Kate thought about how she would handle Marcus. If she was inexperienced, he'd never know. She had to be a lady in public, but hotter than hell between the sheets. She'd read books, she'd talked to girls in the office, she'd spent a few embarrassing hours on the web, she'd raked over all her memories from the relationships gone by; Marcus would need enthusiasm, skill, a sense of the forbidden, plenty of frequency. Today's trophy wife was different, perhaps; you couldn't be a total bimbo. But one thing would never change. Mrs Marcus Broder, by definition, would be a world-class seductress. Without that, you didn't get in the door.

So that night, she was ready. She poured herself one chilled glass of vintage champagne, to take the edge off. Just the one, mind – sloppy wasn't sexy. But she needed to relax. This had to be the performance of her life, starting from the moment the limo dropped her at his building.

Kate turned up for the date in a slinky dress of dusky pink silk that looked almost poured on to her tanned skin. She marvelled at his vast penthouse, with its huge pre-war windows and towering ceilings, building-wide, ten thousand square feet of prime New York skyline, with the greenery of Central Park laid out below them, and every modern creature comfort baked into the walls and hidden under the floorboards and behind the joists. The place looked antique but it sure functioned modern. Hell, her cooing appreciation didn't need to be faked. The apartment was truly spectacular. This is the best kind of foreplay, Kate told herself, And when Marcus's butler served them dinner *à deux* – oysters, a fresh crab salad, a perfect Chablis, and Italian gelato flown in specially from the best little place in Rome: pear and apple flavours, with a touch of bitter chocolate sauce – Kate made certain to remark on everything from the flavours to the eighteenth-century European silver cutlery. She made one further glass of wine, served with the meal, last all evening – not enough to get tipsy, but just enough to relax her, to cause her to lose her inhibitions and focus on Marcus Broder. He was attractive, in that predatory, arrogant way. Maybe there was something missing, sure, but Kate could overlook trifles like that. Nobody was perfect. Marcus was slightly too skinny for her, but she tried to tell herself he was wiry, lean. Like a panther, sleek and sinuous. Hunting her. His face was strong with purpose, his eyes fastened on her. And he knew exactly what a prize he was. When he led her into the bedroom, another magnificent cavernous room, hung with Renaissance tapestries, set about with priceless antiques, and slid her lace shawl off her shoulders, she smiled and unzipped her little silk dress, and it slithered in a heap by her Louboutin heels.

Revealing that she was completely naked. No underwear. Nothing.

Broder was stunned. For a second, Kate felt a rush of triumph. She had actually surprised him. He couldn't move, couldn't speak. Arrogantly, keeping her back straight, the line of her breasts lifted beautifully, her firm, round ass sticking out a little from her slim waist, she lifted her heel and kicked the dress away, and then stood there. Nude. Heels. Long blond hair tumbling down her back.

'Holy shit,' Marcus Broder breathed. He was erect, excited. She could see it through his clothes. 'I want you. I've got to have you.'

Kate slipped from the heels and climbed on to the Chinese silk coverlet that adorned the English four-poster bed. She lay on her back, kicked her legs apart. 'Great. Come and get me.'

He did. And after that there was no stopping them.

What Kate felt, she told herself, was immaterial. There was nothing actually *wrong* with Marcus; no deformities, no kinks. If she didn't feel anything much, so what? She could deal with it. Great sex was probably a myth, she told herself, a fantasy invented by men for porn videos, where the women enjoyed it as much as they did. She tried to ignore the sense of relief she felt whenever Marcus gasped with pleasure and was through with her. And there were plenty of consolations. The excitement of being with him swept her along, the envy in the stares of other women, the limos and private jets, the penthouses and vintage champagne, the gifts of important, expensive jewellery from Tiffany's and House Massot that he would try to give her, and which she always turned down. It was the life she'd always longed for, that her momma had dreamed of, and hell, it was well worth all the work she put in. Including the stuff in the bedroom.

Wasn't this what women had always done? Wasn't this the great unspoken secret of life? Sex was the ticket, the price of admission. And a savvy woman paid up, without complaining. There was no point in dreaming of something better.

Marcus needed her to be hot stuff, and Kate ignored her misgivings. She went for it, all in. She made herself act sexy. Hey, maybe one day she'd start enjoying it like he did. But for now, she told herself, just keep at it . . .

She surprised him in public. Turning up to charity balls then dragging him into a bathroom to cup him, toy with him. Leaning across at a boring charity dinner and whispering a fantasy in his ear till he dared not rise from his seat. Cooking for him at home, then, while he distracted himself on his BlackBerry, stripping and serving his food stark naked. It was always something new, something fresh with her. He was charmed, pleased, impressed. She brought imagination to the whole thing. And Marcus Broder reciprocated in kind. Showing up at her office to fly her to dinner – in Paris. Filling her entire flat with yellow roses, when she mentioned in passing that they were her favourite flower. Since she wouldn't accept jewellery, he sent thoughtful little gifts: books, perfume, a dozen bagels from her favourite store with smoked salmon flown in that morning direct from Scotland. He was attentive to her in bed, playing with her, stroking her, holding her close when they were finished. And Kate knew better than to ever say no. She was available, and made herself seem enthusiastic. After all, it was a giant opportunity. Every time he reached for her. And she seized it.

Outside the bedroom, Kate worked it too. She met Marcus's mother, his only parent, ensconced in an upscale retirement home in Beverly Hills; the old lady was distant, nodding at Kate as though she barely registered.

'She's not all there,' Marcus said. He was edgy, like he couldn't wait to get away. 'Her mind wanders. She won't get who you are. Doesn't recognise me half the time.'

'Do you see her much?' Kate asked timidly.

'I go every season.' His face showed it was not a task he relished. 'Truth is, she's happy here. I pay for round-the-clock care, she's got friends. I have doctors who visit her, check up on staff. We were never that close.'

'You had a tough childhood?'

'My dad was an accountant. Mom was more about him than me.' He shrugged. 'It was OK, I guess. But we've never been the Brady Bunch, you know?'

'We could visit more often. I could fly down . . .'

'She finds it tiring. Exhausting.' Kate looked back at the old woman, already talking to one of her nurses. 'Truth is, I don't enjoy seeing her like this. It's morbid. We both do it, but I don't know who gets anything out of it.'

Kate nodded. 'I understand.'

This was as close as Marcus ever came to speaking emotionally to her, and she didn't quite know how to handle it.

'Well, at least you'll never have to visit my folks,' she joked as the chauffeur pulled away from the manicured lawns either side of the drive. They were heading back to LAX after a single night.

'That's right. You're an orphan.' Marcus lifted his bottle of Evian water to her. 'It's a plus.'

* * *

She knew he was going to propose. Before it even happened. He had booked them on a vacation together, a whole week in a luxury resort in Costa Rica. He had taken the most exclusive suite in the place, and chartered the corporate plane to fly them down. Kate's radar was on full alert. She packed her best dresses: long, clinging silks, tight Gucci or vintage Azzedine Alaia, micro sundresses from the Gap. And bikinis . . . fuller, with structured support, if they walked on the beach; tiny scraps of Missoni string and netting for beside their own private pool. She wasn't sure when exactly he'd do it, so every outfit needed to be perfect. She planned her looks with military care. Borderline slutty if he was the only man in the room, sexy-but-unattainable if they were in public.

'He's going to do it,' she announced to Emily down the phone line.

'He might not,' Emily said. 'Don't get your hopes up too high . . .'

'It's definite.' Kate brushed that aside. 'We *never* go away together for more than a weekend. The press aren't here, they can't get in. He keeps giving me these strange looks. Two weeks ago he asked me how I felt about pre-nups and I said I thought every modern couple should have one.'

'Romantic,' Emily said drily.

'Oh, come on. He's worth hundreds of millions and he's been divorced four times. No way he's getting hitched without one, so that's the sixty-four-thousand-dollar question, isn't it?'

'The hundred-million-dollar one, I guess.'

'Asking me that is like telling me he's going to propose. I laughed and said no woman should object to one unless she was a gold-digger. He smiled. I think I passed the test. A week later he booked this vacation.' Kate cradled the phone in her hand and walked to the huge bow windows of their air-conditioned suite. Somewhere below, Marcus was having a private tennis lesson with an ex-Wimbledon doubles champion. 'He's spent so much money on it, you know, Em.'

'That's hardly unusual.'

'Yes, but this time he went crazy. Took the corporate jet out here. The best of everything, all charged to Broder, Inc.' Kate shook her head. 'I've seen him whip out the black company Amex. And he's going nuts with it.'

'I'm sure his finance director will be thrilled.'

Kate chuckled. 'Don't be square, Em, it's his company.'

'It's got shareholders,' Emily said mildly.

'Well, Marcus does what he wants. Treats that jet like his personal limo service. I watch him write the corporate cheques. Hey, they all love him, right?'

'They certainly seem to.'

Kate gazed down at the view in front of her. She was fascinated by how Marcus just drew on company money, treated it like his own; treated the world like it was own, like everything belonged to him. Even if sometimes actual profits at Broder seemed pretty thin, from the papers Marcus left lying around his room, the emails he sent lying in bed beside her at night, once he was through fucking her. None of that seemed to matter. She kept mental notes; life was one giant piggy bank to the guy, and after all, he was inviting her to share some of those spoils.

Costa Rica stretched out, green and lush, baking in the sun, down to an azure sea sparkling brilliantly in the white-hot heat. It was a long way from Flatbush Avenue, that was for sure.

'And you definitely want it?' Emily asked. 'Truly?'

Kate glanced around her. The soft, snowy white carpet,

thick and welcoming under her bare feet. The bed, hung with Chinese silk and a pale gold satin coverlet. The walnut dresser, the flat-screen TV mounted on the wall, the long fish tank that ran the length of their living room. Every conceivable luxury, and all within her grasp.

'Oh yes,' she said firmly. 'I want it.'

Chapter Seven

She didn't have long to wait. Marcus suggested, after they'd dined in the resort's exclusive private orangery, that she take a walk with him on the beach. All they had to do was walk down four little wooden steps, and they were already on the sand. It was night, still tropical and hot, with cool breezes lifting off the water. Kate sighed with pleasure.

'Man, this is glorious,' she said. She squeezed Marcus's arm. 'Thank you for bringing me here. I could stay for ever.'

'You can't stay for ever. We've got work to do.' He grinned. 'Well, I have work to do.'

'My magazine is very important,' Kate pouted.

'Sure it is. It's nice to be a writer. But your talents are far more suited to other things.'

She hit him lightly in the chest. 'Ssh, somebody will hear you.'

'So what if they do? You're mine.' He paused. 'And I think you *should* stay for ever. Not here, exactly. But with me.'

Kate slowed her walk. Her heart started to pump. Was it happening? Was this actually happening?

Marcus Broder reached into his inner jacket pocket and produced a small black box.

'Oh God,' Kate breathed, and it was almost a true prayer.

Carefully he lowered himself to one knee, keeping the fabric of his very expensive suit just above the sand.

'Kate Fox,' he said. 'You're perfect for me. Will you marry me?'

With a practised movement, his thumb flicked open the lid of the box. A huge, flawless diamond sat there. Kate guessed three and a half carats, and it was flanked on either side by two translucent trillion-cut pigeon's blood rubies, that probably cost more than the diamond. She gasped. That was a hell of a ring.

'Oh Marcus!' she said. 'Oh yes, yes please! Oh, baby . . . !'

He grinned and rose to his feet, tugging the ring from its velvet cushion, then took her hand and slid it on. It fitted her to perfection. Kate trembled, and hugged him, then lifted her mouth to him, kissing him, slipping her tongue inside his mouth, running it under his upper lip, pressing her hand, hidden by her body, against his crotch.

'Let's go home,' she whispered.

'Sounds good to me.' He laughed. 'I've booked the plane for tomorrow. Once we get back to Manhattan, we'll take care of the legal stuff and then I'll book us a ceremony somewhere. I don't believe in hanging around, do you?'

'No,' Kate said fervently. She did not. Kate Broder, that sounded pretty goddamned good to her. Why wait? She wanted the ring, the name, the status. Man! If only it were morning already. She stared lovingly at her ring. She couldn't wait to see this in daylight. 'We shouldn't wait. And I'll sign anything your lawyers put in front of me, sweetheart.' She kissed him full on the lips. 'We're going to be so happy!'

The wedding day was everything she'd ever dreamed. She persuaded Marcus to elope, because she wanted to get the second, more important ring on her finger, and she didn't want any delay over vanilla sponge with passion fruit coulis vs German chocolate cake with hot ginger sauce. Besides, a church would look unbalanced. Emily was the only real friend she had; there was no family, she had no parents, none that counted anyway. She told herself she was prepared to absorb Marcus's world. But when she met his friends and made them hers, she wanted to be Mrs Broder, to be able to demand respect for her position.

'I agree.' Marcus scooped her up in his arms, and she wrapped her legs obediently around him. 'I've done the society wedding to death. Let's try something new.'

They chartered a private jet and flew out to Reno, Nevada. Marcus had chosen the city's most luxurious hotel, the Reno Victrix, for the ceremony, and a minister came to marry them in a room filled with roses of every conceivable colour ... cream to dark sapphire, pale green to blood-red scarlet. The effect was giddy. Kate wore Vera Wang haute couture, created personally by the designer; Marcus told her, in triumph, that he'd ordered it a few months back. He himself chose a Savile Row suit and Armani shoes. His wedding gift to Kate was a serious piece of jewellery, an antique necklace from Paris, a glorious collar of seed pearls and topaz, threaded through with peridot and citrine, that sparkled and glinted in orange, white and green against the cream of her dress. She gave him an antique map of the Roman Empire; tasteful, but not expensive. Exactly what he expected from her.

As the minister said the words, and the glorious immediacy of Nevada's marriage laws took effect, Kate sighed with relief, a long-drawn-out exhalation that seemed to fill her whole body. She kissed her groom, long and hard. Her body was open, receptive. She was grateful.

Wasn't this the high point of her entire life?

Mom had told her to marry money, to marry well. Never to overlook what a rich man could do for you. And she'd done it, a little later than planned maybe, but she'd done it. All those years at school and college. All those carefully chosen dresses and white wine spritzers at the city's most chic watering holes. She'd won, she'd done it. Her kids would never have to work a job, worry about rent, worry about school fees. As Kate looked up at Marcus, in that moment, she hoped she really loved him. Because he was the dream, wasn't he? Wasn't that right?

Her rings glittered on her hand. And Marcus was handsome, powerful, stinking rich. The perfect bridegroom. Nothing could go wrong, Kate thought fiercely, absolutely nothing.

She didn't even want to call Emily. Em might disapprove, and she didn't want to let anything colour her day. Tomorrow would be soon enough. That first day, Kate Broder – that's right, she thought fiercely, Kate Broder, Mrs Marcus Broder – didn't choose to let a single negative thought intrude.

Marcus led her upstairs. For privacy, he had rented the entire top floor of the hotel. They made love in the cavernous suite overlooking the city, then went and had lunch *à deux* in the roof-garden restaurant, which they had entirely to themselves. Kate was full of excitement. She could barely eat. She took care to listen to all Marcus's plans, not pour out her own ideas. It would be bad if he thought she'd got the ring on her finger and was suddenly taking over. She confined herself to staring at him adoringly and running her bare foot up and down his leg, under the table. He'd be ready for sex again in an hour, she decided. All of a sudden her mind had made the shift. From sexy, classy girlfriend to picture-perfect wife. Dignified to outsiders, hot stuff to Marcus, when they were alone. He was her territory now, and she was playing defence, not attack, but she was still fighting, Kate thought.

There were a lot of pretty young women in America. And Marcus Broder was now on his fourth wife. Even today, she could have no illusions.

'So, you'll obviously move in, tonight.'

'Oh. Sure, of course.' Kate frowned lightly with worry. 'What about my stuff?'

'Your stuff? You mean at your apartment?'

'Yes. My clothes . . . I've got some books, my laptop, furniture . . .'

He laughed. 'I'll send an assistant round to bag up all that up and donate it to Goodwill.'

Kate blinked. 'What? But my shoes, my clothes . . .'

'We'll get you new ones.'

'Darling, some of my clothes are nice designer dresses . . .'

'Nice? It's all ready-to-wear,' Marcus said, dismissively. 'My wife shops the collections. And your shoes, well, let's just get new ones. You're starting over with me. I don't want you bringing a lot of clutter.'

'OK. Thank you, sweetie,' Kate said. A flush of heat spread through her body. Donate it all to charity? Start again with haute couture? Brand-new shoes, anything she wanted? She wondered if she should pinch herself. God, if the girls at school could see her now! 'So then I'll just get the laptop. It has some projects I'm working on . . .'

'Working on?' He laughed. 'You mean you didn't quit your job yet?'

'Uh, no.'

'I'll call Fleur for you.'

Kate ran her tongue inside her mouth, nervously. 'You don't think I should have a job?'

'Do you?' He threw the question back at her. 'Tire yourself out for forty thousand a year? So that we can have a hundred million *and* forty thousand dollars?' His eyebrow arched, and Kate shrank a little in her seat, feeling ridiculous. 'Call me crazy, but I'd rather have a woman who's fresh and ready to welcome me home each night. Or who's available at lunch if I want her. Doesn't that sound a lot more fun?'

'Oh yes.' She smiled, ran her hand up his thigh. In the background, the waiters hovered.

'Don't worry.' It was like he could see right through her. 'You'll love it. Shopping, whenever you want. Take a Pilates class. Get your hair done. Let other women slave away in an office; you'll be lying on the massage table in a spa in Fifth Avenue, having two therapists rub at your back and calves. Believe me, this is what people work for all their lives. Even then most of them never make it. You just took a short cut, baby.'

He lifted his head and looked around, and immediately a waiter came over, practically running. The way people always did around Marcus. Ready to jump to whatever he wanted.

'Dessert, sir?'

He nodded. 'I'll take the lemon ice cream with the strawberry coulis.'

'And for madam?'

Kate considered the lemon ice cream. That sounded real good, in the hot Nevada sun. But Marcus had his eyebrow raised, looking at her. She didn't want him to think she would relax, get fat, out of shape.

'Just a fresh mint tea is good for me,' she said. 'No sugar.'

'Yes, ma'am. Right away.'

Marcus smiled approvingly. 'You're right, Kate. This is going to be perfect.'

* * *

She called Emily on the way home, using the sky phone on the back of her seat. She needn't have worried – her best friend was supportive as ever. Happy for her, she said.

'It's what you've always wanted, Kate. You like him?'

'I love him,' Kate said, gratefully. She prayed it was true.

'Then that's just wonderful. And you don't have to put up with Fleur any more . . . think about that.'

Kate did think about it. She glanced down the length of the jet. Marcus was up front, working on something on his wafer-thin laptop.

'So you reckon it's OK? That I don't have a job? You know, Fleur will just be happy she doesn't have to deal with me.' Kate chewed on her lip. 'It's funny, I kind of hate giving her the satisfaction.'

'Don't kid yourself. Fleur will be as jealous as hell of you. And frightened that you'll get her into trouble with the boss.'

That was true. But get her into trouble as a wife did. She would no longer see Kate as any kind of a business threat. If she ever had. And Kate was surprised at how much that idea stung her.

'You don't think Fleur would like that penthouse on Fifth? That rock on her hand? Come on, you *are* what her magazine sells. Think of it that way. She's been secretly hoping Marcus will dump you this entire time. You know it's true.'

'Yes.' She did. Kate breathed out. 'You're right, of course you're right. But Emily . . .'

'I can't believe what I'm hearing.' Man, this phone was good; Em sounded like she was in the next room. 'Kate, this is what you've planned since you hit puberty. Maybe before. And now you've got it, you don't want it?'

'Oh, I do want it,' Kate replied firmly. Yeah, there was no doubt about that. She was digging the private jets even more now she rode on them as of right . . . as *Mrs Broder*. Her rings sparkled madly on her finger in the sunlight streaming through the window, as they soared above cloud cover. 'Maybe I'm greedy. I just want all this, and the old stuff too.'

'Honey.' Emily's sensible tones pulled her back down to earth. 'You say you love Marcus, right? So just enjoy it. Make him happy. You always said you didn't want to work; you've got what you wanted. If he doesn't think you should tire yourself out, listen to that. Put it another way, you're playing in the big leagues now. Your job is Marcus Broder, and rumour has it he's a *very* demanding boss.'

Kate laughed aloud, and up the plane Marcus turned his head to smile at her. She dropped her voice. 'You're a hundred per cent right, as ever. Thanks so much, Em. Please forget I said anything. Let's have lunch tomorrow? Or Tuesday?'

'Whenever.' Emily's voice smiled down the phone. 'You're buying.'

They met for lunch at Sushi of Gari on the Upper West Side, expensive but not outrageous. Kate was already trying to pick venues she thought Emily would be comfortable with. Dating Marcus, it had been a struggle . . . Marcus only ate at the best, and he wasn't interested in making Emily comfortable. In fact, he hadn't been interested in Emily at all.

'Like I told you, the fact that you're an orphan is a plus.'

He was smiling, but the words scared Kate, and the edge in his voice.

'What do you mean by that?' she asked lightly.

'You know. That you come without attachments. I mean, I have plenty of friends.'

He had no friends at all, as far as Kate could see. Like her, there were lots of business acquaintances ... and Marcus Broder lived at a much higher level. His dinner companions were CEOs, congressmen, senators, social powerhouses from the Manhattan scene. Immediately, he'd made it clear that there was no room in their lives for any of the chicks Kate used to take for lunch, girls from the dating scene who were useless now she was married, women from the *Cutie* office, the odd girl from her college days. And Kate made no objection. None of them meant anything to her. Unlike Kate, however, Marcus didn't have a best friend, a real buddy he could hang out with. She tried to tell him Emily was special.

'I remember. She had a magazine. Didn't want to sell it to me.'

Kate smiled, encouragingly. 'That's right, sweetie. I only got you to ask the question to impress you, really. I knew she'd never sell.'

Marcus shrugged. 'So why do you want to see her again?'

'Because she's my best friend. I told you that.'

He sighed. 'We can have dinner. Does she have a date?'

'I don't think so. She's been busy at work,' Kate said defensively, protectively.

Marcus laughed. 'Because she's got an ass the size of Kansas, you mean.'

Dinner was not a success. Marcus hired a private room in Le Bernardin and had it filled with fresh-cut flowers and an off-the-menu dinner prepared. He then reacted to Emily with supreme indifference, answering her questions in mono-syllables, checking his emails on his BlackBerry, and forcing Kate to do all the work. His eyes swept with contempt up and down Emily's soft, curvy figure, her plain black dress from Ann Taylor, and her flat shoes. She wasn't hot and she wasn't rich, and therefore, his attitude said, she didn't matter.

Kate kissed her friend goodbye at the end of the evening, waving her off with a false cheeriness. She turned to Marcus with anger in her eyes, opening her mouth to speak. But there was something in his gaze, a coldness, a rigid set of the shoulders, that scared her, gave her pause.

'No idea what you see in that one,' he said flatly. 'We won't be doing that again.'

'She is a good friend,' Kate muttered, deflated.

'See her on your own time, but I think you might have outgrown her.' Marcus yawned. 'Let's get home, get to bed.'

She knew better than to say anything further. Might have outgrown her? That was perilously close to Marcus telling her to drop Emily. Kate preferred to concentrate on the permission. See her on your own time. Which was exactly what she'd continued to do.

Embarrassed by his boorishness, not wanting to face up to it, Kate made sure there were no more Le Bernardins, no ultra-fancy Manhattan restaurants that screamed about the social divide between herself and her friend. Emily wasn't exactly pushing to hang out with her husband, either.

'He's, uh, he's very interesting,' she said, diplomatically. 'Driven . . . focused on his work, I can see that. If that's what you like,' she added, the hint of a question floating in there.

'Marcus looks after me,' Kate said, and that was enough answer, right? Uncomfortable with the oil-and-water mix, she didn't try to bring them together again.

Besides, if she was honest, there was a tiny plus to the fact that Marcus and Emily didn't get on. It could be . . . not that she admitted it to herself, at least not aloud . . . just a teensy-tiny bit wearing, being Mrs Marcus Broder version 4.0, going to restaurants where dinner cost a week's rent in her old apartment, always perfectly coiffed, styled, wearing the right couture and carrying the correct bag. Meeting Emily was an escape. Like a day pass back to a different life. It was amazing, Kate thought as she pushed her way through the door of the crowded little restaurant, how much she could look forward to grabbing some sushi.

And not only that. Wearing her Gap true skinny pants with the knee-high Armani buckle boots, flat but sexy, and her plain silk Donna Karan tee with the soft cashmere sweater from Banana Republic. High-street stores and ready to wear. What Marcus would consider suitable clothes for one of their staff. But an outfit that relaxed Kate.

'Hi!' Emily jumped to her feet. 'You look gorgeous. Really. It's amazing. Rich suits you.'

'Never mind me.' Kate looked her friend up and down. Emily had lost a little weight, gained a touch of muscle tone, and was wearing a flattering pair of jeans with buttery chestnut leather ankle boots and a fitted navy shirt that showed off her breasts, gave the suggestion of a waist. Her eyes glittered, and her hair had obviously been blow-dried. 'What about you? What's up?'

They ordered. Kate indulged in a spicy tuna roll and some sashimi, since Marcus wasn't there to count her calories.

'Now tell me,' she pressed Emily. 'And don't bother trying to lie. There's a man, isn't there? You have someone.'

'Maybe,' Emily admitted. Their pressed lychee and watermelon juice came to the table, poured over ice with a slice of lime. 'OK, yes . . .'

Kate wanted to jump up and down. She was thrilled, more excited than she'd been for months. 'Who is he? How did you meet?'

'He's called Paul.' Emily sighed happily. She pronounced

the name like it was something exotic and precious. 'He works in magazine distribution. Ran the New York metro accounts for one of the big packagers. He went to Columbia originally; he was going to be a professor, but then he couldn't get tenure, and he'd had this placement on his MBA. Then he ran out of money . . . Anyway, he took a job, and he was good at it, and they promoted him. But he wants to quit. He asked if he could invest some money in *Lucky* . . . we started talking . . .'

'Does he have a lot of money?'

Emily shook her head. 'Just about a hundred thousand saved up. But lots of good ideas. He's smart, he's a really decent guy.' She blushed. 'I kind of like him. I like him a lot.'

'Em! That's *wonderful*.' Kate squeezed her arm. 'You look so happy. Maybe this could be the guy. When can I meet him?'

A look of panic flitted across Emily's face. 'Do you think you guys want to meet him? He's not like Marcus, Kate. He's . . . he's great but he's pretty small-time. Like me,' she added.

'It's OK.' Kate fell over herself to reassure her. 'Just me, maybe. Marcus is pretty busy . . . The three of us could grab some pasta someplace. How long have you been going out?'

'A month,' Emily said. 'But you know, it really feels different with this guy.'

Kate arranged another lunch, that Friday, with Paul and Emily. They ate at a little trattoria in Chelsea, and she was overjoyed to find she liked the guy; he was quiet, thoughtful, entranced by Emily's sweetness and brains and humour. He was short himself, and losing his hair, and it was clear from the way he gazed at Emily that he thought he'd found a great match. He liked her pretty eyes, sneaked the odd look at her breasts; Kate could see his attraction, enjoyed the collected, hopeful side of him, a good counterweight to Emily's natural pessimism.

She hoped it worked out, and somehow she expected it to as well. When somebody is with the right man you can always tell, she thought. Why shouldn't Emily have her own version of the fairy tale?

Because Kate had got hers. Right?

Chapter Eight

Dreams do come true. And they take some adjusting to.

Kate allowed Marcus to sweep her into his world. She was unresisting, enthusiastic, grateful. Her clothes duly went to Goodwill, and she turned up at Fifth Avenue with nothing more than the silk dress on her back and the Louboutins on her feet. There was a perfectly sized pink Chanel suit hanging in the closet, and the next morning, after Marcus kissed her on the cheek and went off to work, a personal shopper called.

'Mrs Broder? I'm Lilly. Mr Broder asked me to show you around. Get you some stuff.'

Kate laughed. 'I think I can do my own clothes shopping, Lilly. I was a contributing editor for *Cutie*. I know fashion.'

Lilly smiled brightly. 'Mr Broder said you might say that, ma'am, but not this sort of fashion. This isn't the stuff they sell in department stores. We've got appointments at the ateliers. That is, if you're not too busy.'

Kate thought of her blank diary. Besides, Marcus wanted this, didn't he? He'd set it up, and that had to be a hint.

'I'm not. It's fine.'

'We have Chanel, Gucci and Prada today. Armani and Versace tomorrow. Those are Mr Broader's favourites. But you can add anything into the mix you feel like.'

101

'Thank you,' Kate said, ironically. 'Nice to know I'm allowed the occasional assist.'

'Certainly. There are a few things I know he likes, but you can choose whatever else you might want.' She added hastily, 'I do know certain styles Mr Broder isn't partial to, so I'll be sure to help you with those.'

'I'll pick my own clothes,' Kate said sharply. The joke had worn thin. 'Thank you for making the appointments. You can arrange payment and delivery if you want.'

Lilly bristled. 'Mr Broder has used me for years. He always has me select—'

'And I always select my own outfits. We're clear on that, right?'

'Yes, Mrs Broder.'

'Excellent. My shoe size is 8, if you want to start there. I like Louboutin and Manolo, but I'm willing to try other things.'

'Yes, ma'am.'

'That's everything for right now, Lilly. Thanks for that,' Kate said, and offered a brisk smile of her own. For a moment the grin on Lilly's face faded, and Kate wondered if she'd challenge her. But her eyes quailed as they met Kate's, and her gaze slid away, down to the floor.

'Yes, Mrs Broder. Our first appointment is at two. Shall I come here?'

'Sure. Just tell Patrick where you want to go, and he'll have the car ready.'

Patrick was the chauffeur – her personal chauffeur, that is. Kate had her own limo complete with driver. Marcus kept a separate one for himself, and Ricardo and Fred drove him in shifts. He did more travelling than Kate.

'Certainly. See you this afternoon.'

'And please call me Kate,' Kate said. She was sorry she'd been mean. There was just something about the woman that put her back up. Or was it really the idea of Marcus? Talking about her with another woman, like this? Conspiring?

Don't be stupid, she told herself. Marcus is just looking after you. Which is exactly what you wanted.

An hour later, her phone rang.

'May I speak to Mrs Marcus Broder, please?'

The voice was familiar, but Kate couldn't place it. And then there was the odd mode of address. Who would refer to her as Mrs Marcus Broder? The Queen of England? But there was a certainty to the clipped tones that would not be denied.

'That's me,' she said lightly. Informally.

'Mrs Broder, this is Alexandra Timpson.'

'Mrs Timpson,' Kate answered. Despite herself, a little thrill of adrenaline ran through her. She had worked on enough mini-features on the queen bees of American society over the years, placed enough photos of Alex Timpson in couture and dripping with sufficient diamonds to shame a Russian empress, not to be impressed.

'I'm a friend of your husband's,' Alexandra said. 'Many congratulations on the marriage. Marcus gave me a call this morning and suggested we do lunch. Would one o'clock be convenient?'

'Of course,' Kate said. Like she had a choice.

'Will Jean Georges do? At Trump Tower?'

It was one of the best and priciest restaurants in the city. Fabulous for people-spotting. Kate understood exactly what Marcus was doing. A little *intime* lunch with Manhattan's reigning socialite; this was her coming-out party.

103

'Lovely. I'll see you there.'

'Yes, dear. Best to be prompt. Marcus tells me you have shopping this afternoon.'

'I'll be there,' said Kate sweetly, although a tiny spot of shame burned on her cheek. Goddamnit, she thought as she hung up. That bitch of a shopper had called her husband. And, obviously, Marcus instantly called in the cavalry.

He was sending in the big guns. Alex Timpson, queen of them all, doing Marcus Broder a favour. Showing his greenhorn wife how *trophy* was done in this town.

Kate licked her lips. Not much fazed her. But Alexandra Timpson made her nervous.

They met for lunch in the restaurant. Alex was already seated at the best table, right by the window; as Kate entered, she noticed a succession of people, older men and stylish women, passing by her, pressing her hand, kissing her on the cheek. Paying tribute. It was feudal, really.

She looked magnificent. No concessions to minimalism. She was wearing classic Chanel haute couture, a custom-tailored sand-coloured suit with cream piping and the signature little gold buttons. She carried a Birkin bag by Hermès, and her feet wore chic little Dior pumps in a silky chestnut. Her hair was immaculately coiffed, as ever, and she wore a discreet necklace of thick gold, the rich orange tone of 24 karat. The engagement ring on her wedding finger sparkled in the sunlight. It was vast, even bigger than Kate's own.

'Mrs Broder,' she said, smiling, but making no attempt to get up. That was Alex Timpson; every move was calculated around her social standing.

'Mrs Timpson,' Kate responded, sitting down as the waiter drew back her seat. She had chosen well, she thought;

a simple Jil Sander shift in dove grey with a gunmetal cashmere cardigan by Tori Burch, and charcoal platform pumps from Louboutin, an Anya Hindmarch clutch and no jewellery. You couldn't compete with Alex. Why try? 'But since you and Marcus are friendly, shall we switch to first names?'

'Of course, Kate.' The older woman inclined her head. 'Shall we order?'

She chose foie gras brûlée with sour cherries and a butternut squash soup; Kate, whose appetite had deserted her, ordered egg caviar and duck breast with cracked Jordan almonds.

Alex made small talk for a little while, congratulating Kate again on her marriage. Marcus was a man of discerning taste, she said. Very demanding.

'He thought it might be a good idea if we spoke,' she said. 'You know, my dear, this is a very particular world.' She sighed delicately. 'It can be savage.'

Kate smiled. The food was incredibly delicious, but she couldn't focus on it. Alex Timpson was simply a force of nature.

'You'll find people can eat you alive,' she said.

'But, Alex, they can't. They can only gossip about you.' Kate shrugged. 'This is Manhattan. Why care what other people say? That's so petty. I mean, within limits, of course.' She thought of Marcus. 'I would never want to cause a scandal.'

'Ah, you see. That – if I may speak quite frankly, my dear—'

'Please do.'

'That is the attitude of a newcomer. You see, doing this wrong *is* a scandal. Having one's peers – the type of people you see at parties Marcus goes to – gossip, and whisper, and disapprove . . . it is a scandal; it focuses attention not on the woman . . .'

'. . . but on the man who owns her?' Kate said coolly.

Alex shrugged, a little slither of wool and silk, her perfect cream blouse moving under the Chanel. 'Now, Kate, that kind of talk is *very* frank. I'd advise you to be a little more measured. Other than with a friend like me, of course. Shall we say . . . on the man that she's with. And our husbands don't appear to care too much about women's things . . . the wardrobe, the jewels, the hair, your girlfriends and so forth. But don't be fooled. In marrying you, he delegates that job. The business titan . . . and his socially perfect wife. The wives of his friends must envy you. His friends themselves must envy him. You are fighting his battles, on another front.' She smiled, her eyes closing as she reached back into distant memories. 'When my husband was still alive, I decided I would win every one of those battles. With clothing, with parties . . .'

'And very successfully.'

Alex didn't bother to deny it. 'There was no reason to change things after he died. He left me all his money, by the way. Just a fraction to his other relatives. He was grateful I'd been such a good lieutenant.' She lifted her glass of sparkling water to her lips. 'Something to consider, my dear. Let's face it. You don't have any traction yet. And dear Marcus has quite a record. To break the mould, you'll need to do a lot better than the last few women.'

'I'm grateful for the intervention,' Kate managed.

Man, this was humiliating. But Mrs Timpson didn't pull her punches. She'd laid it out. Kate would have to do things Marcus's way.

'Getting the ring is one thing, my dear,' Alex said. 'Keeping it is quite another.'

'I understand. Thank you, Alex.' Kate thought with

trepidation about Emily, about her days in jeans. But she wasn't going to give that up. Let them bluster all they wanted.

Still, she guessed she had to turn up for that appointment with the personal shopper.

The next months passed in a whirl. Kate barely had a minute. There was so much to be done. Shopping for couture clothes, working with a personal trainer, getting her hair blow-dried every day. Manicures and pedicures, it all took time. She had lunches and coffees with all her colleagues, and the girls from the magazine were slack-jawed with envy. Emily was a special case, of course. Kate had plenty of semi-friends: chicks from the office she liked to hang out with, a couple of girls on the dating scene she occasionally had coffee with, ladies on the charitable boards that Marcus was involved with. But Emily remained her only true friend. Kate had a hundred acquaintances and only one person that truly mattered to her.

Yet Emily was not so easily available. She was ploughed into *Lucky*, and could hardly get away from the office. Kate loved going over there. It was weird: all the money, all the parties, everything that came with being Mrs Broder, and the most fun she had was when she tugged on her jeans and sneakers and a T-shirt – even if all her T-shirts were Armani these days – and jumped in a cab down to the Village, to head for Emily's cramped little production office. There was no deference there. Emily and her handful of staff – Jake, the graphic designer, sixty and bearded, a hippy genius, and Lucy and Keith, who between them wrote most of the copy, and sometimes Francesca and Didi, the two staff photographers – they all camped in the office, swapping ideas, brainstorming layouts, swearing at each other. Kate joined in with enthusiasm. Hell, she was good at it, and she loved it. And it wasn't really a *job*; she wasn't getting paid. She was just helping out a friend. He couldn't complain at that, could he?

She hung out with Emily, who treated her with the same sarcastic, good-natured friendship she always had. No forelock-tugging, no 'ma'am' or 'Mrs Broder'. One highlight for Kate was Emily and Paul's wedding, when Emily called her at the last minute, shocking her.

'Are you busy right now?'

Kate glanced at her Cartier. 'Sadly, yes. Got to be at Marcus's charity concert in twenty minutes.'

Emily sighed. 'That sucks, because I kind of need you at City Hall.'

'City Hall?' Kate's eyebrows lifted. 'You up on a traffic violation or something?'

'No.' A beat. 'Paul and I are getting married, and we need two witnesses. I thought . . .'

'Hang on.' Kate's heart was pounding. 'I'll be right there. Give me ten minutes.'

It was sheer joy to her to see it: Emily in a tailored white dress, Paul looking slightly uncomfortable in his suit; Paul's friend Tom as one witness, herself as the other. They waited in a functional room with a bunch of other couples, some in jeans and T-shirts, others wearing formal dresses and suits, with the door opening and closing again and again. They ploughed through them like a taxi rank, and when Kate followed Emily into the industrial-looking room, with its strip lighting and bored-looking official standing behind a podium, she was overwhelmed. It was the most romantic thing she had ever seen. Emily and Paul were oblivious, completely oblivious, to the harsh lights, the monotonous voice of the city clerk, the standard instruction to kiss the bride. They repeated their I do's, they exchanged rings, and when Paul took Emily's head in between his hands and kissed her, it was like the world around them had faded, dissolved into nothingness. Kate had tears in her eyes when the clerk handed a radiant Emily her marriage certificate.

It was a million miles away from the luxury of her own wedding. Was it better?

Kate was drawn to the hard work of Emily's office, the happy, exhausted atmosphere of Emily and Paul's apartment. She spent as much time there as she could, ducking out of dinners, leaving parties early, cancelling her manicures and personal shopper appointments, all the little things that Marcus liked her to fill her days with.

But she always made sure to leave in good time, head back uptown, be ready in a little cocktail dress and designer shoes when her husband came home.

Because Emily was right. Marcus was her job.

She soothed him and flattered him. Asked him to talk about his day. That was easy, as he wasn't interested in hers. He would compliment her on her outfit, her hair, her body. Kate found that he carried tension with him, coiled inside like a spring. She worked at easing it. Taking him upstairs, making love, trying to surprise him, keeping things from being routine. And he appreciated that, at least. She tried to shrug off the uneasy feeling that he liked her more after they were done, when she was carefully dressing in one of her new, important outfits, with the blinding jewellery and the shampoo-commercial hair, preparing to hit some society dinner or charity ball and be the hottest wife in the room.

It was vital to Marcus that he present the right image. Kate knew she could never have more than a single glass of wine;

that she had to dazzle all the men without flirting with any of them; that her job was to charm the wives, but just a little, because Marcus Broder's wife wasn't really meant to do the heavy lifting. People were supposed to come to her. That was how Marcus saw himself. And Kate reflected that. She applied herself. She was smart, sassy, sexy in a refined way. They made the gossip columns for all the right reasons. The Hottest Couple in Town. Killer Kate Broder, Queen of the Forbes 400. Society's Sweetheart. They were profiled in *Vanity Fair*, *Vogue*, even the *New Yorker*. And Marcus Broder was happy.

He showed it. Kate started getting gifts. One day when she was in the spa, having a hot stone massage, half falling asleep with languid pleasure, the attendant admitted a female courier from Tiffany's – carrying a huge cardboard box containing a spectacular diamond necklace. There was the mystery weekend, when Marcus told her to pack for hot weather, then scooped her up and flew her to the private island of Necker, just for dinner. There was the Old Master painting from the school of Titian that he bought, to her utter delight, for her birthday. The first cold snap that hit the city, he presented her with an antique silver fox fur coat. If she lifted a finger, it was only to get her nails done.

And in bed, Marcus was patient, careful. He kissed her and licked her and stroked her. He tried to make sure she came, and if she couldn't, Kate touched herself and took care of it. Sure, it went without saying that Marcus had to come. And he wanted sex with her every day. She didn't complain. It was his due, his right. He was taking care of her, in almost every way possible.

Just one teensy-tiny fly in the ointment.

She wasn't happy.

The thought kept surfacing, and Kate continued to shove

it back down. After all, that was just ridiculous, right? She was pampered, cosseted, spoiled, respected. She was the envy of every girl in town. She looked gorgeous, she had everything she could wish for, some stuff she hadn't even thought of. And a smart, handsome, go-getting husband. Momma would be busting with pride, if she could only see her daughter. What's not to like?

'I'm an idiot,' she said to Emily one morning.

It was late November in Manhattan. The last comforting glow of autumn had really faded now, and the city was settling in for winter, bitter, freezing New York winter. Nowhere did cold and rain quite like it.

Kate had her fur coat and hip-length leather boots, but she was wearing jeans and a plain North Face jacket. That plus a black woollen hat tugged down over her ears. Not the most glamorous outfit on earth, but she didn't want to be recognised. The paparazzi were fun for the first three months. After that, you got sick of them.

'I don't think so.' Emily shivered in her own fleece coat from the Gap. She'd lost a little weight over the last year, and looked better for it. Love agreed with her. Kate was so happy to see it. Her best friend was thriving, she was busy, she wasn't comfort-eating. The magazine was still independent, and circulation rose a little every issue. Better, they got critical acclaim. Tons of it. The broadsheets wrote about them, the bloggers quoted them. Emily was the den mother for the new counter-culture. And she just loved every minute of it. There was money, too. Not a bunch of it – she insisted on ploughing all the profits back into the magazine – but enough for her and Paul to buy themselves an apartment, a proper two-bedroom on Murray Hill that even had its own scrap of garden. They were modestly successful, and very content.

Whereas Kate was Queen fucking Midas. Everything she touched turned to gold, but just like the story, it wasn't all it was cracked up to be.

They were walking down Twelfth Street to French Roast. Emily swore it had the best cup of joe in the city. Arctic winds whipped down Sixth Avenue, and nothing would help in the *Lucky* office except some cinnamon coffee. Kate preferred French vanilla. The scent of it was warm and comforting, and mostly calorie-free. Anyway, she relished the off-duty nature of it, standing here with her best friend, carrying her coffee in a cardboard cup. No bone china and no waiters. That was something to be happy about, at least.

'Here you go, girls,' the barista said. He handed over a couple of the precious cardboard cups. Kate breathed deeply, drinking in the rich scent, enjoying being called a girl. The aroma of vanilla and coffee hit her nostrils hard. God, such a simple thing . . . why was she assailed with such a wave of pleasure?

'Thanks.' Emily gave him a ten and waited for her change. 'Look, Kate, you're bored. You're too smart to sit around getting facials and choosing what flowers to have delivered fresh that day. If Marcus loves you, he'll see that.'

'He said he doesn't want me tired out,' Kate said dubiously. They took their coffees and headed for the door. Outside the warmth of the shop, the freezing air smacked them in the face. Kate sipped at her drink; it was hot and comforting. 'And it makes sense. I mean, the guy's just got so much money. What would be the point of my salary? It'd be a joke.'

'Does he want you bored and restless? Maybe the work's worth doing for its own sake. Man, I love *Lucky*. I'd work on it for free.'

'You work to get ahead in life. And I'm already at the top of the tree. Marcus was the fast elevator; he skipped all the other floors.'

'You're wrong,' Emily said flatly. 'Think about it. Bill Gates. Oprah Winfrey. Steven Spielberg. Mark Zuckerberg—'

'Who's he?'

'Founded Facebook.'

'Oh, right.'

'All got one thing in common. Maybe more than one. They're all rich, but they still all work. More money than they could ever spend, but they're in the office. Hey, you know who else does that?'

Kate shrugged. The coffee was so good. She breathed in the cinnamon coming from Emily's cup.

'Marcus Broder,' her friend said triumphantly. 'Why isn't he sitting at home? He could live off the interest on his investments. He never has to do a stroke of work in his life. But you don't see him slowing down. Look, maybe you can get involved in a charity or something.'

Kate shuddered. 'Chair one of those charity balls? With the social X-rays? I don't like those people. Or the five-thousand-dollar-a-plate dinners, I go to enough of them, Em. They're just an excuse to wear your flashiest jewellery.'

Her friend slowed her walk a little and looked at Kate sharply. 'What's wrong with that? Isn't this what you've been working for since you were a kid? The flashy jewellery and the designer handbags? Don't tell me you're regretting it.'

'There's nothing wrong with having money.' Kate ran a hand over her woolly hat distractedly. 'I don't know what the hell's the matter with me. Only that I am bored and I definitely don't want to be some charity patroness.'

'So compromise. Come work at *Lucky* – nobody puts photo

stories together like you. Actually, since you stopped helping out, our circulation's dipped a little. You bring that populist sauce to it. I'm too academic, you know? And we'll donate your entire salary to saving the whales or something. That's charity, but not doing some stupid dinner or whatever. What do you say?'

Kate grinned. 'I say yes please.'

'If you're going to do it properly, not just dropping in at lunch, you need to speak to Marcus.'

Kate nodded her head. 'Yes. Right.' She breathed in deep, nervously. 'I'm sure he'll see sense.'

Marcus did not see sense. He saw red. It was their first fight.

'My wife doesn't work,' he said flatly.

'It wouldn't be work, like putting food on the table. It'd be charity. Come on, sweetie,' Kate pleaded.

'You'd be going into an office. Doing a job. You want to donate to someone? Write a cheque.'

Tears welled up in Kate's eyes. Man, she was tired of pleading with him all the time. 'But Marcus, please. Emily's my friend. It's just something to do while I'm waiting for you to come home.'

'Do?' His sharp eyes narrowed. 'Last time I looked, there was lots to do in this city. Museums. Galleries. Shops. Beauty salons. Go to a baseball game or the goddamn Bronx Zoo. Take your girlfriends with you, I'll spring for the tickets.'

'But she works. And I'm bored,' Kate begged. 'You can't shop all day.'

'None of my other women have had a problem with it,' Marcus snapped. 'And that's why I don't want you doing this. People will say that being married to me is *boring* you.'

'OK.' Kate swallowed the lump in her throat. 'I – I guess

you're right, honey. I love you.' She wanted to believe that. 'Forget about it.'

Instantly he softened. 'I appreciate that. Look, Kate, you're a beautiful woman. Your friend Emily . . .' the disdain was written all over his face, 'she works, she has to. You don't. We've got everything here. It's what you wanted. Try and enjoy it.'

For the better part of a year, Kate did. She worked out frantically. Designed her own dresses and had Manhattan seamstresses make them up. She volunteered one day a week at an adult literacy centre, making sure she was home when Marcus got back from the office. And she did sink herself into plays, movies, art exhibitions. Marcus was right; you could get really busy doing nothing if you absolutely worked at it.

Trouble was, she resented it. And she resented him. She started to find his presence in her bed less tolerable. Even if she never denied him, Kate could not muster up any enthusiasm for sex. And Marcus noticed. His coldness grew. Kate saw Emily privately, without telling her husband. And nine months into it, Emily was hinting she should get a divorce.

'You're not happy.' Her best friend shrugged. 'Kate, you gave it a try. You obviously don't love the guy. And you don't even love the life. Look, what's wrong with admitting to yourself that you made a mistake? Maybe there's a reason the Mrs Broder position comes vacant every couple of years.'

'You don't understand.' Kate twisted her manicured fingers. 'You don't know what it was like for me growing up.'

Emily stared at her. 'Of course I do, I was there.'

'No.' Her bubbly friend was still now, as flat as an old glass of champagne. 'You never came home with me, never saw what it was really like.'

'You didn't want me to,' Emily pointed out gently. 'You were working a night job.'

'It's not that. Mom had already died when we became friends. Things were how they were because Dad left and took all his money with him. Mom . . .' Kate swallowed, hard. 'Mom never wanted that life for me. She wanted me to marry well, to be taken care of. Not to have to work all hours for peanuts, like she did. We were close . . . we had to be. There was nobody else. And Marcus takes care of me.'

'He writes cheques,' Emily replied. 'Is that all your mom wanted, Kate? Do you really think that was the only thing?'

'It was the main thing.' Kate was firm. 'You can be as pious as you like; without enough money there's nothing else.'

'A man isn't the only way to get money, Kate. And nobody needs as much money as Marcus has.'

'Mom would have—'

'This isn't your mother's life. It's yours. You want my two cents? You should divorce him.'

'Divorce him!' Kate shuddered in fear. Her whole mind had been preoccupied with Marcus dumping her, with whether or not he'd take a mistress, maybe more than one. And how she would handle it. She'd been beating herself up because the prospect of a girlfriend, or two, for her husband was a matter of supreme indifference to her. She'd secretly welcomed the idea, because she didn't enjoy sex with him, and maybe that would keep them married. But she, Kate Fox, the nobody from the Bronx, she divorce him? The multi-millionaire?

'I wouldn't get anything. There's a pre-nup.'

'You'd get your freedom,' Emily said mildly. 'That's something.'

Kate panicked. She thought of it all being taken away from

her, the private jets, the designer shoes, the ten-thousand-dollar dresses, the first-class tickets. 'Oh Em, I don't know. I'm used to this life. How can I go back?'

'You'd be surprised what you're capable of. Maybe your energies were focused on the wrong goal. What if you turned them to another one?'

Kate squirmed. She thought what it would be like not to have Marcus in her bed, not to have to deal with that any more. And then she thought what it would be like not to have the bed itself, with its California King memory-foam mattress, or the chic cream and bone decor of the room that went with it, or the huge penthouse in which it was contained. Visions of worrying about the rent, not owning anything for herself, all danced before her eyes. And who would employ her? Marcus *owned* this city.

'I can't.' She withdrew into her shell. 'I just can't.'

'Fine,' Emily said, with that mildness that frustrated Kate sometimes. 'I'm not pushing you into anything. You can't.'

The conversation unsettled Kate. That night, she made love to Marcus with as much passion as she could muster. He smiled slightly, in approval, and it was a huge relief. Kate wasn't ready to bet on herself, couldn't turn her world upside down. She had a great chance with Marcus and she wasn't about to let it go.

And then Marcus Broder brought it all down around her ears.

Chapter Nine

'You must have got it wrong.' Kate stared at Emily, the paper cup of coffee cooling rapidly in her hands. 'There's no way he would do that.'

'Oh, but there is,' Emily told her bitterly. 'Marcus wants to buy *Lucky*. And he's made it clear. This time, I have no choice.'

Kate shook her head. 'This can't be right. He didn't say a word to me. What has he offered you?'

'Terms are reasonable.' Emily shrugged. 'Not even generous. Just reasonable. And a redundancy pay-off for me. He says he'd be looking in a different direction for the magazine, and that there's no point old management being involved.'

'You must have made a mistake,' Kate repeated. A horrible feeling was gnawing at the pit of her stomach. Marcus knew all about Emily, knew what friends they were. He couldn't have done this, could he?

But Marcus Broder didn't make mistakes. And nor did Emily.

'Read for yourself.' Her best friend shoved a sheaf of papers towards her. Printed-out emails. Kate read through them disbelievingly. Em wasn't exaggerating. Marcus wanted *Lucky*; he said he was offering a fair price. No place for Emily or the

119

current editorial staff. Basic redundancy. The tone of the emails was proper, but it was clipped, menacing. She could almost hear him saying the words, see the sneer on his face. 'He knows better than to threaten in writing. But he makes it clear. If I don't play ball, he'll lean on my stockists, my distributors, my advertisers . . .'

I hope the opportunity will arise to purchase Lucky *at market price. But Broder, Inc. is looking to obtain a publication with this demographic of readership, and will, in any event, be seeking to attract similar advertisers and stockists to our own title should a deal not be reached. As* Lucky *is a privately owned publication we believe we could offer significant competitive advantages based on the Broder brand and distribution network.*

Yep, Kate thought. That was a threat all right. If Emily didn't sell, he'd start a rival magazine, discount it to almost nothing, practically give away the advertising. He could steal all her accounts and retailers, and then when *Lucky* folded, charge full price. It was classic Marcus Broder.

'But you're nothing.' She shook her head, wanting to deny the evidence of her own eyes. 'You're a tiny little title. Why does he care so much? He knows we're friends . . .' she finished off, her voice trailing away.

Emily just looked at her. 'Exactly. And maybe he doesn't like that fact. So he's decided to crush me.' She gripped Kate's hands. 'Outside of my relationship with Paul, this magazine is the most important thing in my life. You gave me this, Kate.'

'I had nothing to do with it,' Kate said.

'The hell you didn't. You encouraged me, you made me

think it was possible, that anything was possible.' Emily's brown eyes welled with tears. 'I love this job. It's small, but it's ours, and it's a good thing in the world and—'

'You don't have to sell to me, Em.' Fury, unaccustomed white rage, surged up in her. Marcus was fucking with Emily's *life*. Just to make a point to her. For a second, she hated him for it. 'I know. Believe me. I'll talk some sense into him.'

That night, Marcus had suggested they eat in their apartment. Which usually meant he wanted sex, and wasn't going to wait to leave some dreary opera or benefit in order to get Kate naked.

She let their maid set out the plates and serve the first course, then dismissed her.

'Thanks, Karen. That'll be all for tonight.'

Marcus arched his brow. 'We may want dessert.'

Kate swallowed her rage for a second; she didn't want a scene. Not with the staff around. 'That's all, Karen, and if you could send everybody else home for the night, please.'

'Yes, Mrs Broder,' said Karen, delighted to be getting away before ten p.m.

Kate indulged Marcus, chatting about his day, asking her normal, devoted questions until she heard the front door shutting, the butlers and maids departing. They were finally all alone.

'You're right, I don't want dessert.' Marcus looked at her, and ran a tongue over his lips. God, she was still sexy, and he normally tired of them after a year. But this girl . . . perfectly groomed, like all his women, but with more about her than the rest . . . those jutting breasts, those hot, full lips, begging to be crushed. She was more than good looking; she was fuckable in the extreme. Once he'd ironed out the kinks, she would be the perfect wife. Marcus wanted his arm candy to appeal to other men, and they could always tell which girls were just clothes-horses, and which ones were hot. Kate could infuriate him, but she turned him on, too. He smiled. 'Let's just go to bed.'

'No. Not right now.' Kate surprised herself. Her voice was firm, calm, no nerves about it. 'We need to talk.'

'We need to fuck,' Marcus said crudely. 'Whatever it is can wait.'

'You sent an email to Emily, saying you wanted to take over *Lucky*.'

Marcus pushed his chair back. His cock stirred; he loved to see her eyes flashing fire like this. He enjoyed fighting women before bed. She would surrender; they always did.

'She has a choice. She can sell, or be crushed. I want a title like that. It's how we do business.'

'Not *we*. You. She's my best friend, for God's sake. You're so rich, Marcus.' He noted that; not honey, not baby. Marcus. 'Drop this, please.'

His lids half closed. Now they were where he had wanted to be all along.

'I'll make *you* a deal, then. I'll drop it, if you drop her.'

Kate blinked. 'You have to be kidding. I just told you she's my best friend. Look, I've known her since school.'

'I don't like her.' Marcus was unblinking. 'She's a bad influence on you, Kate. You're my wife. And thanks to that fat slob you're not happy with that role. I get enough conflict at work, I don't need it in my own house. You can get some other friends, she can keep her magazine. Everybody wins.'

Kate laughed, spluttered. 'Please tell me that's a joke.'

'No joke.'

'I'm not going to drop Emily.' Her tone turned to ice. 'Not now, not ever. You don't have the right to ask that.'

Marcus shrugged. 'Fine. Then she can kiss her publishing career goodbye. Like I said, we could do with a title like *Lucky*. Now can we go to bed?'

Kate stared. 'You think I'm going to *sleep* with you now?'

He smiled, contemptuously, his eyes sparkling with lust. Kate shrank back a little in her chair. She had never seen Marcus like this. 'Baby, of course you are. You got what you wanted when you married me.' His hand gestured at the luxury of their apartment, the antique furniture from Europe, the velvet drapes, the priceless Persian rugs. 'You love it all. It's what you were going for.' He lifted his glass, toasted her with Château Lafite. 'And you're so *good* at it. This is your job, your career. Not writing articles and booking photo shoots for peanuts. Your job, Kate Broder, is just to keep me happy.' He swallowed the wine, a big gulp. 'Which is why you're going to get your pretty ass into the bedroom and give me the performance of your life. And first thing tomorrow you're going to call Ms Emily and terminate that relationship. Or I may just terminate this one.'

Kate put her head back and breathed out, long and slow. It was weird how this felt, she thought with a small part of her brain, almost observing herself from the outside. She was relieved. That was the main emotion. Fear, nervousness, excitement, loathing. But mainly just relief. This part of her life was done.

'Marcus, it's been fun,' she said. 'But it's over.'

He stared. For a second, Kate enjoyed the shock on his face. Nothing ever surprised Marcus Broder. But she just had.

'Get out,' he said, quietly.

She squared her shoulders. 'This is the marital home. You can't throw me out.'

'You'll be amazed at what I can do,' Marcus answered, and his voice was ice.

'I'm going across the street,' Kate said. 'To the guest apartment.' They kept a penthouse in the building across the road, two bedrooms, just for guests. Marcus hated the thought of people disturbing his sleep, or hearing him when he grunted and cried out with Kate. It was far enough away, and had its own doorman; she would feel protected from his rage, at least for the night. 'We can talk in the morning.'

'Oh yes. We'll talk.'

Kate looked him up and down. He was too slight, she decided, lean and skinny. Stripped of his power suits and tailored shoes, naked in their bedroom, Marcus Broder was really just a small man.

'I want a divorce,' she said.

Next morning, Kate awoke, disorientated for a second. She wasn't used to the expensive, sterile taupe of the guest apartment. And then it came back to her. Adrenaline flushed her body. She leapt out of bed and into the shower. Marcus was right, it didn't feel like their place at all. It was his place, his, like it had always been.

And her whole adult life was based on a huge mistake.

As the water sluiced over her breasts, her firm thighs, her flat belly, Kate wondered if she was young enough, beautiful enough, hell, strong enough, to survive that. Because the ugly truth was that Marcus Broder – bastard extraordinaire – was right. One hundred per cent right. She had absolutely sold herself to him. And victory had consisted of holding out for the biggest price tag. Would she have married Marcus if he was positively old and ugly?

She rinsed her head, her blond hair flattened and dark about her face from the rivulets of water, the shower massaging her back exactly as she would wish it to. This shower alone had cost twelve thousand dollars. It had a seating area, a sauna, multiple jets, individual temperature control. It did everything short of wash your hair for you. Lined with black Volterra marble and studded with stars and moons cast in eighteen-carat gold, it was gorgeous, and beautiful, and still not good enough to make it to her own master bedroom. And now this shower and every other item of luxury like it was vanishing, like the coach that turned into a pumpkin.

Kate dressed quickly. Last night she'd had the presence of mind to grab a change of underwear from her dresser, a fresh T-shirt, some jeans. Naked was too vulnerable. What if he came across the street, after all, and attacked her? Perhaps that was a wild fear, foolishly exaggerated. But she shivered at the thought. Who would arrest Marcus Broder? Some excuse would be found, an accident alleged. Maybe that she'd got out of control, attacked him. She just didn't feel safe with him so close . . .

Stop it, Kate. Pull yourself together. She grabbed her purse and headed out of the building. Her own home – it still was her home, legally, for a little while at least; she had to go back there, pack a suitcase. Take some basics, and then God knew what. Maybe she'd head over to Emily and Paul's place. But she needed clothes, perhaps her jewels. Some cash, for God's sake. Most likely he'd closed their joint accounts last night.

She glanced at her Cartier. It was quarter to nine; Marcus had probably left the building already, gone to work. Or to his divorce attorney. It wasn't like he didn't have a lot of practice at seeing those, she thought with gallows humour.

The doorman nodded a good morning, but did not meet her eyes. Kate flushed lightly. Word had obviously already got round. The staff all looked her over: dead woman walking. Kate didn't take it personally. They knew which side their bread was buttered, and it wasn't with the short-lived wife.

She took the elevator back to their – his – master bedroom.

'Marcus?' she called.

No sign of him. Thank God. Kate grabbed a large suitcase from the closet where they kept the Louis Vuitton for last-minute trips, and yanked the drawers of her dresser open, grabbing clothes by the fistful. If she could finish packing in twenty minutes, she might get away with it, make a clean getaway until she could clear her head . . .

'Mmm.'

Kate squealed, jumped out of her skin. He was standing there, fully clothed, leaning against the doorway, looking her over. She was well displayed, her cotton T-shirt tight against her breasts, bent over, frantically filling the suitcase.

Marcus licked his lips. 'You do have an outstanding body. And you know how to use it. Would you like to ask me for another chance?'

She turned her head defiantly. 'No.' She had never been more certain of anything in her life. She would miss this world, miss the money, the luxury. But she would not miss him. She looked across the room at her husband, and felt a flush of shame, for herself, for him, for the grubbiness of it all. 'It was a mistake to marry you, Marcus. I'm sorry.'

He was unmoved. 'You will be.'

'I'll file for divorce today.'

He shook his head. 'Women don't leave me. We'll do this my way. I'll file, no-fault, with the pre-nup. You won't contest it. You'll sign the document my lawyers send over saying we have a final settlement.'

Kate opened her mouth to protest, but he brushed it aside. 'I don't owe you a damned thing, but I want to get the divorce. You also sign a confidentiality agreement. No talking to the press. In exchange, I give you a million dollars. Which is a million more than you're worth.'

Kate swallowed. 'Marcus, I . . .'

'You'll take it.' He shrugged. 'What else do you have to live on? You're unemployable, and you're used goods on the marriage market, honey. No other rich man is going to take my cast-offs. I believe you once said that to me. So, a million dollars.' He grinned. 'We both know that doesn't get you to first base in New York, not with no other income. But it's a lot of money in Nowheresville, Alabama, and that's where I suggest you take your pretty tail.' He gestured at the suitcase. 'Hurry up and pack. You get to take one case. Clothes, no jewellery. My driver will be waiting downstairs in twenty minutes. Do we have a deal?'

Her throat was dry. He was right, of course he was. She absolutely needed the money, and a million dollars would soften the fall. She wanted to tell him to go fuck himself. But she had no job, and she was the ex-Mrs Broder, and there was nothing to fall back on.

'Yes.' Her voice was hoarse with the effort of choking back tears, of anger, embarrassment. 'We have a deal, Marcus. I'll be gone in twenty minutes.'

'Where shall I send the paperwork? You checking into a hotel?'

'To Emily's apartment,' Kate said, and had the satisfaction of seeing rage flash in his eyes.

The next few days rushed past. Emily took her in with open arms, and Kate holed up, a prisoner in her friend's place, while the paparazzi gathered on the street outside. When it became clear that they weren't going to get their interviews, they turned nasty. The gossip columns that had fawned on Kate's style and grace openly called her a gold-digger. Blind items ran in the papers branding her a slut. The women of New York society who'd called her all hours of the day and night asking for favours now turned off their phones, as one. Designers started ringing and asking for payment; Kate cancelled all her outstanding orders, then rang Marcus's secretary.

'People are calling me for bills.'

The woman was ice cold. Two weeks ago she'd been giggling and joking with Kate, desperate for the slightest sign of her approval.

'That's not our problem, Ms Fox.'

'I think it is.' Kate was surprised at the reserves of courage she had. 'All of this stuff is connected to my marriage, to the image Marcus wanted me to maintain. Please inform him that if he doesn't settle my bills, he'll find stories in the press of Mrs Marcus Broder being chased for money. Because that's what I am, until the divorce comes through. Not "Ms Fox". As inconvenient as it may be for your office.'

The girl swallowed. 'I'll pass that message on.'

'I bet you will. And pass this on while you're at it. Kate wants him to call off the dogs.'

'Excuse me?'

Kate sighed. 'Look, just put me through to Marcus.'

'That's not possible. He's in a meeting.'

'*Now*, Isabel. Or I'll get right on the phone to Page Six and give them an exhaustive interview.'

'Please hold, Mrs Broder,' Isabel responded, panic in her voice.

Marcus was on the phone ten seconds later. 'Kate, I don't enjoy these silly games.'

'And nor do I. Marcus, I want you to call off the press hounds. We both know you can do it. Ring your friends who own the papers, ring the Mayor, ring your contacts at NYPD. I want this story buried. Send me the million bucks, pay all my outstanding bills, file for immediate divorce and tell the press to forget about me. I want to get my own place, start looking for work. I can't do it with the paparazzi hung round my neck like a lead balloon, OK?'

He paused for a second.

'And what's in it for me?'

'Image. You get a dignified divorce, I leave, the papers stop writing about it, you can start auditioning for the next Mrs Broder. I get on with my life, you get on with yours. The Marcus Broder myth remains intact.'

He laughed unpleasantly.

'There will be no more Mrs Broders. Until one of you proves to me that you're not all greedy whores.'

Kate winced. 'I said I was sorry for marrying you, Marcus. We all make mistakes.'

'Girls like you always seem to make the same one. Still, you're right. I'm tired of you. I don't want to read about you. So I'll get rid of the press. Route all bills to my office. A million dollars will be transferred to your bank account this afternoon. And I've already filed.'

'Thank you. I won't contest it.'

'Of course you won't. It comes with a price tag. And we all know what little Kate Fox thinks about that.'

'Fuck you.' She didn't have to take it any more.

Another laugh. 'You can *fuck* me any time you like. One thing you're indisputably talented at . . .'

Kate slammed down the phone, shaking with rage. At him. At herself. She had never felt cheaper.

'What will you do? Leave town?'

Emily and Paul sat round the kitchen table with Kate. She was red eyed, drawn. They had a bottle of cheap Italian red open, and Paul had cooked some spaghetti and pancetta with a handful of fresh torn basil leaves.

'It's the best thing I've eaten in months,' Kate said.

'What, with all those fancy cordon bleu cooks around?' Emily asked.

'This tastes better.' Kate ate, but slowly. She sipped a little from her wine glass. It was as though her appetite was gone, even if she liked the food. Emily was worried about her. Her friend the butterfly, the sparkling, laughing Kate Fox, had apparently vanished. And the most expensive haircut in the world, the best manicure, the glossy, buttery rich-girl highlights . . . nothing could help that.

Marcus Broder had sapped the life from her. Emily briefly hated him.

'You could learn how to cook it. I'll teach you,' Paul offered. 'All you need is fresh ingredients. And good food is cheap.'

'Cooking's not for me,' Kate replied, with a flash of her old spirit.

God, Emily thought, I hope I'm not responsible. I asked for help with *Lucky*. And she divorced him for my sake. All that money, all that wealth . . .

'And no,' Kate continued, 'I'm not leaving New York. Marcus thinks I'll have to, that he's starved me out. But I'd rather downsize than run away. This city is the only place I've ever really been happy.' She was determined, and it showed. 'I'm going to find a place downtown. A short-term rental. Something real cheap. A studio. Furnished.'

'But you're used to—'

'Doesn't matter what I'm *used* to. I grew up in the Bronx, Em. I love Manhattan, but I've only got a million dollars, and I need every cent of it.'

Paul nodded. It was true. Owning an apartment in Manhattan did not come cheap. Even a one-bedroom would set Kate back at least six hundred grand, and with property taxes and maintenance . . . Maybe she had a year living that way without a job, maybe two. After that, she'd run out of time.

Kate Fox was gonna have to work. Like the rest of them.

'I think that's right.' Emily took a big slug of her wine. She smiled encouragingly at Kate. 'No point in harking back to your old life. You can't afford it any more. It's right to adjust as quickly as you can.'

'Studio flat. Bed Bath and Beyond for linens.' Kate grinned, and Emily was happy to see it. 'I can deal, honestly. This shouldn't be weird. Weird was my time with Marcus. I'll look back on that as eighteen months of madness. This is real life.' She ate some more spaghetti. 'Now I just need a job.'

'But you *have* a job,' Emily said. 'With me.'

'Oh, come on. We were just doing that for fun.'

Emily blinked. 'Fun? For you, maybe. For me, you were vital. Your stuff really helped to push sales. You were *great* at it. I want you, for real. Proper salary . . .'

Paul coughed.

'Proper salary for *Lucky*,' Emily conceded, acknowledging her husband's warning look. 'You know we don't pay a lot. It's not a big glossy like you were used to. I can give you maybe forty thousand dollars.'

Kate nodded, but the disappointment showed on her face. Forty thousand was a pay cut, even from what she was getting at *Cutie*. And she'd had a year and a half out of the scene. It would be regarded as taking a big step down. She swallowed hard.

'That's great, Emily, thanks.'

But at least it was a job, she told herself. At least she was going straight back into employment.

'If you make a serious difference, we can give you some shares in the company,' Paul said.

'I couldn't do that.' Kate shook her head. '*Lucky* belongs to you guys.'

'I wouldn't have it if it weren't for you,' Emily answered. 'And Paul did say only if you make a difference.'

'OK, OK.' Kate grinned, a real smile for the first time in days, and Emily was glad to see it. 'Hell, I'm about to be Manhattan poor. I need to take anything anybody gives me.'

'Then that's settled.' Emily forked up some more of her spaghetti and relaxed a little. Maybe Kate would be fine. Maybe work *would* suit her, if she applied herself to it. Which she never had before. 'Let's just hope Marcus Broder leaves us alone.'

Chapter Ten

The next few weeks were busy. Kate found a place, the next morning, by the simple strategy of renting the first apartment she saw. It was a tiny studio in a nice building in Tribeca, chic, but with barely enough room for the suitcase full of clothes she'd taken from Marcus's place. And they were all fancy dresses, so the same day, she was in the Gap and Emporio Armani, buying the basics of a work wardrobe, which she stored folded in a pull-out drawer that lived under the bed. That was basic, too, barely a double. The place didn't even have a bath; there was nothing but a tiny shower room, and one end of the main space was a little kitchen nook. But at least it had a washer/dryer, so Kate wouldn't have to bear the shame of being seen using a public laundrette, and since the bed was also small, at least the main room was somewhat spacious.

In a way, she loved the tiny little place, as soon as she clapped eyes on it. It had potential, and her designer's eye saw what could be done. The apartment took up a small corner of an old industrial building; on the upper floors there were some really smart and expensive lofts, including a giant penthouse that ran the length of it, owned, so the rumour went, by David Abrams, the reclusive publishing mogul.

Which meant it was the shittiest apartment in an outstanding building. It wasn't for sale, and the rent was high for what it was. But it was furnished, and she could be happy there for a while. There were stripped wooden floors, and a floor-to-ceiling window at one end, one of the original features from its industrial past, more like a wall of glass, really. The whole studio was about a hundred square feet. But it was double height, and Kate could see exactly what to do with it to give it a feeling of grace. She took a six-month lease.

'I'd like to make some changes,' she told the letting agent.

'Such as what?' The girl gave her a brittle smile, her glossy lipstick barely cracking as the corners of her mouth inched upwards. It was a smile that got nowhere near the eyes. 'This is a heritage building. They really don't want tenants messing with it.'

'It would involve a little construction. Some stuff added to the floor. A staircase, maybe a sleeping platform . . .'

'Absolutely not. No nails.'

Kate's eyes narrowed. After Marcus Broder, she could survive anything, and some stupid leasing agent was not about to put her off. 'Miss, you work for the agency. You can't say no. Just convey my request to the landlord. That's your job. And remember I'm a journalist.'

That was an exaggeration, but it did the trick. The girl's resistance crumbled.

'Very well, Ms Fox.' Kate had gone back to her maiden name even before her divorce had come through. Nobody needed the 'Mrs Broder' tag around their neck. 'I'll get back to you. Meantime, until you have permission, please observe the conditions of the lease: no nails, no picture hooks, no sanding the floors—'

'Yeah. Sure. Absolutely.' Kate cut her off. 'Thanks for all your help!'

She walked out.

Lucky was a great place to work. And work Kate did. Her rent was twenty-one hundred dollars a month; that was almost her entire salary. But it was worth it to have someplace good to live, and buy her time while she shopped for the right apartment. Now was not the time to make any expensive mistakes.

Bruised and heartbroken, she flung herself into the job. It wasn't Marcus; she didn't miss him, even for a second. But she was out of love with herself, and her dream, and everything she'd aimed at her whole life. Now it had turned sour. Kate loathed Marcus Broder, and didn't really like herself any better.

Because he was right.

She kept coming back to that thought.

She had sold herself. Like a hooker. Maybe worse than that. Dressing up, styling herself, aiming at a rich guy. It was socially acceptable; some magazines offered it to girls as something to aim for. And Kate's momma had thought that if you had money, nothing could ever go wrong.

But Kate had gotten that money. And lost herself.

Marcus Broder's contemptuous face, his foul words, sang in her ears.

'You're used goods, honey.'

'No other rich man is going to take my cast-offs.'

Kate felt sick when she thought about it. All the clubs she used to go to, all the restaurants she used to eat at. The succession of dates she'd had. Each guy with a bulging wallet. Oh yeah, they would all be talking about her now.

Maybe she should go back to school. Ask the nuns if they had any space in the convent . . .

She grimaced as she thought about it. Man, she'd be lucky to end up with . . . Who? Who wouldn't care that she was the ex Mrs Marcus Broder? The only one without a settlement? Fired after eighteen months?

Maybe she should take up Marcus's suggestion. Forget about hunting for a place. Forget about making the rent. Just head to the Port Authority and take the first Greyhound bus to the middle of nowhere, where she could stretch out her million and be just another girl; perhaps get a job in the local library, or come full circle, teach at a school, tell the young chicks to pull their socks up and button the tops of their blouses . . .

Yet every time she looked out of her window, Kate knew she could not do that.

There was something.

Something small, deep inside her. A kernel of resistance that refused to budge. She was a New Yorker, born and bred. Why let one rich bastard run her out of town?

She liked her new apartment. She loved *Lucky*. Emily was a great friend. The other kids that worked on the magazine got on well with her. At *Lucky*, she wasn't the ex Mrs Broder; she was Kate Fox, and they dug her. Besides, there was the city itself, and the romance of it never left her. The honking horns and yellow cabs, the tourists at the crosswalks, the cops in uniform, the skyscrapers, vast and beautiful, like a petrified forest, stabbing into the sky, looming over her, over Marcus, over everyone. She loved the tree-lined streets of the Village, the urban parks of Tribeca, the crowded delis, the scented coffee in paper cups, the electric billboards in Times Square, the quiet old money on Central Park West.

She couldn't bail. And she wasn't going to.

There was work to do at *Lucky*. A hell of a lot of it. Kate found herself sucked in, totally absorbed. Now she wasn't just playing; she fought for her ideas, argued with Emily, tried to tug the magazine in a more populist direction.

'It's not what we do,' Emily protested. 'We're into social action. We have a conscience.'

'Yeah, and you have a budget. Liberal girls like Louboutins as much as the next chick. Trust me.' Kate grinned. 'Think of it as subversion. You get more people signed up to the agenda if you wrap it in a gorgeous package.'

'Fuck me.' Emily wasn't given to swearing. 'OK, OK. I surrender. Do what you want, one issue only.'

Kate took her at her word. The September issue ran the same features on community activists as ever, but Kate bumped it up with controversy. The Democratic senator who'd consented to give an interview agreed to talk about her favourite lingerie, to help a Victoria's Secret promotion for breast cancer. Kate blew the budget on photography: gorgeous shots of places readers had never seen, a film star's bathroom, a movie director's games palace that filled his entire basement. She conducted interviews herself, got the subjects to loosen up. The senator cracked jokes about her husband's lousy taste in underwear. The film star gave a blow-by-blow of his last therapy session. The director, after a drink, listed his ten most prima donna actors and spilled the beans on some of their more outrageous demands. It was irreverent, chic, a little shocking.

'We need sales.' Kate brushed into the sales department, which was three girls with a phone each. 'This is going to be big. Give me one of those.'

Without even knowing what she was doing, she got *Lucky*

racked out at Hudson News stores all across the city. It was their big break. Over Emily's protests, she doubled the book rate for their advertisers, and trebled it for new customers.

'God.' Emily was almost breathless when Kate showed her the figures. 'Kate. I can't believe it. I just can't.'

'We need more money,' Kate said.

'Honey, forty thousand is all I can afford – I mean, at least till after we sell this issue out, and now the printers are on overtime—'

'I'm not talking about me, Em. I mean the magazine. *Lucky*. It could break through, you know? Become a major title. But it needs better paper, higher-quality photographers, some star writers. It needs production so we can package up fragrance samples and slicks of lipstick. You won't get the big cosmetic houses without it. That needs capital, an infusion of capital.'

Emily paled. 'You're telling me to sell to Marcus Broder?'

'No, not Marcus Broder. No. Of course not. I'm telling you to sell to an investor. And not the entire company either, just some of it. Enough to get some working capital. You'd retain control, Em. You keep as much of the stock as you want.'

'I'll think about it,' Emily lied. 'Look, Kate, I'm just not as into the capitalist stuff as you.' She gave her best friend a hug. 'The last issue was amazing, though. We have never booked as many ads.'

'You wait. It'll fly off the shelves,' Kate predicted, and of course, it did.

A week later she received a note in her pigeonhole.

The landlord would like to see you. Could you come to the supervisor's office, 9:30 Monday morning.

Kate called Emily. Would she mind if she was late in? She really wanted to get this done. In her mind, the apartment was like an issue of the magazine; all she could see was the perfection once she was through with it. The current state of the place was just the starting point, the blank canvas. Except that now she had the idea in her head, the current state of her apartment was actually bugging the hell out of her. It could be so much better, and that was what she wanted.

'Absolutely. Paul and I are taking the train out to Scarsdale on Monday to see his parents. Sylvia will be in charge of the office.'

Sylvia Cotillo was Emily's right-hand girl, the production designer. She wrote copy, styled shots, took photographs, whatever was needed. She was a fierce, ugly woman with a stunning sense of style and a raw sexuality about her, what the French would call *jolie laide*. Kate loved her. She had a husband in Queens who worked in the fire department and was utterly besotted with her.

'Then that's OK. I'll call Sylvia soon as I get out of here.'

'Sounds like a plan.' Kate perked up to hear Emily's laughing voice. It was as though she was sucking all the sugar out of life. The September issue was selling out in every store they sent it to, and now they were in production on the Christmas issue, and advertisers were throwing money.

There were growing pains. Like the poor production for a sale of this quality. But overall, life had never been so good. Emily was almost glowing with joy, and that made Kate feel good. She was part of it.

The building supervisor had an office on the ground floor. It was somewhat luxurious, with blond wooden floorboards and a kidney-shaped desk topped with smoky glass. Kate had been there one time, when her plumbing failed in the first week. The super was a very efficient Latina woman in her fifties, and she got the problem fixed before Kate came home from work.

'Hi.' Kate smiled across the desk at her. 'I got a message to come here and see the landlord. Is anybody from the company around?'

'Oh. Landlord not a company, Miss Kate. He's a person.'

Kate laughed. 'How old fashioned. One guy? I'll talk to him, then, if he's here.'

'Waiting in the back office. Come through, please.'

She conducted Kate round the back of the desk and knocked on a little wooden door.

'Your nine thirty is here, sir.'

Kate grinned. It was odd to hear Ximena calling anybody 'sir'.

'Thanks, Ximena.' The door swung open and a man in a dark suit was standing there, looking Kate up and down.

For a second, she caught her breath.

It's nothing, she told herself. It's just that I'm surprised.

The landlord wasn't the fat, balding sixty-five-year-old Russian she'd been expecting. Instead he was, she guessed, in his mid to late forties. Older than her, in his prime; muscular . . . God, that was a barrel chest. The suit didn't hide it. He had a strong jaw and brown eyes; incredibly thick black lashes, almost like he was wearing mascara. She swallowed, once, at the eyes. And the sweeping, casual look he gave her as those eyes ran across her body.

'Hi. So you're one of my tenants?'

'If you own this building, yes. I'm Kate Fox.'

'How are you.' He shook her hand. His handshake was

firm, tight. 'Ms Fox, I gather you're here just on a six-month lease.'

'Yes, well. A year's rent here is thirty thousand dollars. That's a big chunk of my salary.' Practically all of it but she didn't tell him that.

An eyebrow raised slightly.

'I have savings.' Why was she explaining herself to him? She blushed. 'I just don't want to use them all up. So I guess I have to go buy somewhere.'

The man inclined his head a fraction. 'Fine. But the thing is, we really can't allow permanent alterations. After you're gone, we'll need to rent the place to somebody else. You know how it is. Personal and quirky? It doesn't sell.'

'I can believe that. I won't make it personal and quirky.' Kate leaned forward, into the man's space. Suddenly this really mattered to her. She wanted to convince him. 'Look, mister, I work in the magazine industry.'

'Oh, really now?' he said softly. There was a hint of amusement in his voice, which aggravated Kate. 'You do?'

'Yes. I do. I'm junior partner on a magazine called *Lucky*. You might have heard of it. Or picked up a copy of this month's issue, that is, if you could get any before they sold out.' She tossed her blond hair, sending the buttery, silky highlights tumbling around her cheekbones. 'We've just doubled our circulation.'

'I thought somebody else owned *Lucky*. Can't recall the name, but it wasn't Kate Fox.'

The words were pleasant enough, but Kate sensed the challenge in them.

'Emily's the senior partner. With her husband Paul. Like I said, I have a junior role. But it's working. The title's taken off since I came on board . . .'

She stopped herself. 'What am I talking about? You don't need to know any of this.'

'True.' He smiled down at her. 'But don't let that stop you. It's fascinating.'

'Anyway, my point is, I have style. You could say that style is my job. And that little space needs it badly. All I'm asking is for you to let me in with a carpenter, my expense; let me paint and sand. You have a small space, but with height,' she explained, looking into his dark eyes. She could hardly tear her gaze from them. They were hypnotic. 'I could put in a staircase and a platform to make an office; that would free up part of the downstairs room. Add a sliding bamboo partition; hey presto, it's a one-bedroom. That's worth at least another seven hundred in rent for you. Then you've got natural light in a dusty space. You should sand the floors, bleach them blond. Just like this. I'll add a mirrored wall, and all of a sudden you have this great one-bedroom apartment on two levels, off-whites and creams, very soothing, very high-rent.' She smiled. 'Literally.'

He returned the smile, but it was a little cold.

'You're very persuasive, Ms Fox. If you're willing to bear the cost, you can go ahead.'

'Great.' Kate wondered why he was so distant. She wanted to provoke him, to needle him. 'On one condition. If you love what I do to your property, and you think it has increased the value to you by, let's say, double what I pay in rent, you refund my rent and let me have it for the six months rent-free.'

He laughed; surprised. 'What?'

'I think you heard me, sir. Come on, that's only fair. And it'll be your judgement that counts. What have you got to lose?'

His eyes held hers for a second. Fixed on her. And Kate blushed, feeling a momentary heat starting to burn between her thighs. Quite unexpectedly.

'Nothing,' he agreed. 'I suppose you have a deal.'

Kate extended her arm, shook his hand.

'But don't hold your breath. I highly doubt I'll be giving your makeover that kind of rating. You should be prepared to pay all your rent in full. Like anyone else.'

She arched a brow. 'But of course, Mr . . . ?'

'Abrams,' he said quietly.

'Mr Abrams, right.' Kate suddenly looked up. 'Wait a minute, you're not . . . no, of course you're not.'

'Not what?' he asked.

'Not David Abrams . . . right? I did hear a rumour he lived in this building.'

He released her hand and looked down at her. 'The rumour was correct, Ms Fox. I live in the building. And I own it too.'

She blinked. Wait, this guy was David Abrams? The magazine mogul? The one who shunned the limelight, the . . .

'I thought you were a recluse,' she blurted out.

'No, ma'am. Just a private person. I let the business talk for itself.'

'But your business is magazines.'

He shrugged. 'Yes, principally. But when I see an opportunity, I take it. This building offered me one. I purchased it five years ago.'

'Before the property boom really got going,' Kate noted.

He shrugged, confidently. She tried not to find it attractive. Not to find him so attractive. This was no time for her to be getting into anything, now was it?

'It was industrial. Took me eighteen months just for the permissions to convert. But it was an interesting side project.

Perhaps I didn't have time to finish every apartment.' He caught himself, looked at Kate again, and the coldness returned. There was a pause.

'I gather your last husband was in magazines,' he remarked deliberately. 'As well as other things.'

Adrenaline washed through her. It was as though somebody had taken that tiny, unusual flame of interest and doused it with water.

'So you know,' she said.

'I think most people know. In some ways New York is a big town. In others, it's tiny.'

She tossed her hair back, boldly. 'Well, my past is my own business. As is my settlement. I'm renting here because this is what I can afford.'

Abrams held up his hands. 'Fair enough. It is your business. Thank you for the meeting, Ms Fox. Glad to have you as a tenant.'

She stood up from her chair, feeling belittled, summarily dismissed.

'Thank you, Mr Abrams,' she said. But he busied himself with his papers, and did not look up.

Marcus Broder settled back into his seat, feeling a remarkable sense of contentment. He'd just come out of another routine board meeting. They were so supine, it was hardly a challenge any more. He'd sent the corporate jet down to Costa Rica to pick up a date, and when some piss-ant little non-executive director had dared to challenge him about it, the rest of the board had shouted the guy down. Marcus remembered the man flushing with embarrassment, loosening his collar. He wouldn't want to lose the cushy salary and giant pension pot.

The Costa Rican had been outstanding, too. Sex with her was a real workout. She was flexible to the point of being acrobatic, totally uninhibited. Worth his company's tab this month. Of course, she was too brash, too over the top to be serious. But who wanted serious?

Kate Fox was out of his hair. It had been harder than he liked to admit to forget her, at first. There was something different about that girl. But he didn't dwell on it. Obviously, it freaked him out that she'd walked. Women didn't walk away from Marcus Broder. When he was bored, he dumped them.

Still, his business was powering ahead. Girls were around, girls like Alicia, to help him brush aside the memory. Every trace of her had been expunged from his apartment, the pre-nup was watertight; there was no need to cling on to a ghost.

The dinner tonight was one he'd looked forward to. The New York Public Library's annual charity dinner and dance. Luminaries from across the city flocked to it, and a chance to gawk at Marcus Broder was one of the main attractions. He enjoyed bumping into his contemporaries, the giants of the city's publishing scene. There was Anna Wintour, looking elegant, and Fred Drasner, the great magazine man. Abrams, Inc. had taken over one corner of the room, and across to his left he saw a table full of American Magazines people. All the big names, and a few scattered faces he didn't recognise, some up-and-coming industry types they tended to invite, and—

Marcus Broder's hand tightened around the stem of his crystal wine glass. What the hell? That was her. Right there. Kate, wearing one of the dresses she'd had when they were married, damn, and it was one of his favourites too, that stunning yellow Versace, floor-length like a Greek goddess, trimmed with sparkling silver ribbon and picking out the rich tones in her skin and eyes. She looked like Venus herself in that thing. Clearly one of the dresses she'd grabbed when she'd left.

For a second he was paralysed. He couldn't believe the bolt of adrenaline that shot through him. Like sweat breaking out on his skin, his palms. This was off-script, not meant to happen. Marcus looked wildly around at her table, scoping out any rich men who might be there, might be escorting her. Could he have been wrong? Was there some sucker in Manhattan who didn't mind his cast-offs?

He loathed her. But the thought of one of his peers dating her, *fucking* her . . . that made him feel ill.

He couldn't see anybody obvious.

'Marcus?'

His date for the evening, a vapid socialite from England with connections in Washington, impeccably pretty and well bred, tugged at his sleeve. 'Marcus, sweetie? What's the matter? You look like you've seen a ghost.'

'Stay there,' he muttered, barely collecting his manners. Then he rose, and moved across the room to the American Magazines table. He simply could not help himself. The curiosity was too much to contain.

'Topaz,' he said, addressing himself to the ultra-chic woman at the head of the table, the Italian-American goddess who had been CEO of the company for the last fifteen years. Topaz Goldstein wowed in a scarlet velvet sheath that matched her fiery red-headed bob. 'Good to see you. Joe off tonight?'

'He's getting ready for sweeps,' she replied, shrugging. Joe Goldstein was one of the East Coast's biggest names in television. Together they formed one of the hottest power couples in New York. Topaz was not at all Marcus Broder's type of woman. 'Good to see you too,' she added, with a smile that didn't reach her eyes.

'I see you've got your usual gang of comers,' Marcus went on, forcing himself to look directly at the big boss woman and away from his ex. American Magazines liked to invite new stars of the industry to this event every year. They were well known for it. A futile gesture; half of this year's start-ups never lasted past December. But Topaz kept at it. She was a kind of godmother to new talent. 'Anybody interesting?'

'See for yourself,' Topaz replied drily. 'I think you know at least one person here.'

'Hello, Marcus,' Kate said quietly.

He was forced to look at her, smiled mirthlessly. 'Good evening, Kate. Who are you here with?'

Kate blinked. 'American Magazines.'

'No, honey, he's asking who your date is.' Topaz gestured to the male executives surrounding her. 'Kate came with Paul; he's the husband of her friend Emily. They both work at *Lucky* magazine.'

'Right. I remember.' A sinking feeling appeared in the pit of Marcus's stomach.

'Kate's really turned that title around. You should check out the sales figures,' Topaz added, clearly enjoying herself hugely. 'Surprised nobody's flagged it up to you yet. They're kicking major ass over there. Little magazine not going to be so little for much longer. Gather you tried to buy it; good call. It's worth a lot more now.'

Paul, whoever the hell he was, smiled appreciatively at Kate. 'She's really transformed our prospects, Mr Broder.'

'We're talking about her at American. But then again, the buzz is kind of out there in general.' Topaz lifted her glass. '*Salud*, you two, *mazel tov*. You've got a good thing working.

And there are some other exciting prospects here as well. Lionel runs an independent film title out of his house in Queens, and it's starting to sell into colleges and universities—'

'Yeah, well. That's great. Congrats, Lionel.' Marcus couldn't listen to a second more of this drivel. 'Good to see you, Topaz, Kate. I should go back, my date's waiting on me . . .'

'Don't let us keep you. Enjoy your dinner,' Topaz said sweetly, maddeningly. Marcus boiled inside. He knew he had exposed himself, displayed interest in Kate, practically asked what she was doing still on the scene. But he'd had to know, had to torment himself by asking.

He went back to his own table. But the evening was ruined for him now. The decorative smiles of his pliant date, the caviar and lobster thermidor, the vintage champagne, the tributes of lesser men, ambitious hostesses, hopeful models and single girls . . . none of it mattered.

Almost as soon as he'd managed to forget her, Kate Fox was back. And making a success – an actual success – of her new job. Topaz Goldstein rated her highly, he could see that, even among her year's picks. And Topaz was rarely wrong.

Well, he would take the print queen's advice. He hadn't been following *Lucky* magazine before.

He would have somebody track its every move from now on.

Kate Fox had broken their bargain, as far as he was concerned. She was supposed to crawl into a hole and stay there.

Now she was back on his turf? No. No way.

Marcus Broder was going to fix this.

Kate took the call the next day. On her mobile, a blocked number. She picked up; if it was the press, she could always just cut them off.

'Kate Fox.'

'Kate, this is Alex Timpson.'

It was like somebody had dropped ice cubes down her back. Alexandra Timpson's clipped tones had changed. She was glacier cold.

'What can I do for you?' she said.

'Leave town.'

There it was. That famous Timpson brusqueness. She never minced her words. And now those words were a social death warrant. Kate had been given her advice. Ultimately, she'd rejected it. In leaving Marcus, she'd made herself an enemy.

'I'm afraid I can't do that. I have a job,' she said lightly. 'Not something you'd understand, Alex, I fear.'

'Oh, we all have our jobs. Mine is to make things run smoothly. You have a settlement, I understand. It will go further somewhere else – anywhere else.'

'I earn a wage.'

'And the enmity of your ex-husband. And all his friends,' Alex promised silkily. 'It isn't very seemly, you playing at publisher. You made a choice, Kate. Understand that there are consequences.'

'Yes. The consequence is that I no longer need to care about you, your opinion, or your whispering campaigns.' Man, it felt good to say that. 'Marcus Broder no longer owns me. And despite what you think, he doesn't own Manhattan either.' Kate breathed in, steadying herself. 'I'm not going anywhere. Please carry that report back to him.'

She hung up. But despite the brave words, a little shiver of fear ran across her skin. Marcus was against her. And Alex, and all her little cohorts. That was bad news. But there was nothing for it but to go on. She wasn't going to turn tail and run. She would focus on *Lucky*.

Chapter Eleven

It was infuriating. Kate told herself she didn't care. There were a million businessmen in New York. OK, so not all of them were legendary magazine men like David Abrams, the Jewish entrepreneur from Scarsdale who had refused his parents' wish to become a lawyer, and founded *Toys* magazine from his college dorm, a mid-eighties success story, dedicated to the coolest gadgets a boy could find. It was basic, and raw, and funny. It made millions. Before he graduated, Abrams had funded another two magazines without quitting school. There was *Model*, a fashionista bible, and *Review*, which broke him into the big time. *Review* was a baby *Newsweek* for right-wingers. The story, which Kate had heard a million times, was that left-wing student Abrams was so offended that a student body had decided to uninvite a conservative talk-show host from a campus debate – he raged against the censorship – that he founded a glossy magazine just to give right-wing youth a voice. 'Trying to understand the other side,' he'd said.

That line was quoted a lot. Mostly because David Abrams didn't give interviews. He graduated, and went to work for a medium-sized magazine house, Epic Publications. It was failing, and rather than take a salary, David Abrams raised some cash against his three magazines and bought his bosses out.

Then he turned the joint around. Epic started to print some of the hottest titles in America. Like *Beauty* magazine.

David Abrams became a very rich man. And then he disappeared.

Kate knew this, because she'd been intrigued. At one point, in her former life, she'd suggested to Fleur that they get him in for a fashion shoot.

'Print Man,' she said. 'It'd be great. Put him in some hot menswear, have him holding a copy of *Model*.'

'Sure, if you can find him.' Fleur had snorted. 'David Abrams doesn't do press, Kate. He *owns* press.'

She had never seen him in the nightclubs, never met him in the hot bars. He didn't hang out with rich, lazy New York. Kate had read his magazines with vague admiration, then forgot all about him. She was hunting, and he wasn't available as prey.

And now she'd met him, and he didn't even know she existed. Kate wasn't used to being dismissed like that.

She didn't like it.

In the daytime, she slaved away at *Lucky*. With strong ideas and a good little team, she was building the magazine, growing the sales. Emily guarded the editorial fiercely; it was *her* baby, and Kate wasn't allowed to get too popular, not just yet. But they took on more staff, and there was a plan for a bigger office.

In the evenings, she improved her flat. The craftsmen came in and made a staircase and a platform. Kate had them working on the floor, sanding it down, staining it a gorgeous blond. She sourced all the mirrors herself, the white and cream furniture, little Moroccan accents of glass beads, coins and silver. Everything reflective, and on a cheap budget. It came together, slowly but surely.

And then one night it was ready.

Kate came home from a long day at the office. They had just landed an advertising deal with a major cosmetics firm. All the major houses wanted space in *Lucky* now. With every stop her excitement grew. She was going home. To her gorgeous new place. The workmen would be out today; they'd have fitted the last of her mirrored no-fog tiles in the bathroom. It was time to see the results of her hard work. With labour, she'd spent just six thousand dollars on the whole thing. And the furniture would come with her, if she ever found somewhere to actually buy. Not that there'd been many chances to look. She had filled every waking second with work; work on *Lucky*, work on her place. Right now, she didn't want to have too much time to think.

Slowly, gradually, Kate's self-esteem was coming back. She didn't wake up thinking about Marcus, about how she'd sold herself, about her bleak future. At least, not every day. She was a magazine woman again. Just Kate Fox. Nobody in the office cared. If there had been the occasional glance when she first turned up, a few whispers around the water cooler, that had evaporated. Under Kate's direction, they were selling magazines, expanding, making money. Her staff were getting pay rises. There were more jobs around. Turned out they cared more about that.

The train stopped and she got out at Bleecker Street turning south towards Lower Broadway. She walked fast, striding along the street in her Prada ankle boots and skinny jeans; she had teamed them with an ultra-fine navy and black striped Armani sweater, and it draped lovingly over the swell of her breasts. Her hair, lowlighted with dark streaks adding contrast to her buttery blonds, shimmered around her face in a long, razor-cut bob that highlighted her sharp cheekbones. She worked out, running every day, doing crunches and light weights; it was good for sexual tension, now there was no man in her life, and her body was lean, lithe under the tight clothes; strong, not model thin. Her ass was round and jutted out from her back, but it was high, tight, made for a man's hand. Her arms were defined and beautiful, and she carried herself well, her hips swaying as she walked, breasts bouncing a little.

Men stared as Kate Fox made her way down the street. But she still didn't notice. She was focused. This little apartment project had absorbed her. And tonight it was done.

There was her building, looming up in the twilight, its beautiful pre-war façade sharp against the sky; warm yellow brick set with white stones, the large arched windows that had once lit the factory now gracious, like relics of a more elegant age. She tried to make out where her apartment was, but it was lost, somewhere up there amongst the towering floors. She tried to imagine what it must have been like to buy this building. David Abrams intrigued her.

Which was wrong. She shouldn't care about him. He was a cold, arrogant son of a bitch.

She squared her shoulders and walked inside. The doorman smiled at her. The elevator purred, ready to whisk her up to the ninth floor. It was industrial, functional, like so many in the converted warehouses. I'd fix this right up, Kate thought. If the building was hers. Everybody used the elevator, after all. Spend a little money and make a great impression. It was the kind of touch that enabled you to charge the best rents, sell for the best prices. But her landlord didn't have that kind of attention to detail.

I could fix his magazines too, she thought, and then stopped herself. Sure, there were some rough edges there. But she didn't want to think about David Abrams. He was dangerous territory.

The elevator stopped, and Kate, taking a deep breath, walked down the hall and fished her key out of her bag.

She opened the door.

She smiled.

'And there's one last thing, if you want to do it.' Lottie Friend, David Abrams' efficient, fifty-something secretary, was running through his diary down the phone.

David didn't like to spend too long in his office. Inspiration could strike anywhere. Besides, what was success for, if you had to sit there feeling trapped? He regularly bailed, to go to a play, see a movie, just take a walk in Central Park. He'd had many of his best ideas that way. Tonight he was sitting in his apartment, relaxing on his Ligne Roset couch, staring out at the downtown skyline from the three floor-to-ceiling windows that framed the space. It was vast and cavernous, and he deliberately made it seem even larger by furnishing it with minimal amounts of stuff. A couple of large modern art canvases to cover one wall. Sleek Italian sofas; a wafer-thin HDTV set the size of a cinema screen pinned to one exposed brick wall; and his bedroom, and the guest bedroom, set with very expensive low-slung sleigh beds imported from Sweden. There were two bathrooms, his and hers; his was a wet room, ultra-functional, with a seated shower and body jets that blasted in from everywhere, and small grey putty tiles. The guest bathroom was set in ochre stone imported from Tuscany, with a sunken stone tub, a stand-alone shower stall in warm shades of orange marble, and copper-coloured fixtures. He kept the lighting there soft, and the maids put fresh orchids in the vases every other day.

It was designed for women.

None in particular, of course. Just whoever happened to be the catch of the night. David Abrams didn't nest, and he didn't like women in his space. Girls would be taken home, made love to, treated well. He would leave for his office in the morning with a warm note of thanks, an invitation to help themselves, and a chauffeured car waiting downstairs to take them home.

Mostly, he didn't call back.

Abrams had been married once, long ago. It was a disaster. He was up and coming then, had just sold his first magazine, but all the cash had been ploughed into the company. Still, he was a rising star, and he clearly had money. She was a secretary, working on the first title he took over. Blond – he liked that. An English accent; she was transplanted from the East End. And she was loud and irreverent and fun.

She was also wrong for him. Fun didn't necessarily go with smart. He found that out the hard way. After the sex, he got bored, and he soon found that she partied all day long. She liked to drink, and she flirted with his friends. One month he had a famous actor stay at the house. Although he didn't know for absolute certain, David thought she'd cheated on him, gone straight for the bigger, better deal.

He wasn't having fun. He asked for a divorce. She let him go with minimal fuss. He settled for half a million dollars, and worked his butt off the following year trying to recover his fortune. The marriage had lasted only eighteen months, but it left an impression. That he could not tolerate being tied down.

David Abrams liked women, but he hated being used. The

beautiful New York society girls, always looking over his shoulder to see if somebody richer had entered the club. He dated a few women, always girls from Boston Brahmin backgrounds, heiresses with money of their own. But that didn't work either. They were supine, flattering him, trying to drag him to the altar. He wanted to be challenged, aroused, talked to. Wanted an equal. But none presented themselves.

You could get very jaded, being rich and single in New York. As his magazines climbed the ladder, so did his bank balance. And the women flung themselves his way. Socialites. Models. Girls with plastic, perfect good looks, tits that spoke to the surgeon's art, girls with bags that cost three months' rent in one of his apartments.

He was busy. Work exploded. Print was his passion, his life. He stayed out of the limelight and looked for the deal. After a while he started to experiment, to take small stakes in companies he believed in, to buy real estate. Only to his own taste. And it worked. Life was fun, absorbing, a challenge. Girls were always around, and he didn't deny himself. Nor did he ever promise them anything. If they chose to sleep with him, David Abrams was willing to take it.

He didn't bad-mouth women. He didn't break hearts. He enjoyed them, pleasured them, gave them jewellery, and moved on. Now and then, when his mother nagged him, he half-heartedly tried to date.

It never lasted.

He was single. And in love with his job. And not looking to be a walking ATM. What was the point of bitterness? If you accepted life for what you could get out of it, then New York's beautiful women were something to be celebrated. David Abrams took them at face value. And no further.

'What's that?' he asked. He stirred on the couch, feeling

restless. Time to walk upstairs to his private gym and start working out. He lifted weights, ran almost every day. It was better than therapy, ideal stress relief.

'The super called in from your building.'

'This one?' he asked casually.

He owned four. Renovating the factory had been so profitable, he'd done it again three times in the last two years. A property division was starting to creep up on him, although magazines would always be his heart. Abrams loved money, but he loved ideas even better.

'Yes, sir. That one. A tenant has asked for an appointment tonight.'

Abrams rolled his eyes. 'Ximena should know better than that. I don't see tenants myself, almost never. Let her take care of it; that's her job.'

'You saw this one a couple of months ago. It's a Ms Fox.'

Abrams paused. He sat up, swinging his legs over the side of the couch. Yes, he'd seen her, the little ex-gold-digger in the tiny studio they'd carved out of this building in a little bit of spare space, almost forgotten about. Mostly he'd asked to see her out of rubbernecking curiosity. She was the latest in a long line of Marcus Broder exes, and she must really have messed up. He'd dumped her without any kind of settlement. Guess the guy was getting wise to pre-nups. Why he married them in the first place was the mystery. This girl had barely gone four seasons before getting fired.

Only she hadn't been exactly as he expected, had she?

Pretty, sure.

Maybe more than pretty.

You had to commend Broder's taste. Fantastic tits, a narrow waist and a glorious curving ass. It was the kind of body that crashed cars. But Kate Fox hadn't been quite as supine and adoring as he'd expected. She was feisty, argumentative. Fought her corner. He'd been intrigued, had quietly had her checked out. She was working, really working, at *Lucky*, that cute little mag in the Village. Using her own name. Sales had been pushed up. By quite a bit. He assumed Broder had something to do with it all. Trophy wives didn't mess up their manicures by doing too much hard graft. And the press clippings were there on his computer, in her LexisNexis file: the couture gowns, the diamond necklaces, the penthouse on Fifth, the fabulous private resorts.

Kate Fox hadn't just fallen into it with Marcus, either. Abrams scanned the articles, read between the lines of the blind items in the newspaper gossip columns. She was a girl around town, OK. This trust-fund brat. That rich entrepreneur. Entry level seemed to be three or four million dollars. And she had worked her way up to Broder.

He shrugged. Kate Fox was just another gold-digger. It was merely that her package was slightly more interesting than most.

'I don't want to see her,' he said, abruptly.

'OK,' said Lottie, in the voice that usually meant 'and you're a jerk for that'. 'Whatever you want, sir.'

'You think I should see her?'

'Well, Mr Abrams, apparently you promised her an appointment. Which means if you don't see her now, you'll have to see her tomorrow.'

He bit his lip. 'And what if I don't see her at all? Who says I have to?'

'You can certainly try that, sir, but the problem is, she does actually live in your apartment building. So she can waylay you on the stairs. Or in the elevator.' A shiver of distaste in the woman's voice. 'She might even *knock on your door.*'

He was amused. 'And we couldn't have that, could we?'

'It's not my place to say, but . . .'

'Go right ahead. Say.'

'Well, sir, the young lady does have something of a past.'

I know, Abrams thought. I checked, didn't I?

He was glad Lottie couldn't read his mind. Really, what the hell was he doing research on this chick for? he chided himself. She was just another Manhattan socialite, and they were ten a penny in this town.

'And since you promised her an appointment,' Lottie was still talking, not giving up, 'and she is in fact your tenant, that gives her a very good excuse to come knocking on your front door at any hour of the day or night . . .'

He laughed aloud. 'Like a predator, you mean, wearing a see-through negligee and high-heeled sandals with pompoms on the toes?'

The thought was not completely displeasing. His mind flashed on Kate Fox's knockout body in baby-doll gauze, and he felt himself stir under his tailored slacks.

'I wouldn't put anything past a woman like that. It's such a pity you saw her personally the first time around,' Lottie said.

'So you prefer I see her now. In the downstairs office, at a reasonable hour.'

'Yes indeed, Mr Abrams. Perhaps she'll still be in her work clothes.'

'Don't worry, Lottie. I'll see her in the super's office again. Before she has time to change into a killer miniskirt.'

'Thank you, Mr Abrams. See you tomorrow, sir.'

David Abrams got to his feet and prepared to head downstairs. Interesting, he thought, how he had not really resisted his secretary. It would have been simple enough to delegate this appointment to the super.

But what the hell. He had no plans for this evening. He was bored.

'It's ready.'

Kate Fox was standing in front of the desk, leaning towards him. No miniskirt, but David Abrams thought this might even have been worse. She was wearing a pair of skinny jeans, ballet flats and a clinging, silky jumper that hugged her breasts. He tried not to stare at the V-neck that presented itself, exposing her warm, tanned skin, the delicate line of her collarbone, just hinting at what was underneath, the swell of her cleavage. Her hair swung around her face in a choppy cut. Her make-up was minimal; Abrams had seen enough models to recognise that she just had a tinted moisturiser on, a little warm blush, neutral eyeshadow, a clear lip gloss. It was a fresh, light look that allowed her natural beauty to shine through.

'I was hoping to show you,' she added drily.

Abrams flushed, annoyed with himself. He'd been caught staring at her. Just the kind of reaction a woman like Kate Fox would love to elicit.

'Very well. And Ms Fox, this will have to be quick. I have another appointment.'

'I appreciate you seeing it at all, Mr Abrams,' she said.

Smooth, he thought. She's smooth. He tried to suppress a momentary admiration. 'Let's go see your place. After this, you can deal with the super or the letting agent.'

She smiled. 'But we're neighbours.'

Abrams shook his head, rejecting her little light attempt at flirtation.

161

'We are, but I need to be able to relax in my own home. I'm sorry, but I don't want to be in contact with tenants. I'm sure you understand.'

She shrugged, as though to say it was his loss. 'Come upstairs, then, and we'll get it over with?'

Goddamnit, he thought. Now I feel boorish. What is this woman doing to me?

'Yes. Thank you. That's very considerate,' he replied.

She turned towards the door without a word, and David Abrams got the full benefit of her sensational ass in the tight jeans. Man, it was just like a peach. He wanted to reach into his pocket and bounce a quarter off her. Thank God she couldn't see him staring again. He had to bite down on his tongue to stop himself licking his lips.

Abrams felt restless. Soon as he got upstairs, he'd place a call to one of last week's hopefuls. Maybe the redhead from Murray Hill. She had her own townhouse, so she was worth some money; he wouldn't have to feel guilty about it. Besides, he'd see that she had a great time. He always did.

But right now, Kate Fox was walking away, and her ass was going with her. He coughed to distract himself.

'So, what do you do for a living?' he asked. Pretending he'd forgotten all about her.

They reached the elevators. Thank God she lived too high up to use the stairs. He didn't trust himself to walk behind her.

'Same as you.' She punched the button. 'I'm in magazines. We had this discussion, remember?'

'So we did. But not quite the same as me.' He couldn't resist a little put-down; she was cocky, as well as beautiful. 'I own the magazines.'

Kate inclined her head. 'I'm well aware of who you are, Mr Abrams. You don't need to beat your chest.'

The elevator doors hissed open. He got in and stood next to her. 'Risky attitude, given that you want my approval on this little project of yours. To save half a year's rent.'

'You'll approve it,' she said confidently. 'You wouldn't turn me down just because I failed to massage your ego. You're not the type.'

He glanced at her. She was looking straight ahead, staring into space. Man, she was beautiful, he thought. And not sucking up to him as he had expected. Lottie would be surprised to see this.

They got off at the ninth floor. Kate marched up to the door of 9b, turned the key and opened it.

'There you go,' she said.

David whistled, softly.

She had transformed the space. There was a staircase, planks of wood supported by metal bolts, so that light streamed through it, and a raised platform at the top surrounded by a sturdy fence. On it she had placed a king-size bed and a desk and chair. A slim laptop, a MacBook Air perhaps, was plugged in. It was comfortable, functional. The double height of the ceiling was now reflected in a smooth blond finish to the floor, which she had sanded, lightened and glazed. Furniture was in shades of pearl and cream, with red Moroccan accents to break it up, and the whole apartment seemed open, spacious even. As he glanced around, he saw that she had played with light; there were big mirrors on the wall, patent and glossy surfaces everywhere, accents and lamps in hammered glass. The sunshine streaming through the vast windows was captured and reflected in a million different ways. Kate had thrown down area rugs, cheap but luxurious in texture, cream shagpile and a sheepskin by the architectural lounge chair carved from driftwood that she had positioned under the window, where the bed used to be, for reading.

He moved into the apartment. The reflective surfaces were working overtime. As he crossed into the kitchen area, he never felt cramped. All she had done here was replace his cheap laminate floor with good pale grey slate tiles, and his Corian countertop with snowy granite. Which she could afford, he guessed, because the kitchen corner was absolutely tiny. Only now it was also chic, top of the range.

He glanced inside the bathroom. She had redecorated with a clear plastic curtain dotted with stars and moons to keep the flow of light, placed silvery bathmats on the floor, and hung extra mirrors on one wall. They were amplified by the sparkling mirrored tiles, adding light and the illusion of space to the tiny room. Just cosmetic stuff, but instantly effective.

'I might have put in a corner tub.' Kate spoke up, clearly savouring his reaction. 'But I ran out of money. Hope you understand.'

Abrams shrugged. He had to admit defeat. He might as well do it graciously.

'Fantastic job,' he said.

She beamed. 'So we have a deal?'

'We do,' he agreed. 'No rent. It's a one-bedroom now. I can get double for it.' He looked her over, in the jeans and flats, her pretty face lit up with a smile. Gold-digger she might be, but she was definitely good at this. He thought of his new building on the Upper West Side, a derelict ex-synagogue; it needed a complete refit. 'You're good at interior design.'

She tossed her head, arrogantly. 'I'm superb,' she said.

Man, he wanted to fuck her. No getting away from it. He imagined Lottie Friend's disapproving face and dismissed it from his mind. 'I might have a job for you. Refitting another building I've just bought.'

'Not interested,' Kate said immediately.

He was annoyed at her dismissiveness. 'You haven't heard my offer.'

'It doesn't matter. Like I told you, I'm in magazines. And that's a full-time job.'

'Look, honey.' Time to give her some home truths. 'You're a features editor on a small independent. It's nice, but you're hardly saving the world. You make terrible money, and always have. In this occupation at least.'

Her face flushed scarlet. 'What did you say?'

'Oh, you heard me, Kate Fox. Don't be coy.'

'Fuck you,' she snapped.

David Abrams blinked. Nobody had spoken to him like that in the last ten years.

'You work for Emily Jones. That's it. Maybe you can afford to mess around on no wages, because Marcus Broder left you enough.'

'Excuse me?' Kate said, outraged.

'I was about to offer you an actual position. In a major corporation. At a decent salary. Six figures. Which is more than you're making now.'

'And how the hell do you know what I'm making now?'

He shrugged, enjoying her rage, his own superiority. She had challenged him. And David Abrams was going to put her in her place.

'Because unlike you, miss, I *am* in magazines. And when I want to know something, people tend to talk.'

'You checked me out? Doesn't that mean my landlord is a stalker?'

'Natural curiosity,' he said, unfazed. 'Can you look me in the eyes and say you didn't go and check me out?'

She took a step away from him. 'This is my apartment. Get out.'

Abrams nodded. 'Yes, ma'am, it sure is. And you've transformed it, so it's now rent-free. Your previous payments will be refunded to your account.' She opened her mouth, and he held up his hands. 'I'm going, I'm going.'

David turned on his heel and walked out of her front door, pulling out his BlackBerry as it closed. An email to his letting agents confirmed the new arrangement; a deal was a deal.

What a ball-breaking bitch, he thought. And was infuriated with himself for having let her annoy him.

Time for a palate cleanser. He tapped the phone icon, pulled up the number of Kimberley Deloitte, one of his favourite high-end hookers. Very expensive, very exclusive, and worth every cent. Slim, with plastic breasts and over-plumped lips, she had the most talented mouth on the Upper East Side. And now he just wanted to be taken care of. One of his limo drivers would pick her up, ferry her downtown.

She giggled, promised to be with him in a quarter of an hour. Kimberley never gave him any trouble. She used the guest bathroom, pulled on her clothes and was out of the door within twenty minutes after they were through. She was great, he thought, a friend with benefits, no attitude. Abrams kept a spare stock of jewellery boxed up in a little cupboard beside his bed. He'd open it and find something cute for her, as well as the money already wired to her account. He liked her. A solid gold cuff bracelet, that was one of the more expensive pieces. She could show him a good time and be riding back home with that on her wrist.

No fuss. No stress. Screw the little trophy wife downstairs. Right?

Chapter Twelve

Kate sat in her gorgeous new apartment and fumed. That bastard, she thought, that absolute jerk. Why was she even allowing him to get under her skin?

First Marcus, now David Abrams. Demeaning her job. Laughing at her salary.

And far, far worse, laughing at *her*. He'd stood there, that arrogant son of a bitch, and talked about marrying Marcus like it was her occupation . . .

Kate burned. Marcus Broder's contemptuous words rang in her ear once more. 'No other rich man is going to take my cast-offs.'

Maybe he'd been right. Maybe all this was stupid. David Abrams could not have been more clear in his contempt. He liked her apartment design, but he thought she was playing, messing around, a dilettante rich divorcée with a settlement that covered everything. As if she'd have been in this building, in a minute studio, if that were true.

What was she doing over at *Lucky*? With all her success, she was still earning a salary. Just like David Abrams said. Still treading water. Still working for Emily, on money that had scarely covered her rent, and she'd done all this just so she could put some cash away.

There was the horrible sensation that maybe that good-looking son of a bitch was right. Kate was in her late twenties. Was she wasting the best years of her career? Wasting her life?

She paced up and down her new floor like a tiger, thinking, just thinking. About Marcus. About Emily. About this city . . .

The phone rang. Annoyed, she picked it up. Couldn't they leave her alone for one goddamned evening? She was trying to get her head straight.

'Kate?'

It was Sylvia, in the main office. Emily's assistant. She was sobbing, almost hysterical. Kate forgot about David Abrams, forgot about everything.

'What's the matter? Sylvia, what's happened?'

More frantic sobbing. It was as though she could barely get the words out.

'Have you looked at the news?'

'No.' Fear washed through her. Her palms broke into a sweat from adrenaline. 'Sylvia, for God's sake. What's happened?'

'There's been a train crash,' the older woman wept. 'Metro-North. To Scarsdale . . .'

Kate's heart pounded. Emily's parents lived in Scarsdale. 'Has something happened? Is Emily hurt?'

More sobs. 'Emily and Paul were in the first carriage, Kate. It derailed . . . They're dead.'

Immediate waves of panic and grief assailed her. Kate closed her eyes against the dizziness, against the pain.

'That can't be right.' She was denying it. 'It can't be true.'

Her fingers fumbled for the remote control on her table; she turned on the small TV set she kept in a corner of the room, switched to CNN.

Carnage filled the room. The images leapt out at her. An aerial shot of the train, sprawled across the track, on its side, on fire. Fire engines and crews blasting it with water. Cut to shots of bystanders sobbing, injured being taken off on stretchers. The ground was thick with emergency service vehicles, rubbernecking locals, news crews, hysterical relatives . . .

'How do you know?'

'Her parents called me twenty minutes ago.' When Kate had been preoccupied, fencing with Abrams. 'The cops called them; they found their wallets on the bodies. Mr Jones went down to the site for the ID.'

Kate was weeping now, tears streaming down her cheeks. 'Oh God, Sylvia, oh God. She's my best friend. She's been my best friend for ever. I love her . . .'

'I know. We all know. I'm so, so sorry, Kate.'

'What . . . what about Paul's family?'

'Emily's parents are calling them . . . Kate. What do we do about this place? About the job . . . about everyone . . .'

'Close the magazine for tomorrow. Send everybody an email.' Why are you bothering me with this? Kate thought. She was sobbing, tears coursing down her face.

'And after that? Kate – Kate, please don't be mad. You're the features editor . . .'

Right, right. She tried to pull herself together. There were fifty people who worked on *Lucky*, depended on it for their rent, their food. She was second in command. And right now they were looking to her.

'We'll start work the day after tomorrow. Until I find out who owns the magazine, and what they want to do with it. It belonged to Emily, so maybe it went to her mom and dad, or Paul's parents. We don't know. For now, we'll keep going.

I . . .' She tried to think. 'I have signatory authority on the bank accounts, so we'll carry on. I can make the payroll . . .'

Sylvia cried even harder. 'Thank you, Kate, I know it's awful to be worried at a time like this. I shouldn't, I know that, but you understand . . .'

'Hey. It's your life. People have got bills, got kids.' She tried to be strong, but her voice was cracking. How the hell could she work when her life was destroyed? 'Long-term, I can't guarantee anything, though. It's not mine. I don't know whose it is. Tomorrow I want to call Mr and Mrs Jones, see about the funeral . . .'

She couldn't go on. She broke down. Sylvia was saying she was sorry, again.

'I have to go,' Kate muttered. 'I'll call Mrs Jones,' and she hung up, then sank shattered on to her couch, where she buried her head in her hands and cried and cried until she could weep no more.

Marcus Broder looked at his bedside clock. The LED numerals glowed softly; he had them on a dimmer, so that his insomnia was not exacerbated by too much light.

It was half-two in the morning. But he was wide awake.

The text message had woken him up.

It came from an intermediary. Jack Jones, one of his vice presidents, a mid-level flunky who would never normally bother the boss direct. But Jack kept an eye on various acquisition targets for him. And one that Marcus had asked him to watch closely was *Lucky*. Jones had his spies, his low-level contacts in the magazine's accounts department. Marcus required a monthly email from him. It was one way to track that fat bitch Emily Jones, the girl who had fucked up a perfectly workable marriage.

But then the text. At night. Buzzing in to one of his most private numbers.

Train crash on Metro-North, it read. *Employees say Emily Jones & husband killed. Unclear on who owns magazine property, makes payroll. Staff panicking.*

Marcus had read the text several times. But it seemed pretty clear. He was pleased the junior schmuck had had the courage to send it. No point in waiting until the morning. He put the TV on to watch the news, muting it so his bed partner didn't wake, annoy him with questions.

The girl of the moment slept beside him, her long, slim limbs sprawled over his bed. He would push her back on to her own side but he didn't want her to stir. Let her sleep, and snore slightly in that annoying way of hers. He could get rid of her in the morning.

They had been dating for three weeks. She was very suitable, the daughter of a diplomat in the French consulate. Pedigree, that was what he needed after the car crash that was Kate Fox. He had only agreed to call off the press because Kate's needs dovetailed with his.

Marcus Broder hated being mocked.

Kate was meant to curl into a ball and go away. Which would help him forget that she'd actually asked for the divorce. Even if the world thought it was the other way around.

Instead, she'd chosen the path most likely to enrage him. Staying here. Taking his money. Working, at the job that had wrecked their marriage. Working for Emily Jones.

It was like a deliberate insult.

His spies reported back regularly, until he told them to drop it. Kate was flinging herself into her sad little job. She had rented a modern apartment, tiny but chic, in a smart building downtown, was looking for something to buy. And was somewhat serious. She turned up to her work every single day. And she was selling the magazine. Not that huge a leap, but selling it all the same. She would be a valued member of their team.

He hated it. It was like she'd slotted right back into her old life. Less partying, longer hours, but she was Kate Fox again, like Marcus Broder had never happened to her.

Louise Keroualle, the girl in the bed, just wasn't as good a fuck as Kate. None of them had been. Even though she hadn't been giving her all to him. He knew that, and he resented it. There had been something, under that slim, sexy body, the big tits and round ass, something that marked her out. An urgent sexuality. It chewed at Marcus nights, sometimes, even when he was banging the latest pneumatic brunette from the country club or high-class hooker he liked to indulge in. None of their appreciative moans or extravagant compliments meant as much to him as when Kate would stir and moan in her sleep.

He suspected he had never satisfied her.

And he hated her for it.

He looked at Louise. She was nothing, she was methadone. Did she harbour dreams that he was going to marry her? Man, he'd never be that much of a sucker, ever again.

The worst of it all was that he wanted Kate Fox back. He had unfinished business with her. She was one of his possessions, bought and paid for, but she'd left him, cheated him. And just dusted herself down and went right on. Like nothing had happened . . .

For weeks he'd been thinking revenge.

There were plenty of options on the table. Destroy her in the press. That was a good first step. Now she'd signed the settlement deal and he'd been the one to get the divorce, she had no hold over him, no bargaining chip. If he'd called off the dogs, he could surely put them back on the hunt.

That was one way to go.

There were others. Sue her . . . it hardly mattered for what. His pockets were deep; she had nothing but one paltry million. He could make her spend every last dime on lawyers. Get rid of her job, strangle Emily's pathetic little magazine she took such joy in. He would take it into Broder, Inc. and transform it into everything she hated. Or he could simply put out one of his own and undercut them in every department.

Lots of choices. Lots of ways to bring her down. He could try any or all of them. She would know what he was doing, of course. Marcus indulged in a pleasant fantasy: Kate Fox asking for an appointment, coming back to see him, to beg him for mercy, beg him to let her go. On almost any terms. He might permit that, he thought, stiffening at the thought. He'd make her get down on her knees and literally beg him. And then he'd stand over her and have her give him the blow job of her life. She could suck him every day for a month, and then perhaps he'd let her go to New Jersey and sink into obscurity. Unless he put her in an apartment and kept her on the side, strictly for recreation . . .

What a delicious thought. Kate Fox, broken and humiliated, and at his feet. That was precisely the way it should be.

Broder reached down and stroked himself. He watched the scene on the wafer-thin television hung above his bed, the sound muted, the lights of the TV scene lighting up his bedroom, dappling the naked body of the pretty, boring piece of fluff sleeping in his bed.

It was fate. Lining up behind him, the way it usually did. They called men like him 'masters of the universe'. Tonight that felt literally true. The train crash was playing out on the news channels in an endless loop. Two-hundred-plus fatalities. A senator's wife, an actress, a Catholic archbishop, and several prominent New York businessmen, all wiped off the face of the earth. And with them Emily Jones and her milksop of a husband.

Kate Fox was out of a job. He hadn't needed to do anything.

Idly he wondered who owned the magazine now. Her husband would have been the heir. Were there kids? Parents? A favourite goddaughter? Nobody that knew the first thing about running a print title, of course. He could pick it up for nothing. And he would. *Lucky*, she'd called it. *Unlucky*, more like. He chuckled at his own joke.

Maybe he could purchase it through an agent. Quietly. It would be great to walk through the doors of that office two weeks from now, and see her face. When she realised who the new boss was.

Marcus's fingers tightened into a fist. Look at him. He was thinking about her again, fantasising about her. Wasting time on her. And that would not do. He would have to take care of Kate Fox, far better than he'd done when he dumped her.

Emily Jones was dead. And so was Kate Fox's career in New York.

The funeral was mercifully fast. Emily's father arranged everything at lightning speed, to spare his wife, who was beside herself with grief. Kate discovered herself standing at the side of a grave in a Scarsdale cemetery, tears rolling down her cheeks, while Emily's parents and sister and Paul's family – cousins and aunts – sobbed and moaned as the preacher rattled through his Bible readings. She couldn't bring herself to look at the coffins; she just stared at the ground. Wherever her friend was now, it wasn't inside that box.

Emily had died so young, but she was with Paul, the only guy she'd ever loved. She'd worked at her passion, lived life how she wanted to. Married the right guy. That made her a success. Far more of a success than Kate, with her empty fridge and her sterile million nesting in the bank.

That thought tightened around Kate's heart, was like a band across her chest. It was almost as though she couldn't breathe, and the pain she felt for her best friend was mixed with pain for herself. Paul was a regular guy, and Emily had loved him and was happy with him.

How the hell did I mess up my life like this? Kate thought.

David Abrams came into her mind. His arrogance, his cockiness. And the disdainful way he'd treated her. *You make terrible money, and always have. In this occupation at least,* he'd said.

Man, she would love to throw the money back in his face. Tell him she didn't want the rent subsidy. But she couldn't do that, could she? Didn't have enough money.

So she threw him out of her tiny apartment. And that was all she did. Not the best picture, Kate thought. Because she was still taking his money. And she knew what that meant in his eyes.

Anger and shame mixed in with her grief.

'Kate.' Mrs Jones came up to her. 'My dear girl.'

'Oh, Mrs Jones, I'm so sorry,' Kate managed. She hugged the older woman, but the sorrow was too much now, pumping through her with every beat of her breaking heart. She had to get the hell out of there, but she couldn't, couldn't run away. Not from Emily's mom. 'Emily was my best friend . . .'

'I know that, honey.' Mary Jones wiped her eyes. 'Thank you for all you did for her. She talked about you all the time. She looked up to you, you know.'

Kate shook her head. 'It was the other way round, ma'am.'

'No.' Mary Jones was quite definite. 'She said you were one in a million, Kate, if you let yourself go for it. That you had a destiny.'

Kate's eyebrow lifted, despite herself, despite the pain.

'She said what?'

'Destiny. That you were special. And you just weren't letting yourself be special. I've lost my little girl, Kate,' she sobbed. 'And I know she'd want you to go for it now.'

'I'm so sorry,' Kate repeated numbly, but Emily's mother was lost in her grief, weeping, her shoulders shaking, burying her face in her hands.

Mr Jones, in a dark suit, his own eyes red, came over and steered his wife away, his two hands on her shoulders.

'Come on, sweetie,' he said. 'Let's get you home.'

Kate stood there watching them go. Even in this dark hour Mary Jones had someone to take care of her, and someone she had to look after. Family. A husband.

Kate only had Emily, really. And now Emily was gone.

'Kate?' Emily's dad looked over his shoulder. 'Be in our attorney's office tomorrow at ten. Kohlberg and Green in Scarsdale. For the reading of the will.'

'But why . . . I'm not in the will,' Kate protested. She had an issue to complete, and a staff who were barely capable of switching on their computers. They had suppliers waiting and advertisers who'd paid their cash. That was the thing about life: it went on without you, whether you gave it permission to or not.

Kate needed to sell this magazine, to make her payroll. And that job was the only thing getting her up in the morning.

'Yes you are. You need to be there.'

Kate bit her lip. She could hardly argue with the grieving parents. So Emily had left her a small bequest, some personal items, a picture or something. And she would cry her heart out again when she heard it, but surely she didn't need to be there for the reading of the will. They could just ship those things to her.

But if Emily's mom and dad wanted her there . . .

'OK, yes, sir.' She gave up. One last thing she could do for Emily. 'I'll come, but I really need to get back to the office right away afterwards. I have to finish this issue of *Lucky*.'

'I know you do.'

'Did Emily leave you guys the magazine?' Kate asked, innocently.

'No.' Mr Jones looked down at her oddly. 'You mean you didn't know? She left it to you.'

It seemed like an odd place to have your life changed.

This was clearly the family attorney, Kate thought, small-town, a comfortable room with inexpensive navy couches and *Good Housekeeping* magazine on the table next to *US Weekly*. A well-thumbed copy of the local *Pennysaver*, the listings mag, rested beside them. Framed law degrees from minor schools upstate hung on the walls. But the carpeting was soft, and the office was clean and spacious. There was good money to be made in Scarsdale, handling lawsuits in the real estate divisions, settling provincial divorces, even probate.

It was a million miles from the oak-panelled corridors of her divorce attorney, the stench of wealth that hung around the sharks who served Marcus Broder.

But it was still serious business. Her life was due to change here. She tried to pay attention. Mrs Jones was at home, with a sister; Emily's father and a couple of her cousins had attended the reading.

'Really, it's very simple.' Ezra Kohlberg looked over his glasses at them and smiled, briskly. He'd done this before, and had no sense of drama. A small, wiry man, he spoke quickly. Just giving the family the facts.

Kate could see that this worked for Emily's dad. Stopped him thinking too much. Like organising a funeral did. Humans were clever, Kate thought. They came up with ingenious workarounds for pain.

'It was a simple will. Ms Jones left her entire estate to her husband, Mr Benutto, and he left his to her. But that's not relevant, because the autopsy is clear that he predeceased her. He was sitting further forward . . .' A shadow of agony passed across Mr Jones's face. 'The point is that the will has provision for secondary heirs. That's you and your wife, Mr Jones, since Mr Benutto's parents are dead. Emily left you everything: her apartment, her car, bank balances in two accounts totalling one point five million dollars.'

Emily must have been thrifty, Kate thought. *Lucky* wasn't anywhere close to making profits like that yet. That was saved money.

'And she left her interest in *Lucky* magazine to you, Ms Fox. Including the corporate accounts.'

There was barely enough in there to pay the bills, but OK, Kate thought. She felt a wash of gratitude to Emily.

'Did she leave me a letter?' Kate asked, her voice cracking.

The lawyer shook his head. 'No, ma'am. No letter. I don't honestly think Ms Jones ever expected to die, or for that matter to have these provisions kick in. It rarely happens.'

Maybe it was just as well. Kate couldn't have coped with a note. She would have dissolved completely.

'I can tell you what she was thinking,' Richard Jones said, heavily. 'She actually asked us. And we didn't want it. I got no idea how to run a magazine.'

'You could have sold it.'

'Not interested.' He shook his head. 'Mary and I have always saved, Ms Fox. We don't need to worry about money. I told her I was so proud of her. I wanted her to become a dentist, you know. Like me.'

Kate smiled. 'Yes, sir. I remember.'

'Thank God she didn't. Instead, she followed her dreams. She told us that was because of you.' Tears came to his eyes. 'Look, my wife and I – well, we weren't that fond of you. Didn't approve. You were too . . .' He gestured, making a big circle with his hands. 'Too much,' he concluded. Despite herself, Kate cracked a small grin.

'Anyway, that wasn't my Emily,' he said. 'You were loud, and . . . kind of . . .'

'. . . hot,' the attorney muttered, then shuffled his papers as though he hadn't said anything.

'But she wouldn't listen to us. She stayed with you. And she changed her look some, and then she met Paul. And she got that stupid magazine. I read it once. It's subversive.' He said that with a strong sense of pride. 'She was happy, Kate. You take a lot of credit for that.'

'She was happy because you raised her happy, sir,' said Kate.

He wasn't listening. 'When we persuaded her we didn't want her little magazine, she said it wasn't Scarsdale. And we laughed. And then she said, maybe I'll give it to Kate.'

Adrenaline flooded her. It was like Emily was talking to her, guiding her, telling her exactly what she wanted.

'She said you'd know what to do with it. And you'd make it fun.' He offered her his hand, and Kate shook it, fighting to swallow down the lump in her throat. 'You made my daughter's life fun, Kate Fox. Never think that isn't important.'

He looked at her.

'Now let's see what you can do with her magazine,' he said.

She rode back into town in a daze, in the back of a local cab, because she couldn't bring herself to get on the train. Besides, she wanted to be alone. Wanted time to think.

Lucky was hers now. And she had Emily's words, and her father's, ringing in her ears.

Let's see what you can do.

A shudder of grief ran through her. But something else, too. Fear. And excitement. There wasn't going to be time to mourn. There was only going to be time to pull this thing together. Maybe Emily planned it that way, Kate thought. She'd know what it meant to be in charge of a small indie.

Sylvia's anxious words came back to her. There were the staff, all dependent on her. And more than that, there was *Lucky*. Emily's baby. It had been her pride and joy. She wouldn't want it to crash into the ground. Her parents might have done that, but Kate Fox wouldn't.

She pictured David Abrams offering her a job, sneering at her salary. What would he say now? she wondered. No salary any more. She owned the whole damn thing. With its expanding sales, terrified staff, and barely adequate financing. All *Lucky*'s problems and opportunities had landed right on her desk.

Of course, David Abrams had run his first successful

magazine while he was still at college, a little voice in her head reminded her.

Yeah, and bought and sold five more by the time he was her age.

What if she had focused earlier? What if her work had mattered more? What if she hadn't been looking in the wrong place . . .

Oh, come on, Kate told herself. Stop beating yourself up. David Abrams is one of the most successful magazine men of all time. You can't make *him* the standard. Just decide where you go from here. And stop thinking about him.

He was an arrogant bastard.

And absolutely not interested in her.

Kate shook herself in the back of the cab, like a dog shaking off rainwater. It was time to focus on her job. Maybe later, when she'd healed a little, she could think about falling in love. Try to find an ordinary guy, maybe a lawyer or a teacher. Somebody her own age. Right now she knew she wouldn't be any use to anybody.

Sadness had settled through every part of her, but underneath it, now, there was a new emotion. Excitement. Shock. Perhaps – she felt guilty, but perhaps – just a touch of pleasure. In the middle of all this pain, Emily had sent her a hell of a gift.

Her own magazine. Which her friend had loved, and wanted saved. It actually belonged to her.

It was like life just gave Kate Fox a second chance. And this time, she intended to take it.

Chapter Thirteen

David Abrams spun the chair in his office and looked out of the window. He was easily distracted these days.

To be fair, it was a hell of a window, and a hell of a view. He had offices in midtown, Tenth Avenue, just north of Times Square, and his architects had gotten a permit to change the façade of a landmark building, just for his penthouse suite. A sheer wall of glass, tinted on one side, reflected the neon glories of the square, the huge billboards, the scrolling news tickers wrapped around the skyscrapers, tourists clogging the sidewalks, yellow taxis crawling past the sex bars at ground level. From the outside, it looked like a huge mirror, glittering in the sun, reflecting everything that was going on. A special decision at City Hall was taken to allow it. After careful donations to their political action committees, assemblymen from all sides said that David Abrams was adding to the beauty of Times Square. Seventh Avenue at Forty-Ninth Street, home to one of the city's hottest new entrepreneurs.

Of course, on David's side it was soundproofed, and the city looked almost tranquil spread out below him. The giant billboards energised him, made him want to contribute, to create. They advertised Guess jeans and Maybelline cosmetics, Diet Coke and M&Ms, the New York Yankees, airlines and movies, TV shows and Broadway productions. He *had* to put his office here. It was Times Square, the beating heart of the greatest city in the world. Where you had to compete, had to fight. Manhattan was full of sharks. You moved forward or you died.

All David Abrams wanted to do was move forward. That was why he was back in his office. Working from home, downtown, had suddenly become far too distracting. He cursed the day he had agreed to see Kate Fox. She had gotten under his skin, and every day he rode the elevator to his own apartment he wondered what she was doing in hers. As tiny as his was cavernous. That little slice of light, airy space she had magicked up out of almost nothing.

It bothered him. He'd scythed his way through more girls than usual this last week. But somehow she still kept jumping into his head. For a second, he'd even thought about moving house. Finding another apartment somewhere, in one of his other buildings. But of course that was fantasy. He wasn't going to move just because some chick had a place in his building.

That she'd ordered him out of. And now wasn't even paying rent for. He wondered if he'd gotten the best of that deal.

Still, it was temporary. Kate Fox would be gone soon. It was a real short lease. And then he could rent it to some junior prick of an investment banker and forget all about her.

For now, he was gracing his office with his presence, staring at Times Square, looking at all the busy New Yorkers getting on with their busy lives, powering the greatest engine of the Western world.

'Lottie.' He buzzed his assistant. 'Get me the report on our magazine division. And get Tim Reynolds in here.'

Reynolds ran the magazine side of the empire. Originally poached from Condé Nast, he was urbane and efficient.

'Yes, sir. Right away.'

'And Iris. And Rick Johnson.'

'Absolutely, Mr Abrams.' Lottie hung up. She'd be calling his major executives, summoning them to a council of war. Tim Reynolds was the money man; he was chief financial officer to the whole group. He made sure David didn't overextend himself, kept costs under control. Rick Johnson ran marketing. The group was sprawling; Abrams was conscious of that. He needed Rick around to nag him. And Iris Haughey was the doyenne of *Model* and *Beauty*, his two major women's titles, the reliable powerhouses amongst his magazine stable. Travel and lifestyle came and went, but if you did it right, you could always sell lipstick. Haughey was forty-three, with mid-length curly hair always blow-dried to perfection and a penchant for black silk dresses. Deeply formidable, she was married to a merchant banker with three kids from his first marriage. She didn't need the money. She just loved the power. A woman after his own heart, Iris used chic like a weapon.

Abrams heard she wasn't popular. But she got the job done. Even in a recession, his major titles sailed along, steady in their readership. Where others bled, he stayed the same. It was editorship Tim Reynolds appreciated. Like he said, they could bank on *Beauty*.

And Tim Reynolds was a hawk. He delivered pay deals that attracted the major names, the big writers, the celebrated photographers, all America's best stylists. Abrams was still a small player, but with Tim on board, he kept a good flow of the best talent. All his magazines were in the game, and if any of them failed to cut it, Reynolds was ruthless; he folded the title, and staffers were looking for other jobs. Costs were low here, and production smooth. Because Tim Reynolds didn't do diva. Anybody working for Abrams knew the score.

Within five minutes there was a knock on his door and Lottie Friend had the report in his hands. Within ten, his three senior execs were sat in the high-backed Eames chairs facing his desk.

'I'm not happy.' Abrams watched them exchange nervous glances with each other.

'The division broke even. It's been a rough year,' Reynolds said.

'Sales at *Model* are up two per cent for the quarter,' Iris added. 'We have plenty of ad revenue.'

'Yeah, and sales of *Beauty* dropped three per cent.'

'It's not bad in this climate.' Rick tried to defend her. 'The industry thinks we're doing fine. There's envy out there.'

Abrams stood up, and they shrank back a little in their chairs. His eyes were flashing. His executives knew this wasn't going to be good.

'Fine doesn't cut it,' he said. 'We're treading water. We've stabilised, yes. The difference between you and me, Tim, is I don't think that's a good thing. My ambition wasn't to run a medium-sized magazine group. I wanted to be the new Condé Nast. Better, even. This company needs to be expanding. I want imagination, vision. Not steady as she goes.' He put one hand on the desk. 'Tell me what we need to be doing. What do we shut down? What do we buy? I want to acquire something. Like a new title that has potential to get *talked* about. To blow the industry away.'

'But David, if I may point out,' Iris said. 'You're already a very rich man. And you've done it without taking risks.'

'Rich?' Abrams snorted. 'I don't know what rich is. Marcus Broder is rich. Mark Zuckerberg is rich. We're all just ticking along in our five-million-dollar apartments, being comfortable. That doesn't work for me. I'm ambitious.'

'You can say that again,' Rick muttered.

'So go away. Think strategically. Find me something I might be able to use. A new title, one to make this city sit up and take notice. Let's start with that.'

'Very well,' Iris said, standing up and smoothing down the skirt of her Donna Karan. 'I'll come back to you.'

Rick got up and walked out with her, shaking his head. He obviously believed that steady was fine. Only it wasn't, and David Abrams could see that with crystal clarity.

'David.' Tim Reynolds remained in his seat, one hand pressed against his forehead. Meaning he was thinking hard. Abrams liked to see that; it was why Tim ran the group and the other two reported to him. 'There is one option out there, off the top of my head. I can scout around for possibilities. But there's a new book that springs to mind.'

'I'm all ears,' Abrams said. 'I want an independent that's ready to grow. And massively.'

'Have you heard of *Lucky* magazine?'

Abrams blinked. 'What?'

'*Lucky*. An indie, kind of a new take on *Wallpaper* meets the *Village Voice*. Left-wing politics but lots of quirky stuff too, some fashion, some lifestyle.'

Goddamn Kate Fox, Abrams thought, but said nothing. He wanted to hear an outsider's view.

'Go on.'

'Had a dedicated readership when it started out. Rich liberal kids. Made a small profit. But then it got freshened up by a new features ed. She put in populist stuff, but didn't take out the activism. It's not like anything out there right now. Mixes up the lifestyle stuff with a social conscience. It's kind of subversive.' Reynolds couldn't keep the admiration out of his voice. 'And it's started to sell a lot better. The features ed actually took over the day-to-day a few months ago, and sales exploded. She got it into Hudson News: they were expanding . . .'

'Privately owned?'

'Yes. But the owner died in the Metro-North crash last week.'

Abrams sat bolt upright, as though he had been shocked.

'What?'

'Yes. Her name was Emily Jones. Husband also died.'

'Fuck.' He never swore usually. He thought of Kate, less aggressively. 'So who owns it now?'

'No idea. We could find out. You'd probably want the features ed to come with it. She's been the linchpin of the entire thing. And you know the bizarre thing? She's an ex-wife of Marcus Broder, the most recent one, I think.'

'I heard that,' Abrams said drily. He needed to go find Kate Fox, say he was sorry for her loss. At the very least. 'I guess I need to think about this, Tim. Thank you. Keep looking for other titles.'

Reynolds nodded and walked out. Abrams chewed on his lip. He wasn't sure about this. Work was meant to be a *distraction* from Kate Fox.

Maybe fate was laughing at him.

Kate sat in her boardroom, if you could call it that. A kitchen table at the top of their little building in the West Village. The magazine was run out of eight rooms, and the kitchenette doubled as the place for meetings.

'This issue's gone to bed.' Karl Levin, their accountant, breathed a sigh of relief. 'Thanks, Kate. We booked the ads, the bills are getting paid. But starting next month there are going to be problems.'

She scratched her head. 'I thought we were doing well. The senator's cover . . .'

'We're doing great, as a *magazine*. As a business . . .' He shrugged eloquently.

She sighed. 'Well, I've inherited a business. So tell me about it.'

'*Lucky* needs financing. Desperately. But Emily refused to float it, or sell a stake, or anything.' He grimaced. 'The company's in debt, Kate. This building . . . the landlord raised the rent. And taking on extra staff means more taxes. Our revenue leaves a shortfall, and the new sales haven't fed through yet. It's a cash-flow problem, but it's kind of a big one.'

'How was Emily dealing with it?' Kate demanded. 'There had to be a way.'

'Sure there was. The magazine had a line of credit, and she was borrowed up to her eyeballs.'

'We can keep going.' Kate was determined. 'Sales are on the up; we just need a little time for them to filter through.'

'Ah.' He loosened his collar, awkwardly. 'I'm afraid that after the accident . . . well, the banks have started to press for early repayment of the loan. They can do that, under the terms. Emily was the owner, and they felt comfortable with how things were going under her leadership.'

Kate bristled. 'Emily was wonderful, but I'm the reason *Lucky* has been expanding.'

Damn it, this was her baby now. Had been since the divorce.

'I mentioned that to them, but . . .' Karl flushed.

'Spit it out.'

'I'm really sorry, Kate. They don't want to know. They think you're a . . . a . . . a socialite,' he finished lamely.

Trophy wife. Grasping bitch. It was going to follow her for ever. Colour heightened her own cheeks.

'Then I guess I need to explain things to them.' She stared at the figures in front of her. The neat little black and white rows, so precise and impersonal, hid the scale of the disaster. *Lucky* was running on fumes. And if she couldn't get the money, it was going to fold, sales or no sales.

Kate didn't kid herself. It had happened before to magazines. Happened all the time.

'Set up appointments with the banks,' she said.

'I'm sorry, Mrs Broder.' The manager stared at her over his desk. He was a fat little man, with piggish eyes and a mean streak in his smile. 'You have absolutely no experience. Western City Bank can't be sure you'll safeguard our investment.'

'I have plenty of experience. I started at *Cutie*, and then I took a short career break . . .'

His arched eyebrow told her what he thought of her 'career break'.

'I remember, Mrs Broder. I read all about it.'

Son of a bitch, Kate thought. She bit her lip to stop herself correcting his use of her name. He was doing it deliberately, enjoying her discomfiture. She wouldn't give him the satisfaction.

'Well, I was soon back in the saddle, Mr Jackson. And at *Lucky*. Where, as you may know, I took over editorial, landed the big stories, increased our sales distribution . . .'

'May I be frank with you, Mrs Broder?'

Kate shrugged. 'Why stop now?'

He ignored the sally. 'You're claiming credit for the sales uptick, but nobody can be sure that's true. All I see on paper is a mid-level features writer on a low salary of forty thousand dollars. Ms Jones owned this magazine, she took the risk to set it up, she worked at it since college; we were happy to back her. You . . .' He spread his hands. 'You made, shall we say, other choices.'

'The forty grand was only until Emily and Paul made me a full partner.'

'Sure, Mrs Broder, of course it was,' he said soothingly, patronisingly.

Rage boiled up in her. She fought to control it. 'Mr Jackson, Emily left me the damn magazine. That should tell you something.'

'She left you a pile of debts. Look, your best bet is to try to sell. We'd give you a month to do that. Otherwise we're calling it in.'

'That's insane.' Kate stared. 'By doing it that way, you'll force *Lucky* to close down. We'd fold and you'd lose everything.'

'You know what lending mostly is, Mrs Broder? It's the art of not throwing good money after bad.' He smirked, proud of his little witticism. 'I'm outstanding at that.'

'Well, it's good you can be outstanding at something,' Kate said, as she stood up. 'Because, Mr Jackson, you're one of the most boring, vision-free, petty little bureaucrats I think I've ever met.'

She turned on her Manolos and walked out of his office, leaving him gaping like a fish.

* * *

It was the same story everywhere she tried.

'I'm sorry, we're not interested in new management.'

'We need satisfaction on this debt.'

'The terms of your loan clearly state . . .'

'Ms Fox, you need to pay us. As soon as possible. Within a month at the most. Otherwise the magazine is collateral. You'll sell it.' The banker's eyes were perfectly emotionless. 'Or we will.'

After one week, she was convinced. If she didn't do something right away – immediately – the new start Emily wanted for her, wanted for the magazine, would vanish. And a swift end would come in its place. Her second chance, her new life, snuffed out completely.

'You have to tell the staff, Kate,' Sylvia begged her, her eyes red.

They were locked in the little corner office together. It was a cramped room with a window that overlooked the pipes and ventilation shafts at the back of the hotel behind them.

'At least give them notice . . . they should start looking around . . .'

For all the other jobs that were out there in this dying sector? Come on, Kate thought. Like it would make a difference. One or two would fall on their feet; the rest were out of luck. The magazine was quirky and brilliant, but you couldn't slot that into a new job with *Cosmopolitan* or *Ladies' Home Journal*.

'Nobody's going to look anywhere.' Kate sighed deeply, and rubbed at her temples. The answer had been staring her in the face from the second that banker dropped his bombshell; she just hadn't wanted to face it. 'I'm going to get the finance. Maybe sell a stake, but I'll get the finance.'

'From where?'

Kate sat up straight and reached for her Prada bag, a gorgeous thing in dusty pink leather that went perfectly with her draped mink crêpe de Chine top and skinny blue jeans.

'An investor,' she said, and tried to ignore the flush of colour that dappled her cheeks. 'I think I know somebody who'll be interested.'

Sylvia took in her new boss's discomfiture, the colour in her beautiful cheeks. She groaned. 'It isn't Marcus Broder, is it? Because Emily hated him.'

'It's not Marcus Broder.' Kate got up; there was no point in putting it off any more. 'It's someone else. David Abrams.'

'You're kidding. You actually know him? What's he like?'

'He's a son of a bitch,' Kate said.

David Abrams sat in his kitchen and breathed in the rich scent of cinnamon coffee.

He didn't keep staff. A cook or housekeeper round the place first thing in the morning would have been obtrusive. Gabriella worked six days a week, when he was out, running or working. He liked his house perfect, his floors cleaned, fresh flowers daily, the Porthault sheets washed and ironed every time he used the bed. But he didn't want to see how it was done. Besides, there was something satisfying about fixing his own breakfast. He ran oranges through the juicer and brewed flavoured coffee, letting the heady perfume of it waft through the kitchen. Usually he toasted a raisin bagel and slathered it with cream cheese. If you ran and lifted weights, you could eat whatever the hell you liked.

Abrams saw no reason to deny himself any particular pleasures.

He was in a good mood. Last night's girl had been

spectacular. Eileen was a stripper from Queens, with fantastic big fake breasts and a party attitude. She waitressed part-time at his tennis club in the Hamptons every summer, and the iced tea came with fringe benefits. Abrams had showered her with jewellery and gifts, and she was an undemanding, friendly, easy bed partner.

All women should be like that, right? Not complicated. Prickly. Faking it. At least Eileen was upfront about what she wanted. She enjoyed his body, but she wanted money, gifts, jewels. And in exchange she got up, used the guest bathroom, sprayed herself liberally with the Chanel perfume he laid out for his female guests, and took his limousine back to her own place. She was as uninterested in a relationship as he was. Maybe she had her own guy tucked away somewhere. He didn't embarrass either of them by asking.

Trouble free. Didn't want to marry him, didn't want to argue all the time. He thought of Kate Fox, then added sugar to his coffee, stirred, sipped it. Trying to put her to the back of his mind. There would be other properties out there. *Lucky* wasn't the only one . . .

The coffee was strong, good. He savoured it, skipped food. He wanted to get into the office. It was time to make something happen. He was almost grateful to Kate; she'd made him see that he was treading water.

David Abrams never wanted to be comfortable. He'd made big promises to himself as a kid, and he intended to keep them all.

His BlackBerry buzzed on his Volterra marble countertop. He glanced at it idly. A new text message coming in, from a number he did not know.

Mr Abrams. I'd like to make an appointment to see you. Preferably today. To discuss investing in Lucky magazine. Kate Fox

He almost laughed aloud. It had to be a joke, didn't it? Only it wasn't, he knew that for sure. She really had messaged him. And she was asking for an appointment.

He stared at his phone for a few seconds. Then he took another long sip of his coffee.

Kate gathered her towel around her. Her hair was still dripping wet from the shower, little rivulets of water sluicing down the swell of her breasts. But her phone had buzzed insistently, and she was unable to ignore it.

She stepped cursing from the shower, tugged a luxuriously large bath sheet around herself – some things you just did not stint on – and picked up her iPhone.

'Ms Fox?'

'It is, yes.'

'My name is Lottie Friend. I'm calling you from David Abrams' office. He wanted me to confirm your appointment.'

Kate clenched her fist. God, so soon. He had scheduled her an appointment. That was wonderful. Although he had no idea what she was about to hit him with.

'That's tremendous,' she said, delighted. 'When is he seeing me?'

'At eight forty-five today,' the woman said coolly.

'Isn't that a little late still to be in the office?'

'Eight forty-five in the *morning*, ma'am.'

Kate bit back the urge to squeal. To ask Lottie Friend if she was fucking serious. But she didn't want to give the woman the satisfaction. She'd clearly said *today*. And was happy to lob this little bomb in Kate's direction.

That was twenty-five minutes from now.

'Thanks very much,' Kate said. 'I'll see him then.'

She hung up fast and moved at lightning speed. Her wet hair was tied back in a ruthless ponytail. She applied a slick of tinted moisturiser and bronzer on her cheeks, leaving her eyes and lips untouched. Her workday uniform of black leggings, a T-shirt and a thin cashmere jumper was pulled on; she grabbed her black Lycra socks and a pair of patent leather flats that she kept by the closet for emergencies. That, and dousing herself in Sure Ultra Dry anti-perspirant. She was going to need it.

Kate half ran out of the door, grabbing her bicycle as she went. There would be no time to walk or fuck around with the subway. It was clear to her that David Abrams, that arrogant jerk, was setting her a little test. Trying to unsettle her. It wasn't like he didn't know where she lived. Calling at eight twenty and setting a midtown meeting for eight forty-five? She was supposed to call up, perhaps in tears, say she couldn't do it, beg for another chance. Sure, he'd rearrange, but he'd enjoy her discomfiture.

No freaking way, she thought. She rode the elevator down, twitching with impatience, and shoved her bicycle through the doors before they were even halfway open. Within seconds she was out of the front door, powering up Broadway, her lean legs pumping, weaving in and out of the rush-hour traffic.

Chapter Fourteen

'Kate Fox,' she said, twenty minutes later.

Her face was flushed from the exertion, she knew, and she was barely made-up, and her hair was damp. But there were still five minutes on the clock. That was what counted.

'I have an appointment with Mr Abrams. Eight forty-five.'

The receptionist, an irritatingly pretty blond girl in her twenties, wearing an immaculate cream shift from Dior, her hair twisted up in an elegant chignon, smiled serenely at her. Looking at the girl, Kate wondered if she ever broke a sweat.

'Certainly, ma'am. If you'll just take a seat.'

Kate was happy to. She flopped down on the couch, and tried to get her breath back. Perspiration dewed her skin. She licked it off her upper lip.

'Kate Fox.'

God. She hadn't seen the door open. Kate nearly jumped out of her skin. She put her tongue away and blushed richly.

David Abrams was standing over her as she sat on his expensive couch, looking down at her. He wore a well-cut suit that did nothing to hide the tight muscles of his chest and arms. His hair was dark, flecked with salt and pepper, cut close to the head. He had a strong nose and those incredible brown eyes, fringed with thick, dark lashes, almost startling eyes, that seemed to hold her in place.

He was perfectly calm. And his expression was unreadable.

'You made it.'

She shrugged. 'This is the appointment time you gave me, Mr Abrams. So here I am.'

He gazed at her, and she wanted to shift and wriggle on her seat. She held herself still by a great effort of will.

'It had better be David, don't you think?' he asked. 'Since we're neighbours.'

'David,' Kate said. 'Thank you. Again.'

'Don't thank me too hard. I haven't done anything yet.' He gestured behind him. 'You're slotted in before my first meeting of the day. Come into my office.'

She followed, biting down on her lip to stop herself from thanking him one more time.

'Would you like anything? Tea, coffee?'

Another immaculate staffer, this time older, grey hair cut in a chic bob, materialised from nowhere and opened the door.

'Black coffee would be great, thank you. No sugar.' She didn't really need any coffee, but they were in a dance now, and she didn't want to seem weak or hurried.

'Certainly. And for you, sir?'

'I'll just take an iced water,' Abrams said. 'Come on in, Kate. I take it I can call you Kate?'

'Yes, sure,' she muttered.

Abrams was leading her into a vast, glorious space. She was stunned at the triple-height ceiling, the wall of glass, the view of Times Square stretching out below her.

It wasn't the same as Marcus Broder. There was nothing old money, nothing country club about it. This was brash, upstart wealth, from a comer who was going places.

David Abrams was everything she admired. In fact, he was a fucking legend. She wished he wasn't such a bastard. She wished he wasn't so damn handsome. If that was the right word. He had a cruel, sexy mouth, sharp eyes, a strong nose, not bland, inoffensive movie-star features.

He disturbed her.

'Have a seat.' He gestured to a pair of couches in one corner of the room, facing each other over a low glass coffee table. Kate sat down, thankful she was wearing leggings and didn't have to figure out where to put her legs in a skirt. Abrams sat opposite her. With perfect timing, his secretary appeared again with a small tray of drinks: iced water for Abrams, served in a crystal glass, and a cup of coffee for Kate, in wafer-thin bone china. The scent of it filled the room.

'Jamaican Blue Mountain,' Abrams said. 'You can't get better.'

'Yes, I remember,' Kate agreed thoughtlessly, and then could have kicked herself. She took the cup and sipped, spots of colour burning on her cheeks.

'Mr Broder liked it?'

'He wanted the best of everything,' Kate said flatly. She had fucked up by mentioning it; at least she could show David Abrams that she wasn't going to run from anything.

'I can see that,' Abrams replied. And his gaze travelled across Kate's body, like he could undress her with a glance.

She pressed her legs together defensively. He made her feel vital, and alive. He disturbed her, very greatly.

'I didn't come here to fence with you – *David*. I came here because I need your money.'

He laughed aloud, startled out of his composure. 'Well, at least you're upfront about it.'

'Not for me, you son of a bitch,' Kate exclaimed. 'For the *magazine*. For *Lucky*.'

Abrams regarded her, his eyes now somewhat amused. 'Yes, you said you wanted to talk about me taking a stake. Tell me, you think calling your white knight a son of a bitch is the best way to go about it?'

'Perhaps not usually. But in your case . . . maybe.' Kate tossed her head. 'I know you, David Abrams. I know everything about your career. And I see who you are. You like my magazine, and you're interested in me. That's why you saw me for the apartment thing. You were rubbernecking. And I threw you out, which probably doesn't happen to men like you too often. Let's not play games, because I've cycled more than twenty blocks and I'm tired. You gave me an appointment this morning that should have been impossible to keep. A test, right? But I was here on time. So here's a thought. We stop playing games, I tell you why *Lucky* would be perfect for you, you say yes, and we both make a ton of money.'

Now his smile was unguardedly warm.

'Points for style, Kate,' he ceded. 'I'll give you that.' He settled back against the warm charcoal leather of his couch. 'Of course it was a test. I think you passed. Have you thought about the consequences of what you're doing?'

'I'm saving my magazine.'

'No. You're saving *our* magazine. Because if I bail your ass out, I'm going to own a large chunk of it.'

'I'll still have a majority stake,' Kate countered. 'I'm not offering you the whole thing.'

'I don't do piecemeal deals. *If* I decide to invest, I want fifty-one per cent.'

'Forty-nine,' she said. 'Tops.'

Abrams shook his head. 'It's a great title. You have something really interesting going there. I've done some due diligence already, Kate. No games? Fine. Here's the deal. It's a perfect fit with my stable. We want to shake up the market, and if you hadn't called me, I was going to call you.'

A shiver of pleasure, of relief, ran through her.

'But it's not the only opportunity out there. In business, nothing ever is. And I've been the boss since I was a teenager. I don't work for other people, I don't take a minority stake. Ever. That's non-negotiable.'

She looked across at him. They were so close, their knees were almost touching. He was not about to buckle; he was quite firm. A small buzz of desire started to run through her, despite herself. And the more his eyes looked down calmly at her, not giving an inch, the worse it got.

Kate resisted the impulse to lick her lips. God, no man had ever done this to her. Not Marcus, not the guys who had preceded him. She tried to ignore the trails of desire trawling across her breasts and belly. It's the situation, she told herself. She wanted this magazine, wanted it badly. And she had to supplicate this man for it. It was only natural she would feel something.

'It's my title. Emily left it to me.'

'Yes.' He nodded. 'I only heard recently how this all came about. I'm very sorry for your loss. But I still don't take minority stakes. I am in charge of all my properties. It's the only way I work.'

Kate stiffened her back. She had to pull herself together. It had been an emotional couple of months, and she was overreacting, that was all this was. He would have another meeting in less than ten minutes. She had to get this done.

Act like the boss Emily Jones thought she could be.

'Fifty-fifty, then. Partners. I need your money, we're in debt and the banks will call the loan in. But the magazine is only expanding because of me. I don't want to go back to being a salaried employee. I'd rather try again, start something up from scratch.'

Was that bluffing? She didn't know. What she was sure of was that she wanted *Lucky* to work.

'Fifty-fifty I can live with, on one condition.'

'I'm listening,' Kate said.

She struggled to contain her joy. She started to think he was going to save her ass, rescue her magazine, guarantee the paycheques of all her staff, pay her rent. For the first time, money meant more to her than a fancy dress or a diamond necklace. The sheer power of it, of what it could do . . .

'Like I said, I'm always the boss. Fifty-fifty, if the contract states you work for me. You report to me. And I can fire you as Editor-in-Chief of the magazine. You keep your stake, but not your job.'

'Work for you?'

'Yes. It's mostly a partnership that way.' He smiled, very slightly, in that arrogant way, and she tried not to notice. 'Fifty-fifty. Co-owners. You as editor. It's just that, at the end of the day, I'm the boss.'

'I hate that deal,' she muttered. Part relief, part resentment, part something else.

'No you don't. You'll take it. And you're as grateful as hell.'

Kate got to her feet. 'You don't even know how much I want.'

'I know your debts and the value of the title. We'll thrash out the numbers by this afternoon. You get something else for the keyman clause, of course. You're right, it's principally your talent I'm buying. So if you leave voluntarily, you forfeit your stake to me.'

She bristled. 'Now you're locking me in, David.'

'With golden handcuffs,' he said. 'And I think the words you're looking for are *thank you*. Aren't they?'

Kate put her coffee cup down in its bone-china saucer. 'Thank you for the deal. But you're going to get your money's worth.'

He stood and offered her his hand. He still loomed over her. She shook it briskly, firmly. He was in her space, and she tried not to take a step backwards. She looked up at his mouth. Wondered what it would be like if he kissed her. If he took her.

Stop it, she lectured herself.

'You can count on that,' David Abrams said coolly. 'Your lawyers can expect my call later today.'

'I can't believe it.' Sylvia blinked at Kate. 'You have to be fucking kidding me.'

'Sylvia!' Kate said. The older woman never swore.

'You actually got him to go for it. That's incredible. How much money was it?'

'My stake was worth eight hundred thousand dollars. It's a new magazine, and the debts were almost a million. Abrams, Inc. takes a half-stake immediately; all our bills are paid.'

'Is he going to be here?' Sylvia pressed a hand to her mouth. 'In this office?'

'He doesn't edit any more, if that's what you mean. I'm still editor. But he's CEO of the new company. So yes, I guess he will be in. Sooner rather than later, I expect.' As she was speaking, her iPhone buzzed.

Sylvia squealed. 'Is that him? Is that David Abrams?'

Kate smiled. 'Yep. He'll be by this afternoon, about four, he says.'

The older woman instinctively touched a hand to her hair, but Kate gestured softly.

'No. You look great. And no need to dress up. In fact, don't let's tell the staff. He can take us as he finds us.' She squared her shoulders determinedly. 'David Abrams isn't going to change anything around here.'

He was pleasantly distracted at lunch. Tim Reynolds was excited, unusually talkative, as he went through all the new title would mean.

'A sales force is the first step. And it needs to be specialist. We're never going to be *Vogue* . . . *Wallpaper* is the closest thing, but she's not all about design. There's the pop culture meets liberal journalism . . .'

Abrams nodded, not paying attention. His mind wandered to Kate Fox. Hard, trying to not be impressed. There was something very sexy about the way she'd called him on the appointment. Of course he had been trying to test her. No way she could have made it uptown in that time. He'd just wanted to see how she'd handle herself when she called to reschedule, how she made her excuses. Instead, she'd gotten herself there. Wet hair, flushed face; she'd biked, and that explained how she was dressed. Tight black leggings, flat shoes, a clinging tee. She looked healthy and gorgeous. No amount of expensive styling in a beauty salon could have done that for her.

He replayed her standing up in reception, to follow him into his office. Those leggings were modest enough, covered her from waist to toe after all. But they also left very little to the imagination. Man, she had just an outstanding ass. A small waist you could fit in the crook of your arm, and then that glorious thing, sticking out there, round, high and tight. She was built like a forties pin-up. And her breasts, too. Medium in size, looked natural, just kind of perfectly proportioned to her height. She had a pretty face, oval, green eyed, blonde hair; you could see that even when it was tied back. He remembered what it looked like when she'd met him in the super's office. Thick and smooth. Goddamn, she was a peach. That ass . . . He was getting a little hard thinking about it.

Stop that, Abrams, he told himself. There were lots of sexy women in this city. Quite a few of them had seen the inside of his bedroom. So what was so different about Kate Fox? Wasn't she just another pretty face?

'I want this title to break things open. It's not *Wallpaper*,' he said to distract himself. There was a flash of insight. 'It's *Vanity Fair*.'

Reynolds scoffed. 'Nothing's that big. The days of the groundbreaking book are over. It's the internet age; that wasn't out there when *Vanity Fair* exploded. Besides, you think she's Tina Brown?'

He shrugged. 'Her early work there is impressive stuff. It's odd she hasn't been snatched up.'

Reynolds toyed with his water glass. 'Uh, not to be awkward, but she's not a regular girl, is she? She's a recent ex of Marcus Broder's. And was hardly unknown on the scene before then.'

His words were like a bucket of cold water. Abrams dragged his mind away from the enjoyable cataloguing of Kate Fox's body. Yeah, there was a reason he had despised her.

He hated gold-diggers.

And it wasn't just once with Kate Fox. There was no getting away from that. He'd checked her out. His deputy was absolutely right. She was well known on the scene, rich guy after rich guy.

If he went for her, he'd be the latest in a long line of suckers.

And Abrams was nobody's sucker. Get a grip, dude, he told himself. There are plenty of girls in New York with fabulous asses and athletic legs and full lips, and they come a lot cheaper than a divorce settlement. He had a bunch of the classier ones on speed-dial.

So what was it with this chick?

'You're absolutely right.' He focused back on Tim, tried to be objective. 'So maybe it's good for us. We get her for a bargain. I'm tying that tight into the contract.' He took a mouthful of steak. It was good, rare; he liked the taste of the blood, a primal way to eat. 'Still wonder why she's working so hard on the magazine.'

'It shouldn't be a mystery.' Reynolds obviously disapproved of Kate. 'It's her job. Puts food on the table.'

'But she's—'

'A rich man's ex-wife? Look, it was a real short marriage and Broder's no fool. Word is he kicked her to the kerb with a million. She buys a small apartment, what's left? I mean,' and he chuckled, 'nobody else is going to marry her, are they? At least, nobody important.'

Abrams sighed a little. And there it was, laid out pretty brutally.

'No. Of course not.' He smiled, thoughtfully. 'Might be fun to work with her, though.'

'You're going up there today?'

'This afternoon.'

'But you haven't even drawn up the deal yet.'

'I don't believe in hanging around,' David Abrams said.

* * *

Kate was waiting for him when he arrived. She'd picked a simple business suit, a modest charcoal pencil skirt with a Coco Chanel black and white striped top and low-slung heels. Her hair was out of the ponytail, washed and blow-dried sleekly. She looked every inch the fashionista, but serious; workmanlike.

It was obviously deliberate. He tried not to grin at her.

'So, welcome to *Lucky*.' She shook his hand, briskly. 'These are our offices. I'll introduce you to some of the staff . . . This is Sylvia, our office manager. The place doesn't run without her. And here's Rachel Watson, head of production . . . Lucy Andrews, design . . . Tom Coffey, he runs the sales force, and here they are . . . this is Jake Clement, Janet Marks . . .'

Abrams smiled, shook hands. The staffers were young and earnest, not many of them as hip as Kate. He could see the influence of Emily Jones on the magazine. She'd done the hiring; this was the core she'd put together: liberal, socially conscious young journalists. So Kate Fox was the pop-culture guru holding the sales together, getting the perfect mix in.

It was the mix that made the title what it was. Abrams got that. Not that these kids weren't necessary. There were plenty of magazines out there running features on celebrities, design, avant garde furniture. The point was the serious stuff, the liberal mind in full flight, matched with enjoyable high-end fashion, interviews with a twist, the hippest homes. It was an odd recipe on paper. But those were the titles that made a difference.

'Good to meet you all. I'm sorry for the loss of Emily and Paul.' Abrams held their eyes, kids, all of them. Kate Fox stood at the back of the crowd, watching him through narrow lids. Her face was expressionless. '*Lucky* is a wonderful magazine, but to get where I want it to go, it has to become a lot better. Kate is now Editor-in-Chief.' He glanced at her. 'She'll have a larger budget, and I'm assuming she'll be hiring more staff. Plus, we need new offices. Abrams' magazines tend to go for open-plan, so you can bounce ideas off each other. There's a free floor in my building, Model House, located on Tenth Avenue and Forty-Ninth Street. If Kate's OK with that?'

Kate pressed her lips together. He could see she hated the idea. But the space was almost free; their rent would be ridiculously low. She could hardly say no, could she?

'Sure, absolutely fine,' she replied sweetly. He could almost see the gritted teeth.

'And I'll be working with Kate on some suggestions for colleagues. Meanwhile, great job, everybody, and all of us at Abrams are looking forward to working with you.'

They applauded, and his eye took in the admiration, the suck of breath, the flirtatious looks from the younger women. He was used to it; in print, he was a big cheese, famous, as good as it got. Other magazine houses regularly ran profiles on him.

Only David was unhappy. What others considered complete success to him was a failure. He wanted much bigger than some rinky-dink little proprietor of a bunch of magazines. America was out there, and other men were conquering it.

But sometimes you stepped back to step forward. He had to make his magazine division big and hot again.

Because after that, he was going to sell it.

Lucky included.

Chapter Fifteen

When Kate got back to her apartment, her head was spinning. She was exhausted, drained from the emotion of the day. Word travelled fast out there. The lawyers had hammered out a back-of-an-envelope deal in an afternoon, that went miraculously smoothly; David Abrams kept his promises, and Kate had nothing to object to. She signed the contract, it was messengered up to Times Square, and by six o'clock that evening she was eight hundred thousand dollars richer, paid by cashier's cheque. And now the half-owner, and editor, of a functioning magazine.

She should be happy. She should be thrilled. And no doubt there was relief. David Abrams had saved her magazine at the eleventh hour. Kate had pulled it off, based on her hunch, on how she read the man.

Her inheritance could have been nothing more than a Chapter 7 bankruptcy filing.

So what was the problem? Why was she so goddamned pissed off? Because she'd found him attractive? Or because he was an arrogant bastard who'd come right in and changed everything around in an afternoon?

Kate chewed on her lip. David Abrams was in a power struggle with her. That was the way he worked, the way all these guys worked. He'd laid down his money; he was entitled. But there was more to it than that. He was showing her exactly what he could do, in her house, on her turf. Addressing the staff. Offering to fill her vacancies. Like she could hire, but from his group of candidates.

Essentially, he was saying that he was running the show.

She couldn't allow that to stand.

Carefully Kate undressed and hung up her suit. She stepped into the shower, letting the glorious warm water sluice down her belly and breasts, warming her. Then she grabbed her white towelling robe, dried herself, and stepped into her skinny jeans, royal-blue tee and Capri sandals. Her hair she blasted dry. Then she grabbed her purse, swallowed hard, and headed out the door.

This is dumb, she thought. But she tried to ignore the little voice in her head. David Abrams lived in her building. Hey, like he said, he was her neighbour. That meant something . . .

The elevator banks were right in front of her. She always rode down, out of the building. Tonight, though, she pressed the button for the penthouse. The elevator hissed smoothly upwards, and Kate felt her heart thump a little in her chest. This was stupid. Maybe he'd be out, anyway; there was nothing to say the guy would be there, available. He would probably be having dinner with a girlfriend, or one of his financier buddies, or plotting which newspaper he was going to buy next . . .

This wasn't like most buildings; there was a single door on the penthouse floor, a single buzzer. David Abrams had the entire apartment. And why not, right? He owned the damn building.

Kate pressed the buzzer. She sucked her breath in.

There was a pause. Right, maybe he was out. A mixture of relief and disappointment rocked through her. Then she heard a crackle; he was lifting the receiver somewhere inside.

'Yes?' Abrams said.

'David, it's Kate,' she managed, although her heart was thumping in her chest. 'Sorry to bother you at home, but do you think I could have five minutes?'

'One second.' He hung up, and she heard, very faintly, the sound of his feet padding towards the door. It was thick, reinforced steel, good against burglars, kidnappers, any possible enemies of rich men. Marcus favoured the same kind of set-up.

The door opened, and David Abrams stood there, silhouetted. Without her heels, he loomed over her. He smiled down at her, amused; it infuriated and aroused her.

'Well now. Kate Fox, from downstairs. Come to borrow a cup of sugar, neighbour?'

She blushed. 'You know I haven't.'

'But business hours are over,' he remarked, mildly.

She bit her lip. That was true. Abrams had a way of making her feel stupid, gauche. She lifted her head, determined he should not detect weakness in her.

'Can I come in, or not?' she demanded.

He smiled slightly. 'When you put it like that, I guess you can come in.'

Abrams stood aside, and Kate walked past him. The place was cavernous. The ceiling loomed above her, a third as tall again as that in her own tiny apartment. But it was far removed from that; whereas she had height but no width, this palace stretched for miles, the whole length of the building. She saw views on every side; the place was flooded with light.

Abrams did not have Marcus's wealth. A quick glance took in the decor; everything modern, chic, minimalist. He was a true American and proud of it. She noted the modern art on the walls, the clean, neutral lines of his furniture and rugs; instead of the clichéd white on white, he had gone for a softened palette, shades of oatmeal and biscuit, like he wanted to get out of the way of himself. The couches were ones she would have picked herself; low-slung, square and rectangular lines, probably from Milan, in leather, with large soft pillows in butterscotch. The beige and gold would fade warmly into the sunlight if she were here in the day, and the wraparound nature of the space meant that he would get light in the mornings and in the evenings.

So the colour in the paintings was picked out. Abrams had chosen large, bright canvases, with reds and blues. Kate recognised some of the artists: Jean-Michel Basquiat and Asger Jorn, really high-quality stuff.

It was a deeply beautiful space. Marcus had gone for the obvious, the Louis XVI chairs, the Chippendale sideboards, old-world antiques whose worth you could tell at a glance. It was a more expensive look than Abrams'; tackier, in the context. Marcus wanted to re-create himself as something he wasn't.

Kate acknowledged Abrams' style.

He followed her eyes, gestured to the painting. 'Do you know his work?'

She nodded. 'I like art. Never saw Basquiat outside a gallery, though.'

'Marcus Broder liked the Old Masters?' Abrams enquired.

His mocking smile snapped her back to herself. A shiver of anger ran through her. She was grateful for the shift. It was not enjoyable, finding David Abrams so impressive.

'You know what? Quit bringing him up. I'm divorced. The end.'

He spread his hands. 'Whatever you say, Ms Fox.'

She ignored the dig. 'We need to get some ground rules straight. You think you can come into my magazine—'

'*Our* magazine.'

'Whatever. Fine. *Our* magazine. Come in on day one and tell my staff we're moving offices? That you'll be supplying the people I supposedly hire? What if I want to work somewhere else? What if I pick kids from Condé Nast or Victrix Publishing?'

'First of all, magazine publishing is about more than content.'

Kate was incensed. 'Don't patronise me.'

'Then don't act dumb.' He took a step closer to her, so he was physically in her space, looking down at her. She could see the muscles of his torso sliding about under his shirt. 'I don't just put out good articles. I cut costs, where it doesn't show. I produce on the best-quality paper, I spend cash where it counts. There's space in my building. I'm the Chief Executive. We're not about to waste time and money hunting for a new lease someplace else. You're using my space.'

He was the fucking CEO. That was the deal.

'Fine,' she snapped. 'I'll give you that.'

'Give me that? You have no choice, baby.'

'Don't call me baby.'

Kate waited for him to apologise. Instead, his gaze trickled over her body again, so arrogantly, stripping her with his eyes, taking in the lush swell of her breasts, slowly, taking his time, eventually coming to rest in between her legs.

She felt her breathing deepen. She couldn't help herself; he was turning her on. Her nipples stiffened against the lace of her bra; she felt wet, aroused between the legs. She dared not look down, in case he could see her tighten under her T-shirt.

'You should have discussed it with me first. You don't make announcements to staff. *My* staff.'

'Fair enough. Next time I'll tell you first – how it's going to be,' he said.

'And as for hiring, I'm Editor-in-Chief. That means I pick the staff, and you don't bother me. Are we totally clear on that?'

Abrams grinned. Her turn to scold him. And this time she had a point. He gestured. 'Sit down. I'll brew you some coffee.'

Kate shifted from foot to foot. She'd demanded he let her in; she couldn't be graceless.

'Thank you,' she muttered.

'The kitchen's this way.' He led her through the long, gallery-like sitting room to a vast open-plan kitchen, fitted out with top-of-the-range appliances, everything neat and perfect. There was a table in smoky glass with tobacco-coloured leather benches around it. Kate calculated the table alone would have cost around ten thousand dollars. This world had been hers for five minutes. But Abrams had made all his money himself. Could she do the same?

Make her own money? Become rich? Without relying on a man to do it all for her?

Fuck, she thought. I'm gonna try.

'What do you like? I have the Blue Mountain, various other kinds of coffee.'

'Do you have any decaf? I don't want to get too wired before bed.'

'You, wired?' He smiled lazily at her. 'Now that would never do. How's decaf vanilla?'

'Sounds delicious.' It did. She'd had nothing to eat since lunch, no time, with all the planning up at *Lucky*. Suddenly she felt pangs of hunger shoot through her. Her stomach rumbled, loudly. She creased with embarrassment, her face flushing.

'And you'll eat with me, too.' Kate opened her mouth to protest, but the brown eyes held hers. 'Lunch may be for wimps, but dinner isn't. Come on, it's not like you had plans.'

'I just wanted to talk to you, David. There's food in my apartment.'

'And in mine. You like sushi? I have it delivered daily. Housekeeper puts it in the fridge, throws out what I don't eat. Everything's fresh. You don't have to worry about it.'

'I wasn't.' Kate scouted around, fetched a couple of mugs. 'That's a huge waste of money. And food.'

'So, the limousine liberal doesn't approve?' Abrams said unrepentantly. 'Look, I work damned hard. I've made five million dollars a year for the last twenty years. I don't cook, I don't clean. I've never done a load of laundry since I left college. And I give a ton of money every year to the homeless and poor. Here and abroad. You know what? If I decide to stay home nights, I like supper in the fridge. Fresh. Daily.'

Kate's face burned. When he put it like that . . .

The coffee machine hissed and purred, and Abrams removed the jug from its stand, pouring a heavenly stream of coffee into her mug. The rich scent of the vanilla floated all around her. She added Splenda, stirred, sipped it.

It was wonderful. Kate felt her resolve weaken.

'Fine,' she said. 'You win. Sushi would be lovely.'

'What do you like?' Abrams asked.

Her belly rumbled again. She bit her lip in embarrassment. 'Pretty much anything.'

He opened the Sub-Zero and took out plates, laden with everything; it all looked insanely good. Kate set the coffee aside and grabbed a piece of spicy tuna roll.

It was unusually seasoned, outrageously delicious. She took a side plate, heaped it and attacked the food.

Abrams laughed. 'You're like a starving orphan.'

'As a matter of fact, I am an orphan, in effect.' She swallowed, took another bite of sushi, something with salmon eggs and lemon. Also fabulous. 'And I'm certainly starving. So thank you for feeding me . . . Mr Abrams.'

'I knew that about you.' His eyes steadied for a second, dulling the sparkle when he looked at her. 'I was only joking. I'm sorry.'

'It's OK. Was a long time ago.'

But he pressed her, wouldn't be brushed off. 'How long? How old were you?'

'Dad left when I was small. He isn't dead, but he might as well be. No contact to speak of in twenty years.'

Abrams nodded. 'Your mom?'

'When I was sixteen. I brought myself up after that.'

Abrams carefully selected some spicy eel and yellowfin tuna, slathered them with wasabi. He busied himself eating, breaking eye contact, not looking at Kate in case she was self-conscious, maybe crying. She was grateful for his thoughtfulness. She swallowed hard, against the lump in her throat.

'Define brought yourself up. Who had custody?'

'Nobody.' She was back on safer ground now, and fiercely proud. 'I dodged the system. Forced my dad to send some money to pay the rent on Momma's flat. That was it, though; he never sent anything else, nothing for food or clothes and stuff.'

'Your school? You were at public school?'

Kate shook her head.

'Private. Catholic. Got the nuns to waive my tuition. They were pretty good over there, gave me free meals, supplied my uniform. All that shit.' She shivered.

'And I needed those free meals. I'd sneak out rolls and ham slices or wedges of cheese, maybe an apple, from lunch – went into my book bag. And that was supper.'

Now she had his full attention. David Abrams was staring at her, fascinated, horrified.

'Your father had a duty to support you. Not just give you one payoff and let you go.'

'Right, and the cheque is really in the mail.' Kate ate another piece of sushi. 'Real world doesn't work that way. I had no money to pay lawyers. Didn't want to go to the cops. They'd have put me in a foster home, you know?'

He nodded. 'Sure. I get it.'

'Besides which,' Kate said fiercely, 'I didn't want to take anything else from that piece of shit. Just what I had to. He was a real deadbeat. My mom worked like a slave until some drunk driver killed her, because she married a total bum.'

His eyes were expressionless. 'And you didn't repeat that mistake?'

'Who says I didn't?' She pulled at her coffee, shook her head to clear the cobwebs from it. 'Anyway, I thought I told you never to bring him up.'

'I'm sorry,' he said, softly, looking at her. 'That was a rough time for you.'

'I did fine,' Kate said. She squared her shoulders. 'Bumpy road, maybe. But I found something I'm good at. I need you. For now. But you're not going to steamroller me. From now on, every major decision – like offices – we discuss together.'

'And staff hires?'

'I'll tell you whom I've decided to hire.'

He liked the *whom*. She was classy, this girl. And the story about her childhood . . . it made him look at her differently, as a person, one he could talk to. There it was, right? The insecurity about money, the girl out on her own. The deadbeat dad. Kind of clear why she'd gravitate towards rich guys. What wasn't as clear was why she'd stopped.

Abrams thought of Tim Reynolds, his contempt. And Kate's reputation; that was bad. Getting involved with her would not be good news.

But as she sat at his table, wolfing the sushi, in plain jeans and a T-shirt, her damp hair pulled severely back, no make-up . . . he knew he was going to do it anyway.

'I consult with you on my decisions, you inform me of yours?' he asked, looking at her mouth.

Kate shrugged. 'You have the nuclear weapon. You can fire me. Beyond that, the day-to-day is mine. Otherwise, I may as well just go away and start my own book.'

'And throw away eight hundred grand? Come on, honey.'

She shook her head. 'Tonight I have eight hundred, yesterday I didn't have it. I'll get over it. So, do we have a deal?'

He put his plate down, came around the table. She shrank back a little on her stool, her back arching away from him.

'Sure. Deal. For now. Until I change it. Nervous?' he asked.

Kate looked up at him. Her heart was thumping. She was wet and squirming between the legs.

'No,' she lied. 'Why would I be?'

Abrams stood in front of her. She sucked in her breath, staring at him. Unable to move, like a mouse looking at a snake. He put his hands on her shoulders. She wanted to pull away, to run, but her body wouldn't let her. She just sat there, mesmerised.

'I don't know you,' she managed.

'There's a lot you don't know,' Abrams said. 'But you can learn.' He ran his hands slowly, deliberately down her rib cage, his fingers splaying, slightly, against the swell of her breasts.

'I'm not interested,' she muttered.

'Bad girl,' he murmured. 'You know you shouldn't tell lies.' And his hands moved down her back, kneading the tender knot of flesh below the base of her spine. As she quivered, battling her arousal, the way desire was melting her belly, he moved his hands lower, over the tight denim of her jeans, stroking the curves of her ass.

He's such an arrogant bastard, she thought. She struggled against it. But those dark eyes, fringed with their thick black lashes, held hers, and his muscled chest was bearing down on her, his strong arms were encasing her, and heat, heat like she'd never felt with Marcus, never felt with any other man, was spreading through her body, trawling its little silver hooks through her belly and breasts and dissolving her resistance.

She gasped.

Abrams bent his head, bringing his mouth closer to hers, her lips wet, slightly parted, mutely offering herself to him.

But he didn't kiss her. His lips came down, lightly, teasing, just brushing across hers, and helplessly, lost in desire, she pressed up closer, trying to reach him, to kiss him. Abrams' arms tightened around the small of her back, pulling her to him. Her weight was nothing. Against the thick muscles of his chest, she felt light, feminine. Weak.

Abrams extended his tongue, licked a spot of wasabi off her upper lip.

Kate arched her back, trying to bring her mouth to his.

'What happened to I'm not interested?' he enquired. 'You want nothing to do with me. Don't call me baby. Right?'

Kate squirmed. He brushed his lips backwards, forwards over her mouth. Mercilessly. Waiting for her surrender.

Kate moaned, deep in the back of her throat. She couldn't concentrate, couldn't think. His scent, his overwhelming power, his virility. She was almost dizzy.

'That's better,' he said, half mocking, another tease, like he was saying *good girl*. 'Isn't it?'

She couldn't speak. She couldn't think. David Abrams and his body and his mouth, his gently insistent, probing, teasing tongue. Her world had shrunk to that. Mutely she opened her mouth, and he took her, crushing her lips, kissing her fiercely, his tongue running into her mouth, dancing on hers. Whatever part of her brain was screaming caution, she ignored. Her hands laid flat on his chest, her palms outwards, feeling him, the iron muscles of him. She fumbled blindly at his shirt, popping his buttons, tugging the fabric away from those broad shoulders. His hands came up under the back of her T-shirt, the fingers trailing, tracing lines across her back that made her writhe in his arms, arching her spine, almost dizzy with pleasure. He unhooked her bra with practised ease, and as the straps loosened around her shoulders, she felt those hands come forward, edge under the lace cups and hold her breasts; not squeezing or pulling, just holding them in his hands, warm and full of blood, like he was weighing them, like she was some ancient slave girl in a marketplace being examined by a rich man's majordomo. He ran his thumbs feather-light across her nipples, barely touching them, and they tightened further against the callouses of his skin.

'Take it off,' Abrams murmured, his voice guttural with desire. 'I want to see you. See if you're like I imagined the day you walked in the door downstairs. I looked at you then and I stripped you naked.'

'Arrogant,' she managed.

'And you like it. Don't you? Admit it, Kate.'

She wriggled, and her tits bounced in his hands. He felt a surge of sex, power, pure exhilaration rip through him.

'Admit it,' he said. 'Out loud. I want to hear you say you like it. You like me.'

She gasped. 'You're hot. OK?'

'And you want me.'

'Yes,' Kate groaned. She was beside herself; his hands on her breasts were so sure, and that shirt she had tugged off . . . man, where Marcus had been lean, even skinny, David Abrams was built. He was a guy of exceptional attractiveness, clearly into weights, his biceps lean and toned, the muscles of his chest large, firm under her fingers. His power in the boardroom was perfectly reflected in his naked body. Kate reached down, peeled off her T-shirt. Had the satisfaction of hearing him look down at her and murmur, 'Goddamn.' He wanted her, that much was clear. And she was inclined to let him go with it.

'You've seen it all before,' she challenged him.

'Not like you.' His voice was thick with desire. She could see his erection, strong, thick, pressing up against the buttons of his jeans. He lowered his head to her, kissing her nipples, sweet and tight and full with blood. Then he took them into his mouth, sucking, licking. Driving her mad with passion.

Her Capri sandals slipped from her feet. She stood, sliding

down from the stool into his embrace. He was strong over her, leaning into her, blending with her.

'Now these.' His thumbs hooked into the waistband of her jeans, tugging them off, her panties with them. They slipped from her lean thighs, tumbling into a heap by her feet. Kate stepped out of them, feeling her slightness, her nakedness next to him, still mostly dressed, just bare chested. His arms ran down her back, rubbing all over her ass, cupping it, squeezing it. She was beside herself, frantic with need. Her fingers reached for the buttons of his jeans, tight against his erection, but she was half panting now, and they fumbled. She groaned, frustrated, and he reached down, freed himself. She barely saw it; he was enfolding her in those strong arms, kissing her, taking her mouth, drawing her into him, and she felt him kick away his clothes, and then she was lightly lifted up in his arms, as though she were made out of thistledown, and he slid her on to him. He was so thick, so hard inside her, she was absolutely penetrated and taken, and he murmured her name, gripping her to him, moving her up and down, absolutely relentlessly, and the pleasure, great waves of it, started to gather in her belly and groin, a huge, sweet block of pressure, pushing out and out until she could not take another second, and as she squirmed against him, the orgasm exploded over her, deeper and harder than anything she'd ever felt in her life, taking her out of herself. Her nails were clutching, raking at his back, and he cried aloud and spent himself deep inside her, and it was so good she was dizzy from it; and then finally it subsided a little, and she was there, drenched in sweat, panting, staring into David Abrams' eyes.

Chapter Sixteen

Marcus Broder walked into his boardroom and looked at the collection of men around the table. His gaze flickered contemptuously over them. They sat there in their five-thousand-dollar suits, with their Rolexes and Patek Philippes; all of them rich, comfortable men, but so far below him. Many of them were older, some more than ten years his senior.

But he was the boss. They all worked for him.

The boardroom was in the penthouse suite of his offices off Wall Street. Broder, Inc. had eighteen floors of the skyscraper, including the penthouse, and it was all decorated with classic European art; he had a Renoir in the corporate collection. But the boardroom was dominated by a huge canvas landscape of the Hudson River, looking towards Manhattan, painted in the early part of the century; one of his favourite images, because New York, the whole of it, belonged to him. It was symbolic. At the other end was a vast portrait of himself painted by Daphne Guinness, the renowned Brit artist who normally only worked for presidents and prime ministers.

It was big, designed to intimidate. He loved it.

The faces around the table looked at him eagerly. And why

not? He didn't carry dead weight; there were no worthy losers on the board of Broder. Every one of them brought something to this table. The ex-governor of one state had a lot of juice. So did the senior senator from another. He could probably have got the junior senator for less, but she was a woman, and known as feisty, and Marcus Broder didn't like working with women. Unless they knew their place.

He looked down the table. There had been some pretty wild corporate parties in here. He never hired hookers – that was an easy route to blackmail for some of these chicks – but there were party girls on the scene with a taste for jewellery and blow and a reputation for discretion. A few years back he had livened up one important event by sending a couple of girls into the party as the men played poker and telling them to take care of business, offer themselves around to anybody who wanted some.

He got a momentary hard-on just thinking about it.

The other guys looked up his way eagerly. Marcus Broder did business the old-fashioned way. Sure, they were all very well remunerated, and there was prestige and perks that came with sitting on the board of this company. The chauffeur-driven limos, the stock tips, the party girls in their skimpy dresses, the rides in the private corporate jet that Marcus used like his own personal taxi, getting picked up at the airport's helipad and flown to their estates in Dutchess County or Katonah.

The boss supplied their every need, and they were all owned by him. Simple. Besides, he now had dirt on each and every one of them. Payments in kind, insider trading, sluts bent over the boardroom table being serviced by respectable married men. Marcus Broder kept his little black book, and he kept it well.

So when he needed something, these men were always there.

'We have a small problem,' he said. 'Another company is treading in my space.'

'And what's that?' the senator piped up.

'For some time now I've wanted to acquire *Lucky* magazine.'

There were glances across the table. Impudent fucks. A surge of annoyance washed through him. 'Yeah, yeah, that's the one now owned by my ex-wife. *One* of them. For a year.' He shrugged. 'She came up to the majors for a cup of coffee, couldn't make the grade, got shipped back out to the minor leagues.'

They laughed, dutifully.

That aggravated him even more. It was seriously annoying that this had all happened. After Emily Jones was wiped off the scene, he was meant to go in there, scoop the magazine up, and fire Kate. She hadn't listened the first time. He wanted her out of town, out of his hair.

Only Emily Jones had fucked him, that fat bitch, fucked him again from beyond the grave. Not enough to poison Kate the first time around, ruin her as the excellent, tasty little wife she'd been for the first few months. She'd handed Kate a reason to stay on Marcus's turf, in Marcus's city. Embarrassing him. Doing well with her shitty little title, her sales force. Early days, but doing quite noticeably well. Marcus was too good a businessman ever to underestimate the opposition.

And Kate Fox was his.

But only days after the train crash, while he was still putting together a bid, dotting the i's, crossing the t's, trying to discover who the new owners were, he got the bad news.

Goddamn Emily Jones and her loser of a husband had left the title to Kate.

Not that he worried too much. It was sunk in debt, worse than the Federal Reserve. His research guys told him they could barely pay the rent, make the payroll. There were loans out there, lines of credit.

Marcus stretched forth his hand, did a little business.

The lines of credit tightened and snapped. The banks pulled them in. For a moment he'd sat back and enjoyed the stories of Kate Fox personally touring the offices of various junior pricks begging for another chance. Nobody would give her any.

Lucky was done. It would fold. Kate's little inheritance would be worthless. Marcus had smirked at the thought. There were lots of ways to skin a cat. You could buy the title, or bankrupt it. He wasn't interested, of course, in buying it from Kate. No approaches were made in that direction. She was not to be made any richer; not another cent of the Broder fortune was heading her way, the ungrateful bitch. No, his desire now was to ruin her, just to ruin her. Without *Lucky*, she wouldn't get another job. He knew all the major houses . . .

Or so he'd thought.

She took him by surprise. His mind danced back to the day she'd had the brass balls to ask him for a divorce; him, Marcus Broder. Kate Fox had a nasty habit of surprising him.

He fucking hated that.

Two days, two goddamned days after inheriting that bankrupt piece of junk, she had gone and sold the fucking thing. Half-stake. To David Abrams, that comer from midtown.

Marcus Broder detested David Abrams. He was mid-level rich, started some magazines in college, made some savvy deals, got into property on the side, stock. Marcus's finance guys, scrambling for detail after Marcus rang them to scream at them, came up with a rough figure of fifty million. Abrams' apartment buildings were rented, but mortgaged; he had a small house in the Hamptons, just off the beach; drove a racing-green Aston Martin, membership of Soho House, that was about it. He was far too laid-back, far too relaxed. Nobody really paid attention to the guy, unless it was all the pussy whose hearts he was breaking. There were no seats at the opera, no country clubs up in Westchester, nothing the way Marcus did it. Abrams flew commercial, and apparently rode the subway quite a bit; expected his employees to do it too.

Course, he made less money. Broder was a major corporation. But Marcus had the nasty feeling that Abrams would be low-key if he made a hundred million, even more.

And Kate had gone to him and sold to him. In one day.

Now, thanks to that asshole, she'd be sticking around. *Lucky* had enough money, it had office space, Marcus's friends in the banks were seeing their loans all redeemed. She was in the pocket of Abrams, another powerful, rich man, he thought, despising her but grudgingly respecting the deal. Private company, jointly held between Abrams, Inc. and Kate herself. And she even had fifty per cent.

'Unfortunately, somebody else has gotten there first,' Broder said. 'Abrams, Inc. I don't appreciate that. We've been interested, even before the tragic accident. I think the title would be a perfect fit with our growing print interests.'

They looked at him blankly. 'What can we do about it?' one Goldman Sachs big shot asked.

'Give me your recommendations. Who here knows Abrams? Personally?'

A man at the end of the table stuck up his hand. 'Sold him a building downtown.'

It was Louis Matthews, the owner of the Victrix Hotel.

'How d'you make out?' Broder asked.

'He fucking buried me,' Matthews said, good naturedly. 'I thought it was a good price. He got the rent-stable tenants out, he got a zoning variance, converted the whole place to luxury flats, put eight mil on the value inside twelve months. Paper; he hasn't sold yet. But they're all rented out.'

Broder burned. Fucking kid with his little two-bit deals. 'You know him? Make an approach. We want that magazine. More or less any price. Get him to flip his stake to me.'

'What does any price mean? It's just a title; promising, maybe . . . just one book.'

'It fits my brand. Brand matters more. Like overpaying for a movie star or a hot-shot author. Just make sure the offer's routed through a subsidiary; keep me out of it.' Marcus glanced at the other faces round the table. 'If he won't sell, we're putting them out of business. I don't allow pikers to screw me, you understand?'

'You mean advertisers, distributors . . .'

'Whatever. We have a lot of money in the field. Their writers? Poach them. Treble their salaries. That's fucking chicken feed. We start a rival title. They sell or they die. It's not about the damned magazine, it's about our reputation. Nobody treads on us.'

Heads nodded quickly. Nobody dared challenge him about his ex-wife, about the money this would cost. Marcus Broder got whatever he wanted. Besides which, it was fucking chicken feed, right?

'You got it, Marcus.' The ex-governor spoke up. 'I'll see what I can do. We're all on this one.'

'Good. Get it done. And fast. I want this under way in a week.'

Marcus turned around and walked out. They were losers, overpaid losers, and he had no desire to stand around and shoot the shit with them.

His personal assistant, or one of them, was waiting in the hallway with his greatcoat and briefcase.

'Miss Valdez is in the car, sir.'

'Right.' He grunted. Lola Valdez was his girlfriend for the weekend. He'd dumped the French broad; too boring. Lola was flashy, trash with money, courtesy of a corrupt Colombian uncle who had shipped his younger relatives off to have their cash washed clean in the United States, go to the best schools, mix with good society. There were lots of these gangsters out there: Russians, Nigerians, some South American drug runners, arms smugglers from South Africa, dirty diamonds from Sierra Leone. The scions of families with cash acquired at the business end of an AK-47 came to London, New York, Washington, and mingled themselves clean. Lola laughed a lot and told him he was wonderful in between enthusiastic sessions in bed, where she would pliantly do whatever he asked her. She wore her dresses tight and her breasts were big and perky, a tribute to the surgeon's art, while she had an ass that would do credit to a high-end stripper. Most rich men in the city envied him getting to bed her, and that was enough reason to hang out. For now, she was an acceptable release of tension.

Marcus reckoned he'd be tired of her in six months. He was already scouting for replacements. Trouble was, this shit was bad for his public image. He was older now; how long could he go without being married, without *staying* married? He had no interest in kids, really. But he was keenly aware that a guy in his position required one or two. Heirs to the empire. With a couple of nannies and a stay-at-home wife who knew her place, he could show up to throw a ball in the garden from time to time, maybe read a bedtime story once they were neatly in their pyjamas and ready to go straight to sleep. Summer camps, fancy city schools . . . his wife, whoever she was, could take care of that.

But he had no desire to marry Lola. Nor Louise before her. Not even with the most watertight pre-nup. Who could stand such boring bitches? They were for fucking, strictly recreation.

He'd gotten it wrong a few times. Didn't matter before. But it was starting to. Kate Fox would have been perfect, if she'd just done what she was fucking told. Young, gorgeous, stylish, fun at times, started out with the right attitude, never turned him down in bed . . .

Until that damned magazine.

Marcus rode the elevator down in silence. He was going to work this out. First run Kate out of town, then find some woman, some better woman. And get to work on her, train her the way he wanted her to be.

For now, he was simmering with anger. He thought about Lola. She was riding with him, flying first class. She could suck him, right in the car. He'd slide the privacy window up. The driver would know exactly what he was doing, but Marcus didn't give a damn.

That was why he rode in the back, and his driver ferried him around for thirty-eight thousand a year.

Marcus gave himself up to thoughts of Lola's big olive-skinned tits, her talented, ingenious mouth. That would work. A temporary distraction from Kate Fox and her annoying little magazine.

* * *

The sunlight streamed through the windows, hitting the bed at every angle. Kate stirred in her sleep. For a second, she didn't know where she was. Somewhere comfortable; the bed had a memory-foam mattress and she was held lovingly in it, her back sunk into it. The sheets were pure white, deliciously soft and crisp, and the goose-down pillows cradled her blond head. She was vaguely aware of her hair tumbling about her, free, unfettered, and her body . . .

Her body, naked.

She raised her hands to touch herself, running them over the warmth of her breasts. No T-shirt, like she normally wore at night to sleep. She was nude, properly nude, and in . . .

In David Abrams' bed, her mind said.

Slowly, she turned her head and found that it was true. She was nestled next to him. He was fast asleep, on his side, the big muscles of his chest covered with a smattering of salt-and-pepper hair. His face was peaceful; she stared, studying the strong nose, the square jaw, the hair cut tight against the head, almost a military buzz cut. There was nothing pretty about him. He was virile, and that was it. Kate glanced down at his hands, lying flattened on the bed. The nails were roughly cut, and he had an occasional callous here and there. No manicures for Abrams, and he probably played sports.

He had fallen asleep with one leg thrown across her body. His right knee covered her thigh possessively.

He was gorgeous.

Lust rippled through her, languid but insistent, like a low wave breaking on the seashore. Kate flushed with heat and shame, remembering how he had handled her last night, how he had made her respond. After his first orgasm he'd been ready to go again in fifteen minutes, and had taken his time with her. Barely listening to her weak protests, how they shouldn't do this, what a bad idea it was, office politics, their reputation, their magazine . . .

'All true.' Abrams did not stop stroking her, running his finger lightly up and down her spine, tracing patterns on her back, driving her absolutely crazy, so that she wriggled and writhed for him, asking him to cut it out, and then, when he did, whimpering for him to begin again.

'We can stop if you like. But you don't want to. Do you? I'm right about that one, am I not?'

Kate had nodded her head. But he held her eyes. He would not let her get away with anything, not one thing.

'Out loud.'

'I don't want to stop,' she whispered.

'Then forget all your good reasons. Come here.' He moved closer to her, scooped her up in his arms. 'Bed's this way.'

Kate was unresisting. She couldn't help herself. It was so good; it was everything she'd imagined when she looked at him, talked to him. Maybe this was a terrible idea. Complicated . . .

But she couldn't think, couldn't speak. Didn't want to. Her world had shrunk to his strong chest, his arms, the musky scent of his neck, the stubble on the side of his chin. He was carrying her through the apartment without breaking stride; she saw a glass staircase on copper poles rising to an upper floor, but she wasn't there to admire his place. Her face burning with lust, and shame, Kate buried it in his neck.

She felt rather than saw him kick open the door to a room. And then there it was. His bed. Low-slung, California super-king. The bedroom was vast, but quiet: rush matting for a carpet over an industrial brushed-concrete floor; an architectural folding table with an ergonomic chair; some very fancy Mac laptop with a vast screen. A couple of photos on a table by the bed. Kate's head spun. It was perfect, restful, more copper and beige, warm sunlight shades, softening the functional space. Very luxurious, very spare. She gasped to see that he had placed mirrors over the doors to his walk-in closet; a huge, unsparing wall of reflection, right opposite the bed.

'That's right.' He looked down at her and grinned. 'That way I can see every inch of you. And so can you.'

'I can't watch that,' she begged.

He laid her down gently, very gently, on the end of the bed. He was hard, full of desire again. His hands moved from her back, cupping her breasts, sliding down over the flat of her stomach, moving mercilessly, one finger inside her, touching her, teasing her, stroking the slick nub of her with her own juices.

'Oh! Oh, please! Ahhhh . . .' Kate reared, half screamed.

'You want it,' he said relentlessly.

'Yes! Oh, David, please! Please!'

'Then we do things my way. Flip over. On to your stomach. Raise your head; I want you to see . . .'

Sobbing with heat and need, Kate obeyed him. She was being completely controlled. No man had ever handled her with such authority. It was unbelievable how much it turned her on. She was soaking wet. She felt wildly aroused, submissive, despite herself. He smiled, stood behind her. She lifted her haunches, presenting herself to him, and the sight of her own body, crouched, ready, sent a second flood of longing through her. She could see him, all the iron muscles of him as he stood, tall and strong, behind her, and then, as she pleaded with him, he took her, ramming into her, and she dissolved, shoving herself backwards, bucking, just trying to pull him in . . .

Oh hell, yeah.

It had happened all right. Again, and again. Kate replayed the movie in her head and moaned softly under her breath. Was she insane? Why had she done that? She had to work with this guy. She had to *fight* this guy. She had to make him respect her.

She pressed her fingers to her forehead.

But it had been so good – so good.

Stop that, her conscious brain said firmly. It doesn't matter how good he looks. How good he is. What he did to you . . .

She looked around. David Abrams was rich, and powerful, in his mid-forties, a prime catch. Too reclusive for the nightclub scene, but Kate had been with him now, had felt him, knew for certain, without being told, that he was too strong, too virile to be a monk. There had been plenty of other women, watching themselves in that mirror.

Trouble was, she hated every one of them.

It was tough to look at him lying next to her, sleeping, satisfied. She had surrendered herself, helplessly hot and wet, and her passion had turned him on. Her belly stirred just thinking about it, despite herself. She was angry with her weakness. He was handsome – could you call it that? Maybe not, but attractive, man, so unutterably attractive. She was melting just looking at him, just lying next to him . . .

No. Stop. No more weakness.

It had taken a year for people to stop sniggering behind her back. Kate Fox, socialite, gold-digger, the soonest-dumped wife of Marcus Broder. Gossip-column joke. And she didn't want to be another of the desperate girls trying to land David

Abrams. She knew what he thought of that whole scene, right?

Because he'd so kindly let her know.

Imagine the laughing stock she'd be if she turned into one of those girls. Mooning around after the city's most wanted. Really, *most* wanted, because he wasn't on his fifth divorce, wasn't a corrupt politician or a sleazy, strip-club-going playboy who was just too old to hang in the club. It was weird that he hadn't married, but not her business.

David Abrams wasn't about to marry her. And she wasn't going to be his piece of ass.

Whatever else, she thought, I don't beg.

Not outside of his bed, anyway, her mind shot back, and she blushed.

Besides, the job mattered to her. *Lucky* mattered. Her kudos for getting the financing, for finding Abrams, selling off half the interest, paying the debt . . . Right now she was respected. Her reputation was spreading. She liked those calls coming in from the girls at *Cutie*, where she used to work, from her contacts at *Vogue*.

If anybody knew she'd slept with Abrams, nobody would listen to her. She would be just another New York blonde bimbo, sleeping her way to the top.

The thought made her feel sick. Positively ill. Delicately, she extracted her leg out from under Abrams', pulled away to her side of the bed. The space-age foam mattress absorbed her weight, leaving him undisturbed. That was a mercy. She stood, regarding her naked body in his mirrors, blushing. No time to gawk at herself, no time to lose. Quietly, on tiptoes, she moved out of the sliding glass panel doors that framed his bedroom, padded down the long glass staircase. God, she was naked. She hoped fervently that there were no perverts with binoculars living in the high-rises across the street, because she was framed in his huge industrial windows, no blinds, no drapes . . .

Her clothes and shoes were right where she'd left them. In a heap, at the foot of his kitchen stool. She grabbed them, taking in his apartment. In the far corner, an open door showed her a guest bathroom, designed somewhat out of sync with the rest of the place, golden and soft, obviously made for women. Sexist jerk, she thought; he has a separate space for his booty calls, so they shower and freshen up outside of his bedroom, conveniently near the door. God . . . she had given in, been a slave to those feelings. She blushed to the roots of her hair, burning from the shame of it. She, Kate Fox, was just another of those chicks now, wasn't she? A notch on David Abrams' bedpost, a locker-room story . . .

Screw his shower. She wanted to get out of here, downstairs to her own apartment. Note to self: call the realtor again. She couldn't go on living here. At least there was money now to buy a nice one-bedroom, somewhere far far away from the meatpacking district, somewhere she would never bump into David Abrams again.

Kate tugged on her clothes. Her desire for speed was making her fumble. She thought of her fingers last night, shaking as she tried to undo his jeans . . . Get a grip, she lectured herself, just get a grip. There . . . her waist button was done up, and now she tugged on her socks, jammed her feet into her sandals. OK. Ready.

Desperately she scouted around for a piece of paper. Time to write him a note. There was another desk, further away from the kitchen, near where she had walked in. Kate ran over to it. God, but this was a huge apartment, she thought; she could train for the marathon in here . . .

There were papers on his desk. She grabbed one, turned it over, wrote on it.

Dear David,
I apologise for last night. It was a mistake. We have to work together. I'm happy to do that, not anything else. Guess I'm depending on you not bringing it up.

She put his pen in her mouth, chewing on it, agonised. Should she beg him not to tell anyone? But no, if she did, that would make her even more of a hostage to fortune. She thought of Abrams passing it around to his buddies in the office, at the gym. Whatever the hell he did with his free time.

In any event, I have a magazine to edit and you have a business to run. So I suggest we keep out of each other's way. I'll call you when I know who I'm hiring.

That would have to do. Kate picked up the letter and ran back with it to his kitchen table. He'd have to come here, because his own clothes were on the floor next to where hers had been. Meanwhile, the sunlight of a fresh New York morning was still streaming through these windows. He'd be up any minute . . .

Her heart pounding, her head spinning, Kate raced out of the door to his apartment. She shut it behind her very, very slowly. Then she had a seemingly endless wait for the elevator. When it eventually arrived, she jumped in, relaxed a little. But it wasn't over yet. As soon as she got to her own apartment, she unlocked it, shoving the door shut behind her. She jumped in the shower and blasted herself, shivering because she hadn't even given the water time to warm up. Not that it mattered. She just had to get the hell out of the building. She grabbed a towel, dried herself off and pulled on something fast: a dress, Capri sandals, a light coat. There was emergency make-up in her purse, some tinted moisturiser for touch-ups. She could do that in the cab. She picked up her bag again and within minutes was riding in the elevator, down to the lobby, making a break for it.

Outside on the street she exhaled. David Abrams was up there somewhere, still sleeping, maybe just stirring in his bed. She tried not to think of what a pleasant picture that conjured up.

Be strong, Kate, she told herself. Get over last night.

Get over him.

A yellow New York cab came barrelling towards her, its light on, like a knight on a white charger, riding to the rescue.

'Taxi!' Kate Fox yelled.

Abrams woke up. He knew immediately, before he opened his eyes, that she had gone. The bed felt different. There was no breathing, other than his own.

He sat, slowly, rubbing his eyes. Yeah – she wasn't around. There were no noises coming from his downstairs bathroom. He was puzzled, disappointed. Last night, right before he almost passed out with exhaustion, he'd been thinking it might be fun to take her to breakfast. His favourite diner was a block away, and they had the best omelette with Canadian bacon in the city.

But she was gone. Vanished.

Normally, Abrams was grateful for that. Girls who knew

how to get their pretty asses out the door usually got asked back for rounds two or three, plus they got consideration, the limo rides, the strings of pearls, whatever they wanted. Because he wasn't into attachment, and preferred to drink coffee on his own. In this case, though . . .

It had been good, last night. He was sure she knew that, had loved it as much as he did, felt the passion between them, the blazing, all-consuming nature of it . . .

Man. He ran his hand through his hair. It was never that good, not with any of his other women.

His Ralph Lauren dressing gown was hanging in his en suite bathroom. He reached for it, belted it loosely, went downstairs to retrieve his clothes. Hers were gone, of course. And she'd left a note.

He picked it up, scanned it. *She* had left *him* a note. Normally it was the other way around. Abrams would leave them in bed, with a polite thank-you letter, pointing out the guest bathroom and the waiting chauffeur, promising to call. He always did call; but usually to give them a warm thanks and a brush-off.

He read the note. Anger welled in him, disappointment, annoyance. Kate Fox was treating last night like some minor inconvenience. Like it had meant absolutely nothing to her.

Slowly he walked back upstairs, showered, shaved. He'd lost his appetite for breakfast now. He would go straight into the office. Arrange for the *Lucky* staff to transfer over to his building; somebody else, Tim Reynolds, could call Kate once he'd sorted out the mechanics. He did not want to speak to her. She had poured out her heart to him last night, told him her life, embraced him, then just upped and left. Abrams took inventory of his behaviour towards women. Maybe there was some element of use there, he conceded to himself.

239

But it wasn't like he ever lied to any of them. He made no promises, certainly never talked emotionally.

Listen to yourself. You're acting just like a woman, he lectured himself. He walked to his closet, selected one of his many Armani black suits, no tie, a blue shirt with stripes, cashmere socks, black shoes. Putting this on was like armour. He fastened his Breitling watch to his wrist. It was a bit of a comfort, but David Abrams didn't kid himself. He'd been played by a woman, and he didn't like the dismissal.

She wanted an arm's-length relationship, pure business? Just fine by him. She could have one.

Chapter Seventeen

'Darling,' Lola purred. 'You're in a bad mood.'

Marcus propped himself up on one elbow, to get a better view of her breasts. Her body was first class, like all the women he indulged himself with. She had been something of a pleasant surprise on this trip, Lola. She knew when to turn up, and when to leave.

'It's nothing,' he said. 'Something at work.'

'Poor baby.' Lola leaned forward, warming the organic coconut oil in the palms of her hands. 'Can I help?'

'Just keep rubbing.'

'Mmm,' she said. She leaned forward, her body golden brown, straining against the tiny white triangles tied together with snowy string that served as a bikini. Lola could get away with it. There was barely a hair anywhere on her body, other than her expensive caramel-highlighted mane, that tumbled halfway down her back. Besides, they were sitting at the side of his private pool in the resort's best cabin. Nobody could see her except the ogling waiters and valets who scurried back and forth, serving drinks, changing the sheets on the bed, delivering ironed copies of the *Wall Street Journal*. And Marcus didn't mind that. The help didn't count. Besides, it always aroused him to show off his women to other, lesser men who could never touch a piece of ass like that in a million years. 'Let me help you forget it, sweetie.'

She had a good touch. She was working the oil in between his shoulder blades, rubbing and pressing, her thumbs and forefingers kneading out the knots. Her tits bounced a little against the white triangles. He felt a faint stir, which pleased him, as he'd already taken her once this morning. Below the azure expanse of the infinity pool, past the low wall of his private garden, the landscaped resort stretched out to the sea. He could glimpse the white sandy beaches, see the palm trees swaying in the wind, the lush vegetation on the hills all around them.

It was pretty relaxing.

Fuck it, Marcus thought. I'm a rich man. Seriously rich. None of these little jerks can touch me.

All he needed to do was just wrap up the Kate Fox problem, and then he could go back to enjoying his life.

'Pass me my BlackBerry.' He held out his hand. Lola knew better than to argue. She handed it over, continued to rub him. Her fingers slipped down his spine, massaging the top of his buttocks. They started to creep around his hips, reaching under the waistband of his swim shorts, but Marcus put one hand firmly on her, to stop her. She could take care of that later. And she would. He would have her finish what she'd started, pay his bill in full. For now, though, his mind was on the deal.

'It's Broder,' he barked, when the other end picked up. 'What did Abrams say? I want an answer. Within the hour.'

He clicked the call off and thought for a second. Hopefully David Abrams would not be stupid enough to try to keep an asset Broder, Inc. wanted. He would fold like a concertina and sell.

If he refused, Marcus was not in the mood to be toyed with. Besides, he was a little bored. His corporate star needed burnishing. A big, old-fashioned hostile takeover, the old lion crushing the new challenger. That would suit his purposes down to the ground. Abrams was building an attractive little portfolio, one that would sit well in the Broder empire.

Fuck David Abrams. He would cave in on Kate Fox.

Or he would be destroyed.

'Good morning.' Tim Reynolds smiled briskly as he walked into the boss's office. 'Hope you're in an excellent mood, David.'

'Why wouldn't I be?' Abrams snapped. He depressed the phone button for his secretary. 'Lottie. Coffee. Now.'

'Good,' Reynolds said. 'Because I have some news. You know my thoughts about Kate Fox . . .'

'Jesus,' Abrams swore, and saw an expression of distaste cross his deputy's bland WASP features. 'Sorry, Tim, but I just don't want to hear anything about that woman today. I'm fixing the move into our building, talking to our real-estate guys about sub-letting their office space to save money. You can call her about it. I don't want to talk to her.' Reynolds opened his mouth, but Abrams cut him off. 'Or about her.'

'Glad to hear it. You've come round to my way of thinking, then. She's trouble. Although even I didn't expect her to offend you quite so soon. It's been exactly one day, hasn't it?'

'Are you hard of hearing?'

'No. No.' Tim Reynolds lifted his hands, trying to placate the boss. Abrams was good to work for, but you didn't cross him. 'Sorry. Let me put this without mentioning any names. You've had a call that can take this entire mess out of your hands, and we can do it at a nice profit.'

'Explain,' David said. He had a headache, and wasn't interested in Tim's obscure references.

'Guess whose office called last night?' Reynolds took in Abrams' face. 'OK, don't guess. Marcus Broder's people rang us.'

'We're of no interest to Broder.'

'Until you bought his ex-wife's magazine, David. Now all of a sudden we're best buds with the big boys. He wants your stake. I told him the number, he offered triple. Triple!' Reynolds was beside himself with glee.

'Your coffee, sir,' Lottie Friend said, entering with a silver pot. She busied herself pouring and stirring in his sugars, and Abrams was glad of the distraction.

He needed a moment to think.

Reynolds was still talking. 'Marcus Broder said that *Lucky* was the right title, he wanted to take it forwards, all that stuff. But obviously it's personal. It's something to do with the lovely Kate Fox. He's overpaying wildly for an unproved commodity. Man, she must have had something on her to fry his brain like that—'

'Enough,' David Abrams said. He spoke very sharply, and Reynolds was shocked into silence. 'We don't discuss women like that in this office. Is that understood?'

There was silence. Lottie swallowed hard, trying to disappear with the coffee tray. Tim Reynolds broke out into a light sweat.

'Uh, yes, sure, David. I'm sorry.'

'And we especially don't discuss Kate Fox like that. Here or anywhere else.'

Reynolds bit his lip. 'Why does she get special treatment?'

'Because she's our colleague.' Abrams picked up his mug of coffee and took a long draw on it. 'I just bought that magazine. I'm not selling.'

* * *

Kate was glad of her work. There were plenty of résumés to read, lots of phone calls to make. She didn't choose to delegate any of this. Hiring staff was the key. Besides, a great magazine would get her over the horror of last night.

'Susie? Hey, it's Kate Fox. At *Lucky*. Yes, you heard right. Want a job?'

'Joline? I want a staff photographer. Senior. You interested? Less money, but you won't be doing "the new spring pastels", I guarantee you that.'

'Joshua? I heard Fleur wouldn't publish your piece on the DA.'

'She said it was too controversial.' He grunted. 'Paid me for it, though. It belongs to them.'

'I want you to write as much daring stuff as you like. Name names. You'll be on staff. We'll print it all. Just make sure it checks out.'

'You're kidding me, Kate.'

'Contributing editor. Exclusive to us. Deal?'

The calls went on and on. Some of her targets said no. She couldn't offer the pension plan, the gold-plated employment contracts. *Lucky* was untested. And Kate was aiming high, cherry-picking the best from EMAP, Condé Nast, and Victrix. It was great; it was like cooking with humans. Less cash, more credit. Her employees would have a stake in something worth doing. She wanted the hot celebrity gossip, the ground-breaking exposés, the fascinating studies of new artists, directors, bands. Some of the good people asked for a little more money. That was fine, she told herself. Whatever. She knew what she could pay. Then she would move on to the next candidate. She had no intention of calling up David Abrams, asking if they'd found any more money in the budget for staff. She worked within the numbers he'd given her, no problem.

Throughout the day, Kate glanced at her phone. Kept looking at it.

There were no calls.

At least, not from David Abrams. There was nothing. Tim Reynolds, his Chief Executive, called about moving the office. She spoke to him about that. But where was his boss?

Ignoring her, not bothering to call. The humiliation burned Kate. Yes, she'd left him a note. But shouldn't he have called, emailed, something? Apologised himself? Told her how wonderful she was . . .

Instead, nothing. Abrams was doing a great impression of a Trappist monk.

'Work for you? I'm expensive,' Jacqueline Moltrano warned her.

'I *know* you're expensive. Because you're *good*. You're the one who exposed that Republican judge with the hookers, and the Democrat DA for the tax fraud. We want you at *Lucky*, babe. Besides, you should see our sample closet. It's way more chic than they have at *Cutie*.'

'Because you're picking the clothes.'

'I do have style,' Kate said airily. 'This is going to be a big book, Jacqui. We have production money now, a serious distribution staff . . .'

'Paid off your debts?' she asked, archly.

'Yes, as I'm quite sure you know.' Kate rolled her eyes. If Jacqui wasn't so insanely talented, she wouldn't be on the phone to her right now. She was a writer who hit politicians where they lived. Emily hadn't wanted her because she had destroyed a couple of corrupt Democrats; she'd liked concentrating on right-wing sleaze. But as far as Kate was concerned, a crook was a crook. Big news-making stories sold magazines. Especially valuable to her, because *Lucky* wasn't stocked at every newsstand yet, and it needed to be. Her little magazine was like a struggling actress: talented, maybe, pretty, sure, but needed to get her name in lights.

A kick-ass photo spread, some fashion exclusives, a political career or two exposed to the sun . . . that was where she wanted to go with this.

Hence her call to little Jacqui Moltrano, the lean brunette with the glossy dark hair and the penchant for Herve Leger. Jacqui was hot, if you liked your chicks obvious, Kate thought disdainfully. She wore Manolos, Louboutins or Bottega Veneta on her feet, and Hermès 24 Faubourg as her perfume, and you could spot her coming half a mile away by the way guys around all craned their necks for a better look.

'I did hear something about it,' Jacqui purred. 'David Abrams financed you, is that true?'

'It is.' As you've known for a while, like ever since the ink dried on the papers.

'A really interesting guy. I've seen pictures. Gorgeous. Is he still single?'

Kate flushed. 'I'm sure he is. I've no interest in his personal life,' she said shortly. God, Jacqui was so obvious. Kate couldn't get past it. She admired driven, she admired pushy . . . but Ms Moltrano was just greedy. And obvious with it. A turn-off. Colleagues, yes, she admired her work; but friends? This wasn't going to be the new Emily. That was for sure.

'Really, sweetie? Because *I* certainly do. Is he ever in the office?'

'He came in yesterday . . .' Kate fanned herself with her hand; she wanted out of this conversation. 'Look, Abrams,

Inc. is a big company; he has way more to do than just this magazine. Take the job if you want it. Not just to meet David.'

'David? So we're on first-name terms?'

'I did sell him half my stake,' Kate countered. Wow, Jacqui wasted no time, did she? Zooming in, asking the right questions.

'And who's in charge? You or him?'

Kate's cheeks flamed, but there was no good reason to hang up. Besides which, she told herself, this was exactly why she wanted Ms Moltrano. She'd have made a hell of a prosecuting attorney. Her questions zoomed straight to the heart of whatever you least wanted to say.

Jacqui was Kate's last call today, a must-get. She would be the big superstar writer who could launch a new magazine to the stratosphere.

Kate swallowed her pride. Fuck it.

'He's in charge,' she admitted. 'I'm Editor-in-Chief. I can fire everyone, but he can fire me.'

'Exclusivity clause?'

'Yes. Like you will have, if you sign with us.'

'I don't know, honey.' Jacqueline's languid tone fooled neither of them. This was the business end of the conversation. 'I'm kind of hot right now. Got a great 401(k). Six figures on the salary. They wine and dine me, I get first pick of the party invites. Can you offer me any more?'

'I can't better it. I can only match it.' Kate closed her eyes, hoped she didn't have to deal with Abrams on that. But Jacqui was the only one where it was worth paying the same as the other, richer magazine houses did. 'But we run your stories, all of them. No censorship. We give you the biggest byline ever seen. Jacqui, you'll be the new Woodward and

Bernstein, only in a killer dress. And I'll throw in a new pair of Jimmy Choos *every month.*'

Jacqui laughed. 'You've got style. Tell you what, baby, I think it's a deal. *If* I get to have dinner with David Abrams. One on one. Oh, and I have a one-way get-out clause from the contract at six months. In case you ain't selling any copies. Rent costs a *ton* in this town.'

Kate sighed. 'Tell me about it. Yes to the break clause, no to David Abrams. I'm not his pimp.'

'Not his pimp! You mean you're keeping him all to yourself? Spill, is he next on the list? Marcus Broder II, the Sequel? And all the talk in the newsrooms was that Kate Fox was changing her ways.'

Kate almost gasped at the directness of the hit. 'Hell, no,' she said, speaking much too fast. 'He's cocky, full of himself, if you want the truth, and I wouldn't date him if he was the last single guy in Manhattan.'

That was true. Right? She wanted nothing more to do with David Abrams, outside the office.

'Look around, sweetie. He *is* the last single guy. At least with any cash.'

'OK, fine.' Man! Anything to stop this conversation.

As she broke out into a light sheen of sweat, her palms slippery on the receiver, Kate's sharp mind turned to the problem. She really regretted her lapse, her little slip, with David Abrams. She wanted this job, wanted *Lucky* to work, wanted a second chance at life. And getting Abrams off her back . . . her gut told her it might be a good move. Abrams was dangerous, dangerous to her. If he kept pressing her, she was afraid she might crack again.

Hard-as-nails Jacqui Moltrano was offering her a way out. Hell, be tough about this, Kate told herself. She forced herself to picture David's guest bathroom, separately laid out for women. The lack of commitment, the easy girls. He was a bad boy; he couldn't complain if the shoe was on the other foot. Besides, he could handle himself with Jacqui. And since Jacqui made it plain that she was only interested in cash . . . yes, they deserved each other. Setting David up with Jacqui was the sexual equivalent of the repentant alcoholic unscrewing the tops off all the hidden bottles and pouring the whiskey down the sink.

It'd be the Christians and the Lions in the Coliseum. And she wasn't sure which was which. The point was, it would remove one big, bad temptation.

'I'll set you up with him,' she agreed. 'One dinner, that's all I can promise. And not till you've signed a contract.'

'Messenger it over tomorrow. With a note telling me where our reservation is. This is going to be fun,' Jacqueline said, sweetly. 'Working for both of you.'

'You'll only be working for me. I'm the editor.'

'Absolutely, Kate, whatever you say. I'm sure David and I can discuss all that at dinner. Talk tomorrow. Bye!'

She hung up.

Kate leaned back in her chair, tried to steady her breathing. Oh God. Oh God. She had hired Jacqueline Moltrano. She wasn't sure if that was the best, or the worst, move she'd ever made.

Jacqueline thought she was attracted to David Abrams . . . Well, OK, bad example, she admitted to herself. You *are* pretty attracted to Abrams. Jacqueline thought she was sleeping with Abrams . . . Kate breathed in hard. Start over. OK, Jacqueline Moltrano thought that she was targeting David Abrams as her new rich husband. Marcus Broder II, like she said. And with a thrill of shame, Kate guessed that David Abrams probably thought that as well.

There was only one way out of it. As awful as it was, she was gonna have to call Abrams' office. Actually speak to him again. Because he had to go on this date with Jacqui. Kate needed to sign her, and she wanted Jacqui to believe she was ready to throw David Abrams to her like a sacrificial lamb. Otherwise, Jacqui would spread it all around town that Kate had set her cap at her new boss.

The thought was horribly embarrassing. She physically moved in her chair, wriggling with discomfort. Oh God! Her head was spinning. She really didn't know which was worse, calling Abrams now, or having a motormouth like Jacqui blab to every gossip columnist in New York.

He hadn't called.

He hadn't emailed.

She'd come up to his apartment to discuss work, and . . .

Ugh. Right. Like he'd believe that. He would assume she was throwing herself at him.

And now, after her little note and zero contact from him, *she* had to call.

Kate buried her face in her hands. God! Somebody invent a time machine! She wanted a do-over for last night . . . The quicker she got Jacqui and David together, the better.

The phone buzzed on her desk.

'Kate Fox. What?' she yelled.

'It's David.'

Her heart sped up. Adrenaline dewed her palms. She couldn't control her thoughts. A picture, crystal clear, of him lying next to her, sleeping, the strong muscles of his chest rising and falling, covered in that smattering of salt-and-pepper hair. Her belly stirred with the echoes of pleasure. She replayed how he had turned her over on that bed, handling her so well, with such casual authority.

Her body was a traitor. She bit her lip.

'Hello,' she managed.

Thank God he couldn't see her, couldn't see her blushing, her lips parting, her pupils dilating. She gripped the phone tight, knuckles white around it. Maybe she could bluff this out. She had to, right?

'I need to talk to you. Can we meet?'

'I've hired Jacqueline Moltrano,' she blurted out.

'Really.' For a second she could hear him readjusting, turning his mind to her coup of the day. 'How did you manage that? I'm impressed.'

She thrilled to hear him say that. He was a great print man, a legend. The career girl in her wanted his approval.

'Paid her the same as she's getting now. But she's the only one,' she added hastily. 'Promised we'd print all her stuff, treat her like a star. She gets a six-month break. Signs an exclusive.'

He digested that. 'Very good work.'

'Thank you.' She exhaled. Her job was allowing her to claw back a modicum of self-respect. 'There's a catch, though. She signs tomorrow, but only if I can deliver you.'

There. She had said it. Maybe Jacqui would solve all her problems. Start dating David Abrams, and it would be like last night never happened.

Only problem was, part of her hated that idea.

'How do you mean, deliver me?'

'You're single. You're . . .' She swallowed. 'You're attractive.'

Another pause, then his tone shifted, again. Kate recognised the predator, and desire for him rose in her.

'Why thank you, ma'am. I thought you had decided otherwise.'

She ignored that. 'She wants to have dinner with you. It's non-negotiable, and she's a very pretty girl . . . Please say yes, OK? I need you to do this.'

'Fine. I'll eat with her. Once.'

'Thank you.' She relaxed, fractionally. 'And David, again. I'm sorry about last night.'

'I'm not,' he said.

She swallowed a gasp. 'But it's insane. We can't . . . we're partners. We're . . .'

'You don't want a repeat. You made that very clear.' He was all business now, and she tried to adjust. 'Let's have coffee. There's something I need to discuss with you, privately. And we can clear the air.'

'Sure. Clear the air,' she agreed. And hated herself for wishing he'd try just that little bit harder.

French Roast was his favourite coffee shop, on Sixth Avenue at Twelfth Street. A Village hangout for years, it served every kind of delicious-smelling brew imaginable, from skinny soy-milk cappuccinos to rich Irish-whiskey-flavoured coffee. He ordered a black Amaretto and took a skewer covered with brown sugar crystals to stir into it.

Kate asked for a vanilla hazelnut and added a tiny froth of warm milk, dusted with chocolate powder. They picked a booth and sat down. She sipped at her delicious drink, glad of the excuse to look down. He was devastating up close; the dark suit picked out those incredible eyes; women's heads turned automatically when he entered the room. She was sure hardly any of them knew who he was; David Abrams was a businessman, private, not one of the celebrity rich crowd. But females responded to his sheer masculinity, the presence of him, a lion in a world of sheep.

And she was female. He made her feel it too.

She took a pull of the coffee. 'You wanted to meet?' She glanced around. 'Great choice. I used to come here with Emily.'

He nodded. 'My office took a call today. A bid for my stake in *Lucky*.'

'That's insane.' She blinked, jolted out of her desire. 'The ink's barely dry.'

'Exactly. Ordinarily, nobody would make such an offer yet.'

A wash of fear crossed over her. The warm, wonderful feeling in her belly, the tingle on her skin, dried up almost immediately.

'It was Marcus Broder,' she said.

He nodded. 'Got it in one.'

'He offered you more than you paid.' It wasn't a question. 'Double?'

'Triple,' Abrams told her. 'I told you it wasn't real.'

Her heart was in her mouth. 'You said no?'

'Of course I said no. We're partners.'

She felt grateful, so grateful, so protected, she could have cried. 'David, you could have cleaned up . . .'

'I have plenty of money. I don't do business that way.'

'Thank you.' She swallowed, hard, but her body was refusing to obey her this time. Tears prickled in her eyes. 'I appreciate that. Look, I have to go.'

'Go where?' He glanced at his watch. 'It's seven p.m. You've poached half the city for our book. It's time for a break.'

She looked up at him, weakly. 'I can't stay with you. I'm

– I'm really attracted to you. I need to get out of here. Please.'

He stared. 'I know you're attracted to me, sugar. I was there. We both were. I don't have short-term memory loss.'

'Do you know what Jacqueline Moltrano asked me? If I knew you were rich, and single. If I wanted you for myself.'

His eyes danced. 'And do you?'

'David, she asked me if I got the financing for *Lucky* by sleeping with you.'

'Right. We both know better.'

'And if I date you, the whole town will agree with her. Truth won't matter. Look, David.' She drank some more coffee. 'You got some of it last night. Before . . . before you kissed me. If you even remember that part.'

'I remember everything,' he said, softly.

'Well, your little theory. It was right.' She felt liberated as she said that, and dared to lift her eyes from her mug to look him in the face. Oh, but he was so handsome. So manly. It hurt, this actually hurt, pushing him away. Yet she knew she had to do it. 'About not dating losers like my dad. My mom . . . I really loved her, you know. She was a great mom, till some douchebag drunks mowed her down in the street. But she looked like shit, because she never slept, working two jobs to put me through Catholic school and make the rent. And I was her only kid and she always said she wanted better for me. That I should marry money.'

'So she didn't care how you did at school?'

'Oh, sure. She wanted me to ace it, to pick up those good grades. Because like she said, that way I'd have a career. As backup. In case the marriage didn't work out.' Kate forced a smile. 'And guess what, it didn't. Now I don't know anything, except I'm sick of rich men and I want to do something for myself. I want to be respected. Emily always thought I could be better than I was. That's why she left me *Lucky*. And the second I date you, it all goes away. Anything good I ever do at *Lucky*, everybody will say it was all you, David Abrams, the great magazine man. Who rescued the blonde bimbo. So, yes, you're hot. But I saw your bathroom just for girls, and I don't want to be Miss September. Maybe you can date Jacqueline Moltrano, OK? Do you get it, at all?'

He sighed. She was so beautiful. Damaged, but determined. He loved what he saw in that booth.

And she'd been the best lay he thought he'd ever had. *Ever.*

Trouble was, Kate Fox disturbed him. He was a man who loved women, in general – appreciated them, desired them, enjoyed their company. The one-night stands he preferred, he treated with respect and friendship; never demeaned them, never called them names. Showered them with jewellery and gifts. Hell, who was he to judge? David Abrams didn't believe in the double standard. He wanted no-strings sex, after all, so that put him and the party girls on the same level, in the same boat.

Yet his heart had rarely been touched. The girls he'd actually dated hadn't lasted long. They were all nice, sweet, accomplished girls, and David went through the motions, including in the bedroom. But he hadn't felt a spark, hadn't fallen in love. And after a month or three, it seemed pointless to go on with the charade.

But Kate Fox . . . there was something else there. Sex with her was different. Mind-blowingly, gloriously different. It wasn't her body . . . there were girls out there more to his taste, if he were writing a list on a piece of paper. And it wasn't her technique. For a girl who'd been married to

Broder, she seemed naïve, almost, but receptive . . . so receptive, so hot . . . that was what truly turned him on.

David Abrams sensed that the sex was so great because his feelings were different. The bravery, the determination, the pick-yourself-up-and-start-again, he loved it. He empathised. Even if she admitted she'd married for money. She'd made a mistake, a giant one perhaps, but she was trying to put it right.

He steeled himself. This was crazy. He was getting carried away, and that was something he never did. But he wasn't ready to commit after one night. And he acknowledged what she said, about her career, about the stigma . . . that nice little speech. Unfortunately, she was exactly right. If she dated him, nobody would rate her as a print woman ever again. She might as well walk around town with a scarlet G on her breast. For gold-digger.

Anyway, she was way too young for him.

And she had issues.

And he was her boss.

'I still don't like it,' he said.

'You don't have to like it. You just have to let me go.'

'Very well. Run my magazine. Do a great job.' He stood up, leaving his coffee, and threw a twenty on the table.

Her face fell. 'Are you mad?'

'No. I'm not mad. I'm also not made of stone. If I sit here much longer, nothing you say is going to count for shit. So I'm leaving. In future, we'll meet with other people around.'

He walked out and she looked after him, staring at his back, watching him through the glass panel on the door as he walked away, crossing Sixth, heading towards West Eleventh Street.

Kate wanted to cry. But she bent her head, and finished her coffee. It was time to wake up, time to get real.

David Abrams tried to concentrate.

There was a beautiful woman sitting in front of him, after all. He'd smiled when Jacqui Moltrano walked into the restaurant. Any red-blooded male would have. Not such a penance, after all, to be forced to eat dinner with her.

'Hi, I'm Jacqui,' she said, extending one hand with its long, blood-red nails.

'I'm David.' He stared determinedly into her eyes, which was difficult. She was slim, and showed her figure to best advantage, in a clinging, full-length split silk gown under an attractive red and gold Chinese brocade jacket. The material flowed close to her body, which was a little hard, a little chiselled for David's taste – her arms and lean thighs said she was a workout queen – but you couldn't fault the small, perky breasts and her delicately rounded ass. Her hair was long and shiny and dark, and tumbled round her shoulders in an extravagant big-curl do. She had thick lips, painted fire-engine red, like her dress and nails. The olive Italian skin and dark colouring could pull that off.

Subtle was not in this girl's vocabulary.

'Kate tells me you're going to come and work with us.'

'That's right.' She smiled, slid into her seat, extended one long leg out from the slit in the Chinese silk, giving him a good look at her fabulous pins.

But David's mind was elsewhere.

Goddamn, screw Kate Fox, he thought. Screw her complicated personality and her habit of getting under his skin. He had to stop going over that coffee with her.

She was the one who walked out of his apartment.

She said no. Didn't want to date. Wouldn't give him a shot. What did she expect, immediate commitment? A ring, after one night?

She was infuriating.

But so smart. So beautiful . . .

Will you stop that, he lectured himself. Look at this gorgeous chick right here.

Jacqui was clever – maybe not as smart as Kate, but nobody's fool – but she was hard in more ways than one. Ordering a whiskey sour before they started eating. The defined arms. The bright red dress-lips-nails. The way she extended those extremely impressive legs out at him, like she was offering him fruit on a silver plate.

They ordered food and he made a little small talk. Throughout, Jacqui Moltrano licked her lips, flicked her hair. Flung herself at him. But she was no bimbo; hard bitten maybe, but impressive as a journalist. A big name for Kate Fox to . . .

No. Enough. He needed a distraction, and the merry-go-round of strippers and club girls wasn't cutting it any more. Without something to distract him, he'd be thinking about Kate Fox all the goddamn time. When she had so easily thrust him from her mind.

'So, you seeing anyone?' he asked Jacqui, when they got to dessert.

'No,' she said, smiling brilliantly, leaning even further forward. 'But I'd like to.'

'Really? Who's that?'

'You,' Jacqui answered, as he'd known she would. She could hardly have made it more obvious.

He took a small sip from his wine glass. 'I'm not interested in a major relationship right now, I have to be honest. Just friendship.'

'Maybe with benefits?' Jacqui laughed, shamelessly. 'I'm great in bed.'

He responded to her lack of embarrassment, grinning. This was what he wanted from a girl right now.

'Why don't you let me be the judge of that?' he said easily. 'We could date, if we're on the same page. Have some fun.'

'That sounds real good to me, sugar,' Jacqui purred. She looked around for the waiter. 'Cheque, please.'

Chapter Eighteen

The next few months passed in a blur. Kate didn't leave herself a second in the day to unwind or relax. She didn't want time to think.

First, there was the small matter of moving house. She took a day off with her realtor and walked around the East and West Village until her feet bled. Finally, she purchased a cute one-bedroom flat in a non-doorman building, on Eleventh at West End Avenue. It cost her three quarters of a million, but the maintenance on the place was very low, it had those big windows and high ceilings she liked, and it was spartan and anonymous. Her bedroom was a proper bedroom, not some fancy mezzanine she'd constructed to try to grab a little extra privacy. The place looked out over the river, to the running track and bicycle lanes that ran the length of the city. She loved it. It was small, but not tiny, and she decorated it with warm Afghan rugs, the driftwood chair from Nantucket, a colourful Venetian glass vase with fresh peonies and tulips . . . shades and textures everywhere, so that she was not reminded of Marcus's pretentious antiques or David Abrams' minimalist charm. She forgot the gym, bought a small stack of free weights and a yoga mat that slid under the bed. That worked her upper body, and the river was right on her doorstep; all she had to do was tug on her Nikes and she was flying, downriver to the White Bridge or uptown towards Soho. It was the cheap part of the Village, the very end of the street, blocks away from the Magnolia Bakery or the Village Apothecary. There were rumours of a major rock drummer and his gorgeous movie star girlfriend in one of the penthouses, but they kept to themselves, and mostly it was a quiet, unpretentious place.

Nobody knew Kate. Nobody bothered her.

That suited her fine. Her walk-in closet was not large, but she made perfect use of it, laying her designers out by colour and season, allowing her to pick the most stylish ensembles at a moment's notice. Which, after her daily punishing run, was a major part of her job.

Because Kate Fox was the new face of *Lucky*. And that meant she was a star. The industry was starting to notice. The media were starting to notice. Everything she wore was blogged by fashion websites as soon as she reached the Abrams building, and stepped out of the lift on to *Lucky's* new floor.

She was a corporate asset. It was time to stop being so self-deprecating, and accept the plaudits. Kate dressed *Lucky's* style: a Moschino Cheap & Chic black boatneck dress with the cutest three-quarter sleeves, Fendi heels in olive and a pistachio satchel from J. Crew; or ballerina flats from Chanel, skinny grey cashmere trousers from McQueen and a white cotton shirt from Zara. She was always on trend, on point. People noticed. Fashion noticed.

And for Kate, it was part of the mix. She got up before six, ran three miles a day, came back to stretch, shower and dress. Every other day she headed to Blow at Fourteenth Street, to get her hair dried and styled at the best salon in the city. Eliza

Petrescu did her brows, Katherine Flowers at the Victrix Salon manicured her nails. She turned up to work impeccable. Every day.

And the magazine roared into shape.

After the first couple of weeks, Kate really found her feet. Her new hires turned up. All of a sudden, there was money. They printed on the best stock. Perfume samples were available to new advertisers. David Abrams' staff of dedicated sales experts showed her amateurs how to do it; Kate's people led on content, Abrams took care of business.

And it was an easy sell. Because Kate Fox had free rein. Her ambition was total.

Lucky was a smash.

They ran the sexiest girls on the cover. Not supermodels; they had been done to death. Not movie stars either, with their snooty PR reps demanding this and that, total picture control.

'We don't beg people to be on our cover. They beg us,' Kate said.

Her design team looked at her like she was speaking Japanese.

'Huh?' asked Susie Flemal. She was the new head of production, and she had been kicking ass from the day Kate hired her. Bigger photographs, text wrapped around, colours on the page; everything popped, the entire look was sleek. Serious articles were interspersed with style inserts. Every page was unexpected. 'You can't do that.'

'*Lucky* doesn't understand the word "can't". We don't have one star on the cover. We have three. A model, an actor or actress, and a public figure. Maybe a candidate, a politician, a hero cop, whatever. And the idea is, it's an honour to make the cover here. If you're the model, you're the big thing that month. If you're the actor, then you're the star of the moment. Every month one of the names has to be recognised – maybe you get Sarah Palin or Joe Biden, then you can have an up-and-coming actor. You get Tom Cruise, and you can feature an unknown, brilliant circuit court judge. It's the *mix*, kids. Makes us different from everyone else.'

'My God.' Jacqueline Moltrano looked at her with something approaching awe. 'That might actually work. I'd love to style Justice Sotomayor on the cover and feature her with a supermodel. And Robert Pattinson . . .'

'So let's get to it.' Kate clapped her hands. 'It's an event. Every issue is an event. We don't stand still, we don't phone it in.'

She pushed the team to the limit. Stylists worked late into the night. Brainstorming sessions happened every day. Kate supervised every piece, every article. When Jacqueline Moltrano wanted to expose Rick Castle, the Democratic candidate for Lieutenant Governor, Kate didn't blink.

'He's been very holier-than-thou about relationships,' Jacqui said, walking into her office. 'Only he likes massage parlours. In Boston. Flies out of town every other weekend. Sets himself up with girls, always out of town, out of state. When he was an assemblyman, used to entertain colleagues.'

Kate blinked. 'You got *evidence* for this?'

'Interviews with the girls. One CCTV shot. It's grainy, I don't know if it's legal.'

'And you've been holding it?'

'*Vanity Fair* were afraid of the libel laws. And the privacy issues.'

'Yeah? 'Cause I'm not. You run it, Jacqui. If he bitches about the hidden camera, we go First Amendment, public interest.' Kate almost rubbed her hands. 'What's the worst that could happen? We pay him damages, we become a big giant news story. It'd be worth it for the marketing alone.'

Her star writer smiled. 'I thought you might tread on it.'

'I told you. I don't tread on anything.'

Jacqueline pushed her dark hair out of her eyes. She was hotter than ever today, wearing a midnight-blue Azzedine Alaia and Gucci platform booties, with a tiny Cavalli jacket in navy and sexy, dangling moonstone earrings from House Massot. The lean look focused attention on her va-va-voom curves and endless legs; she had gone hell for leather with her make-up, though: smoky eyes and rich berry blush on her sexy olive skin.

'But you donated to his campaign.'

'Yeah. A lot of money.' Kate shrugged. 'So what. He's a hypocrite. And the magazine comes first. Tell you what, here's a great idea.' She snapped her fingers, excited. 'We're asking Kate Hudson to be on the cover with her boyfriend, Matt Bellamy from Muse.'

'Oh hell, yeah. They're awesome.'

'Hopefully they'll say yes. When I nail them, why don't you ask this guy to pose?'

Jacqueline almost jumped out of her seat. 'That's fucking brilliant. You're a goddess. He's a total ego, he'll do it in a heartbeat.'

'I know.' Kate grinned. 'And we'll have him on the cover of the issue that destroys his career.'

'You're evil,' Jacqui said admiringly.

Kate bowed. 'I try.'

Yeah, she thought to herself. Hell, it was such a giant buzz. Coming up with this stuff, making it happen . . .

* * *

They got him on the cover and the issue made the national news, sold out everywhere. Next month she dropped the exposés and just recorded her three cover stars talking... a governor in the Presidential primary, a young super-model with an astrology fixation, and a reclusive Oscar-winning actor coming back out of retirement for his new movie.

The conversation was hilarious, unexpected.

That issue sold out too.

Lucky trebled its subscriber base. Doubled its advertising rate. They started turning would-be advertisers away. Every fashion label in America was desperate for a piece of them, and Kate kept it new, kept it different, every time.

In ninety days, she turned New York on its head.

Kate Fox was the new name in magazines.

And she loved it.

Only problem was, that was all there was to life. She kept busy – real busy – from morning till late at night. When she finally left whatever party, launch or fashion show she was attending, and got herself back to her place, it was usually eleven. Time for bed, if you got up early to run.

So she minimised those moments when she understood herself to be alone. No husband, no boyfriend. All her less stylish friends on the magazine, in the industry? They were with guys.

Kate told herself a lot of convenient lies. She didn't want a boyfriend. She was too busy for a relationship. She had lousy judgement. Whatever worked that day.

It wasn't like she didn't have offers. The girls at *Lucky* liked the boss. Hard not to feel good about the woman who was raising your wages, giving you the best readership you'd ever had.

'You should meet my friend Jim. He's a doctor.'

'Kate, how about Rocky Grandolini? You know, the director? He got divorced last year.'

'My cousin Sam's an architect . . .'

'Louis Baldeaux is the hottest new professor at Columbia. His classes are packed. Political science, you guys would be great together.'

'Darling,' Jacqueline drawled, 'you need a strong man. Someone strong enough to handle Kate Fox.'

'Like David?' Kate joked, and immediately wished she hadn't. Everybody knew Jacqueline Moltrano had been dating David Abrams, on and off, since Kate arranged that dinner. Jacqui was talented, clever, glamorous, and had all the sensuality of Sophia Loren, with tits to match. Plus she had absolutely no hang-ups about dating the boss.

One evening, when the Rick Castle issue was flying off the shelves, and Jacqui's coup was the talk of CNN and Fox, Kate delicately broached the subject.

'But aren't you worried?' she asked.

'About what?'

'Your big story . . . the magazine . . .'

Jacqui leaned forward into the bar. They were drinking at Soho House, the hottest private members' club in the city. Two major designers had just given them an exclusive preview of the spring collections; it would be crisp neutrals, pistachio and slate, Kate thought, instead of the same tired pastels and florals. She approved. She was working a cranberry juice and selzer, but Jacqui was taking a long, satisfying pull on a double Jack Daniels and Diet Coke.

'David doesn't like women who drink,' was her airy explanation. 'So I don't. Unless he's safely out of sight. Mmm, that tastes great.'

'Aren't you anxious? That people will say it's all him . . . that you're being promoted because of him?'

'Oh, who cares?' Jacqueline took another slug of her drink and smacked her lips. 'You're putting the byline up there. And let them say what the hell they want. I'm dating the sexiest man in New York. They're all just jealous.' She lifted her glass for a toast. 'Brilliant issue, Kate. Thanks for making it happen.'

Kate chinked glasses. 'Hey, no. It was your deal.'

Jacqui took another slug. 'And you hired me, didn't you? It worked out for both of us.' She nudged Kate. 'Thanks so much for making it happen with David. He's been amazing. Kind of reluctant at first, even though I said,' and she held up her hands, red talon nails pointing at the ceiling, '"No pressure! We're not even exclusive! Just having fun!" It was like he had another girlfriend. But when I asked him about that, that's when he committed to a second date. And now we *are* exclusive. We have so much fun!'

'Hey, Jacqui, that's great. I'm really pleased for you.' Kate felt sick. 'You know, he is my boss; maybe we should chat about something else . . .'

Jacqui was oblivious. She wanted to boast. 'He is smart. And funny. And so ambitious. You know, he doesn't even think of himself as rich? Keeps saying what an amateur he is, how he hasn't even started yet. I think he wants to give your Marcus a run for his money.'

'He's not my Marcus. Look, we really shouldn't talk about David, because—'

'But I *want* to talk about him,' Jacqui pointed out, with Bourbon-fuelled candour. 'He's just soooo fucking sexy. And not just in the way he looks.' She nudged Kate again, lowered her voice to a stage whisper. 'You would not *believe* the way this guy is in bed.'

Kate broke out in a cold sweat. At least David Abrams had not betrayed her, had not given her up. He hadn't lain there in bed next to her star writer and laughed about Kate, how helpless and hot she had been under his touch.

'Hey, you know. It was a *great* article. But I have to get home, get to bed. I have to be up real early,' Kate said hastily. She patted her friend on the back. 'Look, see you tomorrow, OK?'

'You're no fun,' Jacqui pouted. 'But OK.' She brightened. 'I can finish this off and call David. And he can finish *me* off. Seriously, if you could see how he—'

'Bye!' Kate sang. 'See you back in the office!'

And she ran out the door.

She smiled slightly, remembering that. Because although David Abrams never talked about it, he was still dating Jacqui, and the occasional grainy paparazzi shot of the two of them leaving some nightclub or other turned up in the Manhattan press.

So Jacqui was the career girl with the dubious path to the top, and her many victims, and their friends, delighted in giving quotes against her, while Kate shone untarnished.

It was exactly what she'd asked for.

It was perfect.

Right?

Abrams sat in his office, reading the figures on his screen.

They were good. Really good.

He ought to be a happy guy.

Lucky was making money. Marcus Broder had upped his offer, come at him with a really great price. Only something inside Abrams refused to throw Kate Fox to the wolves.

Jacqui Moltrano was turning out great pieces at work, and was available in his bed. She was always there, always on tap. He didn't have to comb through his Rolodex.

So what the hell was the problem?

Don't ask, don't tell, his brain said.

Ah, he was sick of pretending. He wanted to see Kate. This stiff-upper-lip thing was for Limeys. She worked for him, she was in his main magazine building close by. If he gave her an executive job, she'd move right into these offices and he'd get to see her every day . . .

Hell, he had a relationship. With Jacqui. Kate wasn't a mind-reader. What harm could it do to see his best editorial talent?

He picked up the phone, dialled her extension.

'Kate Fox,' she said instantly.

'Kate. It's David.'

A tiny pause. Was she fazed because he'd called? He wanted to think so.

'Hi,' she said.

'We should meet. Come over to head office.'

'Sure. You have the other editors in? The board?'

'Just you and me,' he said. 'We don't need chaperones, right? We're grown-ups.'

'I'm pretty busy,' she said reluctantly.

'Be here in the next fifteen minutes. I'm still your boss.'

'Well, yes, sir,' she said, and he could hear the smile in her voice, almost see the arousal on her face. She was so easy to read. And he loved that about her.

Kate thought about taking something with her. A file of shots, a printout of their rising sales. Then decided against it. David

Abrams had access to whatever she could see, and more besides. He was her boss.

They might be partners on *Lucky*, but it was very clear. She was the junior partner. He could fire her. And whereas he had fifty per cent of her magazine, he ran the damn company: all the magazines, all the buildings, every employee on every level ultimately reported to him.

She was an editor.

He was a player.

There were worlds between them. And she tried not to find it attractive. But she failed. Abrams' achievements stretched out before him like a fanfare when he entered the room. They were as much a part of his strength as his iron-like body.

Besides, he knew how she responded to strength.

Real strength. Masculine strength. The type that had turned her inside out in his bed, had marched her mercilessly through a succession of orgasms, had drenched her in sweat, made her scrabble at the bedclothes, gasp out his name, beg him, literally beg him, not to stop.

Kate could do nothing about that. He knew, and he was there, and there was no point pretending.

Hell, she thought, as she grabbed her bag and headed out the door. He was with Jacqui Moltrano now; surely she was taking good care of him. Maybe he'd forgotten all about that night.

Like she pretended she had.

'Mr Abrams, Ms Fox.' Lottie Friend hovered in the doorway. 'Would you like some coffee, sir? Some iced water?'

David looked at Kate. She shook her head.

'We're OK, I think. I want some privacy with Ms Fox.

271

So hold my calls, keep the door closed. We're in a meeting.'

'Yes, sir,' the older woman said. She looked balefully at Kate, but didn't dare to voice anything. 'Absolutely.'

Lottie went out, and the door closed heavily behind her.

They were alone in the office together.

'Have a seat,' David said.

Kate slid gracefully into the chair in front of his desk. Her Versace skirt hit just above the knee, and as she sat down, it rode up an inch, leaving her long legs tapering down to her Stuart Weissman shoes exposed, her slim thighs open to him in their sheer pantyhose.

Hell, she thought. I wish I'd worn a maxi skirt. Or pants . . .

'Yes?' she said. Defiantly. 'You wanted to see me?'

'*Lucky*'s going well. I thought we could talk about it.'

'Certainly,' Kate said, pushing her disappointment back down. She rattled out some statistics, some of their latest triumphs.

'Excellent.' He paused, looking at her, and his gaze burned. It was all Kate could do not to drop her eyes, not to plead with him to stop looking at her like that. She was terrified of showing weakness. 'You should know Marcus Broder has upped his offer for *Lucky*. And made threats; if I don't sell, he may offer for my entire division.'

She flushed. 'If you sold to him, I'd have to quit. I can't work for Marcus.'

'But you can work for me?'

'Sure,' she said instantly. 'You're arrogant, and cocky, and vain, but . . .'

'Why thank you,' he said, with a lazy smile that melted her bones.

'You don't hate me, I don't think. And you seem to like women.'

'Correction. I love women.'

'Marcus is damaged. He hates me. I don't think he likes any women really.' She shuddered.

'Well, don't worry. I said no.'

'But your shareholders?'

'They'll just have to trust my judgement,' he replied.

Kate flushed. Once again, in his presence, she felt small, vulnerable. Once again she was dependent on him for protection. Instinctively she crossed her legs.

'Thank you.' She couldn't help herself. 'How is it going with Jacqui?'

His eyebrow lifted. 'Personally, you mean?'

Kate shrugged. Got up from the chair. She felt too exposed, too open, sitting there with her skirt slithering treacherously and David Abrams looking down at her.

'Yes, goddamnit,' she said. 'I mean personally.'

He rose and moved around the desk towards her. There was nowhere to run. David Abrams came and stood before her, pitilessly, right in front of her.

'I'm dating her. It's not a romantic relationship.'

She was ashamed at the violence of the relief that surged through her body, the pleasure, the evaporation of tension. She breathed out, sharply, and David heard it, and looked down at her.

'I explained to Jacqui what I was looking for before we started. And she accepted things on those terms.'

'I see,' Kate muttered.

'You're not supposed to care.'

'That's right. I'm not.' She shook her head. 'This is weakness . . .'

'You still want me,' he said, and she heard the triumph, the deep, profound satisfaction in it. 'You have feelings for me.'

'No,' Kate muttered. 'Your life is none of my business.'

'Because you don't care, right?'

She lifted her head. Rebellious.

'That's right, damn you. I don't care. What you do with your life is your own goddamned—'

Abrams reached forward and grabbed her around the waist, pulling her close to him with a single movement, his mouth closing on hers, kissing her, relentlessly, mercilessly, thrusting his tongue into her mouth . . .

And feeling her instant, helpless surrender. Her response. Her body heating up under her clothes. Her nipples tight through the prim cotton of her shirt. He could feel them against his chest, feel her hands snaking up to his neck, her melting completely into the kiss . . .

And then she moaned, deep inside her throat, almost tortured, and pushed back from him.

'Oh God,' she whimpered. 'We can't . . . it would ruin everything . . .'

Abrams forced himself to relinquish her. It was a struggle. She was beautiful, and hot, and helplessly his.

'It's your decision,' he said, thick voiced. 'I won't make it easy for you, Kate Fox. I won't force you into anything. When you're clear on what you want, you'll come to me.'

She sobbed, once, then reached blindly for her bag and half ran out of his office.

Abrams stood there and watched her go, watched the door shut behind her. He would have to end it with Jacqui. God knew what he was playing at. Kate was right; this was dangerous, foolish.

Yet the kiss raged in his blood like a chemical reaction. And right now, none of the sensible stuff seemed to matter.

* * *

Lola Valdez reclined on the chaise longue and examined her boyfriend. He was over at the desk, a wonderful, ornate piece from an original Medici *palazzo* in Florence, his space-age style computer and monitor balanced on top of it, and he was staring at his emails.

Problem was, he'd been doing that for the last hour. She stretched, lazily, like a cat, moving her magnificent body underneath its chiffon baby-doll nightdress. It was perfectly pitched to make her look more naked than naked. Her nipples were high and tight, peaking under the gauze, clearly visible. Lola kept the central air in his apartment low, so that she would always appear aroused. She had a tiny amount of lubricant secreted in a perfume vial, in case Marcus suddenly wanted sex. For him, she was always in the mood. Thirty seconds locked in his bathroom, and she was ready to go.

This outfit usually worked. Marcus loved its peek-a-boo nature. It had a tiny trim of feathers, and she matched them to her heeled slippers with the pink fluffy feathers on the toes; all very Folies-Bergère. He would walk behind her and lift the hem, exposing her, and Lola would shudder with pleasure. Or he'd be on the phone, and she'd walk past him, letting him slip his free hand through the front of the sheer fabric, casually squeezing her breasts, cupping them, bouncing them.

She was his toy, and she acted like it. No complaints. No sighs. Which was why, contrary to Manhattan's expectations, Lola Valdez had stuck around on the scene for longer than any of his other post-divorce flings.

'Baby,' she purred. She arched her back, thrusting herself forward. 'Come over here.'

He didn't look round. 'Busy.'

Lola pouted. 'You're always busy. Take a little break.'

Marcus paused and turned on his seat. Basking in his appraisal, she spread her legs, widely, an open invitation. The chiffon parted very slightly, giving him a real good view of the Brazilian she'd gotten that morning.

Her persistence was rewarded. The annoyance on his face faded to neutral. 'Maybe later,' he said. 'I want to finish this first.'

'Sure, sweetie,' Lola answered.

She knew better than to push it. His temper was vile. Frustrated, she flipped on to her stomach. The baby-doll dress rose a little, displaying just the lower slopes of her world-class ass. Normally this would have been enough, would have had him walking over, unzipping, taking her exactly as she lay.

But not today. He was busy. And Lola knew what he was busy with.

That goddamned bitch Kate Fox.

Lola kicked the feather heels. She wasn't the brightest woman in the world, but she had a low sense of animal cunning. It was going to be tough enough to get Marcus to marry her. *He* thought she was the fuck of the moment, his relaxation for a week or two. And he thought she didn't know. But Lola was an expert in men. Marcus's week of pleasure had turned into three, or four, and now months, and she was still by his side, still living in his apartment.

Without him noticing, she had burrowed her way in. She was part of his routine now. She'd got him almost addicted. Only one thing stood in her way: this fucking obsession with his ex-wife.

What was it about the bitch? Lola sulked. She wasn't used to being ignored. And Marcus didn't spend time chasing down the lives and careers of his other ex-wives. Not that any of them had a career. They'd all got fat settlements, and they were living off those. In very comfortable obscurity.

Little Kate didn't have a penny, not really. But she was making Lola's life a misery. It would be hard enough to drag Marcus to the altar. He had no morals, as such, but a real strong sense of himself, his image. Another marriage might make him look ridiculous. And he was determined not to.

But he hadn't counted on Lola. She wanted that ring, and she was going to get it. Marcus was in the middle of her war zone, and he didn't even know it.

The baby-doll nightie was one weapon, and it wasn't doing its job. That was OK. Lola had others. She made it her business, in bed with Marcus, to figure out all his triggers. Like showing up to greet him in a business jacket, heels, and nothing else. He'd let himself into the apartment and she'd walk around like that, ass jutting out, the swell of her breasts clearly visible under the fabric, fetching him coffee, just casually discussing his day as though she were modestly dressed for a PTA meeting. Until he would snap and pull her to him, hurrying her into the bedroom. Or when the weak, submissive side of him came out, and he wanted to be ordered around, pushed back on to the bed, her red talons digging into his shoulders, and have her mount him, grinding down on him, telling him how worthless he was as she took his pleasure expertly out of him. That required a little more acting, because she so ardently despised him for being less than a man, but Lola was up for it. Whatever he was *in* the bedroom, outside it, Marcus Broder kicked plenty of butt. She recoiled from his touch at times, but never showed it; if the sex was lousy, she could always turn her head as she moaned and panted and study the Renoir on the wall, the four-hundred-thousand-dollar dresser from England, or the priceless Persian rug on the floor. Those silk sheets from Paris were enough of an aphrodisiac themselves. It was easy to work herself into a frenzy.

Lola planned on staying.

Phase one was sex. Lots and lots of sex. He could get that from any girl, so she had made it different by studying his triggers. Having him watch porn on the big-screen TV wall-mounted beyond the bed while she lay between his legs and sucked. Whispering filthy fantasies into his ear as she stroked him, just enough to push him over the edge. Surprising him at public events, when she was as demurely dressed as she knew how, taking him into some private corner and exposing herself, putting his hands on her . . .

That much was done. The more he fucked her, the better she knew his buttons. Now she had to morph a little, just a little, into the hostess/mommy side of things. The couture dresses were becoming more staid, longer. She had found a make-up artist who did subtle as well as slutty. And she was acquiring a new look, too, to be donned as soon as Marcus had rolled off her, or pulled out of her mouth: designer jeans, flat little Keds shoes or Capri sandals, Bermuda shorts, cute black and white striped Coco Chanel T-shirts, her long, lustrous hair in a ponytail. She even bought a couple of minimiser bras to wear under her T-shirts from the Gap and J. Crew. As soon as Marcus had come, Lola was going to transform into a wholesome, all-American moneyed mom from Scarsdale or Katonah. And all she needed was a baby to go with it.

Because that was her one ticket to the brass ring. Marcus didn't want to look ridiculous, but he did want to achieve some kind of grown-up status. That meant a child, probably two or three, and a wife to sit at home, host his parties, run the domestic side of the empire. He was looking for someone to play that part. And Lola was determined to ace the audition. She'd already started cooing over babies in the street; she was dressing like a nun after Marcus was taken care of . . .

But Kate Fox, the new hotshot of the magazine houses, Kate Fox was blocking her path. That *bitch*. That fucking *ghost*. Lola sometimes read *Lucky*, if Marcus was nowhere around. It was a great little magazine; she copied the style tips devotedly. Kate Fox knew how to pick 'em. But really, honestly. All she was was a fucking working woman. *Loser*. She had swapped Marcus and his millions for a stupid job. She wasn't as bright as all that, was she now? Lola thought smugly. And Marcus needed to see that, needed to get that Kate was nothing more than a failed trophy wife.

Lola stood up from the couch, slipped the little chiffon scrap of nothing from her shoulders. She had two enemies in this process. One of them was Marcus, who still thought he was going to dump her. And the other was Kate Fox.

She would accept Marcus's total surrender, but first, she was going to need to wipe this other girl off the face of the earth.

She was still wearing her heels. Her nude, tanned body was displayed delightfully by then; the shoes elongated her legs, threw out her ass, and made her breasts jiggle. She wandered over to Marcus, put her hands on his shoulders, started to rub and knead the knots between them.

'Mmm.' He sighed slightly, enjoying it. Her touch was sure.

'You just keep going, baby,' she purred. 'I won't bother you.'

She leaned over his shoulder, imperceptibly. On the screen was a chart, a PDF of circulation figures. Regular and projected.

She could see figures for *Elle*, *Cosmo*, *Vanity Fair*, *InStyle*, and . . . *Lucky*.

This was one tiny part of Marcus Broder's empire. But it was taking over.

It had to stop. Marcus needed to get on with his life, so Lola could get on with hers.

She slipped to her knees, then to all fours. That got his attention. He glanced down, grinned. She felt his hand stroking down her back, touching her ass, caressing her.

'What the hell are you doing?' he demanded, but without any real anger.

'Nothing,' she said sweetly. 'You don't mind me, Marcus. Just keep doing your work. I'm just like radio music in the background. You won't even notice me.' Then she knelt between his legs, unzipped him, and as he fondled her head, got straight to work.

Chapter Nineteen

'I had my doubts.' Tim Reynolds stood in the boardroom at Abrams, Inc. and surveyed the other faces. There were some non-execs, a retired State Supreme Court judge, an economist from the IMF, and the former head of M&A at a top city bank, and then the home-grown chiefs: Tim Reynolds, Iris Haughey, and David himself, sitting at the head of the table. 'I thought that it was a punt, that Kate Fox would be flaky. But despite taking a few risks, keeping our corporate counsel busy' – he smiled – 'sales are through the roof. More to the point, *Lucky* is the next big thing in magazines. We already have imitators. There's *Patriot*, which is trying to mimic the mix but coming from the right. They like it on the net, but not on the newsstands. I give it three more months. Then there's *Fall Report*, with Fleur D'Amato at the helm. Fashion with an edge.'

Iris Haughey snorted. 'I've seen beachballs with more of an edge. Fleur should never have moved from *Cutie*.' She preened. 'Not that she could touch our numbers at *Model* and *Beauty* . . .'

'They've dropped a little,' David Abrams said.

The others looked at him. Abrams rarely spoke in board

meetings. He preferred to listen, and then make the decisions, almost on his own.

'Yes,' Iris admitted. 'About fifteen per cent.'

'Dating from when?'

Iris squirmed. She could see what David was driving at, they all could, but she hated to admit it. She named the month.

'That's when Kate Fox left to marry Marcus. And the replacement fashion editors they brought in didn't work. She brought ten per cent of the readers in just on her articles.' David smiled slightly. 'That's impressive.'

'You can't prove the correlation,' Iris snapped.

'Play nice,' Abrams said, coolly. Iris was feeling threatened, but he didn't give a fuck. *Model* and *Beauty* were his bread and butter, but they hadn't lifted their sales in six months. Iris liked to talk about the recession, yet when Kate was faced with the same circumstance, she came up with something great.

Iris sulked. 'Fine. But it's rough on all *mainstream* beauty titles right now. Kate's doing very well – *in a niche market.*'

'How many more units does she have to sell before it turns into a mainstream title?' Abrams asked.

'Give it one more year,' Reynolds said, smiling. 'It really is an exciting moment in the industry. Also, David, you did well with the exclusivity clause. *Vogue* and *Elle* have both offered her a huge jump in salary.'

'You're forgetting, she owns fifty per cent.'

'Yes. And I think you should sell to Marcus Broder,' Reynolds continued. 'It was a big offer to start with. We can get even more now.'

'Sell? You're insane.' Abrams said.

Reynolds coloured. 'Think of the shareholders. It's a no-brainer; it would give us an injection of cash.'

'Thinking of your stock price?' Abrams asked. 'Kate's a winner. I'm not selling her to her ex-husband.'

Reynolds winced at the dismissal.

'No. Don't sell. My recommendation is that you buy her out,' said Donal Redson.

The Irishman was fifty, with red hair and piercing pale blue eyes, and he had been one of the best guys at his previous bank, for David's money, until they let him slide for being too old. He was glad to sit on the board of a coming company, and Abrams held his advice as cheap at the price. 'This is seen as a great deal for you, David. But you want more than just a big stake. It's Abrams, but it's not. Because it's not part of our magazine division; it's separately owned. You want the whole thing.'

'How much should we pay?'

He shrugged. 'About four million dollars?'

David almost spat out his cinnamon coffee. 'I know it's risen in value, but I gave her eight hundred thousand.'

'It's the hottest new magazine around. Sales are off the charts. To be honest, it's probably worth more than that, but you're about the only serious buyer, so you get it for a bargain. Anybody else can only purchase a fifty per cent stake, but you can have the whole thing. So you should get in there.' Donal smiled expansively. 'Once Abrams owns *Lucky*, we'll have the two strong, solid performers in mass market *and* the explosive new young title. You've got reliability and imagination. Yoked. That makes the magazine division much more valuable.' Another grin.

David nodded. He ran his eyes down the list of figures. 'I'll try to buy her out. And I want to promote her.'

'To what?' Tim Reynolds asked. 'She's already Editor-in-Chief.'

Abrams looked at Iris. 'I'm thinking she should have a wider-ranging role. I intend to make her a senior vice president.'

Iris went white. The smile was wiped off Tim Reynolds' face. They were both senior VPs. It had taken fifteen years of industry prominence to rise that fast.

'She has no experience,' Reynolds said.

'You were just praising her to the skies.'

'Yes, David, for early performance. She's not up to corporate responsibility.'

'I've been impressed,' Abrams said. 'I promote on results, not seniority. We're not the federal government.'

'Kate Fox is a loose cannon,' Iris said. 'You can't be serious about this, David.'

'I don't joke about business.' If their egos were hurt, he really didn't give a fuck. He stood up. 'Thanks, guys. See you next quarter.'

Night had settled over the city now, and it was cold, really cold. Nowhere did winter quite like New York. You could dress like an Eskimo, and the cold still had a way of sinking into your bones, freezing your blood. Abrams always gave big donations to the homeless shelters for the season, but you could throw as much money as you liked at the problem; every year, some poor drunk bastard fell down and froze to death.

Still, David liked the winter. It was good weather for thinking.

He was sitting at one of the best tables at No Quarter, one of the fanciest restaurants in the East Village. He loved it because it was at the base of the High Line walkway, the old elevated rail tracks that some clever bastard had decided would make a great raised park. Now the area was a wild grasses garden, with plants choking out the ugly disused rail tracks. Couples, kids, old people, half of Lower Manhattan loved strolling there in the summer. For Abrams' money, it was one of the most romantic walks in the city. And he liked the feeling of being lifted, away from the traffic, the crowds. It was a little island floating in the sky, and a good idea that made a tangible difference. Things like that pleased Abrams no end.

It was great when it worked.

It wasn't working with Jacqueline Moltrano. Ever since that kiss with Kate, the contrast was just too great.

Abrams sighed and looked at his Rolex. Jacqui was due here quarter of an hour ago; the girl was always late. Just like she was loud, and brash, and drank too much. But she was also incredibly smart, and fearless; she had a great imagination; she was good in bed, and fun, laughed a lot, always ready to try new stuff. She liked his money and didn't lie about that, which somehow made it OK. She was a real New York broad, Jacqueline, a fireball from Brooklyn. And definitely gorgeous.

He was grateful. It had been a fun few months. But he was using her, and he didn't like himself for that.

Jacqueline Moltrano, that big-breasted, sleek-haired, stylish, brilliant Italian-American, was nothing short of bodacious. Every man in the city could see why he'd be with her. And being with her so publicly meant that nobody – nobody at all – was looking in the other direction.

At his star of the moment, Kate Fox.

David wanted to get over her. She was right, it was insane, the idea of them together. She'd be a serial gold-digger, he'd be a sucker, it was fouling your own doorstep, it was horribly bad for business. So he'd reluctantly gone on the forced date with Jacqui, and then decided she was a lot of fun, the perfect palate cleanser.

Only he was starting to have a horrible feeling that Jacqui was falling in love with him.

Just as he was falling for Kate.

'Baby,' Jacqui said one night, rolling on to her stomach and propping herself up on her elbows, giving him a fabulous view of her sweetly dependent breasts and her firm, tight Italian ass sticking up in the air from the slope of her back. 'Do you think we're doing this right?'

Abrams had lifted his brows. 'What? Sex with you is terrific.'

Her face fell just slightly, and he wondered if that was the most tactful way to put it. It was the truth, though. Sex with Jacqui was wild, messy, liquid, loud and a great way to pass an afternoon or an evening. He didn't feel any further connection, but so what? He liked her, she liked him, and that should really be enough. They had *fun*. He received pleasure from her body, her mouth, her enthusiasm. And he clearly gave it back to her. That was the kind of deal David Abrams could live with.

'Oh sure. Sex is great.' Jacqui sighed with appreciation. 'But I think there's more for us now. It's been kind of a while. Your place here, it's nice . . .'

'Thanks,' he said drily.

'But we could do better, don't you think? There are some great townhouses out there. The Village . . . the Upper East Side, the Upper West . . . I passed one the other day in Murray Hill, for sale by owner. It wasn't that big, maybe three and a half thousand square feet, but they said it had a garden . . .'

A nasty feeling coiled in the base of his stomach, but he kept his face calm and pleasant enough. 'Whoa,' he said, as gently as he could. 'Easy there. You're practically picking out curtains.'

'Not curtains,' she said, making a baby-face pout. 'We'll have blinds. More modern.' She stood up and sashayed over to the bathroom – she'd been using his bathroom since their second date – wiggling her full, pert butt in a way he particularly liked. 'I'm going to start talking to realtors. No commitment, OK? But let's just see what's out there.'

That was the first time in a long time David Abrams had trouble sleeping.

No commitment was OK. Seeing what's out there was not.

Jacqui had different ideas from him. And all of a sudden, this was no longer fun.

A little bit of guilt gnawed at him. It was easy to see that she was enjoying herself, not so easy to admit that clearly she wanted more. Jacqui had been perfect for him, had given him enough sex and pleasure that he could numb his feelings for Kate Fox.

And those feelings had been growing. Even before the push to move in together, he had been struggling with himself. Kate was pretty, but so were lots of girls in this town. More than that, she was fierce. The determination to put right what she'd done in her life, that was something to see. After all, she had turned him down. And furthermore, there were no dates with other rich men. There were no men at all. Kate was a workaholic, kicking ass all over town. Watching her score the big writers, the legendary stylists, watching her come up with the new, exciting cover concepts – all this was sexy as hell to him.

She never stood still. Every fresh issue, the girl did something new. *Lucky* wasn't just hitting the radar; she was making news. It was groundbreaking. Kate had kept the core concept of a counter-cultural champion, but she'd glossed it up, made it a stylish, rich, aspirational marker on the nation's newsstands. *Lucky* was becoming the official bible of America's champagne socialists, and Kate's 'money with a conscience and a Brazilian blow-dry' was the hottest recipe out there.

He dug it. He dug *her*. The kid reminded him of him. Maybe that was the problem. Lusting after Kate Fox, nineteen years younger than he was, perhaps that was just a big case of narcissism. She was . . .

'Sir.' The maître d' showed up to his table, bowing from the waist. 'Your guest is here,' he said, appreciatively.

'Thanks,' Abrams said, wrestling his mind away from his young editor. He got up and kissed Jacqui on the cheek.

She was wearing a fabulous Prada evening dress in peacock-blue silk, teamed with a glittering sequinined clutch from Ferragamo and towering Prada heels in navy velvet. A satin trench coat from Versace, azure blue with buttons of rough chunks of lapis lazuli, completed the million-dollar look. Her dark hair was swept up on the top of her head in an artful up-do, and diamond drop earrings hung from her lobes. Her lips were slicked in some berry-coloured gloss, and her eyes had been made up by a professional; they were spectacular, with neon greens and violets and a bold line of black liquid eyeliner, so Jacqui looked like a dusky Egyptian queen.

It was a look for a goddess, nothing subtle about it. He breathed in. This would make it harder . . .

'You look wonderful,' she purred.

He was in his standard black Armani suit.

'Thank you. Look who's talking, though. You're breathtaking.'

He had to be polite, but he desperately wanted to get off the topic now. Prolonging this could only hurt her.

'Hey, I like to dress my best for my man,' Jacqui said, and tossed her head, sending the diamond droplets sparkling in the light. 'What is this? A special celebration? Did you find a place to buy?'

Abrams twisted. 'Let's order dinner.' He didn't want to be interrupted by a waiter at the crucial moment. Too much potential for a scene. 'I know what I want.'

'Why don't you order for me?' Jacqueline asked. 'I bet you know all the best things here.'

Normally this would have pissed him off. Kate Fox wouldn't have done the helpless fawn act, he knew that much. But tonight he jumped on it like manna from heaven.

'I'd love to do that.' He turned his head, and a waiter came running.

'Yes sir, Mr Abrams?'

Jacqueline almost writhed with pleasure. She loved it when people recognised David. It reflected so well on her. He could see her revelling in the prestige, the status.

'We'll both have the steak frites,' he said. He'd need the red meat just to get through this. 'Medium rare, err on the bloody side. And make sure the fries are crispy. A bottle of sparkling water and a bottle of the Guidalberto 2005. Two side salads.'

'And for your starter, sir?'

'No starter,' Abrams said. He passed the waiter a fifty, subtly, folded in his hand. 'Ask the kitchen to serve us promptly.'

The man glanced down at the money. 'Yes, sir. Absolutely. We will be with you momentarily.'

'I love it,' Jacqueline exulted. 'Baby, you just can't *wait* to get me home, can you?'

God, Abrams thought. Please be quick with the goddamned steak.

He lifted his water glass to her. 'We'll wait for the food before we talk, shall we? Tell me about your day.'

'Oh, I was just at a *Lucky* strategy meeting.' Jacqui smiled. 'Kate came up with another great idea for the March issue cover.'

Now he was interested. 'Yeah?'

'Instead of having the cover stars interview each other, she's going to have them photograph each other. Tom takes pictures of Arnold, Arnold shoots Sarah . . . they all talk about it inside . . . but I'm doing the interviews, so the story will go back to serious profiles.'

'Very good,' David agreed. He liked the idea a lot. 'Tell me more. How will you interview Arnold? What's your angle?'

'The exposés have already been done, and they slid off him. I want to get at what he thinks of all the Republican candidates for President over the last decades. Get to him to rate them all, Pres and Veep nominees. The Arnold Scorecard.'

Abrams grinned. 'That's fantastic. Everybody will buy it. Go on . . .'

'And then the human angle . . . It's always about women, so I thought I'd ask him about his kids. Individually . . . Arnold the dad, the father . . .' She talked about her ideas, fluttering her eyelashes, looking to David for approval.

'Love it,' Abrams said, eventually. He did. This was good stuff from Jacqui, which was why she was a star, why Kate Fox had done so well to hire her. *Lucky* was batting a thousand, and it would continue to do so, apparently. He looked at the sexy woman sitting opposite him, and all he could think of was Kate . . .

'Sir,' the waiter announced.

That fifty bucks had worked wonders. The food was here. He set the plates down before them and fussed about opening the wine, waiting for Abrams to taste it, all the little rituals of service. David raced through them, and the guy got the message, beating a hasty retreat. He finally cut a forkful of steak; it was delicious, good and bloody, and the fries were dry and crisped to perfection.

'This is fabulous,' Jacqui said, taking a minute bite of hers. 'You have the best taste, honey.'

There's no point in dragging this out, Abrams told himself. He had to just do it. Why play dumb, withdraw from her, stop calling? Let the woman figure out she'd been dumped?

'Jacqui,' he began. 'You're a wonderful, beautiful woman, and over the last few months we've had such a great time . . .'

'Oh my God,' she gasped in ecstasy, covering her mouth with her hands. Her voice rose to a girlish squeal. 'Oh David! Oh my God!'

Fuck, he thought, panicking. She thinks I'm going to propose.

The waiters were watching them. They were circling the table like vultures, talking to themselves; great publicity if reclusive David Abrams got engaged in their restaurant.

'No.' He couldn't take it any more, couldn't do it subtly. 'It's not like that. Jacqui, I've had a wonderful time, but it's not going to work out between us. Not long term. We need to break up.'

She breathed in, sharply. Then her eyes narrowed. At least she wasn't asking him to repeat himself, telling him she'd misheard, all those awful verbal games.

'Guess it's too much to hope that you're kidding?' she said.

He shook his head. The worst was over now. He tried to ignore the fire flashing in her brown eyes.

'But that's nuts. We have great sex. We're friends, for God's sakes.'

'And I hope we still will be,' he said hastily. 'I just don't feel anything more. And you want to develop the relationship in ways I don't. It's better we say we had a great time . . .'

'David, stop saying that. The past tense.' Her eyes filled with tears now, and he winced. 'Look, maybe I was going too fast; we don't have to move in together yet.'

'No. We can't set the clock back. I – I just don't have those feelings for you. And I never will.'

'How do you know.' She wiped her tears away, angrily. He was grateful to see the anger. Tears were a woman's keenest weapon, but it would do no good to let her win the battle. She had already lost the war.

'I just know. Long term, I know. My feelings for you are just not at that level. They'd have changed by now if they were ever going to.'

That did it. A deathly silence settled over the table. Jacqui pushed her fries around with her fork. Her pretty features were now hard with rage.

'Is there someone else?' she demanded.

He shook his head. 'No.'

'There has to be, there fucking has to be.' She was almost spitting. 'Why would you give me up otherwise?'

'I haven't cheated on you.' Abrams just wanted to get the hell out now. He hated this part of it, often dated a woman weeks more than he should just to avoid it. Dinners like tonight were why he had switched to the party girls in the first place.

'Maybe not in your body. But in your mind, there's some woman you're thinking of. I know it, I can just tell.'

'I'm not in a relationship with anybody,' he evaded.

'That's not what I asked.' She focused in on his weak spot, his choice of words, as though she had a laser beam. 'Who is she? Who do you like?'

'It doesn't matter.' He shrugged. 'She's not interested, she told me. That's not the point. The point is that you and I aren't suited, Jacqueline, not as lovers, anyway.'

'See?' She made a fierce gesture, and her eyes were glittering with triumph. 'You just admitted it. There is somebody. I deserve to know *who*. You're humiliating me in front of all these people.'

'There's no humiliation. We're having an amicable, civil conversation. Like adults.'

'*Who is she?*' Jacqueline shrieked. 'I want to *know*!'

Now everybody was staring. Abrams saw the maître d' wavering, wondering whether to come over. David Abrams was important, a player, half a celebrity, but they had a full house here. He swallowed hard. Nobody wanted the embarrassment of being thrown out of one of Manhattan's smartest dinner joints. When she calmed down, Jacqueline wouldn't want it either. He had to save her from herself.

'That's enough,' he said, sharply. 'I'm not discussing her with you.'

Jacqui's cheeks burned red with fury. Her dark eyes narrowed to slits.

'I'm not stupid,' she said. 'I know exactly who it is. It's my boss, isn't it? The new wunderkind in magazines. The female version of you, ten years ago. It's Kate Fox, little Miss Perfect. The reformed gold-digger.'

David stared at her. The urge to deny it was strong, but

Jacqui was right, she certainly was not stupid. She had figured him for his obsession with Kate. As careful as he thought he'd been. Kate was such a strong personality, Kate was around all the time, he did business with her . . .

Besides, along with the embarrassment, he was getting angry himself. He'd been straight up with Jacqui all the way. Told her he didn't want a relationship. Now she was making a scene. Why should he deny Kate, lie about Kate? She'd been strong, staying away from him. He thought that had cost her something. Right now he didn't feel like denying her, just to propitiate this bitch who was acting like she owned him.

'Right. But like I told you, she's not interested.' He turned firmly to the waiter. 'Cheque, please.'

'Yes, sir,' the man muttered. Two further waiters whisked away their full plates, and the first was back with the credit card machine in seconds. Jacqueline sat bolt upright in her chair, staring at Abrams, daggers of fury in her eyes.

'I see,' she snapped, as the men fussed around her. 'The little WASP girl from the Bronx? Already proven marriage material. Not interested, right, I bet. I picked up on the thing between you two the first time I spoke to her.'

'You didn't pick up on anything.' Abrams received his receipt back. 'Let me put you in a cab, Jacqueline . . .'

'Oh, she's smart all right,' she said bitterly. 'She's playing the long game with you. Playing at a job until you rescue her ass from the maintenance payments on her apartment. You think she's your mirror image? Forget it. As soon as you propose, it'll be kids and a stay-home mom. What could be smarter than to work for a little while? And the brilliant thing is, she used me as her cover. And so did you. Were you both laughing at me?'

'Nothing went on.' What a fucking nightmare. Abrams stared at Jacqui. 'I asked her out, she said no way, the end. I can't discuss this any more. She's my colleague.'

'And so was I,' Jacqueline added. 'You'll regret this, you son of a bitch. I'll find my own goddamned taxi. Tell your fucking *girlfriend* that I quit. I'm through making her rich.' And she stormed out of the restaurant, shoving past the chairs of other diners as she went.

'Sorry about that,' Abrams murmured. He tipped the maître d' a hundred, waved away the man's condolences, and headed out of the restaurant, scanning the street carefully to make sure Jacqueline Moltrano was nowhere in sight.

She was not. He exhaled, headed across the intersection to the base of the High Line, climbed up the stairs, and joined the anonymous diners walking home. It wasn't crowded like in the summer. He had space to breathe, space to think.

Jacqui was a little crazy, but women went nuts when they were dumped. Maybe he'd messed it up. But there was no good way to do it. He rationalised that at least it was over now; maybe she could go away, heal. No serious harm had been done, right?

Only he wasn't sure. Her anger had been something to see. And Abrams had a sinking feeling about having mentioned Kate Fox. Jacqui was Kate's big-name acquisition, her star writer. Now she'd resigned, quit on the spot. This could get messy, and he'd dumped Kate in it . . .

Whatever. *Lucky* was the brand now, and it was bigger than any one piece of talent. That was something he was sure of. Anyway, in a few weeks Kate would be more to his company than just the editor of one magazine.

Look, dude, he said to himself. Fuck Jacqui, really. You tried to be civilised. You treated her with respect, you didn't cheat on her. There's no obligation to keep going out with a girl you're not into. Hopefully she sees that, but it's honestly not your problem . . .

That sounded good to him, and he smiled slightly, putting Jacqueline Moltrano away in his mind. She was done. Now the question was, what was he going to do about Kate Fox? Promote her – that was already a done deal. But date her?

Date. The word sounded weak, even to him. They had a high-octane connection, he and Kate. That one night, he had never forgotten. How unutterably responsive she was, almost wild in his arms. How it felt to watch her struggle with herself, and lose that battle, and just surrender to passion, total, ecstatic passion. He could handle her with authority, and his slightest touch on her skin caused her to quiver with pleasure, almost to explode.

He was already hard, just thinking about it. He wanted to take the girl, love her, have her. Desire for her had been sublimated by frequent bouts of sex with Jacqui, but it had never been the same thing, right? Which was why he was walking home tonight a single man.

Kate was an addiction. One night with her, and already he was hooked. Man, you are in trouble, he told himself. She's not real. She's just a young girl with a good attitude who looks up to you. It was passion, or lust, or infatuation. You need a mature partner who . . .

It was no good. Kate Fox might not be real, the whole relationship might be the dumb idea she'd assured him it was. Only it didn't actually matter, because his blood was up, and he wanted to have Kate Fox, to put her through her paces in ways she'd never even dreamed of. She was different, different from other women, and Abrams wanted to take it further.

His life had always been that way, he thought, as he picked

his way through the thin stream of walkers on the High Line. The grasses were frosted over, silvery and beautiful against the cold night air. Below him, the city with its taxis and neon billboards lit up the dark sky. It was bitter, freezing, but David Abrams felt nothing but exhilaration. And it wasn't just a matter of freeing himself from a relationship that wasn't working. It was all about Kate, all about his future . . .

Chapter Twenty

Kate turned her key in the lock. There, she was home. Her apartment welcomed her in from the chill of the hallway; low maintenance, they didn't heat the common areas that much against the icy winters in this city. You needed a good imagination in fashion, planning the late spring editions just as winter was hitting its stride, picking out camel coats and cashmere tights in red and green plaids when summer's heat was starting to roll across the city. *Lucky*'s editions were planned months in advance. Kate was thinking about silk tees in mink and dusty rose shades matched with metallic beiges and pale golds, and yet the editorial suites were full of women in merino polonecks in bright jewelled colours, skinny leather pants from Marc Jacobs and Miu Miu, and sky-high ankle boots from Proenza Schouler. She herself was wearing something more comfortable, still stylish, like she had to be every day: beautifully cut chocolate wool pants from Balmain with an Emilio Pucci nutmeg silk blouse, mahogany leather gloves from Lanvin, and a chestnut brown cashmere sweater from Mulberry, along with a Hermès scarf in classic brown and orange that accented her rich palette. Her boots were Gucci, sturdy leather platforms, and they gave a sexy kick to her walk. That was how you stayed warm and chic in the freezing meat locker that was Manhattan.

But she was home now, and didn't need to impress anybody. With a sigh of relief she peeled off her clothes and put them in the dry-cleaning pile. A housekeeper came once a week to dust, change the sheets on the bed, and do the little jobs that Kate had no time for; each week her dry-cleaning miraculously appeared, hung up back in her closet, under the seasonal colour-code structure she had invented. She thought briefly of David Abrams, how simple it was for him to dress in the morning, and then lectured herself. She really didn't need to be using any old excuse to think about the guy.

Once her work clothes were put away, Kate slipped into a comfortable pair of tight black leggings from H&M, her gloriously soft Ugg boots, and a Gap T-shirt. She moved to the fridge; there wasn't much in there, and she couldn't be bothered to go out foraging for food at this time of night. She'd fix herself a smoked salmon sandwich, maybe, have that with a peach and a glass of Pouilly-Fumé. The alcohol might help her to switch off.

Her phone rang. Kate almost jumped out of her skin. Very few people had this number, and even fewer called her late at night.

She grabbed the receiver. 'Yes?' she said.

'It's David Abrams.'

Her heart started to thud. Pathetic, she lectured herself. You have got to get over this.

'Is something the matter?'

He never talked to her one on one. Only with other executives present. And she wished he wouldn't start now. It was too hard, too much of a tease.

'We've got some business to discuss.'

'Can it wait till tomorrow? I'm exhausted. Another long day. Besides, I don't want to talk to you on our own,' she said, and then blushed beetroot. Why the hell had she gone there? Admitted that?

'Sure you do,' he said, easily.

'No, I don't.'

'I broke up with Jacqui Moltrano,' Abrams said. 'And by the way, she quit working for you. That's the message I had to pass on.'

'Why?' Kate managed.

'Oh, she quit because I admitted I was breaking up with her because of how I feel about you. Now, would you like to tell me again how you never want to speak to me alone?'

Kate breathed in, hard.

'You – I – uh . . . I'm sorry,' she muttered.

'No, you're not. And nor am I.'

Kate froze. Her palm holding the phone was dewed with sweat. She wanted to admit everything to David. How often she thought about him, how her body craved him. How watching him work filled her with such admiration, such hero-worship, that sometimes she crawled into a bathroom stall just to touch herself a little.

'We shouldn't do this,' she whispered.

'Kate,' David said, and there was that confident, arrogant amusement in his voice, that mocking tone, teasing her, like he was standing right in front of her, like he could see her down the phone, face flushed, lips parted. 'I want to hear you admit it. You've been thinking about us. Since that night. Like I have. Now be a good girl and tell the truth.'

Desire rushed through her, so intense she felt dizzy.

'Yes,' she muttered.

'And so have I. So how about that? You want to do

301

something about it, finally? You think maybe it was harder to pretend nothing happened than you thought?'

'I just got changed,' Kate said weakly. 'I'm not dressed to go out.'

'Fine. I'll come to you.'

'To discuss business, whatever it is?'

She could almost see his dismissive shrug. 'Business first. That will take five minutes. You say yes or no. Either way, after that we're making love. No excuses, Kate, nowhere for you to hide. I'm coming over there to have you. If you invite me, that's why. I can do business in the boardroom tomorrow, if necessary. With chaperones. Got it?'

She licked her lips. He was merciless, absolutely direct.

'Yes,' she whispered.

'Are you inviting me over? Be explicit, Kate. I'm done with games, and so are you.'

And so she surrendered, and all the pain and fear evaporated, and she took the risk.

'Yes, come over, I want to see you,' she blurted out, and a mixture of joy and fear rose up in her, and she found, to her amazement, that she had tears in her eyes.

'That's good,' Abrams said, and she heard the deep satisfaction, the triumph in his voice. 'That's a good girl. Sit tight. I'll be there in twenty minutes.'

By the time Kate showed him in, she was halfway to being a basket case. Pacing her place, wondering if she should change, make herself up more, do something, slip into a negligee . . .

But there wasn't time. Anyway, she wasn't sure what Abrams' taste was. And the truth was, she was just too nervous to make any decisions. Her stomach was doing somersaults with lust and butterflies, her palms were sweating, her heart was racing . . .

There was barely enough time to drink a glass of iced water in a futile attempt to calm down. And then there he was, at the door, her buzzer was sounding . . .

'Come right up. I'm in 10F.' Kate buzzed him into the building. Oh God! The best she could do was kick off her Uggs. Now she was barefoot, and wearing a tight pair of leggings that left nothing to the imagination.

But what the hell. He had seen it all anyway. Had taken her on her back, her belly, had those legs wrapped tight around him like a wrestler, desperate to suck him in. He had viewed her breasts from every conceivable angle, weighed them, stroked them, kissed them . . . he had luxuriated in every inch of her body, like he owned it, like she was already his . . .

Yes. Abrams was right. Kate had never forgotten it. Tried to, but failed miserably. And now he was on his way up here.

She twisted her fingers. And then the knock on the door.

Kate opened it. He was wearing a dark suit, the same one she'd seen him in, briefly, at the office, hours earlier. Her heart had leapt a little even then.

Now it was out of control.

She glanced down. He had a small case in one hand.

'Washbag,' he said. 'Change of clothes.'

'Right,' she whispered.

This was it. He was prepared, he was staying over. Sleeping here. Adrenaline rocked through her.

Abrams lifted a brow. 'Can I come in?'

'Oh. Sure. Absolutely.' Kate blushed, and stood aside. He moved towards her, shutting the door behind him, dropping his case. Then he opened his arms, folded her in there, deep, pulling her to him, soothing her like she was a skittish horse.

'There,' he said, laying one hand against her pounding heart. 'It's all right now. I'm here. It's going to be all right, Kate.' He kissed her, lightly, just a soft kiss, a promise of more. 'It's going to be great.'

Emotion overwhelmed her. She felt weak with wanting, weak with need. Her knees buckled beneath her, but Abrams' strong arms were there, folding her to him, picking her up. He kissed her again, more purposefully, his tongue probing her mouth, gently, insistently. Kate opened her own mouth to receive him, the sensation of being kissed turning her on so she could barely breathe.

She had just enough strength left to form the thought *My God, I'm falling in love with him . . .*

They kissed, and he held her tight, his arms around her, until gradually she started to calm, and her heart slowed, and the nerves evaporated, and it was just him and her together, with the world spinning round them.

Eventually he let her go from the kiss. She pulled her head back slightly, raising her fingertips to touch her mouth. Wonderingly.

Abrams was looking down at her, and his gaze burned her, and she could not even hold his eyes.

'Look at me.'

She raised her head for a second, then dropped it again. It was as though her desire was written all over her. She just couldn't do it.

'We're going to have a tough time being in a relationship if you can't even look me in the face,' he said.

'I know. I'll try.' She looked right at him, and the colour surged in her cheeks.

'God, you're passionate,' he said, marvelling at her. 'You have no trouble looking my way in the office. None.'

'That's different.' The mention of work steadied her for a second. 'It's just the job.'

He kissed her again, but briefly, on the lips, and ran his hand down to her shoulder blades. 'Let's talk about work,' he said. 'Get that out of the way.'

'OK.' Kate moved to her little kitchen. 'Do you want coffee? Nothing fancy here.'

'I'll send you over some cinnamon coffee,' Abrams said. 'Decaf, maybe. It's late.'

'I can do that.' She busied herself fixing a pot. It gave her a thrill of pleasure to be doing that for him, to be serving him domestically, even in so small a fashion.

'So *Lucky*'s been doing great.'

'It has, hasn't it,' Kate agreed. No point in false modesty; she had been busting her ass.

'You're a natural. But there are two things wrong with this picture from my point of view, and I want to fix them both.'

'OK,' she said, warily.

'Oh, and Kate?' Abrams smiled a little. 'Whether you say yes or no doesn't matter to me. I mean as far as our relationship is concerned. I'm going to start dating you. So there's no right or wrong way to answer.'

'Fine.' She selected two mugs, some sugar.

'*Lucky* is a property that Abrams, Inc. owns fifty per cent of. It's not our biggest seller, probably never will be. You don't occupy the space of *Model* or *Beauty*. But it's making all the noise. My plan's working out; you've attracted attention to my magazine division again.'

'So far, so good.' She handed him his coffee.

'And that's my problem. We only go so far. I want *Lucky*, the whole thing. I want your fifty per cent.'

'Absolutely not.' Kate shook her head fiercely. 'In fact, I've been thinking about going back to the banks, to get the money to make *you* an offer. *Lucky*'s my baby . . .'

'You know what? You want a lesson?'

Kate shrugged, smiling. He was grinning down at her. Once again. David Abrams, publishing legend, legendary son of a bitch. So goddamned arrogant and in her face.

'Sure,' she challenged him. 'Give me a lesson. Make me sell this to you.'

'What, you think I can't?' He folded his arms, pleasure on his face as he looked down at her. Kate could not help herself; a small point of heat started to burn between her legs. He was so certain he could win this. And her stomach churned, because she thought he could as well. But she would not give in to him, make it easy for him. Somewhere in the belly of her, she wanted to defy David Abrams with all she had. Fight him with every ounce of her strength and intelligence. And if he came out on top, then she would have to accept it.

'Yes. I think you can't,' she said.

'Then you should understand that *Lucky* is not your baby. It's not anybody's baby. It's just a magazine – one magazine.'

'My friend Emily's title.'

'She enjoyed it. Loved the job, even. But it was just one magazine. After a while, she'd have seen it. Emily was a social activist at heart, just like you're a magazine girl. She would have moved on to Democratic politics. And you're going to move on to magazines, Kate. Not just one book.'

'Go on,' she said, slowly.

'*Lucky* was the start. If you can transform that magazine,

you owe it to yourself to go for more than just one. We want the title, so it's fully within our stable, the ritzy star of our magazine division. You should supervise a bunch of our other titles. Find out if you understand the modern American print market. I have a fitness title, I have a cookery magazine, I have a homemakers' bible for the older woman. Sales on all three have been plateauing. Even Iris tells me she can't advance her sales on *Model*.'

'That's bullshit,' Kate said immediately. 'It's steady because she's not trying anything new. She's OK with mediocrity. For that matter, so are you.'

He held his hands up. 'So the only question is, are you ready to step up? You own fifty per cent of what's become a hot property. I will buy you out. Your share isn't worth as much to any other buyer, because it's only fifty per cent, but to me, it's a hundred per cent. Selling to me makes you rich.'

'Rich?'

He shrugged, grinning. 'Somewhat rich. Tip money, basically. Richer than you are now, anyway.'

'Tip money,' she repeated.

'Four million dollars. And don't try to negotiate. You're hot, but your sales are still at the upper end of niche. Four mil is a good price. Like I said, anybody else only buys fifty per cent.'

Kate gasped. She was incapable of pretending to be cool. 'Four million dollars?'

'Yes, ma'am. But you sell the magazine, no strings attached. I have total control, editorial and otherwise. And since Abrams will be buying the cool factor in *Lucky*, to boost our magazine division, there will be a watertight non-compete. You don't get to work for any other magazine company or even start your own for a full five years.'

She stopped gasping. 'Now you're getting serious.'

'I don't waste millions, toots.'

'Maybe I like magazines. Maybe I like running *Lucky*.'

'So here's the second part of the offer. You sign the non-compete when you sell me the book. But you do have a new life, a corporate life. Serious stuff. I will make you a senior vice president at Abrams, Inc. That puts you on a level with Iris, and directly under Tim Reynolds. You get a seat on the board.'

Kate's mouth fell open. 'I'm not even thirty years old.'

'Too young? I was chairman of the board before I was thirty. Mostly because I started the company. Your job would be practical; whipping my editors into shape. I want a little of that *Lucky* magic across my divisions.'

'Iris will resign,' Kate warned.

'So let her,' Abrams said at once. 'This is business. I don't carry passengers. My sense is that you can do better.' He took a long sip of his coffee. 'It's a package deal, Ms Fox. Sell me the magazine, sign a non-compete, become a player in my company. The worst that can happen is that you quit and sit on your ass for five years, with only four million dollars for company.'

Kate laughed aloud.

'That's a hell of an offer, David.'

'So the answer's yes?'

She threw her hands up. 'Yes, of course it's yes. Thank you.'

'Don't thank me. It's a great deal, for both of us. I have plans for the magazine division, and you're going to help me get there.' He watched her warming her hands on the coffee. 'You going to finish that?'

'Why?' she asked, nervous again.

'Because we're done with business now, aren't we?'

Kate was almost dazed. 'But it's such a big thing, such a giant step.'

'Yes, and that's how people make it in this world. The bigger the move, the simpler it should be to decide.'

'Is that how you work?'

He nodded. 'I don't second-guess myself. Maybe I get things wrong, but I make decisions fast and then I stick to them. If you try something and it doesn't work out, that's the time to change it. Not dithering around trying to make up your mind whether to test things out. You just took a leap of faith. Now forget about it, and move on to other things.'

'What other things, exactly?'

He looked around the kitchen. 'Have you eaten?'

Kate shook her head. 'I've got no appetite,' she whispered.

'Normally I would argue.' He moved closer, gathered her to him. 'Not today.'

Kate lifted her head. His strong arms around her, pulling her closer, reassuring, just holding her. Her heart had sped up again. She was almost trembling with desire for him now.

'This is different, isn't it?' she asked.

He almost laughed. 'What do you think? I tried, you know. I tried to get over you. Your point was such a good one. Like we weren't suited, and there was the Marcus thing . . .'

She stiffened, but he kissed her again.

'Relax. I'm over it. Nobody's perfect. We expect girls to be perfect, and they're not. You worked amazingly hard, you're your own woman. I know gold-diggers, baby. I know trophy wives. You're neither. If you had been, you'd still be with Marcus now. And God knows, he's richer than me. You *do* know that, right?'

Kate smiled, broadly. To hear him say that was incredible. It was as though he had reached down, and with the strength of his arms, lifted an anvil from her back. Her early life, her mistakes, they were washing away. David Abrams believed in her. So it no longer mattered if every single other man alive did not. He was the world to her. She could no longer fight her feelings, and she didn't want to.

'I don't need anybody. I've got four million dollars,' she joked.

'Like I said, tip money.' He kissed her full on the mouth. 'That can pay for half of our beach house, how about that? This is not about money. It's us.' He paused. 'I can't stop thinking about you. That's all.'

'David . . . God,' she said. 'It means everything . . . you mean everything . . .'

He scooped her up in his arms, lightly, easily, and carried her into the bedroom, Kate weak and unresisting against him. She could barely move. Abrams laid her down gently, peeling the clothes from her, and dropping them on to the floor. He didn't wait long enough to undress himself; clothed, he crouched over her. She gasped, and his smile turned predatory.

'I've waited for you long enough.' He took her wrists, one in each hand, and pinned her to the bed. 'Isn't that right, Kate Fox? Do you admit it?'

She nodded, gasping. 'Yes! Yes, oh, David . . .'

Waves of lust crashed through her. She parted her legs, ready for him, and he lowered himself, kissing her, sucking, stroking, holding her, and then finally he was tearing at his own clothes, and she lifted herself up to him, and when he took her, Kate was so hot, so overwhelmed, she literally could not help herself, and her orgasm started, relentless, beating through her, a vast, sweet wall of pressure, until as she thrashed helpless underneath him it exploded across her, making her dizzy, shrinking her world so there was nothing in it but her and him, plunging into her, calling out her name, until finally it subsided and she was kissing and licking at the strong muscles of his chest, as his grip tightened on her back and he groaned in bliss and erupted inside her.

Chapter Twenty-One

Marcus Broder sat in the back of his limousine. He was still now, still as a statue. The anger at Kate Fox, at this fucking stupid situation, had hardened into stone. Months he had sat there and watched as she made a success of *Lucky*. There was no point in soft-soaping it, she had done very well. If he had an editor like that among his own titles, they would have been promoted by now.

His hand had hesitated on pulling the trigger. Abrams was sometimes seen around town, and he was fucking that Italian piece of ass, Jacqui Moltrano, a real bitch of a journalist, doubtless absolutely fucking great in bed. He got a twitch in his pants just thinking about it. But Lola was better, and you could take her anywhere. Hard to socialise with a chick who might have done a hatchet job on half the guests at any given Hamptons party . . .

Still, Jacqui Moltrano was with Abrams. Kate Fox wasn't. He never saw her in the papers with any man. And she was sticking in her little box. He despised the lack of ambition, of imagination. Maybe it wasn't worth getting in a big corporate fight with David Abrams. Marcus worried it might tip people off that he was concerned, that Kate Fox bothered him in some way.

Marcus Broder didn't worry about any mere *woman*. He forgot them, moved on to fresh meat.

Only Kate had stuck around. Making her own money. Making it hard to forget about her.

Today was the final straw. He scanned the *Journal* again and again, but every time he read it, the story stayed the same.

Lucky for some, the headline read. *Fox moves up at Abrams, Inc.* And then, in smaller print: *Mogul and editor suddenly close allies.*

Nausea churned in the pit of his stomach as he read the horrible innuendo over and over again. At least they couldn't prove anything.

A short while ago, Kate Fox was celebrated as the newest wife of industry titan Marcus Broder. The socialite was never out of the press, her hairstyle and wardrobe the subject of gossip column mentions and paparazzi shots. But after their quickie divorce, Fox discovered a second life as Editor-in-Chief of Lucky magazine. A title she inherited from her roommate Emily Jones, who died in the Metro-North crash near Scarsdale.

Initially burdened with costly production, high debts and inadequate sales, Lucky *looked like a small business that had disastrously miscalculated its growth. Hours from bank foreclosure on their lines of credit, Fox managed to sell a stake to Abrams, Inc. At the time, wagging tongues asked just what her sales pitch was. What is indisputable is the success Fox has made of the offbeat title. With a heady mix of left-wing politics, celebrities and style, almost every edition under her editorship has made state or national news. The growth of the magazine in a flat market has been the sector story of the year . . .*

Marcus snorted. How much did Abrams pay them to run this fluff? It was a goddamned press release, word for word.

Now comes the inevitable second act. Abrams, Inc. announced today its purchase of the remaining half-interest in Lucky, *absorbing the whole property into its small but significant stable of steady performers, for four million dollars. Editor-in-Chief Kate Fox has also signed a cast-iron five-year non-compete covering not just magazines but the entire print industry. Further tying her in to Abrams, Fox leaves day-to-day at* Lucky *to become a senior vice president at the group. She will now supervise* Lucky *and eight other titles, leaving only* Model *and* Beauty *in the direct charge of Iris Haughey. 'We're excited,' says helmer David Abrams. 'Kate will now be bringing that magic touch to other, even more commercial titles in the group. We believe she has a great future ahead of her.'*

That bitch has nothing ahead of her but early retirement, scandal and obscurity, Marcus Broder thought furiously. He was angry at himself for letting it get so far. There was nothing for it now but all-out war. Abrams was going to find out what happened when you refused a polite offer from Broder, Inc. It was time to take the kid to school.

But not everything is rosy in the garden. There are rumblings this evening that long-time doyenne of Abrams' most profitable titles, Iris Haughey, is unhappy at Ms Fox's rapid advancement. Also, Mr Abrams and Jacqueline Moltrano, Lucky's star writer, have ended their romantic relationship. It remains to be seen what this will do to profitability and visibility on the shelves . . .

Broder crumpled the paper in his fists and threw it on to the floor of the limousine. His driver would tidy it up later. He was used to people picking up after him. Only right now, in the corporate jungle, he had to pick up after himself.

'Take me to headquarters,' he said.

David Abrams would not know what hit him.

Kate Fox woke up late.

David had gone. For a second, she felt a slight panic when she glanced at the empty space, the crumpled sheets in the bed beside her. Like all her fears churning in her stomach; like he really was too good to be true, had used her, had run away.

For the last four days they had been locked in together. Having sex, cooking for each other. Talking late into the night. He'd announced Kate's sale of her *Lucky* stake the morning after he first came over, and it had been a delicious feeling in the office, accepting the congratulations of her co-workers at *Lucky*, shaking his hand and sedately referring to her expanded role 'under David Abrams'.

Kate loved the job, and she loved her life right now. And she was head over heels for David. When she woke, his presence in her bed, in her heart, swam into her consciousness like a delicious dream, like she was a child again and every day was Christmas morning. It was maybe the first time she'd been completely happy since Momma died. Kate wasn't used to joy, not pure, clear, clean joy of the heart like this. She couldn't quash her lingering fear that it was too good, that she wasn't meant to be this happy, that it would all come crashing down around her.

And now she'd woken up and David wasn't there to hold

her. He was gone. Nowhere in sight. The familiar voices started to bubble in her head, black fingers of fear trailed round her heart . . .

But then she saw the note, left right there on his pillow, and all the dark feelings vanished like mist under a rising sun. She grabbed it.

Morning.
Thought I'd let you sleep in. Left you something for breakfast.
Don't be late. We've got the board meeting today, to confirm your promotion.
PS It seems I've fallen in love with you.

She clutched the scrap of paper to her heart. Overwhelming feelings rocked through her: love, relief, sheer exhilarating pleasure. She jumped out of bed and raced to the shower, where she washed in barely two minutes, scrubbed her hair with two-in-one shampoo, and was towel-drying it thirty seconds later. Oh God! Half-nine already. She reached for her favourite vintage Versace suit, black wool with the tight skirt, the military jacket and the gold buttons, and added opaque Wolford tights and some structured platform heels from Dior. Her damp hair was attacked with her power dryer and a paddle brush – it wasn't twenty-five minutes at Blow, but it would have to do – and she hurriedly applied her standby Laura Mercier tinted moisturiser and Chanel bronzer, with light, shimmery eyeshadow – a golden rose shade from L'Oréal – and her favourite, daring Rouge Argent silvery pink Chanel lipstick. It was a sun-kissed look, her smooth skin and blond hair framed by the structured precision cut of her all-black outfit, which she teamed with a small, chained black Matthew Williamson satchel bag. Anything more would be too much; Versace buttons demanded subtlety everwhere else in the outfit.

She checked herself out in the mirror. Perfect. She looked years younger than she was. Not sure if that was a good thing, today of all days.

But it was love, it was joy, it was David Abrams. Her career and her love life merging together in one glorious peak. She glowed, and she knew it wasn't just the perfect foundation and well-matched cosmetics, or the spritz of gloss that finished off her home-made blow-dry.

She was happy. Really happy. In a way she had never been before. Not with Marcus, not with any of the rich boys who preceded him. She was in love, completely, totally, head over heels in love with David Abrams. It was a risk, a giant risk, and maybe it wouldn't work out, and her work and her heart and everything were all tied up together and it was a huge mess and it was glorious and oh, God, Kate thought, I love, I love, I love my life!

No time for breakfast. She was late. But she poked her head into the kitchen to see what David had left her.

There on the counter was a toasted bagel with lox and cream cheese, a cup of freshly squeezed orange juice from the deli round the corner, and a cooling Styrofoam cup on which he had written 'Cinnamon' in magic marker.

Kate reached up and dashed away the tears that had formed in her eyes.

No time for that.

She was a major executive, as of this morning. And she was needed for work.

Lola Valdez was dressing very carefully. She had enough time for it – Marcus had barely stuck around this morning long enough for her to go down on him. Last night too he had come to bed distracted and distant. She knew what the problem was, without having to ask. Rumours had floated around the scene yesterday, and Marcus muttered something about it last night.

Kate Fox. A promotion. Senior Vice President at a rival group. When Lola booted up her MacBook Air this morning, light and slim like she kept her body, and headed over to the *Wall Street Journal* she immediately knew what the problem was. Not that Lola cared about the *Journal*. Or business. But it was Marcus's bible. All she had to do was enter the name of her rival, and then she had all the information she needed.

Because Kate, long out of his life, pretty little Kate Fox, the girl with no money, no background – she was Lola's rival. That was clear enough. Marcus had rushed out of Lola's arms this morning, and remarriage, even to such an obviously suitable sexy mommy candidate like Lola, was now the last thing on his mind. What was she going to do about that? was the question of the day.

Increase her efforts.

Kate Fox did not know it, but Lola Valdez had been targeting her for months.

She selected today's choice. A tea dress in royal-blue silk from Robinson Valentine, made bespoke for her in good old London town, along with very old-fashioned matching navy silk stockings, held up at the top by a lacy garter belt from La Perla. This was matched by a Scottish cashmere cardigan with pearl buttons from Mulberry and a thick string of real South Sea pearls, the size of marbles, from Mappin & Webb, punctuated by little balls of eighteen carat gold encrusted with diamonds. She even picked out a tiny brooch from Garrard, the Queen's jewellers, a delicate spray of coral, emeralds and sapphires on an ivory circle. In a second she would call downstairs; Marcus had agreed to hire a full-time beautician, who arrived at the house at half-seven and hung around for Lola to need her. Helen would apply Lola's make-up, subtle being the watchword of the day, and then she'd be ready for her first appointment.

Lola twirled in the mirror. Yes, she looked elegant, maternal chic, the essence of the trophy wife she'd like to become. With her jet-black hair blown out and curled under at the ends, and her exquisite face adorned still further with professional make-up – nothing but the best touched Lola's skin; it was Crème de la Mer slathered even on her feet, La Prairie on her face – she would look simply unbeatable. She would wear a fur coat out and carry a Hermès Birkin bag; she was going the whole goddamned hog. And she thought she would have a sympathetic ally.

She picked up her bedside phone and punched in the number to the staff quarters. It was just like a hotel in this place. You dialled room service, your hairdresser, your chauffeur, whatever the fuck you wanted. That was what real money did for you. And Lola *loved* it. Seriously, fuck all this bullshit, it was time to close the deal. *Mamacita* was in the house.

'Send Helen up, please. Right away. Hair and make-up. Tell her she'll need to move fast. I want a driver standing by as soon as we're done. I have an appointment at the Algonquin, and I don't want to be late.'

As she replaced the receiver, she smiled at her own cleverness. The Algonquin . . . the perfect place to see a writer. Correct?

Before Helen arrived, Lola stepped into her walk-in closet and moved to her safe, the one in which she kept all of

Marcus's little presents. There was the diamond and ruby cocktail ring, the solid gold cuff set with bezels of pink sapphires and conch pearls, the aquamarine and moonstone necklace, the tremendous, important drop earrings of pigeon's blood rubies the size of pebbles in 24-carat gold. Most were from Cartier or House Massot; put them all together and she had two years' living expenses, at least. But Lola was holding out for the simple small ring from Tiffany's she'd said she wanted. Nothing flashy, just an internally flawless round brilliant set in platinum, at oooh, four or five carats, cut to perfection, nothing there but the firework blazing on her hand.

And there, under all her current baubles, was the file that was going to get it for her. The work of four or five of the city's highest-end private detectives. She pulled out the thin manila frame and went through it. Pictures . . . emails, two burned DVD discs with CCTV footage from a nightclub and a restaurant. All the fabulous, trashy half-prostitution of Ms Kate Fox's previous life.

Lola sighed for a second. If only there had been something more. Just a little more . . . a stint as a high-class hooker, a drunken sex act in an alley, some footage of Kate Fox stripping off at college, anything really. Sadly, the girl had apparently avoided men altogether after dumping Marcus. She had made the move. Fool. Giving up this for what, for a job? A stupid *job*? And during all that time, Kate Fox had seen no other men . . .

Until a few nights back.

Lola stared lovingly at the newest photos in her collection. David Abrams at Kate Fox's building. Kate at his. In at night, out in the morning. And finally the pure gold . . . Kate in Abrams' arms, half bent back, on the street on West Eleventh, her arms snaked around his overcoat, oblivious to the cold in an utterly passionate kiss.

It was a stirring picture. Lola had felt a treacherous warmth in her own belly as she studied it. But she thrust that thought away from her now. This picture was the gold, this was the one that would bury Kate Fox, bury David Abrams with her. And finally pull Marcus Broder into Lola's grateful arms. Because this picture was going to activate Lola's secret weapon. It had all come together at exactly the right time. Lola congratulated herself; the earlier pictures had arrived beforehand, but it was a weak story then, and she'd kept digging, let it season. They knew how to do revenge in Colombia, she congratulated herself. It was in the blood.

There was a knock on the bedroom door. Helen Coachella was there to take care of Lola's hair and make-up.

'Come on in,' Lola said graciously. She wanted the staff to speak well of her. She tipped generously, picked her own clothes up from the floor, sometimes. When you were aiming for the brass ring – or the platinum one – you did not allow any little things to stop you. Even servants.

Time to get ready. Time to go.

'I can't believe it,' Jacqueline Moltrano said.

Lola nodded sympathetically. 'I'm afraid it's true. She's not a good woman, Ms Moltrano. Really, she's bad news.'

She looked at Jacqui with satisfaction. The girl dressed well, for a poor woman. Maybe a little slutty, a little like Lola had dressed before she smartened up. Today she was in Zac Posen, a fantastic wool dress in a ballsy shade of emerald, with dove-grey tights and Louboutin snake heels. She also had a sexy, swinging Roland Mouret cape laid over the arm of her polished wooden chair.

'This is a betrayal.' The colour was high in Jacqueline's dark Italian cheeks. Her chestnut eyes had narrowed with rage. 'She *knows* how I feel. I told her about him. I poured my heart out to her!'

'I'm sorry,' said Lola. She wasn't. 'It's really too bad. Anyway, I thought you'd want to know.'

Jacqueline wasn't listening. 'And Abrams . . . that son of a bitch. He told me Kate wasn't interested in him, that she had turned him down flat. Were they sitting there together, laughing at me? Plotting how to make me look like a total fool?'

Lola held her tongue. It was better if the girl figured it out herself. Lola understood that Jacqueline, like Kate, was far more intelligent than she herself was. But smart people could act dumb, lots of times. She didn't have to be the genius here. Just understand what Jacqueline was, and use her.

'What's your interest in this?' the girl demanded.

Lola was ready. Of course she'd ask this question. And she knew better than to lie.

'She used to be married to Marcus. And she's embarrassing him. He tends to get . . . worked up. I feel he can move on better once Ms Fox is out of the way.'

'Move on, as in marry you.'

Lola didn't flinch. 'That'll be up to Marcus. I'm certainly in love with him.'

'Uh-huh. Sure you are.' Jacqueline's tone was full of cynicism. *Stuck-up bitch*, Lola thought, but she smiled sweetly because she needed her. 'And you knew enough to bring this to me.'

'Marcus reads a lot about the magazine sector lately. I saw you'd quit at *Lucky* after you broke up with David.'

Jacqueline nodded. She took a sip of her tea; they had

ordered tea and cakes, although it didn't quite fit, and Lola suspected Jacqui was more a dirty martini sort of girl. She herself would kill for a shot of tequila, but it didn't go with the mom-to-be image, so she gritted her teeth and tried to enjoy the Earl Grey.

'I wasn't going to fucking work for him. Making him rich. Richer,' Jacqui acknowledged bitterly. 'Or *her*. After he said he was thinking about her. I mean, she's kind of pretty. She's OK. Nothing sensual about her, you know?'

Lola nodded fervently. As a Latina, she empathised with the gorgeous dark beauty of Jacqueline Moltrano. The boring blond housewife look of Kate Fox – what was it men saw in that? Did she even know how to give head properly? Lola doubted it.

'She got *four million dollars* for the other half of *Lucky*,' Jacqueline snapped. 'That money was made on the back of *my* cover stories, *my* concepts.'

The writer had only been one ingredient in the cocktail, Lola thought, but didn't say. Instead she nodded, sympathetically.

'Who exposed the crooked pol and put him posing on the cover? That would be me,' Jacqueline said. 'And yet it's fucking Miss Kate who gets the four million. Her *own money*.'

Lola nodded again, this time sincerely. 'Yes,' she hissed.

That was the part that could not be put right. Kate Fox now had millions of dollars of her own fucking cash. Job money, career money. Even if David dropped her like a stone, she had earned something of her own. And although it was chump change in the world of rich husbands – four million a year was nothing; you could barely get a half-decent apartment in Manhattan for that – it was hers, and it was something. If she managed it carefully, Lola thought outraged, she could probably live well here for fifteen years.

What a nightmare. Even more important, then, that Jacqui Moltrano give her *lots* of incentive to get out of Dodge.

'Nobody knows that David Abrams is with her,' Lola said. 'At least, not yet. This deal is the news of the day. Looks like there might be a, what do you say, conflict of interest.'

'Yeah,' Jacqui said, thoughtfully. 'What else do you have?'

'Oh, the standard,' Lola answered. She passed across her file. There were photocopies of everything at home. 'These are shots of her from before Marcus married her. You see, there she is with Lucius Cohen. And Josh Bernstein. And Paul Grazio. You follow me?'

Jacqui nodded wordlessly. It was easy to see. Both girls had been there before.

'There's a pattern,' Lola said piously. 'I mean, many women work very hard.' *Suckers.* 'They don't need to be competing with a girl who—'

'Save it.' Jacqueline laid one manicured hand over her co-conspirator's. 'For the headline.'

'Then you'll run with it?' Lola asked, feeling the relief and triumph boil up in her. This was like a race, like the Olympics. And she had just successfully passed the baton.

'Oh yeah.' Jacqui took the folder, put it in her glossy chestnut leather Coach briefcase. 'I'll run with it all right. It'll be my little Valentine to Mr Abrams. And his board.'

Chapter Twenty-Two

'Ms Fox, good morning.'

The receptionist gave her a neutral smile. It was like she couldn't keep up the normal edge of hostility, Kate thought. The girl sat there in her simple Jil Sander shift and her freshwater pearl necklace and looked at Kate, approximately her own age, but on her way to the boardroom.

As of right.

'Mr Abrams told me this is your first time at a board meeting?'

Kate nodded. Tried to look calm about it.

'They normally arrive about quarter to. The agenda will be laid out on the table. You're welcome to go in there now. Somebody will bring you a water, if you want one,' she added, as though that would be a terrible imposition.

'Actually, I think I'll have a coffee,' Kate said. She'd decided she wasn't in the mood to be pushed around by secretaries and assistants any more. David Abrams had made her his senior VP and she was going to act like it. 'Mr Abrams keeps cinnamon coffee here. He's recommended it to me. I'll have one of those, black, two sugars. And if they have pastries in the kitchen, a croissant, too.' She didn't want her stomach rumbling. 'As quickly as possible, please; better to have finished it before the meeting starts.'

And she smiled firmly at the astonished girl and moved into the boardroom.

It was next to David's office. She'd been here before, of course, but only as a guest, to explain herself when they were taking stock of whatever outrageous concept she was doing for the cover, or when the corporate legal counsel wanted to hear about Jacqui Moltrano's latest no-holds-barred exposé, as the career of some politician or CEO came crashing down about his ears.

There were the same floor-to-ceiling windows, a small desk in one corner with a chair and computer terminal, and nothing else but a long, lean table in solid mahogany, surrounded by sleek, ergonomically designed chairs in dark green leather. Not that they were needed; meetings didn't usually last too long in David's company, she knew that. He got the information, made the decisions, and that was it.

It was a vast, spare room, all the focus drawn to the views of Times Square below them. It buzzed with money, with power. This was David, this was his company. It all belonged to him. Right now, at the peak of her career, Kate was still only a small cog in the giant wheel of his fortune.

She felt a charge of arousal race through her. Her body tingled, her nipples tightened. She was glad of the slight padding of her bra, the thickness of her jacket. The echoes of what David had done to her last night were still sounding in her body. She wanted him so badly. She wished she had a fast-forward button to the end of the day, so they could be in each other's arms again, naked and comfortable . . .

Not now, Kate, she lectured herself.

The door opened as she sat down in one of the mahogany chairs, towards the end of the table, and a secretary entered, bearing a little tray with her coffee and a croissant. She set it down resentfully in front of Kate.

'Thank you,' Kate said, with a brisk smile. She was past caring. It felt like a victory. Her space filled with the warm, rich scent of cinnamon – of course David had the best. And it reminded her of him. As she tore up the croissant, and ate it quickly, she felt her stomach settle, her nerves calm. No point being ravenous at her first board meeting . . .

'Good morning.' A tall, thickset man was striding into the room. Kate jumped up; she recognised him, red hair, fifty.

'Mr Redson? Good to see you.'

Kate offered her hand, and he shook it, smiling slightly that she had known his name.

'It's Donal. Congratulations,' he said.

The door opened again, and two more men entered.

'Mr Clayton, Justice Rodgers,' she said. 'How do you do? I'm Kate Fox.'

The renowned economist and the retired judge looked her up and down. There were no bouquets here; they weren't exactly throwing her a tickertape parade, Kate thought to herself. But neither was there any overt hostility.

'How are you, Ms Fox?' The judge asked, in a voice that rasped with whiskey and cigarettes.

The economist nodded, and shook her hand. Kate felt her stomach twist slightly; the butterflies were flittering away. And then the door opened again, and there he was. David. In a dark suit, looking absolutely gorgeous, his close-cropped salt-and-pepper hair and thick black eye-lashes picked out by his clothes. He smiled slightly at her, acknowledging her, and the briefest of looks passed between them.

'Welcome, Kate,' he said. 'You know Tim, Iris and Rick, don't you?'

'Absolutely. Of course.' She nodded at Tim Reynolds, the company number two; his smile was level, as was Rick Johnson's. Iris Haughey said 'Hello,' in a voice that could have frozen alcohol. She was wearing battle armour, too: a Chanel suit in classic eighties red and gold, with neutral Wolford tights and a pair of towering Manolo pumps. A Kate Spade clutch hung off the edge of one shoulder. She was pulling a pair of cream lambskin gloves, lined with cashmere, from her hands. Kate noticed the tiny Fendi logo; Iris Haughey was clearly a lady who rode first class.

Everybody sat down. Donal Redson placed himself next to Kate. Very deliberately, Iris Haughey sat opposite her.

'If we could come to order. The first item on the agenda today is the purchase of *Lucky* magazine and the attendant promotion of Kate Fox to this board. I'd like a resolution passed affirming my decision as Chief Executive,' David said. Not looking at Kate, he explained his thinking to the board. He was short, decisive. She thrilled to hear it. God, but it was a turn-on. David Abrams was something else . . .

'That's where we are,' he finished. 'Questions?'

'Four million seems like a lot of money,' Tim Reynolds griped. 'For a new title.'

'The way it's torn up the market? We need it to be an Abrams thing.'

'I don't have a problem with you buying the title,' Iris said. '*Lucky* has done well. Of course, it remains a niche player. I certainly object to Kate Fox becoming a senior vice-president of the company.'

She crossed her arms and glared at Kate across the table.

Adrenaline shot through Kate, prickling against her palms, but she said nothing.

'On what grounds?' David asked. 'You didn't raise this at the last meeting.'

'I said I wasn't happy.'

'But nothing that would rise to the level of a formal objection,' he replied. 'What has changed?'

'You actually went ahead with the silly bloody idea. I thought you'd at least consult us first.' Iris gestured dismissively. 'Kate has edited *one* magazine where the mix was already in place when she stepped in. It could be luck, it could be Jacqueline Moltrano's stories . . .'

'I hired Jacqueline,' Kate said.

'And she resigned,' Iris spat back. 'There was a six-month break clause, wasn't there? So Abrams' new property has just lost its star writer. *Lucky* will have to compete against her new employers, whoever they are. I hear Fleur D'Amato has come back with a *much* fatter offer.'

Kate glanced at David, but his face was impassive.

'That was Jacqueline's personal decision,' she said. '*Lucky* has much more to offer.'

'I wonder,' Iris said acidly. 'It's not proven, like *Model* or *Beauty* – my titles – which are steady *long-term* performers. It's insane to make you a senior VP. You are not on the level of me or Rick.'

Rick Johnson nodded, then caught sight of David Abrams' face.

'She is a bit young . . . untested,' he added nervously. 'But if you think best . . .'

'So I have my two senior VPs objecting,' David said quietly. 'And without notice. Tim?'

Tim Reynolds glanced from face to face. 'I think we should hear the rest of the board.'

Kate looked at David. His face had settled, in a way she had never seen before. It was like granite. Under all the excitement and sexuality, she now felt a shiver of fear.

'Certainly,' David said. 'Justice Rodgers?'

The old man looked over at Kate. 'Iris, you've been flatlining,' he said bluntly. 'This company needs new blood. She's it. I vote aye.'

'That simple?' Iris snapped.

He shrugged. 'Most things are.'

Donal Redson nodded. 'Me too. Furthermore, I think Abrams, Inc. is lucky to have picked up the hottest thing in the industry. It's a good deal. And I'm not particularly thrilled by the ambush thing today.'

Mike Clayton, the economist, shrugged. 'I think Kate Fox is a highly talented editor, but Iris has a point that she's untested. I trust your judgement, David, so I won't vote against – but I'm going to abstain.'

'Interesting,' Tim Reynolds said. He looked at Kate, and she saw the shutters come down in his eyes. 'It seems your appointment – would-be appointment – is getting mixed reviews, David. As your chief financial officer and second in command, I think I've got a duty to listen to more seasoned heads. I'm going to vote against. Kate, your promotion will have to wait until another day.'

Kate stared from face to face. Iris's eyes were bright with triumph. Even Rick Johnson seemed smug and contented. And Tim Reynolds was looking at her calmly, clinically, as though she were something in his way, something that had to be removed . . .

That was three votes. Against two. Humiliation boiled up

in Kate. She was a rich woman now, but one on a non-compete clause, one without a career, without a passion. The announcement had been made to the press already. She would be a laughing stock by lunchtime. And it was shaming to David too, she realised, that his lieutenants were voting him down, challenging him. He'd brought it up before, and nobody had threatened this – that was clear. But at the crunch, they were voting no, telling him no, and she was done . . .

'Just one second.' David Abrams held up a hand. His voice was calm. Terrifyingly so. Kate drank it in, his attitude, the way he leaned back in his chair, not forwards, like he was completely relaxed. But his spine was very straight, and she sensed that predatory side to him, that hunter, and shivers of pleasure, of desire, ran all over her skin.

She suddenly knew he was going to get her out of this. That he was going to *protect* her.

'I also have a vote.'

'It's traditional for the chairman not to vote on these occasions, David,' Tim said quickly. 'When the will of the board is clear.'

'But I've never been a traditional guy,' David Abrams said. 'Been a liberal since college. When I founded *Model*, Iris. *I* did. Not you. You run my magazine. Maybe you forgot that.'

'We're not in college now, David.' Tim attempted a brisk smile.

'No. We're in the boardroom. Of my company. And I am a member of that board. I can vote. I vote aye. Which makes it three-three. And as chairman, I have the deciding vote on a tiebreak. Aye again.' Finally he looked down the table at Kate. 'Welcome to the board, Kate. We're glad to have you.'

'Speak for yourself,' Iris Haughey shouted. 'If you do this stupid thing, David, it will totally humiliate me.'

'We've voted. That's the end of it,' David said.

'Then you can have my resignation,' Iris replied. 'I suppose you'll want me to work out my six months' notice?'

Kate stifled a gasp. Iris Haughey had been at Abrams for ever. She was a legend in the business. She looked miserably at David, sure she was the cause of all this trouble.

'Not a bit of it,' David said easily. 'I accept your resignation, which saves me the trouble of firing you. Kate, congratulations. You are now Editor-in-Chief of *Model* and *Beauty*.'

She looked across the boardroom table at the man she loved, who was so calm for her, so cool under fire, and she wanted to rise to the challenge. To be everything he'd seen in her. Outside the bedroom, as well as in it.

'Thank you, David,' she said. 'I look forward to it. I think there are a number of changes we can make in style and content that should boost sales right out of the box. There's been a lack of imagination, and fashion doesn't stand still.' She stared coolly at Iris. 'Should Ms Haughey still be here? After all, she has resigned.'

Next to her, Donal Redson breathed in sharply, but a slight smile creased his features.

'Absolutely right,' David said. 'It's been nice working with you, Iris. We wish you the best in your future endeavours. Goodbye now.'

He leaned back as Iris gathered her papers together in front of her.

'You don't need those,' David said. 'They're Abrams property. Just leave, if you would, and hand your pass in at the front desk. An assistant will box up your personal items and they will be biked to your apartment within the hour.'

'You can't do this to me!' Iris shouted. 'I have the right to work my notice!'

'I suggest you check your employment contract again.' David's voice was absolutely inflexible. Kate could hardly bear to watch, but her eyes were fixed on him, and she could not tear them away. 'Iris, if you are not out of that chair and out of the door within the next thirty seconds, I will call security to have you removed.'

'You are a goddamned son of a bitch, you know that,' Iris spat. She got to her feet and looked right at Kate. 'And you are a gold-digging whore. And if the whole world doesn't know that yet, don't worry. They soon will.'

She turned on her heel and stormed from the room.

The boardroom sat, frozen. But Kate kept her eyes on David. He was not in the slightest disturbed. He was calm, cool.

'Tim,' he said.

The male heads in the room lifted at once. Scenting a problem. Scenting danger.

'Have you anything you would like to tell us?'

Tim Reynolds leaned back in his own chair, aping the boss's movements. Clearly, he was not about to be such an easy win as Iris.

'Not particularly. Your decision is clear, David. I can accept that.'

'It's intriguing to me that you raised your objection without prior notice.'

'I'd had time to think about it,' Tim said easily. 'This board meeting seemed the appropriate juncture.'

'Was it appropriate to discuss this with Marcus Broder?'

The blood drained from Tim Reynolds' face.

'I haven't,' he said.

Kate struggled to remain calm. David Abrams reached into the folder before him and withdrew two sheets of paper.

'These are the call logs to your office. I had them delivered to me this morning, about ten minutes before this meeting started.' He passed them around the table to his left, starting with the judge, who glanced over them and passed them on. Kate received them in turn. Broder's calls had been highlighted in yellow marker. Wordlessly she offered them to Reynolds. He refused to take the pages; they sat on the table in front of him, a splash of white on the dark wood, accusing him.

'As you know, gentlemen – Kate – Marcus Broder made us an offer for our share in *Lucky* magazine. We turned him down. A few days ago it came to my attention that Broder, Inc. may be mobilising to buy the public stake in our company. I own only forty per cent. It is technically possible that he could take Abrams over.' David smiled thinly. 'I therefore rather object to my CFO speaking to Broder's office about my board decisions.'

Tim Reynolds looked from face to face. They were hard against him.

'It's not that,' he blustered. 'I was warning him off. I saw no reason to bother you with those conversations, David . . .'

'You've worked for me for fifteen years,' Abrams said, as though he hadn't spoken. 'And you do this because I make one decision you don't like?'

'I'm telling you, it was nothing to do with—'

'Tim. Please.' David smiled thinly. 'You know those messages companies have when you call the switchboard? Your call may be recorded for quality assurance purposes?'

Reynolds paled.

'That's right. We have one of those. As you know, or maybe had forgotten.'

Abrams reached to the phone in front of him, punched the speaker button, and tapped in a few numbers.

'Call station 02. Timothy Reynolds,' said a soothing computerised voice. 'Call log Thursday, second September. Three forty-two p.m.'

'First step is to get her off the board,' Reynolds was saying. 'He won't expect that at all.'

'Good.' Kate jumped. It was Marcus; such a long time since she had heard his voice. 'She's an extra vote for him that I just don't need.'

'David never gets crossed. It's still his company. That will shake him. Next I corral the rest of the board into accepting your offer. And after that it's with the Securities and Exchange Commission when you announce the five per cent stake . . .'

'I'll take care of that side of things,' Marcus said smoothly, patronisingly. 'You just deliver the board. And Kate Fox.'

The call clicked silent. Tim Reynolds sat there, in the boardroom, his face now an ashen grey.

'In the interests of company decorum, I expect you to resign very quietly. Long career, time to step down. That sort of thing,' Abrams said. 'You are also tied to your non-compete clause. The slightest attempt to enter business again, in any company, and that tape goes to the regulators. And the DA. As do all the other tapes, of which I have hours.'

'David, you can't deny me the chance to work elsewhere,' Tim Reynolds gabbled. 'I've got two kids in college. A mortgage . . . the summer house is—'

'Part of your past,' David Abrams said. Kate could not tear her eyes from him. He was as cold as a snake, and just as focused. The immense rage she sensed pouring from him was all the more terrifying because of how still he was, how physically calm and relaxed he seemed. 'Let's hope you built up some assets, Tim. I think it might have slipped your mind how much it costs to live in New York. When you fly first class on my company's dime and dine at Le Gavroche and Inn on the Park, you tend to forget about the little stuff. After fifteen years working for me, you shouldn't even have a mortgage. But those Savile Row suits and the Armani shirts don't come cheap, do they? Or that Breitling watch.' He chuckled. 'Expensive tastes have to be paid for. And Nancy's stint at Harvard Law . . . costs a lot. As will Janey at Vassar. Presumably you put something away. Not that I give a shit. All that's your problem now.'

Reynolds stood. 'Those are my shares. And the board's. Yes, I was happy to talk to Marcus Broder. You are making a fool of yourself and this company.'

'Oh, really,' David said.

'It's her.' Tim Reynolds pointed viciously at Kate. 'That fucking girl. One magazine and you've become obsessed. She must be a hell of a lay, that's all I can say, David.'

Abrams slammed his hands on the table, so hard the papers and coffee cups shifted on the wood. 'Get out. Before I throw you out.'

'You gave up Iris Haughey. You neglected a valid offer from Marcus Broder. That could have made us all a lot of money. An overpriced offer . . . you wouldn't even talk to him.' His eyes red now with suppressed tears, his voice high in pitch, half hysterical, he turned to Kate. 'Seriously, honey, you must be one *magna cum laude* piece of ass. Within five years you've fried the brains on both Broder and David Abrams. How much do you charge? Because I might want a pop myself . . .'

Abrams got to his feet, strode around the table, and picked Tim Reynolds up by his lapels. 'Don't touch me! Don't touch . . .' Reynolds shrieked, but Abrams' thick arm went back, and he punched Reynolds hard, viciously, once in the solar plexus. The other man crumpled over, winded, gasping, tears springing from his eyes, unable to talk.

'David . . .' Kate said, timidly. 'Should I . . .'

'Leave? No. You stay right there. We have a meeting to get through.'

She nodded.

'I'll sue you,' Reynolds was gasping. 'I'll sue you, you fucking bastard . . .'

'Why don't you try that?' David Abrams agreed equably. 'This entire meeting has been recorded too. Then we can also release the tape of your comments to Kate to the press, and the whole of New York can see you as woman-hating scum who can't fight like a man and prefers to run crying to the cops. We can add that to the convictions I will undoubtedly secure for fraud. Believe me, I can take a rap on the knuckles for punching out a piece of shit like you. The pleasure was cheap at the price.'

Reynolds struggled for air and groaned.

'Be a man. Get to your feet, leave the room. Or security will assist you from the building. And not like they would have assisted Iris. You have till the count of ten. One . . . two . . .'

Groaning, whimpering, Reynolds stood. He seemed to shrink back, away from Abrams, who had not moved out of his space.

'No! I'm going.' Reynolds stumbled towards the door. 'You were always this way, David. I don't know why this is a surprise to you. You should think about the things people say behind your back. That you're selfish, that you're a driven son of a bitch, a real cocksucker. Months ago you were going to dump the fucking magazine division . . . You have no plan, no thought. This isn't a big company, and with you in charge it will never be. You don't listen to me. You don't listen to anyone . . . We're all just ballast to you, just your lieutenants, just your fucking *staff* . . . It's really all about you, the great and powerful David fucking Abrams.'

'When I was twenty years old, I started a magazine,' Abrams said quietly. 'When you were twenty years old, you were in lecture class, taking notes. When I was twenty-one, I hired my first employee. Lorna Williams. She was my secretary. I gave her stock, because she took the job at a reduced rate to help me out. She retired six years ago and she's worth three times what you are. That's because at twenty-one you were somebody's employee on a top graduate salary. You know what, Tim? That's America for you. Those who take the risks get the rewards.' He smiled coolly. 'That's because risk comes with a downside. You just took a risk. Broke the habit of a lifetime. Unfortunately for you, you lost. Get out.'

Reynolds, red faced, had reached the door. 'You haven't heard the last of me,' he said.

'Oh yes I have. Everybody's heard the last of you.'

The door swung open, and two burly security guards in the company's colours were standing there waiting.

'No need to touch him,' Abrams said. 'Just see that Mr Reynolds doesn't get lost on his way out.'

'Yes, sir,' one of them said. Reynolds took one anguished look back at David, but the second guard closed the door in his face.

'Man.' Judge Rodgers was the first to speak. 'That's better than TV, David. Got to hand it to you, you know how to put on a show.'

Abrams returned to his place and exhaled. For a second, Kate looked at him, agonised. She desperately wanted to rise, to go to him, to touch him. But this was business, and she knew she could not comfort him now. He would have to deal with it, all of it.

His career, his company, he had poured his life into it. And now it was shaking. Because of her.

So she reached out to him the only way she knew how.

'Justice Rodgers, Donal, Clayton. I think this represents an opportunity.'

The remaining faces at the table turned towards Kate. She stiffened her spine, and whatever turmoil she felt in her heart, she sat on it. Now was not the time. She wanted to show David Abrams that she could be worth it.

I want to show myself.

'There are names we can secure for the women's titles. And I'd like to commission big new covers for the next issues. Whatever's in place, we junk. I will edit those myself. With the deputies. A new look, across the board. We announce we mean business. *Model* and *Beauty* are crying out for it. What you want here is a news story.'

'This can't be about whatever you did at *Lucky*.' Donal Redson spoke up. 'I'm here for business, not for magazines, but I do understand you don't take all that left-wing stuff and drop it into a beauty mag. Unless we want sales to fall through the floor.'

'That's not what I propose.' Kate felt her heart rate slowing. In fact, she was comfortable, she realised, calm, cool in doing her job, her actual job. Because she was good. Better than good. She was a natural editor. And David Abrams had just handed her her shot at the big time.

She loved him for it.

And she was going to deliver.

'We stick to the essence. That's what I did at *Lucky*. It was doing OK when Emily first brought me in. I just took the soul of the magazine and expressed it in a way that would sell. So let's take *Model*. How do we make it the story? What gets it out from under *Vogue* and *InStyle*? It sits in the centre because it can't really compete, it's got nothing new to say. Where's the niche?'

'You tell me,' David said, and now the anger was gone from him, and a wide smile was playing on his face, a genuine smile, one that reached his eyes.

'It'll take me more than one new cover to figure that out. For now, we want to start with a big story. That means PR. And a way to do that is to go with size. Lots of talk shows, lots of daytime TV coverage when *Elle* ran a photo shoot with a plus-size model. Talking about America, anorexia. Let's go one better.' The idea seized her, and her words tumbled forward, passionate and excited. 'I want to put a size fourteen girl on the cover. Sixteen, if she's a Brit; their sizes go larger. She should be naked. We'll pose her like Eve. Fig leaves on her breasts, her groin. Or maybe like Venus on her shell, if we get a long-haired chick. Call it "The Real American Woman". That's your strapline. Right on the cover.' They stared at her, mesmerised.

'Oh, and one thing more.' Kate smiled; she was on a roll. 'The cover photo shouldn't be airbrushed.' That would be a first – a cover that was untouched. 'And then, all through the mag, we keep up the theme. Zero airbrushing in the editorials. The aim is to show girls how the beauty industry tricks them, makes them aspire to a level they can never reach. *Because it's not real.* We run features on teens and eating disorders. A tell-all from models addicted to coke to stay thin. What it's like to live on a regime of Diet Coke and cigarettes.'

'The Real American Woman.' Abrams grinned. 'I can see that on *Regis and Kelly*.'

'Better. You'll see it on *Oprah*,' Kate said. She was confident now, enthused. 'The coverage will be huge.'

'Great. Go do it. And the other stuff? Our style magazines?'

'Can't go for the big news angle there, but I'm going to lead with something that'll grab the consumer. Money. "Your new room for a hundred dollars – style on a shoestring".' She gestured, sketching in the air. 'Dramatic before and afters. And some kind of new feature: "Personal Shopper". Every month, we line up a celebrity, give them a budget, have the celebrity make over one room in a reader's house. Angelina Jolie takes a grand and gives Eileen Woods from Alabama a new kitchen. They'll absolutely go for it.'

The men nodded. A couple of them sat upright. Kate felt power, all of a sudden, felt her own talent, her competence, as though she deserved to be here, as though David Abrams had done a good job when he picked her out.

It was heady.

'Let's run through the other items,' David said. He wound up the meeting, and they were through.

Kate stood, feeling awkward. She came around the table, shook hands with the men there, accepted congratulations. And finally was face to face with David.

Lust curled in her belly like smoke.

He looked down at her. His face was neutral, calm, but his eyes crackled fire.

'Congratulations,' he said, shaking her hand. 'Send me a memo this afternoon on the new titles. And don't talk to the press.'

She nodded. 'You got it.'

Even the slightest touch of his hand on hers and she was slick between the legs, her body opening towards him like a flower towards the sun. But she couldn't let them see, couldn't let the other board members know. She had to prove herself first.

'Catch you later,' she said lightly.

Her new office was one floor below his. At least there was some respite; she didn't have to see David every minute, Kate thought, as she stepped out of the elevator.

'This way.' An elegant receptionist whose name tag said *Meeta* was leading her through a series of open-plan offices. Writers were running around, racks of clothes being wheeled in and out. There was a lot of loud talking, assistants running around, photographs being shared. On her right-hand side, through walls of faintly tinted glass, she saw the offices of *Model* and *Beauty*; on her left, there was *House Style* and three of their other, smaller magazines: *Soundcheck*, the music glossy, and *Gamer Heaven*, the computer games title, bumped up with *Modern Traveller*.

The hubbub quieted a bit as Kate moved through. She could see their conversations stopping, see the reactions as she arrived.

'This will be your office, Ms Fox.' Meeta opened a door at the end of the corridor.

Kate gasped. 'You're kidding me.'

It wasn't as grand as David's, but almost. The same floor-to-ceiling windows; huge, blow-up covers of the women's titles; a black and white photo study of models in a changing room; large tiles of polished black granite, angular snow-white couches and a back-lit smoked-glass coffee table. The desk was carved of solid ebony, and topped with a huge computer monitor, with an ergonomic chair in the back. To the side, Kate glanced through an open door at a full bathroom; she could see a stand-alone shower and a vanity top with a mirror, covered in lights.

'Iris liked to do her make-up,' Meeta said. Kate looked over to see an assistant, snuffling and wiping her eyes, packing up some cardboard boxes in one corner. 'This was her office, of course. It's yours now. That's Sylvia-Elise. She's getting Iris's personal effects together. She was Iris's assistant.'

The redhead looked up balefully at Kate.

'I'll leave you to it,' Meeta announced, turning and walking out.

'Hi,' Kate said.

'Hello, Ms Fox,' said Sylvia-Elise. 'I should tell you I've asked personnel for a transfer. Iris Haughey was a great boss.'

'How long did you work for her?' Kate asked neutrally.

The other girl tossed her head. 'Five years.'

'As her assistant?'

'Yes. And I took care of her in every way,' Sylvia-Elise announced proudly.

'But she didn't take care of you,' Kate said.

'Excuse me?'

'You heard me, I think. Five years, and you're still an assistant. You see, if I had a great assistant who looked after me in every way, I'd promote her. Do you like fashion?'

The girl shifted on her knees, staring. Obviously discomfited.

'Uh . . . sure. I mean, it's my passion. It's why I loved the job. *Model* is such a great magazine, and Iris—'

'It was started by David Abrams. Iris was a good editor.

What I want to be is a great one. And I'll need an assistant who does more than make my coffee.' Kate's eyes flickered over the kneeling girl. 'Iris gave you a lot of stuff from the sample cupboard, didn't she?'

Sylvia-Elise nodded. 'How did you know?'

'Because you're wearing that fabulous Emporio Armani leather jacket from last winter with that skirt, it's Patrizia Pepe, I think, from Florence. And those mules, those are Jimmy Choos.'

The girl's mouth dropped open.

'See, I love fashion too. And I know you do. But there's more to it than wearing free clothes. You want to write, you want to spotlight the hot pieces? Then you have to get on. And Iris stuffed your mouth with Prada.'

'I never thought of it like that,' Sylvia-Elise said.

Kate shrugged. 'I've lost my editor. It's going to be a really busy couple of weeks. We have to put various magazines together, make a giant splash, hire new people for each title. I'm going to need a great assistant. Better than that, a world-class one. I just don't have time for feuds. If that's you, great. If not, and you want to be transferred, I'll get someone else and it won't go on your record. But if you want to stick with me, we've got work to do. Starting today.'

Sylvia-Elise got to her feet. She looked at Kate with new respect.

'I guess I want to stick with you.'

'Good. Then get the deputy editors of *Model* and *Beauty* in here. And find me a list of the top ten plus-size models in America . . .'

Chapter Twenty-Three

Marcus Broder smiled to himself. It was all coming to a head. That fool Abrams! He would turn this offer down? Crazy, far more than his stupid little group was worth. Adrenaline pumped through him. Enjoyable, really. You got to the top, you got comfortable. It had been a few years now since Broder had crushed another player. His reputation on Wall Street was solid, but for how much longer? He'd been living on his laurels.

People weren't afraid of Marcus any more.

Well, all that was about to change.

He glanced around his enormous walnut-panelled office. The furniture in it would have graced the White House. Broder, Inc. was a public company, profitable enough, but it did everything first class. Marcus used the company jet like a taxi; even his assistants flew business. Marcus had art on his walls that would have been at home in a major gallery, and he liked to indulge all his tastes. European antiques. Bespoke suits. Vintage champagne. A three-star Michelin chef on the premises, cooking lunch for the board, or for his most important meetings. And of course his pay. Fifteen million a year, plus bonuses. That put him in the top thirty CEOs in America. And the shareholders didn't mind, as long as he kept motoring, kept up the flashy deals. Really, the company was a bit like Trump, he mused, grinning at the thought. Overpriced. But the stock market was a *market*. Your company was worth what someone was prepared to pay for it. A mini-conglomerate like his, with tentacles everywhere, fingers in pies, it was easy to fudge the accounts; lots of promise, lots of brand value in there, stuff you could account for but never have to prove. He wasn't stupid enough to lie in his accounts. Marcus Broder just enjoyed valuing intangibles.

His name, his reputation, that was one of the biggest.

So by crushing Abrams, Inc., he was doing everybody a favour.

Himself. His stock price. Abrams' shareholders. Everybody, really, except David Abrams himself.

And now, because of his precious little bitch of an ex-wife, that gold-digging slut, because she'd gotten under Marcus's skin, because the thought of her flirting with Abrams – the younger, coming guy – drove him nuts, he had a golden opportunity. To do some real good work. To not only buy Abrams' well-positioned little company but to drive down the stock price first.

He couldn't bankrupt the guy. But Abrams wasn't smart like Marcus, who took very little of his pay in stock, and who long ago liquidated his major holding in Broder when the company hit one of its boom-to-bust peaks. Marcus liked greenbacks, dollars, gold bullion. He didn't bet on Broder – hell, he knew the real state of the bottom line. They were doing great, just as long as the market held up. No, he preferred solid, portable assets. His prime property in New York and the Hamptons and the huge penthouse in Monaco, where he planned to retire, flipping the bird to the USA and its taxes. Why should he subsidise welfare cases and pointless foreign wars? Forget it. But David Abrams was one of these younger men, still in his forties, naïve enough to romanticise business.

Just because Abrams, Inc. bore his name, he was freaking wedded to it. His wealth was in stock. He did it the old-fashioned way, ploughing profits back into the business. Growing organically. Flying commercial, no private jets, and even his board members didn't go first class. All very laudable stuff . . . Marcus yawned. Rookie mistake by a boy scout. Should pay attention to the little line at the bottom of those private broker commercials you saw on CNBC.

The value of shares can go down as well as up.

As David Abrams was about to find out.

It was fire-sale time.

The phone rang on his desk. His senior assistant, Olivia. She was a cool beauty, twenty-eight, private girls' school then Vassar, glossy chestnut-brown hair that she wore in a chignon, legs that went on for ever and a great pair of tits. All the secretaries in his firm were easy on the eye. There was an unspoken hiring policy. You had to be intelligent and competent, but without a nice bouncing rack you didn't get in the door here. Marcus had a reputation for it. And of course he had the pick of the crop.

'Sir.' He didn't encourage familiarity. It stirred him when pretty women were forced to act deferential. 'I don't know if you'll want to take this call . . .'

'Who is it? I have the press conference in twenty minutes,' Broder said.

'Yes, sir. It's somewhat related. It's Ms Jacqueline Moltrano. She's working on a major article for the *Wall Street Journal*.'

'About what?' Broder was wary. He didn't enjoy anything

other than puff profiles. The *Journal* could be awkward.

'It's an article on your ex-wife, Ms Fox.'

'Not interested,' he snapped. Fuck, great tits or no, Olivia was going to have to go. Didn't the stupid broad understand how he operated?

'No, sir, she's all ready for print. She says she has evidence of an affair between David Abrams and Ms Fox . . . has some of her past boyfriends on the record . . . wondered if you had a quote or a comment . . .'

He grinned. 'Interesting.'

An affair?

Could David Abrams really have been that stupid?

Buying her stake in *Lucky* for a ton of cash. Overpromoting her. Turning down a generous offer for his magazine division . . .

He remembered briefly, keenly, how Kate had been in bed. Willing, pliant, always ready to go, with that va-va-voom body that could have turned on a statue. But not that hot, not that slutty. Not like Lola, who had a range of tricks in bed that would have shamed a Parisian call-girl.

Was she worth it?

That movie, that picture. It wouldn't go away. Had she been different with David Abrams? Wilder, looser? *Had she actually loved him?*

Marcus looked down. His knuckles were clenched white on the receiver.

What the hell did it matter. David Abrams had just made his task a thousand times easier.

'Put her through,' he said.

David Abrams stood in the office corridor, looking longingly at the elevator. He wanted to summon it, ride down one floor.

Just one little floor. Go and see Kate, see how she was doing. But he dared not. It would be radioactive.

His blood was still up from the board meeting. Man, what a clusterfuck. He was only mad at himself for not spotting it sooner. When vultures like Marcus Broder decided to pounce, they didn't hold back, didn't let you go. He should have assumed Broder would try to turn one or more of his key people.

He'd trusted Tim Reynolds. That was a weakness. This was business, where trust was as much use as yesterday's front page. He was taking risks, betting on himself, on Kate. Reynolds wanted the easy option. Your colleagues are not your best friends, he told himself.

Iris was almost a relief. She was past it. Treading water. She needed to go.

The elevator arrived, and he stepped in, punching the number for the ground floor instead. A few of the key shareholders, fund managers with institutional stakes, had already heard the news on the grapevine. They wanted a meeting, and David was prepared to give them one. Better to strangle discontent at birth.

His thoughts returned to Kate, far above him now, in her office, putting together the new issues of his magazines, cooking up something special. He'd gone into business with her so he could get *out* of business with her – beef up his magazine division enough to sell it, and for a way better price than Broder was offering. But the guys waiting for him in the lobby would not see it that way. Not if they knew . . .

Thankfully they didn't; nobody did.

That she was his lover. More than that, his girl. Already his girl.

Abrams thought of Kate, and his heart did a slow flip in his chest. When exactly had he fallen in love with her? It was lust at first sight, that was for sure. But he had dismissed her as everything he hated in a woman. Grasping, a gold-digger, willing to sell herself for money . . .

She'd had a lot to prove.

And she had done. Hell, what a star she was. What a goddess. He was so proud of her. It was impossible to stop thinking about her, to stop himself from going after her. In the end, the sheer life force of Kate Fox had overwhelmed all his reservations.

Man, Abrams thought. Forget falling in love. I'm completely in love with her. I think . . . I think I might actually want to *marry* her.

She wasn't an angel. Screw it, nor was he. But that first time, in his kitchen, when she'd opened up to him, opened her heart like a flower uncurling under the sun, maybe he'd understood why she did it. Something in him unfroze that day. Because for men like him, rich, powerful men, there were always girls, weren't there? Always pretty, pliant, sexy chicks, as bitchy or submissive as you wanted them. The city was a supermarket; he could select any one of them. But Kate was worth thirty, forty of those girls. She was brave, and hard working, and a little messed up, and sparkling, and stylish, and selfish, and imperfect and he was so deep into it now he could hardly see . . .

'Mr Abrams.'

David looked up. There was a woman in the lobby of his building, dark haired, expensive dress, very tight, Herve Leger, some corner of his brain suggested. The bandage style showed off an impressive pair of breasts. The raven hair was done up in a chignon; he half jumped out of his skin at the familiarity of it.

'Jacqui?' he asked disbelievingly. 'What are you doing here? What's with the "Mr Abrams"?'

Damn, how had he ever been into this girl? Her tight, obvious style, the hardness of her face, that could have been so beautiful otherwise.

'I'm here in a professional capacity,' she snapped. 'Marcus Broder is live on CNBC at this very moment speaking to your shareholders. He suggests that you're putting personal pique and spite ahead of your stock price. Is that the reason you turned down his offer?'

Abrams looked for the security guards. They should have stopped this shit. But she was here, in the downstairs lobby, and nobody had thrown her out. It would look bad to try to do it now.

'No. We can get a better price for our magazines. Broder undervalued them.'

'On the figures, he offered nine times earnings. A great price in a recession.'

'We can take our magazine division further.'

Jacqui nodded, and he relaxed slightly. This was simple; he could handle her.

'You had a stormy board meeting today. Your appointment of Kate Fox lost you Iris Haughey and Tim Reynolds.'

'Kate has assumed Iris's responsibilities,' David answered calmly. 'On Mr Reynolds, I have no comment at this time.'

'So you have given this very young woman, who inherited control of one magazine, direction over your entire magazine division? Placed her on your board and lost two respected board members of many years' standing?'

David Abrams smiled. He looked down at Jacqui Moltrano, a direct challenge.

'That's right. And it was a good decision. I have every

confidence that Kate can juice up one of my main divisions. That she can repeat the magic she showed at *Lucky*.'

'Do you have every confidence that she can juice *you* up, Mr Abrams?'

He stopped dead. 'What?'

Those dark eyes were cold, glittering. Like a snake's.

'Well, you're having a sexual relationship with her. Isn't that right? Kate Fox is your lover?'

For once in his life, David Abrams was lost for words.

Jacqueline Moltrano, his former squeeze, his ex-girlfriend, ex-lay, ex-date, ex-employee, was smiling up at him with venom, a hatred and loathing that knocked him backwards.

'Oh, that's right, David,' she said softly. 'We have the pictures. And come tomorrow morning, so will the whole of Manhattan.'

Holy shit, Abrams thought. The blood in his veins turned to iced water. This was bad, it was real bad. He started to mull the problem, the shock. Kate, he thought. This is going to break on her like a tidal wave.

'I don't discuss my private life,' he said.

'Well.' Jacqui smiled again. 'I guess that makes one of you. Because by tomorrow, you'll be the only guy in Manhattan *not* discussing your private life. What do you say to shareholders who might ask if you couldn't have given your serial golddigger some flowers or a diamond brooch, instead of control of your magazines?'

He looked down at her. 'This doesn't suit you, Jacqui.'

'It suits me fine,' she bit back.

'You're still single,' he pointed out, and had the satisfaction of seeing her eyes narrow in rage. 'You want a comment? Kate was the best girl for the job. Period.'

'Good luck explaining that to your shareholders in the

meeting room down the hall,' she answered. 'See, I took the liberty of dropping in on them earlier. You really don't have too much security on this level. Unlike at your board meeting.'

Abrams swallowed the question he wanted to ask, but she read it in his face, and laughed.

'How did I get in? Just announced myself to reception as an assistant to Mr Watson of the Farthing Trust. It only requires a little imagination. Perhaps Kate Fox has the same motto. Anyway, I digress.' She gave a triumphant little laugh. 'I showed them some of the pictures, gave a little update on your board meeting . . . a sneak peek at tomorrow's paper. You'll have to wait and pick up your copy. But I can say they found it all quite enthralling stuff. I think you'll find they want to have a little word with you . . .'

'Security,' David Abrams said sharply.

Two guards moved over from the reception area.

'This lady has no business in the building. Escort her out, please.'

'This way, miss,' one of them said.

'Oh, don't worry, boys, I'm going,' Jacqui said, smirking. 'And so is he.'

David Abrams stood and watched her go, a horrible sinking feeling in the pit of his stomach. He thought again of Kate, briefly. Then he turned around, and walked down the corridor to face his major shareholders.

Wall Street was buzzing.

The analysts were crawling over the deal. They liked what they saw. Traders swooped, grabbing every last share in Abrams, in Broder.

'It's a perfect fit.'

'The real question is why he didn't do this years back.'

'Abrams is prime takeover material. Medium-sized magazine division . . . great baby steps in property . . . a majority stake *is* out there.'

'And you know, Lucia, David Abrams will have a real struggle on his hands to keep control of his company. He owns a minority stake at this point . . . investors large and small appear to be furious at the lurid allegations surfacing this morning in the normally sedate *Wall Street Journal.*'

'That's absolutely right, Chuck.' The gorgeous brunette looked across at her co-anchor. 'The Street is all over this story. Mixing revenge, money and possible romantic liaisons with what looks likely to be a bitter takeover battle. David Abrams and Marcus Broder are the David and Goliath of the corporate jungle, with medium-sized Broder looking to swallow the smaller, dynamic operation of Abrams, Inc. But the two men have more in common than magazines and money. The *Journal* is alleging that hotshot editor Kate Fox, recently promoted at Abrams . . .'

'And causing a stormy boardroom resignation drama involving some of the key players there,' said Chuck, grinning to camera.

'. . . that Ms Fox is secretly the lover of Mr Abrams. She's also the ex-wife of Mr Broder. The story running in the *Journal* today would not be out of place in a TV soap opera.'

'Senior editor Iris Haughey was apparently driven out by Abrams' promotion of his alleged lover.'

'And respected CFO Tim Reynolds, a fifteen-year veteran, also resigned, apparently in protest at Abrams turning down the rich offer from Broder.'

Lucia smiled into the camera, her glossy raven hair tumbling around the creamy skin of her face. 'What investors and analysts will make of it all, we've yet to find out.'

'Actually, following this morning's pictures of Mr Abrams and Ms Fox kissing outside her apartment, we hear that one of the hedge funds is poised to sue Abrams, citing corporate mismanagement, nepotism and deception,' her co-anchor smirked.

'Certainly a fascinating backdrop for a takeover battle for one of the Street's more exciting small companies. Because Marcus Broder announced today that he is increasing his offer to shareholders of all sizes, bidding now not just for Abrams' magazine division but for the entire company. He's made it clear that management changes would be mandatory. Should Broder succeed, David Abrams is definitely out.'

'And now moving on to our other major story – government gilts. Are they in trouble, Lucia?'

Kate lifted her remote and flicked off the TV. She felt sick, sick to her stomach. In the glass-walled palace of her office – Iris Haughey's old place – the staff were deliberately avoiding her, heads down, eyes averted. This was a magazine. It felt like a mortuary.

She walked over to the windows. Down at street level you could clearly see the small knot of journalists packing the sidewalk. There were a couple of camera crews, too. This story appealed to everybody from society gossip columnists to the finance writers.

She had to hand it to Jacqui. The girl had done a hell of a job.

There was David, hung out to dry.

And Kate's past. Come back to haunt her.

She had the *Journal* spread out on her desk. Printed in full colour, there were the damning photos, surrounded by Jacqui's classic little sneaky, sarcastic story: Kate outside her own apartment, bent half backwards, kissing David Abrams goodbye in the early morning; the building where she'd first met him, that he owned; Abrams sneaking into her place, a baseball cap pulled down low, late at night; Kate in an haute couture gown of ostrich feathers and satin, wearing an important ruby suite of jewellery on her ears, throat and fingers; Kate in a tiny, barely there leather mini-dress, outside one of New York's hottest nightclubs of five years ago, a trust-fund brat on her arm; Kate with a New York Mets shortstop; Kate with a record mogul; Kate with a real-estate titan; Kate with five other rich men. Always wearing something tight and revealing. Always in teetering heels. Showing plenty of cleavage, wearing dresses that were snug round her ass. Fashionable enough not to be totally cheap and slutty, but nevertheless, the photo essay's message was very clear: Kate Fox was New York's most successful gold-digger.

And David Abrams was a hell of a sucker.

Her face went crimson as she looked at the story. Her life in pictures. The snotty words that accompanied it.

At Cutie *magazine, Ms Fox held a very junior position, that of contributing style editor. Her salary was a modest forty thousand dollars a year. Yet people familiar with the situation told the* Journal *that Ms Fox would habitually drink at New York's most expensive watering holes clad top to toe in pricey designer clothes and shoes . . . the succession of rich men on her arm, it is assumed, providing the solution . . .*

Jacqui had slid the knife in but good. It was the perfect hatchet job.

And worse, Kate thought, because it was goddamned true.

While Kate partied, her friend Emily Jones worked. The success of Lucky *magazine is the sole professional triumph laid at Ms Fox's door and the ostensible reason for her promotion. But the magazine's founding ethos, staff, writers and sales force were put together by somebody else. Although earning far more, Emily wore clothes from the Gap and stayed home nights. Yet Kate Fox has received all the credit for the long-overdue expansion of an already successful venture. Analysts will rightly ask if this deserves the massive instant promotion she has apparently received from yet another lover . . .*

Where was David? Since the story broke, he hadn't called, hadn't texted. It was chaos on the upper floors of the building, assistants running, the phones ringing off the hook, his corporate counsel fighting fires. Nobody was talking to her. And Kate didn't dare ask. He could be locked in a room with yet more lawyers; he could be meeting the big investors, talking to his distributors, investment bankers, the brokers, anything.

And why would he call me? Kate wondered, miserably. He had risked everything, and they'd been caught, and now it was all crashing down around them. It was just a disaster. And as David Abrams had picked up that paper, and been confronted with the ruin of his company, he would have seen everything that was laid out now over her desk, the damning pictures, her entire life in photos . . .

All the rich boys. The moguls. The gold-digging. Waiting for the big fish, Marcus Broder, her very own mega-millionaire Prince Charming, the guy who was supposed to save her life . . .

And who was about to ruin that of the man she loved.

This was stupid. So goddamned stupid. Marcus didn't need

this company. It wasn't about Abrams, Kate knew that. It was about *her*.

There was a back way out of the building. She buzzed her assistant.

'I'm going to leave the office for a little while.'

'Yes, Ms Fox,' the girl said, in carefully neutral tones. Nobody was going to argue with her about that, were they?

'My phone will be off.' She didn't want to talk to any journalists right now. 'Just take messages. Say I'm in a meeting.'

She was about to be. One of the most important meetings of her life.

Chapter Twenty-Four

Man, this is a fucking nightmare.

David Abrams was not given to exaggeration. Even in his head. But the picture of panic on his executive floor was not a pretty one. His investment bankers huddled in a group at one end of his office, barking into their cell phones. His lawyers were at the other, sitting on some temporary desks hastily brought in for the purpose. Even his personal broker had turned up.

'Stock's rising. Two eighths in the last five minutes.'

'Broder's upped his offer!' a banker yelled back from the corner. 'Seventy-five a share!'

'Fuck. The Wassteins are selling,' another one called to Abrams. 'I can't talk them out of it.'

Damn. The Wasstein brothers owned eight per cent of his stock. They were a huge stakeholder.

'Get me Jacob Wasstein,' David shouted to his assistant. She punched some numbers into her phone. He could see her pretty face pinched and nervous from the tension. Her job would not survive his departure.

'Ah, his girl says he's on another call right now,' she almost whispered. 'Can he give you a call back?'

Wasstein was blowing him off. David pressed his fingers to

his forehead. One by one, the shareholders were peeling off, heading to Broder. If he couldn't stop the rot, his company, his life's work, was about to be taken over.

'No! He can't call back! Tell him it's urgent!' he snapped.

He watched as she tried to argue with some chick at the other end of the line.

This wasn't good. This wasn't good at all.

Kate rode uptown in the back of a yellow cab. It was a tiny, brief oasis of peace. The driver was Lebanese, and listening to a CD of Middle Eastern music in his car, which smelled of cigarettes. Kate wore a New York Mets baseball cap, a plain black T-shirt, jeans, sneakers; clothes she kept in her gym bag, just in case she needed to change. Never had done before. This afternoon, she was glad of the anonymity.

There were other things in the world . . .

Oh, to hell with being philosophical. Not today there weren't.

This was stupid, what she was doing. A crazy gamble. Marcus Broder was in his element, playing the corporate raider, the merciless titan, the big swinging dick. And it was over her, it was all over her, that these two major players were marshalling their armies.

She choked back a hysterical laugh.

It's me, Kate thought. I'm Helen of Troy!

It hadn't ended too well for Helen, though, had it?

But she was in this cab. On her way to the Upper East Side. To Marcus Broder's house. To see him, to fling herself on his mercy, to try to stop him. The end to this story hadn't been written yet.

* * *

'I'd like to see Marcus Broder,' Kate announced to the receptionist.

Boy, said out loud, it really sounded dumb. She was doing all this on a hunch. Based purely on his habits from a few years ago. When they'd been together, after a big morning press conference Marcus wouldn't usually go to his office. He'd come back home, lie on his bed, take calls there. Normally with Kate curled up next to him, toying with him, pleasing him. And he'd want sex in the middle of it. He was charged up. He'd only go back in to his office later.

'Who may I say is calling?'

'This is Kate Fox.' There was no point lying about it, coming up with some kind of elaborate scheme. Marcus would either see her or he wouldn't. 'His ex-wife.'

'Just one moment.' Not a flicker of excitement on the face; the woman was very good, with her neat battleaxe-grey bun and her crisp navy Chanel suit. 'Will you have a seat, please?'

Kate perched on one of the imported Portuguese sofas, gold wood with plush red velvet upholstery. She had chosen these for Marcus herself, for the lobby of the house. Just like a hotel or an embassy, visitors were not instantly admitted. There was a system. And knowing his love of antiques, she'd suggested somewhere flashy for them to wait.

Now she was perched on one of the solid, elegant little things herself. Waiting. For an audience. For his favour.

'Ms Fox.' The receptionist was in front of her again. 'Will you come this way, please?'

Kate stood, and followed her through the familiar front hallway to the elevator bank. Of course a house like this had its own elevator; she had ridden it with Marcus a thousand times. There were two cars, one for guests, and one that led straight up to the master floor, Marcus's private suite. The receptionist was showing her to the second one.

He had said yes. He was going to see her. He would back off. Everything was going to be OK.

For a moment, the relief hit her so hard she felt dizzy. She stepped into the elevator car, and smiled for the first time that day.

The receptionist pushed a button.

As the brass doors slid shut, she said, 'Mr Broder isn't in. But his fiancée, Ms Valdez, is. She would like to see you.'

Before Kate could say anything, the doors had locked shut. And the elevator was lifting, smoothly, directly, straight to the penthouse.

'I'm afraid it's obvious, David.' Judge Rodgers shook his head as he glanced around the carnage in the office. The ticker on the giant CNBC screen was reporting every mover and shaker as they declared their hands. And for every bank or pension fund that stuck with Abrams, two were ticking over to Broder. The stock price rose, kept on rising. Broder's was steady. 'We'll be lucky if the company survives the day. Your only chance is to go out there and put it right.'

Abrams bit his lip. 'Yeah. OK. Put it right how?'

Donal Redson was pacing up and down. These were the two most trusted members of his board. Finally, he'd put in a call to Kate, but she was nowhere to be found, her number rolling straight to voicemail. Not like her to chicken out. He certainly appreciated the strain, but there was something about her he'd responded to, or thought he had. Guts. Toughness. A willingness to stand up, no matter what the circumstances.

Not today. His little vixen had run to earth.

'Go out there. Call a press conference of your own. Say it

was a mistake, that you understand the nepotism allegations.'
The judge leaned forward. 'Fire Kate Fox. And for that matter,
dump her too.'

David's eyebrow lifted. 'Relationship advice, Judge?'

'Son, I'm a plain-speaking man. And those photographs
kind of speak for themselves, don't they? Don't be a fool. Lots
of great-looking chicks out there. Lots of editors, too.'

Abrams felt sick. He turned to Redson. 'Donal?'

For a long moment, Donal Redson didn't speak. Then he
turned and looked them both in the face.

'Where is Kate?'

Abrams blushed on her behalf. 'Nobody can find her.
Maybe she's hiding out from the press.'

Redson shook his head. 'That's bad. That's not leadership.
But if you want my two cents, you don't fire her today. She
edited a great magazine, she was breaking new ground, she
was the best thing to happen in print since – well, man, since
you. I think you go steady, and you back your own hunches.
You may want to make a statement to that effect.'

'That's insane,' Judge Rodgers snapped. 'I have stock.
Marcus Broder is offering a good price . . .'

'Sell me your stake,' Abrams answered immediately. 'I'll
give you a dollar a share more. Since you've been so strong
on the board.'

They both heard the past tense.

'Done,' the judge replied. A sense of weariness crossed his
face, and he shook hands with Abrams. 'I'll have my broker
call. And I won't make a statement or speak to the press.'

'Good news,' David answered. 'Maybe this thing is finally
turning around.'

But the pit in his stomach was still there.

Where the hell was Kate?

* * *

Lola Valdez sat opposite Kate Fox and smiled, a rich, deep smile. She was elegant, dressed to kill in a floating Missoni dress topped with a little cream Prada cardigan, and Kate Spade kitten heels in oatmeal leather that looked great against the delicate olive of her skin. Her private hairdresser had blown out her locks naturally, keeping the curl bouncing, and her rich seventies playgirl look was complemented by light make-up, just some gloss on the lips, gold shadow on her lids, bronzer swept over the cheeks.

And here was the legendary Kate Fox sitting in front of her, the bogeywoman of all her nightmares, and really, what was she? Just some intellectual bitch with her hair in a ponytail, wearing jeans and a T-shirt. Good body, base-ball cap, nothing to write home about. She could be some stylish MILF out for a stroll in a suburban mall. Style goddess? Forget it.

But the tiny worm of doubt in her ear whispered that Marcus still hadn't laid this ghost.

'I never thought you'd show up here,' she said. She moved her hand, so Kate could see her new engagement ring. A giant sparkler from Tiffany's, natural pink, incredibly rare. Once she'd playfully fessed up to Marcus about the whole Jacqui Moltrano link, he'd proposed on the spot, calling her his baby, his clever little asset. He laughed, enjoying her obsessiveness, saying she was the first woman who'd actually been *useful* to him. Once Kate was gone, they could get on with their lives together. 'Those are some balls.'

'I actually only want to speak with Marcus,' Kate replied. 'To ask him if he'll back off.'

'Back off?' Lola laughed. 'Back *off*? That's what *you* were supposed to do. At the start, when he asked you to. About that shitty magazine. *Amiga*, you must be nuts. *Loca*. All this, and you throw it out?'

Kate looked at her. 'You're welcome to it, honey. The price was too high for me.'

'And after he settled. He could have crushed you, but he even gave you something. You didn't fold. You didn't just *go* away. You stayed. And you *bothered* him. Understand?'

'That's Marcus's problem,' Kate replied. 'I wanted to use my intelligence. He couldn't handle it. Be careful what you wish for, Ms Valdez. You'll earn every cent.'

'You're just jealous. Because I can hold him.'

'I left,' Kate said quietly. 'As I think you know.'

'Then because I didn't make such a stupid mistake,' Lola spat. 'Oh, you think you're so fine and so clever, with your stupid job. Like this doesn't take intelligence. Like *this* is easy.' She flashed the ring. 'It's hard. A whole lifetime of hard. And you were getting in my way, all the time in my *fucking* way. So no, he puts this to bed. I think maybe you find it hard to get another magazine job now. Maybe your Mr Abrams is not too happy if you blow up his company, his life. You think somebody else will take that chance?' She tossed her head. 'Don't blame Jacqui Moltrano, she just does her thing. *I* spoke to her. *I* told her what to write. You need to understand, you have to *leave*. I want to get on with *my* life.' Lola shrugged. 'Marcus gets rid of you, of David Abrams for fucking you. Gets a new company. Everybody loves him again, the papers, Wall Street. Everybody. I get a ring. Everybody's happy, except you and Abrams. But you can still make love to him, maybe that will be good enough.' She laughed. 'Because we know you must be pretty good at that, honey. You have a hell of a record.'

Kate stood, her face flaming.

'You were too late to meet Marcus here. I took care of him about an hour ago. He's back in the office already. Maybe you should turn on your phone. It's too late, you see, almost too late. I don't know much about finance, but I've been learning. The little stake that's out there? It's heading towards Marcus.'

Kate was already walking away, half running to the elevator. She punched the button, Lola Valdez's words and laughter ringing in her ears.

'It's over, honey,' she cried. '*Adios.*'

Times Square was thick with reporters. David Abrams could see them clearly from where he stood, staring down into the street from his glass-walled office. It was a battle, a goddamn war room up here. Moment to moment. He was buying shares, leveraging his own properties, hoovering up the small investors, some hedges, pension funds. Holding back the tide of Broder's money and brokers, one deal at a time. Staunching the flow, maybe, slowing him down, but that was all he could do; every hour Broder beat him back, every hour he crept closer to that majority stake . . .

His people yelled in the background. He was hoarse from talking, needed a break, just a minute. He looked down.

Suddenly the little knot of reporters and camera crews swivelled, like somebody had poured treacle into an anthill. There was a disturbance; they moved away from the building, swarming around a small figure that had just stepped out of a cab.

'It's Kate,' shouted Abrams. Instantly he picked up his BlackBerry, dialled her number. Expecting voicemail. But she answered, and he could hear her, just, over the raucous shouts of the journalists in the background.

'Hi. You upstairs?'

'Yeah,' he said, and suddenly found himself smiling, ridiculously, just happy at that moment to hear her voice. 'Where the hell have you been?'

'Out,' she said lightly. 'This is kind of a mess, huh?'

'Kate! Over here!'

'Ms Fox! Ms Fox! Any truth in the rumours that . . .'

'Kind of,' he said loudly, to be heard over the reporters. 'Come up to my office.'

'No. I think I have a better idea.'

'We need to fix this,' he said adding, because he wanted to, 'I love you, you know. I'm in love with you. I'm staying with you.'

'And I love you too.' There it was, that momentary catch in her voice, but it was gone almost as soon as it came. 'And we do need to fix it. I'm going to fix it right now. I suggest you turn on your TV.'

'Kate, get up here,' he said, but she was gone.

David turned back to the room, which had gone awfully quiet. Then he shrugged.

'I think we better turn on the TV,' he said.

Kate Fox stood on the pavement in front of the reporters, and the mikes, and the camera crews. She took off the baseball cap, and smiled, and shook out her hair. The gesture sparked an explosion of flash bulbs, cameras popping, questions being shouted.

She held up her hand.

'Ladies and gentlemen,' she said. 'If you'll allow me, I'd like to make a statement.'

'Are you going to resign?'

'Quitting, Kate?

'Is there corruption?'

'Did you sleep your way to the top?'

'Actually, it's not so much of a statement,' she said, and gave them another big smile. Amazing, now that she was going to do this, what a relief it was, what a sense of relaxation she felt. 'More of a story. Yes, kind of a bedtime story. Human interest, really. The sort of thing I'd publish at *Lucky* and we'll be doing more of at *Model* and *Beauty*, under my direction. Which is why they'll start selling again. So I suggest you listen up. Especially those of you with shares in Broder, Inc. You see, what I think this situation needs is a little dose of the truth.'

She took a deep breath, the questions quietened, and the cameras started to roll.

In his office, David Abrams shook his head.

'I can't believe it,' he said. 'I just can't believe it.'

His traders turned away from the TV and looked at their screens. 'The Brauns are staying with us,' one guy yelled.

'And Smithfield Capital.'

'Ellen Lazarus's people called. They want to know if she can get her shares back . . . same price.'

'No way,' David said, grinning. 'They're mine now. And what's Broder trading at?'

'It's down,' his investment banker said. 'Dropping. Like a stone.'

'But we're up,' Abrams answered, and laughed.

Kate was starting to enjoy herself now. As an editor, she was used to being behind the scenes, except when it came to fashion.

But today she was front and centre. In one corner, Marcus,

Lola and all their money and power. And in the other, Kate Fox, with the truth.

I know a good story, she thought. She took a deep breath, and began. 'Was I a gold-digger? You know what, ladies and gentlemen? I absolutely was.'

A gasp ran through the crowd. More photographs popping. The reporters literally struck dumb. Kate gave them the potted version. Her childhood, her mom. Fear of being poor. The easy way out, and how hard it was.

'I'd like to apologise to Marcus Broder,' she said, looking them all in the eye. 'I never should have married him. I didn't love him. But on the other hand, he didn't love me. He wanted beauty and style. Marcus's image is very important to him.' A well-placed little sigh. 'And I'm afraid he was happy, until I departed from the script. Gold-diggers are supposed to marry for it. Not go down into their own mines. But my friend Emily Jones gave me a shovel, and turns out I did it better than I thought I could.'

They were listening. Every one of them.

'You know the story of *Lucky*. You also know who David Abrams is. Yes, I fell in love with him. And he fell in love with me. We both thought it was a mistake. And we both didn't care. For the record, I still love him. And I'm excellent at my job. Despite the *Journal*, those things aren't incompatible. Somebody who did care, though, was Marcus Broder. Because I wouldn't fade away. And this is all about him. So I'm afraid a lot of good people, small investors, senior citizens, have got caught up in today. I'm real sorry, but you have to ask Mr Broder about his motivations.'

'Kate,' one woman interrupted. 'Jane Hendricks, CNN. You made a cryptic remark about Broder's stock earlier . . .'

'Yes. Typical girl, I'm afraid; it's taken me so long to get to the point. You see, I went over to Marcus's house earlier, to ask him to back off. His new fiancée told me she had collaborated with Jacqui Moltrano's story – as you all know, Jacqui used to date David – and that Marcus would not stop till David's company was broken. Now you see, that is a woman fighting her corner. But I'm afraid I can't allow her man to hurt mine. It's all kind of Tammy Wynette over here.' She laughed, but nobody joined her. The reporters were standing, staring, willing her on, their tongues practically lolling in their heads. This was so epically juicy, Kate thought they might pass out.

'And it occurred to me, when I saw that a fiancée on a mission – to get me out of Marcus's life, out of the magazine business, out of town – can do so much damage, that I did actually have an earlier incarnation. The one you read all about this morning in the *Journal*. Yes, I was a trophy wife. Marcus Broder's wife. And the thing about wives,' and now she looked directly into the camera, so that America would see her, David would see her, Marcus would see her, talking straight to them, one on one, 'is that they really know where the bodies are buried. So here's the skinny, ladies and gentlemen, here's the headline story, and I suggest you Dow Jones types get your analysts on the phone to investigate what I'm about to say . . . Broder, Inc. is horribly overvalued. The books are next to junk. The spending is hidden under the carpet. Marcus treats the corporate jets like his taxis. He used to boast about it at dinner. Let me tell you about the liabilities of the pension fund . . .'

In his fortress office, panelled in walnut, Marcus Broder was staring transfixed, horrified, at the screen. His bankers said nothing, his traders were silent. But the lights on his phone bank were blinking away like the Starship *Enterprise*.

Shut up, bitch, shut up! he thought.

But Kate Fox just went on talking. Directly to him. Like they were the only two people in the world.

'Uh, Mr Broder.' One of the traders spoke up, a kid too young to know better. 'I think you should know, sir, the market's taking a bit of a dump on your shares. They, like, just dropped two dollars . . . two fifty . . . wow, what's going on, they lost almost four dollars a share . . . holy shit, look at this . . .'

An hour later, it was all over.

Broder, Inc. had its shares suspended. The Street looked into what Kate had said, found some telltale signs. Politicians started to appear on the TV screens. The SEC announced an investigation. Abrams was safe; the stock eased off its highs, but stayed steady. At the close, David was able to breathe out.

Kate was in the room with him. They had applauded when she came in, and she joked, and smiled, like the whole thing was nothing.

'It's just my plans for the "Real American Woman" issue of *Model*,' she grinned, and Abrams was so proud of her he could hardly speak. He pulled her into his arms, and kissed her, kissed her long, kissed her hard.

'Closing bell.' He looked down into her eyes, not caring about the others in the room, who were staring at them both. 'Goddamn, you are one tough cookie to date.'

Kate lifted her mouth to him, feeling his lips warm against hers, firm, insistent. Her belly caved in with love and lust.

'Can we get out of here?' she murmured.

He laughed. 'That's the best idea I've heard all day.'

Epilogue

They curled together in Abrams' bed, watching ESPN on the TV. *Baseball Tonight*, the one place nobody would be talking about either of them.

'You made me a lot of money.' He kissed her forehead. They had made love three times, and for now, just for now, he was sated. 'Stock is at a five-year high.'

'I'm glad.' She cuddled against him. 'You know, maybe I should quit. I don't think I'm cut out for this, David. Working for you, I mean. I think I just want to love you.'

'But you're great at it.'

'I can be great somewhere else. Condé Nast were on the phone. They think I'm the new Tina Brown.'

'No.' He laughed. 'You don't quit. I do.'

'What?'

Kate sat bolt upright, and he leaned down and kissed each of her breasts. For a second she felt a stirring there. God, was it possible? Again?

'At the end of the day, I got an offer. Not a hostile one. For my entire company. Big conglomerate, media interests. And yes, they want you as part of the package.' He smiled, softly. 'It's a good number. I'm seriously thinking about it. Just selling the whole goddamned thing, and maybe starting again.

Real estate is more fun for me. With a big pot of cash, I could do some interesting stuff.'

Kate smiled. 'A two-career couple. I like it.'

'A two-career marriage,' he said, softly.

She blinked, but her heart soared. 'What? That's insane. We've only been dating—'

'Screw dating. You've been in my life long enough. From the second you walked into that shitty little office downstairs, I think I knew.'

'It's fast . . .' she protested, but her heart wasn't in it.

'I love you,' he said, simply. 'I love your guts. Your passion. Your smarts. Your ass, come to that. Did I tell you you have a great ass?'

'About fifty times this evening.' She took his face in her two hands, and covered it in kisses. 'David, I really love what I do . . . I want to work . . . I'm a career girl.'

'I know,' he said. 'And it's one reason I adore you. Because a girl like you is the ultimate trophy. Twice as good as any man I know. You know, Kate, I think you were a little tough on that trophy wife thing today. Why don't you give it another shot?'

'I'll think about it.' She kissed him, reached down, stroked him, felt him stir. Pressed her body against his, overwhelmed with joy, with hope, with love. 'But right now, you're gonna have to sweeten the deal.'

'Oh, I am, am I?' he asked, taking her beneath him again, his mouth closing on hers, pulling her into his arms, into his kiss, letting love sweep across them both, washing everything else away.